I0633942

SHADOWFAE

AETHEAON CHRONICLES
BOOK FOUR

LEONARD D. HILLEY II

CHAPTER 1

*R*oble rode Bleys while Lehrling followed close behind on his new steed, Patch. In her faery form, Shawndirea sat on Roble's shoulder. She zapped pesky, buzzing mosquitoes with little green bolts of magic. The crippled mosquitoes spun and spiraled in clumsy descents before crashing to the ground. She giggled with triumph.

Roble shook his head. "I thought you never took pleasure in harming other creatures."

She scrunched her nose and grinned. "As the Butterfly Queen, I rule and protect butterflies. My charity does not extend to troublesome mosquitoes. Besides, the farther into Woodnog's quagmire we travel, the more we expose ourselves to greater risks of disease. Mosquitoes deliver such pestilence in our realm."

Roble glanced at Lehrling.

Beneath Lehrling's blonde beard, his rotund cheeks dimpled a smile and he nodded. He laughed heartily. "She's right."

"How about in your realm, my dearest?" She placed her tiny hand against his cheek. "You also have these pests. Do you go out of your way to protect them?"

Roble shook his head. "No. Millions have died due to insect vectors and mosquitoes are the primary culprit. Ticks are equally dangerous for spreading disease. But, I've the feeling we'll encounter worse than these bloodsuckers."

"Definitely," Lehrling said. "Far worse."

The twisting path narrowed. A large, polished wooden sign hung from a post. Embedded at the base of the sign, a yellow Elfstone illuminated the elegant lettering: '**Woodnog Swamps: Dangers Unknown**'.

Roble chuckled and shook his head. "That sign's supposed to fill travelers with fear?"

Lehrling frowned. "It should."

"Such a sign only builds my curiosity," Roble replied.

"Because you're an Overlander. The fool-hearted—"

"Is that how you view me, Lehrling?" Roble grinned. "Fool-hearted?"

"N-o-o-o," Lehrling said in a teasing tone. "Not at all. Those who've lived in our realm hold no doubts about the warning being true. Unknown dangers are our greatest risks. In a day or so, you'll understand."

Shawndirea crinkled her nose and laughed until she snorted. "A day or two? I'd say Roble will understand much, much sooner."

Beyond the sign, the lush green trees and vines became sparser. The ground was dull brown and almost barren, except for the black acrid pools of water. The land appeared cursed. Absent of grasses, sprigs of sharp-edged sedges clumped the edges of the stagnant pools. Biting flies buzzed and crawled along the horses' neck. The horses huffed their disdain. Finding a place for the horses to graze might prove impossible in these swamps.

Compared to Woodnog's forests where all flowers, trees, vines, and mosses were blessed by the Fae's magical touch, almost anyone who left those woods would be overcome by apprehension once they entered the toxic bogs and scarred land. Anyone except an Overlander who loved science, studied fauna, and flora far more than his mind gave him caution. He loved discovering new species.

No sooner had they rode past the sign than did the sun averted the path before them. The gray sky held no hint of sunlight. A constant dusk shrouded them.

Behind them, on the *other* side of the sign, the sun's rays continued to break through the forest canopy. Chill bumps prickled his arms. They'd crossed an unseen dividing barrier, somewhat equivalent to good vs. evil, day vs. dusk, or Heaven opposite Hell.

Thunder rumbled in the distance with a brief, faint shimmer of cloud-to-cloud lightning. Insects chummed. Strange birds cried from hidden places in the thick clumps of yellow-brown grass. Winged pixies rode on dragonflies' backs. At first glance, Roble didn't notice the pixies, but when two pixies jousted one another, his eyes became keener. He marveled at things he'd never seen in the Overlands. Or, had he simply been blind to their existence?

A dark cloud of gnats swarmed the path. Roble cleared his throat and covered his nose and mouth with his tunic. The stench of the acrid air tightened his throat. His eyes itched and burned, and Lehrling rubbed his eyes, too. The quagmire displayed every unwelcoming invitation possible, seemingly hopeful for outsiders to flee.

An occasional drop of rain plopped on the dark swampy mire and browning fauna. *Blip!* Yellow haze floated like a thin vapor with outreaching tendrils that resembled searching ghostly fingers.

"It'll rain soon," Lehrling said.

"Soon?" Roble held up his palm and grinned. Several large raindrops struck his glove. "Seems it already is."

"It always rains in these swamps," Shawndirea replied.

"Hasn't rained here in quite some time," Lehrling said.

"How can you tell?" Roble studied the sticky black mud, which was tacky enough to grip a horse's hoof and prevent it from galloping from a dangerous encounter.

Lehrling laughed. "Because you wouldn't see *any* mud. Everything would be underwater. You'd barely see the dried grass blades."

"Ah."

"We should've gone with Riese and aided in overthrowing King Obed," Lehrling said. "That'd be the best retaliation for the destruction the Vykings heaped on Hoffnung."

"That's ambitious for an old man, don't you think?" Roble chuckled softly.

"Old?" Lehrling pointed a stern finger at Roble. "I might be old—"

Roble laughed. "I'm only joking."

Lehrling found no humor in the statement, though he shook his head and shrugged it off with a slight grin. Lehrling's hand involuntarily went to his ribcage, his eyes grew distant, and Roble assumed Lehrling thought about his fall from the horse in Icevale that almost killed him.

Roble held a fondness for Lehrling, much like an uncle he remembered from his childhood.

Lehrling kept a jolly smile and offered kind advice. Any advice the man gave, Roble took it to heart since he was a stranger in Lehrling's and Shawndirea's world. Lehrling never had to take Roble under his wing, and he could've easily dismissed Roble's ignorance as too bothersome to educate. Such, however, wasn't Lehrling's nature.

Lehrling had accepted Roble like a son. Perhaps this affection had only begun due to Bausch's untimely death or that Roble had saved Lehrling's life from certain execution at the hands of the invading Vykings? But regardless of the true reason, Roble was thankful to ride with Lehrling. Roble doubted few humans in Aetheaon would have bothered, except to perhaps find a way to rob and kill him.

Lehrling held his ribs for a moment, glanced at Roble, and apparently realized Roble questioned whether Lehrling was experiencing pain again. Lehrling quickly lowered his hand and offered a slight grin, before looking away with slight embarrassment.

"I'd rather be doing a million other things at this moment," Roble sighed and changed the subject. "This swamp's the last place I care to venture."

"As opposed to the Black Chasm?" Lehrling asked.

Roble half grinned and shook his head. He'd almost died inside the Black Chasm. If not for a magical portal somehow opening nearby and a stranger pulling him through, he'd have never survived. Thus, this was part of his reason for wandering into the quagmire. Fate was not to be ignored. Deep down, Roble expected he'd return to the Black Chasm in the future, and he'd need to be wiser and better informed in what enemies he might have to fight.

Roble sighed. "Okay, the swamp is the *second* to last place. But I can't ignore Lez'minx's invitation."

"Don't view it as an invitation. Lez'minx didn't *suggest* you find and visit his temple." Lehrling's brow furrowed brow. "I'm under the impression the consequences are quite severe, should you decline to meet him."

"That's the feeling I got, too." Roble's hands tightened around the reins. "It was more a threat than hospitality."

Lehrling sighed. "I'm afraid Bausch's fate might've occurred because he chose *not* to seek him out."

"You think he was supposed to?"

Lehrling shrugged. "He never mentioned anything about it to me, but he became more apprehensive about death after we left Icevale on our journey to Glacier Ridge. He never told me much about his armor, either, though I had asked."

"I didn't wager any agreement for this armor," Roble said softly. "It was by chance and due to an unfortunate circumstance I happened upon it. I regret Bausch lost his life. Perhaps if Shawndirea and I had arrived earlier than we had, we could've prevented his death."

"No matter. We cannot change the events set behind us," Lehrling said. His eyes saddened. He cleared his throat. "Fate brought you to rescue me. Your timing and arrival were no accident. Bausch's time had come, for reasons I'll never understand, and given the circumstances, Bausch would've wanted you to have his armor."

"I hope so," Roble said in a low whisper.

"I know so." Lehrling forced a smile of confidence. "It's a shame you never met him. I sorely miss him. A void has hollowed a place inside my heart. Sometimes I awaken from a dream and immediately look for him, hoping his death was nothing more than an extended tragic nightmare. He's gone in spirit but he lives in my heart and mind. The pain of missing him, however, won't easily go away."

"I imagine not. Such losses never fade quickly. But me wearing his armor doesn't oblige me to serve Lez'minx. I plan to make that clear whenever, *if*, we find his altar."

"I warned you not to take the dead wizard's rings, remember?" Shawndirea said. "Lez'minx might insist on more obligations from you because of that."

"I'll outright deny his requests," Roble said firmly.

Shawndirea and Lehrling responded with surprised expressions. Silence hung in the air for several long seconds.

"Even if it requires your death?" Lehrling asked.

Roble's eyes narrowed. "What life would I have if I'm bound to a deity I don't know or one I don't trust?"

"You're being quite selfish. What about me? Us?" Shawndirea pouted. "If you're dead, there's no *us*."

"Are you saying I should worship a strange god?"

Shawndirea beamed a slight grin. "*Who* ever said he's a god or that he wants to be worshipped?"

Roble frowned. "Isn't he a god?"

"He *proclaimed* himself to be a god, but that's entirely different than actually *being* one. For all we know he's a deranged wizard or mage," she said. "Most likely, he's a demigod."

Lehrling's eyes widened. "I never thought about a demigod. Faery, you may be right."

"What's a demigod?" Roble asked.

"Offspring born from a god and a mortal," Lehrling said.

"That's possible?"

Lehrling nodded.

Roble remained silent for several minutes, as he took in the information. "Why would a mage or wizard pretend to be a god? That'd be impudent."

"How so?"

"Placing him or herself to be a god when he isn't?"

"You think someone will punish him?" Shawndirea asked.

Roble shrugged.

"Who could?" Shawndirea asked.

"Someone with more power. Maybe one of the real demigods?"

"Sorcerers with great magical abilities tend to think themselves invincible and godlike, and often torture others into submission," she said. "Demigods tend to think differently. They crave adulation through seduction rather than absolute control. They'd never force others to worship them, but they would bless those who freely do."

"Lez'minx doesn't act like a demigod," Roble said.

She shook her head. "No, he doesn't."

"True loyalty is never gained through manipulation," Roble said.

Lehrling chuckled. "No, but people suffer oppression sometimes in order to eat or live another day."

Roble's jaw tightened. "True. Folks under duress get their wills bent and broken, but I'd rather die fighting a tyrant than live my life as a mindless puppet."

"Aye. Not something I'd expect an Overlander to say."

Roble faced Lehrling with a broad grin. "Some of us fight to the death without cowering or flinching, not only to defend ourselves but those we love and hold dear. Those of us with a spine and heart, that is. But about half the population from my realm bleat like mindless sheep following whomever shouts the loudest, regardless of the lack of rationality or common sense. There should be a moral outrage by people, but seldom does it arise."

"Seems those people are like a lot of the ones in most of our peasant villages," Lehrling replied. "The longer you live among us, the more you'll see everyone tends to be the same regardless of city or race."

"I suppose that shouldn't surprise me," Roble said, sighing.

CHAPTER 2

The pathway into the quagmire sloped downward. The ground became soggier. Puddles of black water pooled around the greenish-brown, clumps of grass. Bubbles rose in the soft mud and popped. Pungent gases irritated their noses and the backs of their throats. The bubbling, gooey mud and dark waters resembled a pot of rumbling water about to boil over.

The swamp progressively claimed the road. They'd need to rely on landmarks to find their way back. But since all the trees and underbrush practically looked the same, it might prove impossible. The occasional lampposts had either toppled into the swampy water or the Elfstones had been stolen.

Roble wondered if Lez'minx offered protection for Roble risking his life to find the altar. He doubted it. Other than voicing his demands through a dead wizard, Lez'minx remained silent. Could he see where Roble was? And if Roble had chosen *not* to seek the altar, would Lez'minx even know?

These thoughts made Roble question Bausch's death, but he'd never voice this to Lehrling for fear he'd offend his new friend. Had Bausch's death occurred at the hands of Lez'minx? Or if Lez'minx had made similar demands of Bausch, had Bausch's fear in not paying homage been the true reason for Bausch's demise?

From what Lehrling had told Roble, Bausch was a seasoned knight, trained by Lehrling, and most likely, he should've defeated three or four Vykings. At best, he could've fended them off long enough for he and Lehrling to escape. But, he had failed. Had he gotten sloppy? Or had his secret fears sapped his bravery.

Lack of confidence was easily recognized by one's enemies or competitors. Of course, Bausch might've sacrificed himself and hoped to save Lehrling's life. Lehrling had already suffered severe injuries. Perhaps being a man of nobility, Bausch surrendered to see Lehrling spared. But, as Roble had seen firsthand, that wasn't the case. Had Roble and Shawndirea not arrived when they did, Lehrling's fate would've been death. Hoffnung would have lost two Dragon Skull Knights.

"You're quite silent," Lehrling said. "You having doubts about this journey?"

"Not so much the journey as finding our way back," Roble replied.

Lehrling chuckled. "It's not hard to get lost in these swamps."

"I agree."

As a biologist in the Overlands, Roble had done a lot of exploration on the other side of the Aetheaon's veil, but never had he trudged through a place without a map or without some foreknowledge of the terrain. The only technological benefit he truly missed about the Overlands was GPS. In some ways, without GPS to guide him, he was blind. Adaptation, in the world of science, was the only way to survived. In Aetheaon, he'd only survive by making similar adjustments.

The rain droplets pelleted harder.

"Rain's setting in," Roble said.

Lehrling nodded. "It's the wet season."

Roble shook his head. "Perfect timing."

Lehrling laughed softly. "But isn't that always the case?"

Roble smiled and nodded.

"If we hurry, we should return home before heavier rains refill the swamps," Lehrling said.

Eyeing the darker recesses of the swamps where the large cypress-like trees towered, the sensation of being watched overshadowed Roble. A chill shot down his spine. He tugged his horse's reins and stopped to study the swampy forest.

9

"What's wrong?" Shawndirea asked.

"Something in the shadows of those trees," he whispered.

Lehrling glanced in the direction Roble was staring. "Did you see something?"

"No. It's just a … feeling. What lives in these swamps?" Roble asked.

"Lots of things," Lehrling replied.

"No, I mean, are there enemies or predators I need to know about?"

"To be honest," Shawndirea said. "Few humans or other races ever venture into these swamps."

"That's comforting," Roble said softly.

Lehrling nodded. "The swamps tend to frighten folks from entering more than the old sign's warning."

"Understandable," Roble said. "That doesn't answer my question. I've encountered numerous creatures ever since I entered your realm. They're so bizarre I'd never convince people in the Overlands they actually exist. Surely you have some knowledge of what's out here, besides mosquitoes and sprites."

"Nothing more than rumors," Lehrling replied.

"What kind of rumors?"

"Giant lizards walk and talk like humans," Lehrling said with a slight grin. "They wear armor and carry spears and clubs."

Roble's brow narrowed. "By your grin I can't tell if you're being honest or spinning one of your tales."

"It's true," Shawndirea said. "They're *not* mythical. They exist. But few who've encountered them ever escaped with their lives."

"But some escaped?"

"Yes," she said. "Those who did were never the same."

"Bards retell these stories in Woodnog taverns and in the southern kingdoms," Lehrling said. "The men who survived became raving madmen and unable to cope, dying shortly after reaching Woodnog and telling their stories to the medics and healers."

Roble frowned. "Died? From what? Fear? Since my arrival in Aetheaon, I've seen things I never would've believed existed—"

"Venom killed them," Shawndirea said.

"Venom?"

She nodded. "The Lizard-men's bites contain a poison no one's ever survived. Well, at least no human. Who's to say how it might affect a different race."

"Which is why few humans make such a bold journey into the swamps," Lehrling said.

"*Bold* isn't the word I'd use after learning about this," Roble said.

Lehrling ran a hand through his blonde beard. "Perhaps, desperate is a better word. Generally, thieves or murderers flee into these swamps to escape prison. It's a gamble, I suppose. The poisoned ones who survived long enough to reach a tavern outside the swamps have been miscreants. Prison would be more preferable than dying from their toxic bites."

Roble said, "Why didn't you tell me about this *before* we traveled so far from Hoffnung?"

"Would such knowledge have kept you from seeking Lez'minx?" Lehrling asked.

Roble thought for several moments and shook his head. "No."

Lehrling chuckled. "I didn't think so."

"I'd have still come."

"See?" Lehrling grinned. "So what's it matter?"

"Mental preparation is all," Roble replied.

"What do you mean?"

"I like to fully evaluate the circumstances before I act. It's good to have a planned escape route in certain situations."

"There's still plenty of time for that," Lehrling said, smiling.

"Not as much," Roble said. "We traveled several days before we reached these swamps. And now, we're venturing into the heart of them? Certainly, you can understand why I'd rather plan ahead. Hell, I'd have even liked to listened to some of the bard's tales."

Lehrling grinned. "Their stories change half the time, depending on the tavern or how much they're drunk."

"Well, then, at least *part* of their information is true, right?"

"Not always," Shawndirea said.

"How is it that these bards even got the information from the dying victims?" Roble asked.

Lehrling released a hearty laugh and his grin widened. His laughter echoed across the swamp. "These bards are worse than the morticians waiting for the ill to die. Bards who tell haunting tales aren't brave enough to *actually* visit places like this to get firsthand knowledge. Instead, whenever they hear of someone surviving bizarre incidents, they flock outside where the deathbed is housed, hoping to learn more."

"And this benefits them how?" Roble asked.

"A good story is well rewarded. Gold coins, drinks, food, or perhaps an innkeeper's hospitality for a free night's stay," Lehrling said. "Tale-weavers are beggars dressed in fancier clothes."

"Most bards are little more than parasites," Shawndirea said.

"Unless," Lehrling said, "the bard has faced the danger or accompanied a journeyer in such an episode, which is rare."

"How do you know if he or she is telling the truth?" Roble asked.

"That's the real mystery," Lehrling said. "You can't ever really discern if it's true or not, as their livelihoods depend on how well they spin their stories. Some bards actually tell legitimate tales, about the ordeals they've encountered along their travels, or the mishaps of being robbed by highwaymen."

"Are they not highwaymen themselves, if they're lying in order to get free food, lodging, and gold?" Roble asked.

Lehrling shrugged. "I suppose one could look at it that way. The tales don't matter though. Few bards are ever quieted, regardless of the tavern."

"Why's that?"

"Peasants lead uneventful lives," Lehrling replied. "As such, they're looking for something more adventurous, even if it isn't necessarily true. Mead to soften their aching muscles, and harder ales to erase the torment of facing the coming day. That's why the poorer folk listen to the worst tales without squabbling over the minor details. They seldom complain about the taste of their drinks, either, which is why tavern owners are willing to pay a shilling or two of gold or even more, if the bard's tales are highly sought after. As long as the bard can lull their minds into a place where they're not faced with the depths of depressive misery, they earn their keep traveling from town to town."

Roble nodded. The same was true with depressed folk in the Overlands. They were given to their technology, which had progressively worsened over time, snatching away more and more valuable time without people even noticing. Once computer technology dominated his society, Roble craved to find a place where he could live a primitive life without cellphones, computers, and other time sinks. This proved to be why he had no problem adapting to a realm where these things didn't exist, and he *hoped*, they never did.

He grinned. He didn't possess any adequate descriptions to explain the world he had left for Aetheaon. While he loved the simplicity in this realm, he had sacrificed other benefits, which were laws that better protected people from being killed by enforcing severe repercussions to those who murdered others. Unlike Aetheaon. So, he needed to remain vigilant at all times.

"What are you smiling about?" Lehrling asked.

Roble shook his head. "Nothing. It's not important."

"You're not finding humor in what entertains the poor, are you?" he asked.

"Of course not." Roble's smile faded. He stared at the edge of the mired swamp at the line of old trees. His horse snorted and adjusted its front hooves on the ground, possibly agitated at their delay in traveling. Roble patted the side of the horse's neck, and watched the fog or mist hanging between the massive tree trunks. "Have you thought of where we'll camp for the night?"

"Nightfall is hours away," Lehrling said.

"How can you tell?"

"Trust me. You'll know."

"But when dusk settles, and we're in a place like this, where would we camp?" Roble asked. "Nothing remotely hospitable here. With this steady rain, we need shelter. Those trees won't protect us from the weather."

"Rest assured," Lehrling replied. "We won't set up camp in an area like this. Nor would we want to. Far too dangerous."

"My point exactly," Roble said. "Any idea where those folks encountered the Lizard-men?"

"No," Lehrling said. "But I've a feeling it was much deeper into the swamps than this. Otherwise, Elven scouts and rangers from Woodnog would've reported them as a threat to their kingdom."

"That makes sense," Roble said.

Shawndirea stood on Roble's shoulder. "It's doubtful the Lizard-men would risk being sighted by anyone."

Roble said. "So, those men who were bitten traveled quite a distance into the swamps?"

"Indeed," Lehrling said.

"It's not possible," Roble said evenly.

Confusion set in Lehrling's eyes. "Why not?"

"Poisoned? And these victims managed to drag themselves through all this muck and dark waters to reach Woodnog? That's impossible. They'd have been delirious long before they found their way out of the swamp."

Shawndirea's mouth twisted as she thought. "Are you implying these Lizard-men live closer to Woodnog?"

"No. I've no idea about that," Roble said. "Logic indicates that if these men were bitten so far from civilization, they'd have never gotten out of the swamp. They'd most likely have died by drowning or something eating them. These swamps are filled with creatures capable of poisoning bites."

"You're probably right," Lehrling said. "However, these men swore it was Lizard-men that attacked and captured them."

Roble sighed and then nodded. "No sense arguing over what they saw, as we don't know for certain. We've no way to verify it. They might've sworn on it, but if the poison was already affecting their brains … it might only be a hallucination. But consider this … what if some of these Lizard-men lurk in the deeper pools of water and attack whenever a traveler happens by?"

Lehrling whistled slightly. His eyes widened with fear. "That's possible. They'd probably have scouts, too."

Roble eyed the dark trees engulfed by thickening fog for several moments. The wind howled, and the raindrops drummed heavier on the mud and sedge blades. The bird and insect songs drowned beneath the pelleting rain, and hushed in their retreat.

Lehrling shivered. "The air's suddenly colder, which isn't normal this far south."

"Why do you keep staring at those trees?" Shawndirea asked.

"That's the direction we need to go," Roble replied.

"How do you know?" Lehrling asked.

"I'm not sure how to explain it, but this armor seems drawn in that direction."

"Drawn?" Lehrling said with a half laugh. "Your armor is *alive?*"

"No, but it *is* enchanted," Roble said. "It adapts to the weather and keeps me comfortable regardless of extreme temperatures. Perhaps the seamstress is somewhere beyond those trees."

Lehrling pointed to the path ahead of them. In places where the mud was thinner, rocky cobblestone protruded. A fallen lamppost covered with thick moss rested across the old path. "Looks like an old road."

Roble nodded. "I see it. We should cross to those trees before the water rises."

Roble tapped Bleys' sides, and the horse moved forward. With a howl hidden in the wind, a bright greenish-blue light of a wisp zipped past them and disappeared into the dark trees.

"What was that?" Lehrling asked.

Roble shrugged. "I've a feeling we'll soon find out."

CHAPTER 3

"*W*as that a wisp?" Roble asked.

Shawndirea nodded. "I believe so. It *wasn't* a faery."

"Looked like one to me," Lehrling said softly.

"A warning? Or an issue to follow?" Roble asked.

Shawndirea giggled. "Probably neither. Wisps don't offer warnings to humans. If anything, they do the opposite. Only a curious fool follows a wisp through a dark swamp. Wisps are a mischievous lot. They might lead someone to a preset trap. However, at the rate of speed that one's traveling, it's *fleeing* from something."

"Like what?" The hairs on the back of Roble's neck stiffened.

"Let's not wait around to find out," she replied.

Roble offered Lehrling a look of concern. Lehrling glanced back at the trail, gave a slight shrug, and nodded.

"It's best we hurry," Lehrling said.

Roble nudged Bleys' flank to encourage the horse to pick up its pace. The horse refused to move any faster than its own stubborn speed. Bleys had never ignored a command before, so its hesitation concerned Roble.

Looking closer, Roble understood why. Camouflaged in the mud and the old clumps of sedges were tapered knee roots with sharp protruding tips. He winced. Those pointed roots could permanently lame the horse should it step directly on a sharp point. The horse would have to be put down. Roble couldn't stand the thought of losing Bleys. Since the horse was keener to their surroundings than he, Roble chose to let Bleys find his way through the tree roots.

Roble pointed at the protruding roots. "Careful."

"I see them," Lehrling replied. "Quite common for the trees in deeper water. The drought's the only reason we see them. Once we reach drier ground, we won't see so many."

Roble nodded, even though it was information he already knew.

"The terrain changes a lot," Lehrling said.

"Looks like wasteland to me," Roble replied.

"For some." Shawndirea smiled slightly. "Don't be surprised to learn that the places humans despise are paradise for different races."

"Like the Lizard-men?"

"This habitat's far more suitable for them," she said. "But I wasn't referring to them in particular."

"Then what exactly?"

She sighed. "We don't know. The quagmire has never been fully explored. So no one knows."

"I see." Roble studied his surroundings. He wondered if the wisp might circle back.

Stuck in the thick mud beneath the shallow water of these desolate swamps were the countless skeletons of those who entered and never found their way out. Due to the partial sunlight, it was impossible to base direction from the sun's position. He hated to imagine what the swamps were like once the night claimed it. He hadn't planned to be here long enough to find out. But, plans were often disrupted regardless of his intentions, especially in Aetheaon. Harsh environments wrought unexpected obstacles. The marshlands leading into the swamps *weren't* any exception.

As they rode into the dark cover of the large trees, misty wisps meandered around the thick tree knots. The sporadic raindrops increased in tempo and number. The droplets drummed against the wide canopy leaves and sluiced into long streams that splashed into widening pools of the deceptive black water. The pools might only be inches deep or they could plummet several feet deep. The deeper pools might contain tangles of sphagnum moss that could ensnare a person.

He worried about quicksand, amongst other things. The possibility of encountering predatory animals or thieving highwaymen was likely.

The sky darkened. A flash of lightning flickered from cloud to cloud, and shimmered with a bright strobing effect. A sudden cool breeze shook the overhead branches and freed the clinging raindrops from the leaves. The effect was similar to having small cloudburst doused on them.

Roble pulled the hood of his tunic over his head. Shawndirea slipped inside beside his left ear. Turning his head slightly, he gave her a slight smile. She wore her armor cut from the material of Bausch's armor that Roble had taken it off Bausch's dead body. The small piece of leather had form-fitted her perfectly. The section of leather he'd removed from his armor had instantly repaired itself.

Neither could ever deny the armor was enchanted. Before he fully understood and accepted the power of magic in Aetheaon, he perceived the essence when the armor clung to his near freezing flesh. Now, they traveled into the heart of the swamps to find Lez'minx; the one who presided over the magic bestowed on the armor. Or so Lez'mix wanted them to believe.

Roble remained torn on the acceptance of the *god's* demand and boast, except for a couple of things. One, the armor protected him from the weather regardless of the climate, and the rain was repelled and didn't attach to the material. The second reason was harder to explain. He sensed the armor was being drawn toward a source deeper in the swamps. Though Lehrling had joked about the armor being alive, Roble didn't want to admit the armor was like a living entity, and longed to be reunited with its maker. The thought worried him. Could this tugging inadvertently influence his decisions without his knowledge?

When Roble had attacked and killed the Vykings who had taken Lehrling into custody, Roble didn't recall his actions. Lehrling had thought Roble was Bausch, and Roble had efficiently used his throwing knives without the slightest hesitation. In the Overlands, he'd have second guessed the thought of killing another. But, he didn't flinch or hesitate. He acted in kind.

Roble marveled at the armor's adaptation to the climate, but for some reason, when he had worn it in the Black Chasm, the poisonous air had almost killed him. Those who had accompanied him into the chasm died much quicker. The armor had probably resisted the toxins somewhat. If he'd fashioned a mask to cover his nose and mouth, would the poison *not* have affected him? Or was the armor alive and less susceptible to the poison? He puzzled over the likelihood. Perhaps the armor fought to keep him alive, and the longer he remained in the chasm, the armor was slowly dying, too?

These questions burned inside his mind, but he didn't plan to return to the poisonous chasm to test any hypothesis.

"You're awfully quiet," Lehrling said.

The statement jarred Roble from his thoughts. He rebounded with a slight smile. "I'm studying our surroundings."

Lehrling shook his head and grinned. "You're a deep thinker, aren't you?"

Roble shrugged.

"That's a good thing." Lehrling turned his attention to the path and whistled a soft tune.

Roble's heart and mind raced at seeing all of the unusual fauna, most of which were unlike any plants he could identify in the Overlands. If he took these to his home, most would be unknown in his botany field. Should other botanists learn about them, it'd garner thousands of botanists' attention from around his world. Attention was never something he craved. He'd be thrilled to share his discoveries with his colleagues, if to only see the awe on their faces. Of course, revealing such unknown plants into his former world of science would be met with undying pleas to reveal *where* he found them. He couldn't risk others finding and venturing through a rift in the veil that separated his world from the Realm of Aetheaon. The dangers were too great for either side.

When Roble found Shawndirea, his colleague, Deiko, had witnessed her capture. The encounter was met by Deiko's sudden violence to steal Shawndirea. Deiko had been willing to commit murder to obtain her and pulled a gun on Roble.

Roble realized afterwards that if ever he returned home, he must be covert and never allow anyone to see or learn of his visit. He wasn't certain if Deiko had given up his pursuit in finding Roble. Surely, after all this time, he had, but the lust for fame and fortune in his former colleague's crazed eyes was unmistakeable. Should Deiko ever find a way through the veil to Aetheaon, Roble doubted the scientist would survive a day.

Shawndirea scooted closer to Roble and leaned against his cheek.

Roble stared at the growing pools of water at the edges of the disappearing pathway. How many had died in this dismal spot, trying to find their way out? How many had been robbed and murdered? Dead, decaying bodies were most likely in the muck. Their carried secrets died with them; buried and lost to time. Death would not reveal their secrets or give up its dead ... Unless? The Plague-bringer.

Roble hunched forward on the saddle and glanced at Lehrling. "Whatever possessed Bausch to come to such a dismal environment for armor?"

Lehrling wiped water from his brow and shook his head like a dog shakes its coat. "Roble, your word choices betray you in our realm. You stand out more than a dragon adorned in feathers would."

Roble frowned. "What do you mean?"

"I've paid attention to your phrases during our journey. Commoners here—even the nobles or any aristocrat for that matter—don't use the words you do to describe our surroundings."

"You expect me to change the way I speak?"

"Not entirely, no," Lehrling replied. "But, pay attention to how the folks around you talk, and in turn, carry on conversation at their level. I've no doubt your apprenticeship in your realm is far higher than our own, but unless you wish to draw suspicion from others about your origin ... keep in mind, few in Aetheaon are fond of those from the Overlands."

"So how should I speak?"

Lehrling chuckled. "Just ask the basic question. Did you not mean, 'why did Bausch come to the swamps to get his armor?'"

Roble nodded. "Yes."

"Then ask the question without adding upscaled words. It'd be rare for us to encounter royalty in our journey to Lez'minx's temple."

Shawndirea leveled a harsh glare at Lehrling.

Lehrling blushed. "Present company excepted."

"You realize if I'm a queen, Roble's a king?" she asked.

Lehrling released a long sigh, flashed a forced half smile, and nodded. "I understand, Shawndirea. I'm not questioning that. Shouldn't he blend in than immediately reveal he's different than the rest of us?"

She shrugged. "I never care what others think, least of all the commoners that might cross our paths. So what if he sounds or acts differently? The fact he *is* different is what drew me to him and many reasons for why I love him."

Lehrling raised his hands in surrender. "Yes, m'lady."

"Don't mock me."

"I'm not. I swear it to the goddesses."

"We're wasting time," Roble said. "What led Bausch into the swamps for this armor?"

Wiping rain from his brow, Lehrling shook his head. "I've no idea. If he found a tailor in these swamps, I don't know where he gained the information in how to find the person."

Roble sighed. "I'd turn back except I don't think it's in my best interest."

"I agree," Lehrling replied. "Sometimes a bit of suffering is better than an agonizing death."

Roble laughed. "No argument here."

"Shh," Shawndirea whispered. "Stop the horses."

Lehrling and Roble exchanged concerned glances, and gently tugged the reins.

"What is it?" Roble and Lehrling said in hushed voices.

"It may be nothing. With the rain, it's difficult to know," she whispered. "We've left the sanctity of Woodnog's Forests and have entered the swamps. Dark Fae reside here." She slid into the front pocket of his leather vest. "It's best that I'm not seen."

"Why?" Roble asked.

"For the same reason the Ratkin took me. But worse, my mother has enemies here; those in the Unseelie Courts."

"But you renounced your claim to the throne," Roble said.

"To them, that doesn't matter. They'd do almost anything to cause her and our kingdom grievance. Since I'm married to you, a human, the

Unseelie would see us both dead," Shawndirea replied. "Or, they'll kill you and take me prisoner. Either outcome is unacceptable."

"Then it would've been best for you to stay in Faybourne," Lehrling said.

Shawndirea shook her head. "No, Roble's new to our realm. I cannot bear living without him. I'd never forgive myself if I let him travel to find Lez'minx without me and something horrible happened to him."

Lehrling frowned before giving a half grin. "Don't you think I've enough experience to keep him safe?"

She nodded. "Of course, from other humans, Elves, and Dwarves. But not when it comes to the dark Fae. You've never dealt with their kind before. I assure you."

"It seems to me, young faery," Lehrling said, "your presence draws more attention to us than had you not come at all."

"The fact he's an Overlander captures their attention even more than myself."

"Fae can detect that?" Roble asked.

"Of course."

"How?"

"Your lack of familiarity with our realm," Shawndirea replied. "Curiosity beams in your eyes. At your age, that's highly uncommon for any traveler. The Unseelie might kill me and persuade you to join them."

"Why? I'm human, not Fae. Besides, your mother doesn't hide her hatred for me. I've no doubt these Fae would agree with her distaste," Roble said.

"To the contrary, my love," Shawndirea said. "They'd greet you with open arms and hope to birth offspring from you."

"What?" Roble's brow rose.

"My mother and I are from the Seelie Courts, which takes pride in keeping our bloodlines pure and not tainted with other races. That's why she hates you for marrying me. Our children won't be pure by the Seelie's standards," Shawndirea said. "The Unseelie have no problem breeding with species outside of their own. Once they discover how much she hates you for marrying me, you'd be a prize for them to enslave to become one of their own."

"*Enslave?*"

"Yes. They can control you with spells. It's a bit harder in our realm. But if they enticed you in the Overlands, you'd remain theirs until they tire of you. You ever hear of a faery ring?"

He nodded. "Yes. A ring of mushrooms where a mythical—"

Shawndirea beamed a half smile and shaking her head. "It's *not* mythical. It's how the Unseelie capture humans from your realm and bring them to ours. The ring under a full moon and during their ritual dance opens a portal to our realm. Should any foolish human step inside the ring … they're spellbound and delivered to Aetheaon. The Unseelie long for diversity within their courts, which is a direct contrast to ours. Anything to offend our courts is a triumph."

"Since you brought me to Aetheaon, are you Unseelie now?" Roble asked.

She gasped. Fury darkened her widened eyes. "How *dare* you!"

"Easy." Roble swallowed hard. Her sudden anger unsettled him. The beauty of her eyes was masked by the swelling darkness of her pupils. "I only asked because I want to understand the laws you abide by. I wasn't making an accusation."

Still fuming, she breathed heavily. Slowly the darkness in her eyes faded, but she didn't hide her offense. She spoke through gritted teeth and bit her words with iciness. "I'm *not* Unseelie, nor will I *ever* be. I hold allegiance to my own, despite what my mother thinks or vows or accuses. I've never faltered. Perhaps I don't view things like she insists, but you're the one I'm to be with."

"I feel that way, too," Roble replied. "We're destined to be together."

"And more accurately," Shawndirea said, "*you* brought me into Aetheaon after destroying my wings."

"That's true."

"And!" She scrunched her nose. "*You* insisted on doing so. Not me. Believe me, the last thing I ever expected was to have my wings shredded in your net. It was painful. I'd never have sacrificed my wings to *snare* you to come to my realm."

Roble nodded. "Must we rehash this again? I thought this was settled."

"It was, until you said what you said about me becoming Unseelie."

"I didn't say you *are*," Roble said. "I only questioned if perhaps that's why your mother—"

"In her eyes, she'd say I've fallen from the Seelie Courts. She'd be the first to make me an outcast since I've denounced the throne. But on principalities, it's not true. The whole reason I warned you about the Unseelie and their habits is so you'd be less likely to reveal where you're actually from. But your eyes continue to be filled with wonderment at the least uncommon thing." She feigned by widening her eyes and placing her hands against her cheeks. "Oh, my! *That* leaf is purple and indented—"

"Okay, dear, you've made your point." Roble cocked a brow and glanced at Lehrling.

Lehrling laughed. "She's right. It's hard for you to mask your surprise at the things we take for granted. And you don't speak like us, lest you forget."

"I suppose you'll keep reminding me of my speech. But my constant curiosity isn't something I can hide. Nature's always intrigued me and even more since I'm surrounded by fauna and flora unknown to me." He glanced at Shawndirea. What's common for you is uncommon to me. I can't ignore the diversity."

"Those are the moments you make us the most vulnerable," Shawndirea said.

"So true," Roble replied. "I'll try to hide my surprise a bit better."

"A lot of our plants and animals are dangerous," she said.

"Ours, too."

Shawndirea shook her head. "No, I'm not talking about poisonous. Some have magical abilities that are far worse than poison."

"Magical plants?"

"Yes. Cursed ones."

"Here?" Roble asked.

Shawndirea nodded. "*Especially* in the swamps where the Unseelie live. These outlands wall the south of Woodnog to the Misty Sea. The Black Chasm walls Woodnog's western border, which is why the Elves are so protective of their forests. These swamps are not only dangerous, but they bury things. Lost cities, temples, and crumbled libraries with magical tomes have been swallowed by the mire. More gold is under the quagmire than in most Dwarven vaults, but won't see the greediest Dwarf trying to obtain it."

"Why not?"

"Ghosts and angry spirits are overly protective of the possessions they've lost," she replied. "The Unseelie creatures are even worse."

Roble took a deep breath and glanced around the edge of the trees. "Is this your way of trying to get me to turn back?"

"No. But you should know the odds."

"True, but all of this information you've withheld from me until now? Why wait to tell me?" Roble asked in an even tone.

"I hoped the need never arose," she replied.

"And it has?"

"Yes," she said softly.

"Why?"

"I don't know *why*. But I sense the darkness of my rivals, my mother's enemies."

Lehrling shifted in his saddle. His eyes widened slightly. "Perhaps we should head on while there's still light so we can find a suitable place to set camp for the night."

"I agree," Roble said. "We're wasting precious hours of what's considered daylight here."

Lehrling laughed.

Roble frowned. "I wasn't joking."

"Trust me. You'll *know* when it's night."

"I imagine so, which is why I want to get as far as possible while we can."

A high shriek pierced through the steadily thrumming rain.

"What was that?" Roble asked.

Lehrling shrugged. His eyes narrowed, as he stared into the dark trees.

Shawndirea ducked inside his vest. "Unseelie. They've attacked something."

"Let's go." Roble tapped his heel to Bleys' flank. The smartest thing would've been to head the opposite direction. But for Roble, he didn't like the idea of retreating when a painful cry beckoned unknowingly for help. He had to know if he could help. Sometimes, though, saving a victim wasn't in one's best interest.

CHAPTER 4

*F*rustration rose inside Roble. The horse refused to move any faster, due to the tree knees and the uneven pockets on the watery path. Even though he recognized the possible danger for Bleys, he worried they'd never outpace whomever or whatever was watching them. Should they be attacked they wouldn't have adequate time to defend themselves and possibly die. He could run faster through waist-deep water than the horse walked on the path.

A bright greenish flash of light emitted around a narrow bend within the towering, moss-covered trees. The light glowed brighter and the pain-filled scream rose in timbre for several moments before it faded into a whisper.

Roble tugged the reins. Ahead on the path, pinned against a bent dead tree trunk was a wisp. Crooked narrow fingers wrapped around its throat. At first glance the fingers resembled tree roots spindling around the wisp's neck from a deformed clump of mud. Then the mass beside the tree moved.

The grotesque creature stood hunched over and held the wisp captive. Large hairy moles protruded through the thin layer of oozing mud dripping down its back. Its skin was the same shade of brown as the mud, and had it been night, he could've walked right past the creature without ever having seen it. Even more alarming was how easily it blended into the soggy earth in the marshier places to attack unsuspecting passersby.

A third arm dangled between its shoulder blades, lifeless and useless, the cruelty of deformity, and the arm swayed slightly. The slimy beast raised a sharp blade carved from a crude stone into the air with its left hand. Within a breath of movement, the creature appeared ready to kill the wisp with a swift downward plunge of the blade.

"Stop!" Roble slid off his horse.

"What are you doing?" Shawndirea whispered from his pocket.

Roble ignored her.

Startled, the beast turned and snarled. Its oddly shaped mouth—filled with rolls of broken, crooked teeth—curled into a grimace. Slime oozed from the sides of its mouth. Huffing through its narrow mouth, it offered a guttural growl and slowly lowered the blade. Its head wobbled side to side as its narrowed eyes attempted to get a better view of Roble but even during its curiosity, it didn't release the wisp.

The light surrounding the wisp continued to fade. The creature's hand sparkled, and seemed to be draining the wisp's magic and life.

"Blah!" The thing widely waved the rock dagger at Roble.

It had long thin arms and spindly legs, but its overly exaggerated, round body jiggled and sloshed like gelatin whenever it moved its club-like feet. If this mud creature had a neck, the blubbering rolls sagging beneath its chin hid it well. The thing resembled a glob of clay haphazardly put together out of proper proportion by a small child. Its anatomy was almost humorous except the creature was *alive*.

"Roble," Lehrling said softly, sliding off his horse. "Don't approach it."

"I have no intention of getting any closer." Roble slid a throwing dagger from a sheath on his belt.

Roble stepped atop a more even piece of ground where he could throw the knife without anything obstructing his aim.

The creature growled fiercely. Its mouth partially closed and twisted. Green spittle sprayed through its teeth. Drool dripped in long sticky streams from the sides of its mouth and wherever the spittle fell, the plants browned and withered.

"Acid?" Roble glanced at Lehrling.

Lehrling nodded, grabbed his horse's reins and Bleys', and led the horses safely outside the creature's spitting range. "Yes. Come on, Roble. Mount up. We'll head a different direction."

Roble shook his head. "I can't let it kill the wisp."

"Don't be a fool," Lehrling said. "We've no quarrel with this creature."

The light from the wisp dimmed. The tightened hand around the wisp's throat radiated a greenish glow that traveled halfway up the creature's bent arm. The creature was absorbing the wisp's energy and magic.

"What is it?" Roble asked.

Lehrling shook his head. "No idea."

Shawndirea peered from the vest pocket. She frowned and studied the creature. "It's a bogshee."

"Is this the Unseelie you sensed?" Roble asked.

"No." She shook her head. "It's not Unseelie. It's a swamp monster."

Roble glanced around. "Then where is what you felt?"

"Nearby. Leave the creature and let's go," she replied.

"It's draining the wisp's power," Roble said.

The bogshee gnashed its uneven teeth together with a grating sound that sent shivers down Roble's spine. It reared its wobbling head in a threatening manner. A gurgling sound, a loud belch, and a gush of acid phlegm spewed onto the ground, which burned and consumed any vegetation it touched.

Splattering raindrops, bit by bit, washed more of the mud from the bogshee's slimy skin.

Roble stared in near disbelief, something he had promised Lehrling and Shawndirea he would not do, but how could he not be astonished? The bogshee was an abnormality without any logical explanation for *why* it even existed. *In my world*, he reminded himself. He wondered if this thing had pulled itself out of the marshland after the rains began.

"So?" she said. "Is a wisp worth risking your life for?"

"We should let it die?" he asked.

"Normally, I'd say to rescue it. But if the bogshee reaches you or Lehrling, it'll kill you before you can defend yourself. You see what its spit is capable of doing, right?"

He nodded.

"Understand this," she said. "The acid reacts differently with human flesh."

"Differently, how?"

"It never stops burning through your flesh. It's a painful death. I've seen the outcome only once, but not on a human. An elf."

"From one of these?"

She nodded. "Yes. So let's go. Please. I understand your want to help other creatures, but you don't *want* to get near the bogshee."

Roble held his blade between his index finger and thumb and chuckled. "I don't need to get any closer. Look at it. It can't possible move faster than I can throw."

Shawndirea sighed. "Looks are deceptive, my dear, or haven't you *learned* that yet?"

The trapped wisp cried softly and emitted a short blast of light, as the bogshee absorbed its fleeting energy.

In seconds, the wisp would be dead. Its life probably ended whenever its last ray of light was snuffed. Disregarding the warnings, Roble flung the knife and struck the bogshee's thick round gut. Half expecting the blade to bounce off the creature's skin, he was surprised when the knife plunged deep into its flesh.

The bogshee didn't react in pain. Instead, it glanced at the protruding hilt of the knife with the briefest curiosity. The massive layers of jiggling blubber congealed around the blade. Greenish ooze leaked from where the skin split open. The stomach muscles quivered, causing the ooze to spill faster. The bogshee stiffened, suddenly acknowledging the foreign object lodged in its flesh as something unwanted. It snarled angrily for a second. Its eyes widened, and a softer whine came from its mouth.

The bogshee's stone knife dropped to the wet ground without a sound.

"Mum-duh!" it said in a dull voice. It grabbed the dagger's hilt and tugged the blade free. The greenish goo gushed and spilled on the ground. The roundness of its stomach shrank.

Its eyes glanced at Roble with confusion and almost pleaded to understand what was happening. The bogshee returned its attention to the liquid spilling from its abdomen. It mumbled sounds without meaning and released its hold from around the wisp's neck before collapsing to its knees.

The wisp gleamed only a second longer and slid into a crevice in the tree's bark.

The bogshee sat in its liquid entrails, more confused than in pain or anger. It seemed a unintelligent creature, and other than its odd need to drain the wisp of its light, it acted rather docile. Even so, Roble remained cautious and drew his sword. Shawndirea's warning rang in his ears. Although the bogshee was injured and perhaps near death, he had been surprised by other creatures before. He wasn't going to risk his life, especially not with Shawndirea inside his pocket, because if he died, she most likely died, too.

Lehrling pulled his sword and stood beside Roble. "You think it's dying?"

Roble shrugged. "I was about to ask the same thing."

Lehrling sighed. "I've never seen one of them before."

The bogshee's lips drooped into a sad expression. It placed a hand to its leaking stomach, cupped a handful of its blood, and stared at it. A few seconds later, life drained from its eyes and it fell on the ground in a mixture of blood, slime, and mud.

With a slight tinge of remorse, Roble swallowed hard. He didn't understand the creature's motives other than to feed on the wisp's energy. He knew nothing about the bogshee's nature and whether or not it was hostile toward humans or only pursued wisps. He took a step forward.

"Careful," Shawndirea said softly.

"It's dead, isn't it?" Roble asked.

"I honestly don't know. It could be faking, hoping you'll let your guard down and come close enough for it to attack."

"How could anything live after losing so much … I want to say blood, but …" Roble grimaced.

"I think it's dead," she said. "But let's not take the chance of me being wrong."

"Let's go." Lehrling returned to the horses.

"Not yet," Roble replied.

"Why not?"

Roble tightened his grip on his sword. "I want to see if the wisp is still alive."

"It's most likely dead, don't you think?" Lehrling asked.

"We don't know unless we check."

"That's true of the leaking acid bog beast, too."

"Listen to him," Shawndirea said.

"I am, but if that wisp is still alive—"

"Roble, *please*," she said, "I understand your want to protect innocent creatures that fall victim to predators, but this world is strange to you. In your world, predators and prey both exist, correct?"

Roble nodded.

She said, "In this realm, not everything's clearly good or evil. Since we're in an area where there's more darkness than light, you cannot trust what you see."

"I know," Roble said. "But look."

The wisp flickered tiny rays of blue and green.

Shawndirea sighed. "It's almost dead. There's nothing we can do."

"Shouldn't we at least try?" Roble asked.

Lehrling glanced at her and rolled his eyes.

"I saw that," Roble said.

Lehrling gave a sheepish grin.

Rain sluiced from the trees. Flickering lightning brightened the sky for a moment.

"You're wasting time, Roble," Lehrling said. "Either you're prolonging your encounter with Lez'minx or deep down you realize the best thing we can do is to turn back."

Roble shook his head. "I assure you neither is the case. But if we can rescue this little creature, I cannot walk away."

"Remember when I said the wisp was fleeing from something?" Shawndirea asked.

Roble nodded.

"Then our delay is allowing its pursuer time to reach us. The bogshee was draining the wisp's light and magic, but it did so out of opportunity. It wasn't *what* the wisp fled from. The wisp chose the wrong place to hide and rest. Quite possibly, she never saw the bogshee before it captured her."

Roble's eyes flicked to the bogshee's corpse. "I would've never noticed it, had it not moved. It blends into the swamp's surroundings quite well."

She offered a slight smile. "Yes, it does."

"Should we expect more of them?" he asked.

"They're rare creatures," she replied. "With the storms settling in, it might've taken the opportunity to find a new mud pool to habituate. The dry season has ended. The storms from the seas will continue for several months, which means we'd best hurry while the levels of water in the marshy swamps are low. None of us want to be stuck in Woodnog's swamps for several months."

"I agree," Roble said. "Can I at least check on the wisp?"

She puffed her cheeks and slowly expelled the air in a long exasperated sigh. "I'm surprised you fought in the Battle of Hoffnung without offering aid to the ones the Vykings maimed."

"War's different." Roble frowned. "Vykings were the enemy. This—"

"The wisp could be friend or foe, and in these swamps where the Unseelie reside, most likely she's a foe," Shawndirea said. "For the life of me, dear, I don't know how else to explain this. I love you for your caring heart, but if we stop along the wayside every time a creature is suffering, we'll eventually fall prey to worse things than a bogshee."

"Duly noted," he said.

Roble eased to the side of the path where the bogshee's shrinking body slowly sunk into the wet soil. At the rate of its decomposition, he didn't fear it'd attack. However, the acid it had spewed was something they needed to avoid. While the rain might eventually dilute the acid's potency, how much water would it take?

Stepping around the green acid pool, Roble walked off the path and through several small shrubs until he reached the tree where the wisp's light flickered from inside a deep crevice of the bark.

Roble sheathed his sword. He peered closer, trying to see the wisp's body. With his right hand, he reached for what he thought might be one of its feet.

"Don't!" Shawndirea said.

He pulled back his hand. "What? Why?"

"Use a stick or something to free it," she replied. "But don't touch it directly."

"Why not?"

"Some of the bogshee's acid might be on it? Besides, even near death, it might've enchanted itself with any sort of defensive spell strong enough to kill a human or bewitch you."

"Never thought about that," he replied.

Shawndirea shook her head. "If I didn't despise the Overlands as much as I do, I'd insist we moved there so you don't kill yourself due to your ignorance of our realm."

Roble laughed. "It takes time to learn and adapt."

"Few survive the transition, my dear," she said softly. "Granted, you learn fast, but it takes only one blind mistake to get you killed."

"That's true for anyone," he replied.

Roble pulled a broad leaf from one of the shrubs and found a narrow, dead twig and snapped it from the side of the tree. Gently, he used the twig to work the wisp free from the crevice and allowed it to fall on a leaf. Then, he moved the wisp and leaf to a fallen log where he could examine the creature closer.

For what beauty the brilliant glow had given the wisp during flight, its true visage was a hundred times more grotesque. In some ways, the wisp was more hideous than the bogshee.

Roble couldn't help but wonder if the extreme illumination was meant to conceal the ugliness of its features in order to lure others to follow its radiant glow. Humans typically were flawed to be attracted to beauty and dispelled by ugliness. What pleased the eyes, most often, were the things humans actively sought, and Shawndirea's advice was most accurate. He had wanted to help the creature because of its adorned brilliance, but deep inside, he really wanted to help it because he had accidentally destroyed Shawndirea's wings when they first met.

He peered at the gasping wisp. Its eyes parted slightly, and were blacker than obsidian. No color like the radiant light it displayed during flight shown in its eyes. Its hawkbill nose and pointy teeth were not features he expected to see, either. Warts covered its face and body and its withered skin made a raisin look smooth.

"What's wrong?" Shawndirea asked.

"Nothing," he said softly. "Why?"

"You're repulsed. At least your facial features reveal your evident distaste."

"I—I expected the wisp to be beautiful like you," he replied.

She blushed. "I imagine she was at one time, but the bogshee drained her light. Without her light, her life and beauty are extracted, too."

"So she was beautiful before it sapped her radiance?"

Shawndirea shrugged. "There's no way to rightly know, my dear. So, what now? It's not going to live. Nothing we do will restore her powers or her radiance. That's forever gone."

Roble nodded and accepted her observation. "Should we wait and bury it?"

"What? No," Shawndirea replied. "Nature takes care of its own."

"Why was the bogshee stealing her light?"

"Not sure. Could be a source of strength as it moves from one mud pool to another."

The wisp gasped. Whispered raspy words escaped its narrow mouth. The words were a phrase and it repeated them a second time. Its body jerked as its last breathes were spent in a sharp laugh. After its dying breath, the tiny body shriveled into a small pile of dust.

"What'd it say?" Roble asked.

Shawndirea swallowed hard and looked in his eyes. "It's a trap!"

CHAPTER 5

*R*oble turned to run to where Lehrling stood with the horses, but before he took a step, the tree limbs were aglow with hundreds of wisps.

"It *is* a trap!" Shawndirea gasped. "Roble, Lehrling … run!"

"I don't advise it," a voice said from high in the trees. "Unless you wish to die where you flit."

"Dirk?" Shawndirea searched the trees to locate him. She frowned.

The male faery glided from his perch in the shadowed trees and hovered inches before Roble. A smirk twisted Dirk's narrow lips. His nose twitched slightly and he stared in a condescending manner.

Shawndirea stood and climbed from Roble's vest pocket. Fury tightened her face and her fingertips glowed fiery green.

"What do you want, cousin?" she asked.

"Your mother's dismissal from the throne," he replied. "I appreciate you denouncing your claim to replace her, which makes it much easier for me to assume her place. But it's time she abdicates."

"She'll never allow you to rule in her place, nor will I," Shawndirea said.

Roble's hand slid to his belt within inches of another throwing dagger. He gave Lehrling a side glance, A half dozen faery guards hovered around Lehrling's face with their swords drawn and their blades aimed at his eyes.

Dirk laughed and flitted upwards, apparently ensuring he was outside Roble's immediate reach. "You have no say in such matters, former princess."

"I'm *still* a Queen," she hissed.

"Not to Elvendale's throne, but to those little precious butterflies you hold … oh, so, dear." He cupped his hands together and pressed them to the side of his cheek. A moment later, he lowered his hands to his side and fury darkened his eyes. "I, however, aspire for so much more."

"Mother presides over Elvendale," Shawndirea said.

"Istrell's no longer mentally capable to oversee Elvendale. I have you to thank, my beloved cousin. Your decision to pair yourself with this … *human* from the Overlands, has shattered her resolve," he laughed. "You've reduce her to a sniveling sot."

Shawndirea's eyes widened.

"Oh? You didn't know?" Dirk offered an evil grin with an equally degrading laugh. "Yes. *You* turned her into a wine bibber. So, thank you and congratulations! I've always been aware of the wedge between you two. Your rebelliousness over the years has spewed her contempt, but now, oh, her mind cannot function, so she numbs it with the strongest wines Elvendale produces. However, if you ask me, I've the suspicion she adds something a tad stronger with the kick of Dwarven stout."

"That's difficult to believe," she said.

"Believe it." Dirk burst into a short bit of laughter. "After your beloved survived his venture into the Black Chasm and you married him, she's sunken even deeper. If you don't believe me, ask Feather."

"Feather? Where is she?" Shawndirea crossed her arms and studied the trees.

Although offended by Dirk's words, Roble kept his silence, but warily watched Dirk and the other faeries with their swords drawn. The other faeries seemed preoccupied with Dirk's heated conversation with Shawndirea. With Dirk's continued bickering, Roble looked for an opportunity to attack.

"Oh, no, you can't ask her *here*," Dirk said. "Feather's practically become the daughter Istrell no longer has. Who are we kidding? The daughter she *never* had. Your mother has placed unmeasurable trust into Feather. Feather displays the perfect etiquette any mother treasures in a daughter. They've bonded quite well, which is a damn shame actually."

"Why's that?" Shawndirea asked.

Roble slid the tip of his dagger from its sheath while Dirk beamed his full attention at Shawndirea. The rain increased its tempo and the rhythm of the droplets seemed to have made it difficult for Shawndirea and her cousin to hear one another. Dirk hovered closer, and Roble hoped the distracting rain allowed an opportunity where he could successfully fling the dagger with enough accuracy to clip one of Dirk's wings.

"Why's it a shame?" Shawndirea asked. "I've known Feather my entire life."

"The shame is Feather's grown fonder of your bitter old mother, if you can imagine that. Convincing Feather to poison your mother's wine has grown impossible. She outright refuses." Dirk hovered and rested his hands on his hips. "In spite of her being engaged to me, too. Oh, and please accept our invitation to attend the wedding."

"I'm amazed your wings allow you to fly in the midst of this rain," Roble said.

Dirk regarded him for a moment with a cocked brow. With a sneer, he said, "Yes, I imagine so. Such minor things keep the simpleminded entertained, don't they?"

"Actually, I'm more inclined to believe your inflated ego keeps you afloat."

"My, my, he's a testy one, isn't he, Shawndirea?" Dirk mocked with a yawn. "You know how to pick one, and such a pity he's no match for me in combat."

"If that's a challenge—"

Dirk tilted his nose upward and dismissed Roble with a slight wave of his hand. Several faeries with swords swept from the trees and stood behind Dirk. Their horrid faces were like that of the dying wisp or something often haunting one's nightmares, but some of their facial features were even worse, misshaped, and pocked. "Face it, Overlander, you're outmatched. Perhaps after you've had several years of training,

I'll not embarrass you so badly. Whatever she sees in you is beyond any Fae's comprehension. Now, cousin—"

"*Why* are you in the Woodnog Swamps?" Shawndirea asked. "You must reside in Elvendale if you have the slightest hope to ever be crowned and take the throne, even if you are of the proper bloodline. Has my mother exiled you again?"

"Phht!" Dirk's eyes narrowed. "She'd never do such a thing!"

"She did once before," Shawndirea said.

Roble chuckled. "And he calls me, *testy*?"

Anger creased Dirk's brow. "Over a minor misunderstanding. I've gained new favor in her eyes since you've married this filth from the Overlands."

Roble's jaw tightened but he held his silence.

"Is that so?" Shawndirea shook her head. "Not likely, since you're trying to kill my mother in order to assume the throne."

He shrugged. "*Only* to speed it along. Nothing more."

"Then you ought to be by her side, learning your duties, and not out here in the swamps where the Unseelie reside—" Her eyes widened.

Dirk smiled. "Ahh, I wondered when you'd make the connection, dear cousin. I've joined myself with the Unseelie Court, and I'm building an army that despises Istrell, which has been far easier than I imagined. Your mother has never been a friendly soul, now has she? My alliance with the Unseelie should come as no surprise, since you've decided to do so as well."

"I haven't," she said. "Nor would I ever."

"Marrying outside your kind, to a human?" He winced. "That fringes on the border of *becoming* an Unseelie. Ghastly and frightening."

"You should fear my husband," she said.

"Fear him? *Him*? Ha! Why?"

"He could squash you like a slimy slug. Roble, you should do so." She clasped her hands together and fluttered her eyelids. "Please? I insist."

"Should he make one sudden move, I'll—" Dirk said.

"What? Kill him?"

"No, I wouldn't do something *that* brutal. I would only command my newfound guards to spear out his eyes. That'd crush his spirit and perhaps wither your heart by having a blind husband."

Roble frowned. "As much fun as it'd be to see you attempt such an attack, we must be on our way. I'm tired of standing in the rain, listening to your pompous prattling."

"Oh, you and your human friend can leave," Dirk said, "but Shawndirea's coming with us."

"No. *Not* going to happen," Roble said.

"No?" Dirk snapped his fingers.

Dozens of wisps suddenly blared their bright shimmering lights in the trees, which revealed more armed faery soldiers eagerly awaiting Dirk's signal to attack.

"Don't be a fool," Shawndirea said. "I'm not going anywhere with you. Besides, why should I?"

"It's not a request. I'm taking you as my prisoner. Perhaps when your mother learns you're in my custody, she'll hand the crown over to me. With a bow, mind you, and *not* a curtsey."

"She won't."

"You've placed an enormous amount of animosity between the two of you," Dirk said. "However, when she learns your life's in jeopardy and your human husband did nothing to prevent it, she'll intervene. Regardless of her words, her heart aches for you. She'll do whatever's necessary to save you."

Roble flung his dagger and nicked Dirk's shoulder. The blade continued in a blur and lodged dead center in one of the hovering soldiers behind Dirk. The dagger spun off balance and the hilt struck the tree. Clutching the blade pierced through its chest, the dark faery plummeted to the ground. The weighted dagger was like an anchor pulling the faery's dead body under the mud.

"Oh, you'll suffer for that." Dirk sneered.

The stones set in Roble's rings glowed and caught Dirk's immediate interest.

The bogshee's corpse suddenly wailed and its body moved. Words thundered from its mouth. "It's you who'll suffer, Dirk, if you attempt to harm any of them."

Roble's brow rose in surprise. "It speaks?"

The entire band of faery soldiers turned their attention to the bogshee as it pushed itself slowly to its feet.

A confused expression crossed Dirk's face. He flicked his gaze from the bogshee to Roble. His eyes revealed his brief moment of fear. "I could've sworn you killed that thing."

Roble met Dirk's confused eyes and shrugged. "As did I."

"This—this is your doing?" Dirk pointed at the bogshee. "How?"

"While I'd like to take credit, I'm afraid, I've nothing to do with it."

"But your rings," Dirk said.

Roble shrugged. "What about my rings."

"They—"

"Your only warning," the creature said.

"Or what, pray tell?" Dirk asked with a sly grin. He slashed his sword through the air and faced the bogshee.

"I'll rid Aetheaon of the disease you are! Roble's under my protection. Don't be a fool. Be on your way."

"I don't take kindly to threats, especially from a … a piece of talking swamp sludge."

"Fool!" The bogshee's eyes glowed yellowish-green.

The dark faeries behind Dirk suddenly dropped their swords and clutched their throats. Seconds later, their lifeless bodies dropped to the wet, marshy ground. The wisps' lights brightened until they couldn't withstand the sudden surge of energy building inside them. Their tiny bodies exploded and left behind glittery, splattered gobs.

Stunned and overcome with fright, Dirk's eyes widened. More dark faery soldiers fell dead in the mire. The remaining few fled and left Dirk hovering in place. His eyes indicated he was unsure of whether he should attack or flee.

"Who are you?" Dirk nervously sheathed his sword.

"Lez'minx."

"Are you Seelie or Unseelie?"

"Neither. But your doom is near at hand."

"What are you?"

"It's best you *don't* know."

Shawndirea smiled. "Do us all a favor and end his life like the others on the ground."

The bogshee's strange eyes focused on her. "That, dear faery, I'll gladly do, *if* you'll swear your allegiance to me."

She frowned and crossed her arms. "Then, no. He lives, for now."

The bogshee's head wobbled slightly. It returned its attention to Dirk. "Very well. You're spared for today, Dirk. But should you cross their paths anywhere in these swamps again, I'll know, and you'll die a more horrible death than your former allies. Understood?"

Dirk swallowed hard and shook his head.

"Now, *go!*" the voice bellowed.

Dirk turned, cast a defeated glance at Shawndirea, and disappeared in a quick dart through the trees.

"Continue on the path you've chosen," Lez'minx said. "You'll find me soon enough."

"By continuing onward to find your temple," Roble said, "I hope you aren't expecting my allegiance."

"Since you possess items I've blessed, I hold your allegiance already," Lez'minx said. "Never forget that. You've my protection, for now. Don't suffer my wrath like those fallen at your feet. Until we meet again."

The bogshee fell face first in the mud and lie silent and still.

Roble held a sword in his right hand and a dagger in his left. He walked toward the bogshee.

"No, Roble, don't," Shawndirea said. "You can't trust it's completely dead. Lez'minx might use its poison on you."

"I'm not going to bother it."

"Then what are you doing?"

Roble sheathed his sword and dagger. He knelt near a dead Shadowfae assassin. He untied a small coin pouch from its belt and placed it on his palm. The pouch grew in size, and the coins rattled when he shook the purse. He poured out several coins, shook his head, and chuckled.

"Gold?" Lehrling asked.

Roble shrugged.

"What's humorous?" Shawndirea asked.

"Perhaps you should see for yourself," Roble replied.

Shawndirea flew and lighted on Roble's forearm. Lehrling hurried to stand beside Roble and inspected the coins.

"The nerve. How dare he!" Anger creased her brow.

"Seems his mind is on overthrowing Istrell. He's already minted coins," Roble said.

Shawndirea seethed. "I should've had Lez'minx kill him. Dirk had best hope our paths never cross again."

Roble held up the largest gold coin. Dirk's side profile was centered with a caption that read: "King of Elvendale."

CHAPTER 6

*R*oble swung onto the saddle with the coins still in hand.

"Throw them away," Shawndirea said.

"Why? We can always melt them down for the gold."

Her eyes narrowed darker. "I'll not have you carry any emblem where he's labeled himself the king of my homeland."

Roble tossed the coins and watched them sink in the muck.

"Thank you."

Roble shrugged but didn't reply. He took several moments to observe the darkening, swampy terrain. Lightning flashed. Raindrops pattered atop the leaves, the bent trees, and the several dozen, dead faery soldiers. Thunder echoed, as though it were the closing curtain for the events that had transpired.

He didn't know whether he should be flattered that Lez'minx had intervened before the situation had turned into a bloody assault or if Lez'minx's protection had somehow been more to demand Roble's undying loyalty and obligation. But had Lez'minx not acted, he, Lehrling, and Shawndirea had been greatly outnumbered. Roble wouldn't have hesitated to put his life on the line to save Shawndirea and prevent Dirk from taking her captive.

Even though the soldiers with Dirk were small faeries, their swords were, no doubt, sharp enough to inflict severe injuries, perhaps even fatal ones.

Roble thought about the threat Dirk had made, about blinding him as a punishment for marrying Shawndirea. The more Roble thought about this, the angrier he became. Such punishment was far greater than death for Roble. He'd be forever robbed of seeing Shawndirea's beauty, which was greater than any gem or treasure Roble had ever beheld. Dirk's choice for punishment was quite cruel. He and Dirk's paths would eventually cross again, and whenever that meeting occurred, Roble refused to be as gracious as he was minutes earlier. Dirk had drawn the magical line, and Roble planned to cross it with pure fury.

Scattered across the tree branches and against higher areas of the tree trunks were glowing splattered globs where each of the enemy wisps had exploded. Roble shook his head. Their remains almost resembled paintballs that had missed their targets, and for a moment he thought about the comparative humor, but then he realized, nothing's humorous in war, which was Dirk's intent. With Roble being married to Shawndirea, this would become a war he couldn't ignore. He had an obligation to protect Elvendale by marriage, even if Queen Istrell openly despised him. Elvendale was Shawndirea's home, and by marriage, his.

Aetheaon offered a lot of things, the chiefest of which seemed to be the constant unrest between opposing forces. He had already fought in one battle, and risked his own life for Queen Istrell by scouting foolishly into the Black Chasm to prove himself. In hindsight, he should've refused her challenge, as it had done him no favors and hadn't gained her approval.

Roble gently tapped Bleys' flank and used the reins to guide the horse to the narrow path that led deeper into the swamps. With the water steadily rising in the swamps, precious time was fleeting. Nightfall would soon settle.

Glancing at a soaked Lehrling, Roble said, "What's your thoughts on Lez'minx now? Is he a demigod or a god? Surely no wizard or mage could perform such a feat."

Shawndirea moved from his pocket and sat on his shoulder. Before Lehrling offered a reply, she said, "I'm not sure."

Slight fear widened Lehrling's eyes as he looked at the dead faeries. "It's unsettling to say the least."

Roble nodded. He held his reins loosely and allowed the horse to lead at its own cautious pace. "While I don't fully understand the differences between a god and a demigod, he seems to have godlike abilities."

"In what way?" she asked.

Perplexed, he glanced at her. "You saw what he did. He somehow knows exactly where we are, knew we were in danger, and he intervened. Doesn't that make him omnipotent or omnipresent?"

"Not necessarily," she replied. "He might've detected your enchanted armor."

"That's disturbing," Roble said softly.

"Or," she said, "it could be your rings. Remember, I warned you *not* to wear them?"

"Yes, you did."

"Roble, did you not notice the gemstones on your rings glowed right before Lez'minx made his presence known to all of us?"

Roble frowned and looked at the rings. He wore the ruby ring on his right hand and the large topaz on his left. After several moments, he shook his head. "No, I didn't. They really glowed?"

Lehrling nodded. "Quite brightly. Dirk noticed. I'm surprised you didn't."

"I was more concerned about how to protect Shawndirea from being taken." He gave her a side-glance. "If Lez'minx's not omnipotent, how'd he kill all those soldiers and wisps, even though he wasn't physically present?"

Lehrling wiped rain from his brow with the back of his hand. "I must admit, in spite of everything else, that was mortifyingly impressive."

"No argument here," Roble said. "But anything lesser than a god or demigod … Could a wizard or mage even be capable of such a feat?"

Shawndirea pursed her lips. "Magic has no limits, but for one crafting magic from a great distance and actually capable of maintaining control, he or she must be seasoned far longer than I've been alive in order to do what he did."

"So he's a god?"

"I can't absolutely say," she replied. "Based on what we witnessed, it's more plausible than not. However, we don't know where his temple is, if he has one, or where he currently resides. If he's closer than we expect, it's less likely he's a god and he's trying to impress or intimidate you. If nothing else, he wanted our attention and loyalty."

Lehrling chuckled. "He has mine."

"He asked for your allegiance," Roble said to Shawndirea.

"Not something he'll ever get, even if Elvendale and my mother would be safer with Dirk dead. The temptation to accept his offer was enticing. If Lez'minx killed Dirk, Dirk's blood wouldn't be on my hands."

"Those faeries Dirk had with him. They don't resemble any of the ones I met in Elvendale."

"No, they're dark Fae or more commonly known as Shadowfae from the Unseelie Court."

"So Dirk has chosen darkness over light?" Lehrling asked.

"It would appear," Shawndirea said with disappointment.

"Why would he do that?" Roble asked.

"Because none of my mother's soldiers would dare oppose her rule. They'd risk their lives for her and our kingdom. Coups are never acceptable or successful within the Fae kingdoms."

"None have ever tried?" Roble asked.

"Tried, yes. But loyalty to the crown and our beloved queens never falters," she replied. "Generally, if any scorned faery wishes to cause an uprising, they're killed immediately the moment he or she whispers a hinted plot. Such an execution is never viewed as murder in the Seelie Court. My mother has pardoned several soldiers over the past century."

Roble thought for several moments. He pushed aside a leafy branch as he rode. Beads of water showered from the leaves. In spite of the cold rain, he remained dry underneath the armor. Even his beard and hair were not touched by the rain. The same held true for Shawndirea with her tiny armor made from his.

Lehrling, on the other hand, was drenched. His hair was matted and his beard resembled a frayed wet rope from having wrung out the water several times. He looked miserable but never offered complaint.

Glancing at Shawndirea, Roble said, "Doesn't your mother worry about other faeries killing someone they disliked and then accuse the faery as being guilty of treason?"

"With the exception of Dirk and a few others like him, our honor and valor is prized highly."

"What changed for him?" Roble asked.

She shrugged. "Jealousy? Resentment? He roamed Aetheaon with other humans, rather than ... it hurts me to say ... our own."

"Humans corrupted him?" Lehrling asked.

"Yes. He allowed greed to consume him."

Lehrling grinned slightly. "I can see that."

"What makes Dirk think he could obtain Elvendale's loyalty if he gathers an outside army and attacks? Even if he succeeded in killing Istrell, he would never gain favor from those who have served her," Roble said.

"You're right," she replied. "He won't."

"Then why pursue it? Why not build his own kingdom?"

"Pride, greed, and his growing bitterness," Shawndirea said.

"Why's he so bitter?"

"Jealousy toward me since my mother deemed me to replace her, despite my numerous protests."

"Dirk knew you didn't want the throne?"

"Of course. It's no secret. Long ago, he and I once were close, like brother and sister. We shared our thoughts, expanded our dreams with one another about our futures, and during one of those conversations, I revealed I never wanted to assume my mother's place on the throne. Not long afterwards, he grew distant."

"Why?"

Shawndirea bit her lower lip, deep in thought. "I'm not quite certain for his reasons. About a year later, mother exiled Dirk."

Lehrling frowned. "For what reason?"

"No one informed me. Around that time was when my mother and her sister came at odds. Perhaps Dirk had shared with my aunt, Aerlene, that I didn't want to the throne. You remember Aerlene in Woodcrest?"

Roble nodded. "Yes."

"Until I found her at Woodcrest, I thought she was dead. My mother lied and spread the rumor quite convincingly," Shawndirea said. "She and Dirk were exiled at the same time."

"Why'd she allow Dirk to return?" Roble asked.

"I'm not sure. Mother didn't inform me about a lot of issues after our heated exchange about me refusing to assume the throne after her passing. I suppose she might've entertained the idea of having him take the throne. But, he's the last Fae she'd ever want to see rule over Elvendale now, which she confided to me."

The overcast skies became darker, gloomier. The rain showed no sign of letting up. Thunder loomed in the distance.

"What about Feather?" Roble asked. "How does she play into all of this?"

A smile brightened Shawndirea's face. "Feather was like a sister. We spent the majority of our youth playing in the castle. We were best friends. That is, until she learned of my ability to heal and rejuvenate butterflies."

"Why? What changed?"

"She did. Jealousy, mostly, as I was capable of something she wished she could do. She resented seeing the butterflies flock to me and ignoring her."

"What are the chances we'll see Dirk before we return to Woodnog?" Roble asked.

"Next to none," she replied.

Lehrling chuckled. "I've never seen anyone go from such arrogance to cowardice in a split second. I'm quite certain he teared up."

"He's arrogant," Shawndirea said. "He's always been. Once he recovers from his shock, he'll eventually become so again. The biggest problem comes after the Unseelie discover all the dead Fae and wisps Lez'minx left behind."

"They'll blame us or Dirk?" Roble asked.

"That depends on whose story the Unseelie believe. Dirk wasn't the only one to survive. Those who escaped before him, had also witnessed what happened."

"Shouldn't that prevent Dirk from recruiting more Unseelie?" Roble asked.

She nodded. "For a while, at least."

A rustling breeze shook blankets of cold raindrops from the leaves.

"Do you know what worries me the most?" Roble asked.

"What's that?" Lehrling asked.

"If Lez'minx knows exactly where we are and when we are in trouble, is he listening to our conversations?"

Lehrling's brow rose. "I never considered that. If so, he knows all of our conversations."

Panic widened Shawndirea's eyes. "Get rid of those rings. I warned you not to put them on, and you did so anyway. I should've expected such from a human male. Always so stubborn."

Lehrling and Roble chuckled.

"It's *not* funny!"

"We have another problem," Roble said.

"What?"

Roble tugged at the ring on his left hand and then tried to remove the one on his right. "They're stuck. They won't come off."

"You might need to use some oil," Lehrling said.

"No, I don't think oil would work either."

"Why not?" Shawndirea asked.

"They won't budge at all, like they've become a part of my fingers and fused to the bones. These have no give."

"Why didn't you listen to me?" Seated on his shoulder, she pulled her knees to her chest and hugged them. "You're linked to him. I warned you."

A chill shot through him. Again, he tried to pull each ring off. "What can be done? Surely there's a way I can get them off my fingers."

"Let me meditate."

CHAPTER 7

*D*uring the next half hour, they rode in silence. Roble attempted to remove the rings several more times without any success. His fingers ached and swelled. The swamp became darker. Nightfall. Roble tried to hide his apprehensiveness. They needed shelter higher than the rising swamp water. A lot of narrow paths were disappearing.

Shawndirea eased to Roble's ear and whispered, "Ride alongside Lehrling and take his hand."

"Wha—"

Before he finished his thought, she flew into the air and lighted on Lehrling's shoulder. She apparently whispered the same thing to him.

Lehrling exchanged confused glances with Roble, but they did what she requested. She landed atop their joined hands and raised hers above her head. She mouthed soft words that only she knew what she was saying.

A bright green orb of light encircled her. The warmth and radiance flowed from her and up Roble's arm. After the light subsided, she flew upward and returned to Roble's shoulder.

"There!" She grinned with triumph and nodded. "That should help."

Roble tried to remove his rings, but neither budged. "It didn't work."

She giggled and shook her head. "The spell wasn't to get the rings off."

"Then what?" he asked.

Lehrling rubbed his wrist where she'd stood when she cast the incantation. "My hand and wrist are awfully warm. What'd you do?"

"A buffer spell to prevent Lez'minx from hearing our conversations," Shawndirea replied.

"Did it work?" Lehrling asked.

"Of course."

"How can you be certain?" Roble asked.

"Look at your rings."

A greenish sheen coated both rings. Beneath the glow, each stone gleamed, trying to break through her spell, but the shield she placed over the stones prevented their lights from shining through.

"I've encapsulated his magic with mine. For now, at least. Once he learns I've blocked his connection, he'll display some sort of angry fit." She smiled. "But, I'm not too worried about that."

"What if it's my armor and not the ring?"

"Not likely."

Lehrling frowned. "Why not?"

"The armor was fashioned specifically for Bausch. Lez'minx insisted Roble take these rings, which was why I warned Roble *not* to wear them. The rings were meant for you, as possibly magical spy glasses to keep tabs on you, or us."

"I hope your spell has blocked his ability to listen to us," Roble said. "The rings haven't loosened at all."

"They're fused to you, for now."

"Is there no way to get them removed?"

She nodded.

"How?"

"The easiest way is if Lez'minx reverses the spell," she said. "The other alternative is to find someone with stronger magical abilities, which could prove more difficult."

"It's doubtful I can persuade Lez'minx to reverse it," Roble said. "He seems to like the idea of having me as his servant."

"Of course he does," Shawndirea said.

"I refuse to swear my allegiance to him," Roble said. "Whether I possess the rings and armor or not, I never submitted myself to him. It's entrapment. We made no agreement beforehand, and I've no intention of ever doing so."

"Look ahead." Lehrling whispered and pointed.

The narrow path darkened and became wetter. Threaded tendrils of fog drifted through the trees and slithered like smokey snakes tightening their grip around the tree branches and trunks. As the fog engulfed the swamp, pairs of glowing red eyes peered from the canopy and the holes of hollow trees. Had Shawndirea not cast her spell over the rings, would these creatures have appeared? Was Lez'minx using their eyes to spy on Roble's whereabouts?

The rainfall decreased its pattering, but the air grew colder. The narrow path between the trees vanished beneath the fog.

"Nightfall's near," Lehrling said.

Roble glanced at him. Lehrling had drawn his sword and lay it across his legs for quicker access. "We've no choice but to keep going. We can't camp here."

Several thick snakes meandered through bent ferns, slinked, and disappeared beneath the black water.

"You're right. It's too dangerous to camp near the water or under the thickness of tree branches," Lehrling said.

Looking at Shawndirea, Roble said, "Any suggestions?"

Shawndirea said, "We keep moving until we find a place in the open. Perhaps old ruins or an abandoned cottage where we can start a fire without the rains extinguishing it. We need fire, not just to keep warm, but to deter the beasts of the night."

"We have a problem," Roble said.

"What?" she asked.

"The path has ended."

Shawndirea frowned and stood.

Lehrling rode up beside Roble. "Eventually, we'd encounter something like this."

"Like what?" Roble asked.

"A slow moving creek. So slow in fact, one might mistake it as a flooded part of the swamp, but we must cross it."

"To where exactly?"

Lehrling squinted and pointed. "Do you see the bog island?"

After several moments of intense inspection, the mossy bank of a small piece of land materialized. Roble nodded. "I'd have never guessed."

Lehrling grinned and laughed softly. "Lots of places are hidden in these swamps, as I told you earlier."

"Any idea what's on the island?" Roble asked.

Lehrling shook his head. "Only one way to find out."

"I was afraid you'd say that." Roble sighed and nudged the horse's flank gently with the heel of his boot. He wondered if the horse would even step into the water. He'd had a hard enough time convincing the horse to move any quicker through the areas where the tree knees jutted upward.

"Be careful," Lehrling said. "I don't think it's too deep, but since we can't see the bottom, that's no guarantee."

"Tell that to Bleys." Roble patted the side of the horse's neck.

Bleys hesitated at the edge of the water. Leaning its head forward, the horse took several deep breaths and sniffed the water's surface. Apparently sensing it was safe enough to cross, the horse stepped into the water. The water sloshed. Peeping frogs at the edge of the island ceased their singing.

Several bats flitted through the tree limbs. They swooped and arced upward, before gliding downward in a near circle while they caught skimming insects on the water's surface with their teeth.

By the time the water washed over Roble's knees, the rain had slacked and the clouds parted. The pale, yellow moon peered through the veil, but for only a few seconds.

Shawndirea slid from Roble's shoulder into his pocket.

"Everything okay?" Roble asked.

"Will be better once we're away from the hungry bats."

"They don't eat faeries, do they?" Roble asked.

"No, but our wings sometimes confuse them. They've mistakenly attacked smaller Fae. Doesn't take much to kill one of us or … destroy our wings. I don't want to risk it, so I'll stay out of sight for a bit."

Roble nodded. The horse's feet apparently no longer touched the bottom and it swam forward. After a few seconds passed, its feet touched the soft swampy mud, gained traction, lunged forward, and walked onto the island's bank.

The trees along the island's edge were thicker, massive oaks that towered higher than the spindly trees and saplings along the swamp trail. The ground was drier, harder. The horse's hooves made odd noises. Instead of walking on compacted soil, the horse walked onto old, wooden planks.

"Any idea where we are?" Roble asked.

"No," Lehrling said. His horse stepped from the water. "Perhaps long ago a small village resided on this island."

What appeared to be an old cistern was cracked and part of the rock wall had collapsed. Near it was a moss-covered, log outline of what might have been a stable. Dry, brittle ivy vines kept the remaining decayed logs in place.

Roble swung off his horse and led it by the reins. "Looks like several old huts near what's left of the plank hamlet wall. Doesn't appear to be a temple or a place to worship."

Lehrling lowered himself from his horse, stretched his back, and nodded. "No one's lived here during my lifetime."

Shawndirea peered from the pocket and shook her head. "Lez'minx isn't in this rundown place."

"I didn't expect him to be," Roble said. "But it looks like we've found a place to set up camp for the night."

Lehrling led his horse to a fallen beam and wrapped the end of the reins around it. He opened his horse's saddle bag. "I'll feed the horses, if you gather some dry wood. That is, *if you find any* dried wood."

Roble ran his hand through his beard and then, he pointed. "That building's probably the best place to find some. The roof's nearly intact."

Roble broke off pieces of the dried, ivy vines and stooped to take several rotted branches off the ground. Old brown weeds stood in the cracks of the aged, crumbling cobblestone. None of the foliage was green. He snapped several dead weeds, which were oddly dry.

Looking around, he frowned. None of the old stones were wet at all. With all the heavy rain they had ridden through, this abandoned settlement was bone dry.

Lehrling said, "This was most likely a fur trading outpost at one time."

"Wonder why no one's resettled it?" Roble asked.

"It must get flooded a lot. Or, those Lizard-men are real and preyed on them. Can't all be fables, can they?"

"I suppose not. Some truth is often found in farfetched tales."

Shawndirea took to flight. "I'll scout the perimeter to make certain we're the only ones on the island."

"No bats to worry about?"

She flung her hands upward. "I'll be okay. I cast a spell to mute the sound of my wings and send their vibrations several feet away from where I am."

"I'll start a fire in that fallen hut." Roble pointed at the small shed-like structure where one corner of the wooden fence had been.

She nodded and took to flight.

CHAPTER 8

Shawndirea flew along the edge of what had been the small island's hamlet wall. She skimmed above the wall and beneath the cover of the tree branches, hoping not to attract the attention of hungry bats or night birds.

Somewhat frustrated by Roble's pursuit to find Lez'minx, she was glad to get a few minutes away from her husband and Lehrling to sort through her thoughts alone. She loved Roble dearly, and nothing would ever alter her decision to have chosen him to wed and father their children. However, he continued to make rash decisions or failed to follow her advice at times when he should have listened. Of course, he *was* a human and reason sometimes fell on deaf ears. Even she understood this. It didn't matter if he were from the Overlands or had been born in one of the human cities in Aetheaon. Humans were bullheaded and needed to experience mistakes, often *repeatedly*, before the knowledge sank through their thick skulls. Sometimes they suffered and endured great consequences because they kept trying the same failed procedure without ever seeing a change in the final result. Thankfully, Roble had better sense than most, and when a trial didn't work, he didn't repeat the same method. He sought a different solution. Yet, his actions had been what had placed them in their current circumstances.

"Why'd you have to put those rings on?" she said softly and yet fumed. "I told you. I warned you. And now, look at where we are."

When Lez'minx had first made his presence known, he instructed Roble to take the two rings off a dead mage's fingers. She insisted that Roble not touch the rings and leave them. His logic in leaving them made it possible for someone with darker intents to possess them. The logic was sound, except instead of pocketing them, he put them on without taking her warning to heart. Since nothing noticeably strange occurred, he never removed them.

The armor Roble had taken off Bausch's corpse to wear had subtlety enticed him. Since it protected its wearers against extreme temperatures, trading for armor without this enchantment was impossible. The armor saved both their lives from the frigid climate around Glacier Ridge. Roble cut a piece of the armor large enough to cover her, and when she wrapped it around her, it form-fitted her body.

She sensed its magic, which wasn't essentially a darker magic, but the undertones weren't solely from the light, either. A part of her intuition warned her to shed the material. She should've discarded the garment immediately, but due to the harsh weather, she couldn't. She was too cold. With tattered wings and her injuries, she was minutes away from dying without the armor. The same was true for Roble. His thin clothing could never have shielded him from the cold.

Even though she sensed the enchantment, she never expected to pay homage to Lez'minx for wearing the armor. Bausch must have vowed to do so. But Roble hadn't. Those details had died with Bausch. She couldn't discern his reasons behind why he'd sought a magic leather weaver to construct his armor but then chose to flee with it. Such was theft and the price had been his life.

Roble couldn't be blamed for taking the armor to survive. She doubted anyone else suffering through the same situation would have done any differently.

As far as owing any homage or allegiance to Lez'minx, they owed none. A fact she was prepared to point out whenever they found his temple. Roble had not sought the seamstress who had pieced it together and blessed it, so Lez'minx couldn't demand anything from them. Its discovery had come during a combined moment of fortune and misfortune.

But the rings ...

Shawndirea shook her head and bit her lower lip.

Had Roble not placed them on his fingers, they could've left the rings at Lez'minx's altar. Roble needed to find a way to remove the rings to break free of Lez'minx. Her magic wasn't powerful enough to perform such a ritual. The best she'd managed was blocking the god's view through the gems. How long it lasted, she didn't know. Lez'minx, no doubt, would be furious for her spell. She wouldn't be surprised if he found and scolded them for meddling *before* they reached his temple.

Is he a god?

Shawndirea slowed her pace and glided closer to the broken wall where she noticed several broken statues outside the crumbling rock front of a deteriorated home. With caution, she hovered at the entrance. Crude stairs descended beneath the floor. In a ray of moonlight, a pile of large gleaming skulls and bones littered the floor and down the stairs.

She glided closer. At first glimpse, the bones appeared old. But near the top of the stairs, a track of green, gooey slime trailed down the stairs and was smeared on the walls. Fresh crimson blood remained on several bones. Recent victims.

The cellar's cooler air wafted toward her. She gagged and placed her hand over her nose and mouth. The rot of decayed flesh triggered nausea at the back of her throat. She refused to further investigate the cellar, not that entering was a wise thing to do. Whatever had been killed at the center of the stairs was dragged downward only a few days earlier. So, the predator lurked below.

Pushing backwards against the air, she flitted upward. They weren't alone on the island. Something lived underground. From the numerous skeletal remains, the predator was of considerable size. Whether intelligent or purely instinctual remained to be seen. She hoped they were off the island before they encountered it.

She glanced toward where she'd left Roble. The faint moonlight obscured his position. He'd yet to build a fire.

For several seconds, she contemplated returning to Roble and

Lehrling. She worried the creature might be creeping around the island, but probably not. The concentration of clean bones in and around the stairs meant the creature was more opportunistic than stalking. In the chance it wasn't in the cellar, she decided to finish searching the perimeter of the falling wall, just in case.

CHAPTER 9

*P*ursing her lips, Shawndirea flew behind the building with the cellar to examine the former island wall. She had only examined one full wall during her flight and a portion of the wall where Roble and Lehrling were setting up camp for the night. With something living in the old shack's cellar, she wanted to make certain the cellar was the only place they needed to worry about overnight.

Flying slowly, she kept a keener eye for fallen walls or trees where more predators could hide. It was strange the heavier rains weren't falling on this part of the old settlement. No moisture touched the island at all. The windblown rains swirled beyond the tree line and the island's hamlet wall, but the area beneath her remained dry.

Lightning flashed around the island's border and over the swamps, followed by heavy thunder. During her scouting, she had been too busy to notice, but all the walls and collapsing thatched roofs were dry. All the vegetation and trees were dead, dried out. Without the rain, her exploration was easier, but the air was unseasonably cooler than the surrounding swamp, which troubled her.

An uneasiness settled over her about the island.

The island's cursed.

This explained why no one resided here. The creature in the cellar might be the result of the curse. Or someone had placed a guardian on the island to ensure the place remained desolate, and thus, eliminated any future claims or settlements.

Her curiosity about what lurked in the cellar escalated. With evidence of recent victims, possibly only days before, the creature was quite alive.

Hovering above the hamlet wall, she glanced across its north side and then toward the building housing the cellar. She flitted back to the front of the building where she could see the cellar stairs without fear of getting attacked by what resided below.

She re-examined the bones scattered down the stairs. In the dark shadows, the stairs turned right at a ninety-degree angle and descended.

The shiny goo resembled the ooze trails slugs left behind as they crawled. Almost hidden in the small pile of bones was a rusted sword with holes eaten through the blade. Small portions of chainmail were nearly nonexistent under the bones. Whatever had killed these victims had dissolved them with its acid.

A strange bubbling, gurgling sound echoed down below. She rose higher and kept her attention on the turn of the stairs. Whatever was hidden down in the cellar seemed to be waiting for its prey approach it. The ooze was only on the steps. None blotched the floor outside the stairwell. Sensing its approach and worried it sensed her presence, she darted over the building to the wall.

With renewed determination, she set to discover what else was hidden on the island. Since the creature or creatures didn't seem to leave the protection of the cellar, she wasn't too concerned it'd find its way to Roble and Lehrling. This gave her time to inspect the rest of the island.

While flying, her mind revisited her major concern.

"Is Lez'minx really a god?" she whispered.

After he wiped out dozens of the Shadowfae, it became obvious he wasn't Seelie or Unseelie. He had no worry about repercussions from the Unseelie Court. Otherwise, he'd have been more sparing or cautious in dropping them. He held no fear of them, and almost daringly challenged their power. Perhaps he sought to war against them? She'd almost favor that, provided it didn't involve her. However, he might be successful in masking his ties to either side.

But as to whether he was a god or not, she didn't know and wouldn't know until after they found his temple. He might be a demigod posing as a god, or a demented wizard wielding magic she'd never known a wizard capable of performing. Of course, Aetheaon possessed an over-abundance of demented wizards and mages. Using magic for long periods of time stressed one's mind. The use of magic never came free. A price was demanded, and sometimes, the continued reliance of using magic claimed one's sanity.

Anyone, even Shawndirea, paid a price for the use of magic. She wasn't burdened like other practitioners because her gift to repair butterflies' wings extended their lives. In return for the blessings she bestowed to these fragile beautiful creatures in nature, no cost was required. But, should she use her magic to severely harm different races, unless in self-defense, she could become weakened and vulnerable, so she chose her battles carefully.

Her mind drifted to Dirk and renewed her burning anger toward him. Lez'minx had offered to kill Dirk along with the rest of the Shadowfae aligned with her cousin, provided she pledged her devotion to Lez'minx. The temptation remained overwhelming. She hoped she'd successfully masked her momentary yearning for Dirk's demise and how his death would remove the heavy burden he'd plagued her family and Elvendale with.

His death liberated Elvendale of Dirk's dark heart and his obsession to claim the throne. Had Lez'minx killed him, his death couldn't have been traced to her. His blood wouldn't be on her hands. She had other means to deal with Dirk without Lez'minx intervening. She refused to sacrifice her mind and soul to Lez'minx. She valued those more.

Of course, Shawndirea was thankful Lez'minx had interceded, as she, Roble, and Lehrling had been greatly outnumbered. While the ending might not have been with their deaths, Dirk held no qualms about rendering permanent injury and deformity to Roble, just to spite her. She was proud Roble never flinched. He stood ready to fight, which was surprising, considering he was an Overlander. Roble had not been in Aetheaon long enough to understand that even the smallest races were capable of inflicting severe pain or could maim him for the rest of his life.

Seeing Dirk flee like a frightened child was an amusing reward all its own. His immediate death would not have been nearly as satisfying. His smug demeanor had been crushed by imminent fear. Like Lehrling, she'd seen tears forming in Dirk's eyes.

In hindsight, they should've bound Dirk and taken him prisoner. Since he was an active threat to the queen and Elvendale, he should've been dealt with accordingly. However, with him as a bound prisoner, their journey would've been far more complicated and taken more time.

While Shawndirea had her differences with her mother—a vast canyon divided them—Shawndirea couldn't allow her mother's murder. No anger or bitterness toward another deserved death. Eventually, she figured, some sort of truce could be drawn between she and her mother but not in the immediate future.

Regardless of the current circumstances, she couldn't allow Dirk to take the throne. With the evidence of Dirk's sinister plans, Queen Istrell would execute him in such a way, the entire Fae population in Aetheaon would shutter. His death would become a stern warning to all future Fae children and set them on their best behaviors for life.

Since Dirk was aligned with the Shadowfae and was trying to build an army to overtake Elvendale, everything the kingdom held sacred would be forever tarnished should his invasion succeed.

But after what Lez'minx had done in the swamp, she doubted Dirk could rebuild his meager army anytime soon. His next step was to plead his case before the Unseelie Court and explain the reasons for the deaths of the dark faery soldiers that had pledged to serve him. Dirk might not even survive such a trial, as his recruiting had probably been secretive. And should he survive, she doubted he'd find many Shadowfae eager to follow him unless he were capable of proving himself able to protect them. If anything, Lez'minx would become better known in the swamps, especially to those who had no knowledge of him.

In some ways, Shawndirea wished she'd never renounced her right to Elvendale's throne. Her stubbornness to obtain independence might plummet Elvendale into utter chaos once her mother became too old or physically unable to rule. Since Dirk was an opportunist, he recognized Shawndirea's departure from ruling Elvendale as something he could capitalize on. However, even his mother was unlikely to dub him as the new ruler.

Elvendale had always been governed by a Queen regnant. It was unlikely Dirk's claim would be accepted by the Elvendale's general population. Not freely at least, which was possibly why he'd chosen the Unseelie to enforce his rule. Even then, her mother's guard would not have allowed it without a battle, and that seemed to be what Dirk hoped for: A war destined to rend the peace Elvendale found as the substance of their foundation.

Since Shawndirea had wed a human from the Overlands, which was far worse than marrying a human within Aetheaon, her right to rule Elvendale was tarnished, even if she decided to claim the throne. Her mother's indignation stemmed predominately from this issue, more than anything else.

Roble had questioned Shawndirea's allegiance and Dirk insinuated that Shawndirea crossed over to the Unseelie Court after marrying outside the Seelie Court. The more she thought about it, the more she recognized that perhaps she had unknowingly done so. In order for her to claim her right to the throne, she must dissolve her marriage to Roble, which was something she refused to do. Or, Roble's death freed her to rule in Elvendale.

While she wouldn't necessarily put it past her mother to attempt to have Roble assassinated, Dirk—on the other hand—would probably do anything within his power to keep Roble alive to prevent Shawndirea from reissuing her right. Irony at its best, or at its worst?

Although Dirk had openly threatened Roble, it was highly unlikely he wanted Roble dead. It further complicated matters for Dirk's ambition to rule Elvendale, because it immediately ushered Shawndirea to be next to ascend rule in Elvendale. So regardless of Dirk's attempt to form a coup, he unwittingly become Roble's ally, further dividing Dirk from Shawndirea's mother.

Shawndirea could plead her case before the Royal Council and hope they'd consider allowing her rule, even though she was married to Roble. It was doubtful she could sway their hearts and minds to side with her, but it was worth trying. Otherwise, she would face the decision of watching everything she loved within Elvendale collapse forever by her staying with Roble, or allowing herself the broken heart of letting him go. Both were tragic fates. Neither were favorable, but her love for Roble outweighed the two, which was selfish on her part.

Thousands of faeries' lives depended on Elvendale being ruled fairly under the structure of Order. Sadly and strangely, she was beginning to understand the reasoning behind her mother's outrageous anger. She realized it wasn't unfounded or outrageous at all.

Had her stubborn streak been too overpowering for her to notice? She frowned and pushed the thoughts to the back of her mind.

CHAPTER 10

*S*hawndirea flitted from open door to open door of the crumbling shacks. Her mind drifted toward Feather. She and Feather had been friends their entire lives. She loved Feather as a sister, and Feather's only flaw was her gullible nature. She was quick to believe what someone told her and trusted others too easily. Shawndirea could not count the number of times she set Feather straight concerning minor things.

Dirk must have discovered Feather's vulnerability, which was probably why he chose her to be his Queen. Or, at least, he deceptively convinced her of his fake love and promises to lure her to his side. His faux praise could've smitten her. Feather always envied Shawndirea's ability to heal butterflies and her princess role. So, the idea of being Elvendale's next queen thrilled Feather.

However, Dirk probably overlooked one trait about Feather: Feather held family loyalty to a fault. Since Istrell was like a second mother to Feather, Feather would never betray Elvendale's queen. While her actions to defend her family were admirable, they could prove to become deadly. Should Dirk's *love* turn to repugnance, he'd kill Feather without a second thought and in such a way, no one would ever place the blame on him.

Shawndirea couldn't allow that.

A flame lit at the other side of the former hamlet, and immediately caught her attention. She paused to look over her shoulder. Semi-dried kindling and other wooden materials slowly rose in flames. The rising fire revealed the outlines of Roble and Lehrling. She smiled.

While Roble could survive quite easily in the Overlands, she realized the dangers she had placed him into by bringing him to her realm.

He was smart, strong, and devoted; qualities she admired. But, naive ... wasn't *quite* the word she'd use. In her world, though, he faced obstacles he'd never face in his own. Things he never imagined could exist. Sometimes his bravery bordered more on facade than actual courage. If she detected it, others in Aetheaon did as well. Perhaps he was attempting to keep a bold face during his confrontations to assure her he was capable of living in her world and protecting her. The only problem was he didn't possess the understanding or know how to properly react when attacked with magic.

Lez'minx was an obstacle Roble wasn't prepared to confront. With Roble's defiant attitude, he might not survive. She didn't want to say, to him at least, that he needed *her* protection, but in truth, he *did*. Had Roble not placed the rings on his fingers after she sternly warned him, she might not question his vulnerability. His failure to heed her demand and accept her knowledge wasn't simply because he was human. It was because he was an Overlander human. His independence was most likely the reason for his petulance. Eventually, she reasoned, he'd mature and become more cautious; provided he *survived* their encounter with Lez'minx.

Given adequate time, he'd figure out these things on his own. Until then, she'd have to keep a watchful eye to ensure his safety. She hoped protecting him didn't bruise or shatter his ego. Not that he lacked self-confidence or he'd begrudge her for intervening in situations he believed himself capable of handling, but men often took offense when others fought in their place, as it showed weakness.

Shawndirea admired Roble for his decision to confront Lez'minx and reject his offer. Roble indicated his refusal to succumb to Lez'minx's demands or to give his allegiance for the *gifts* blessed by Lez'minx. She believed Roble when he stated he'd resist steadfast, but she also knew he didn't understand the ramifications.

Outright refusal at the temple, if such a temple existed, would be costly. Perhaps deadly or worse, a horrible disfiguring or agonizing curse. Roble held no grounds for negotiation since he had chosen to wear the rings. That troubled Shawndirea. He accepted the rings as gifts, so pleading ignorance wasn't a bargaining chip. With the rings affixed to his fingers, he couldn't deny wearing them. In her mind, she recognized the binding spell Lez'minx had placed on the rings. Once worn, they couldn't be removed, except after death or unless Roble was somehow pardoned from the spell's effects.

Such a spell was underhanded because curiosity ate at the mind, especially *human* minds, and a shady sorcerer thoroughly understood those types of temptations. Bright shining gems and rings enchanted with magic were coveted by all in Aetheaon. Regardless of how much one sought to ignore their beauty or entertained the thought of what magical power they possessed, the longer one held onto the trinkets, the more likely the person succumbed to wearing them. Not to witness their sparkle against their flesh, but to wield the power within. The subtle snare seldom missed its prey.

In Roble's case, the rings had fused to his flesh. Now, he must face the consequences. Either to serve Lez'minx or to die.

But there must be an in-between. Some way to get Roble freed from Lez'minx's hold.

At the moment, she could think of nothing to alter Roble's servitude to Lez'minx, which angered her.

After several more minutes of searching the cracks and crevices in the fallen wall and crumbling buildings, she found no evidence of life except for themselves and whatever occupied the cellar. Could they camp throughout the night without becoming prey?

Shawndirea sped her flight. Once Roble and Lehrling understood they were not alone, they could come to a decision on what must be done. With nightfall, they couldn't leave the island. Greater dangers were outside the fallen walls of this hamlet. Without knowing the identity of the beast, they didn't know its strengths or weaknesses. It might already know of their arrival and awaited the perfect time to emerge and eat them.

CHAPTER 11

*R*oble cupped his hands around the dried, sedge blades. Lehrling struck a match against the cobblestone and lowered it the brittle sedges. Roble blew softly against the tiny flame. After the fire began consuming the leaves, he placed the rising flames beneath a small heap of broken twigs and dried grass. "I'm confused, Lehrling."

"About what?"

"We rode through pouring rain, rising swamp water, and yet, this entire place is bone dry? These old vines and tree branches should be soaked."

Lehrling shrugged and placed a feed sack over his horse's mouth. "Beats me. I expected this place to be foul with mud and muck like the rest of the swamp."

"Do you know the name of this place?"

"No." Lehrling sighed. "I've never traveled far into Woodnog's swamps. Most refuse to travel through the swamps when a better, quicker, and *safer* route lies just to the west. Why place yourself into a hazardous terrain when it's not necessary?"

"I understand." Roble kept his attention on the growing fire. He added a larger stick on the fire. "You know of anyone who has chosen to explore these swamps well enough to know them?"

"A fellow Dragon Skull Knight, Geowren, often traveled through these swamps, but that was years ago."

"Is he still alive?"

Lehrling ran a hand through his drying hair and frowned. He expelled a disappointed sigh. "No one knows. Well, no one in our Order, that is. Erik knighted him on the same day he knighted me. After Erik's death—or perhaps his disappearance—since rumors circle that Erik might be alive, Geowren disappeared into the swamps."

"For what reason?" Roble asked.

Lehrling shrugged. "The Goddesses only know."

"Hmm." Roble grabbed more dried vines, snapped them, and placed them on the fire. "Isn't that a bit odd?"

"In Aetheaon?" Lehrling laughed. "Not if you knew him."

"Is it a coincidence he'd vanish around the time King Erik did?"

Lehrling frowned. "Is that an accusation because—"

Roble shook his head. "No, nothing like that. But if someone actually killed the Hoffnung's king, isn't it possible for others in the Dragon Skull Order to have been targets, too?"

"I imagine that's possible, but until Waxxon's overthrew Queen Taube, our Order never suffered threats for who we are and the king we served. Since Lady Dawn christened you into the Order, you serve the Crown as well."

"Yes, with my life."

Lehrling approached Roble and clasped a firm hand on his shoulder. "Aye, I believe you do, which is quite remarkable for an Overlander."

"Why's that?"

"You're not from our realm but yet, you offer your loyalty to defend a kingdom that's not your own."

"It is now," Roble said.

Lehrling smiled. "Yes! But, my point is most in our realm wouldn't have bothered to do half of what you've done for Hoffnung and the queen."

Roble chuckled. "The majority of people in my realm would die trying to find their way to return to the Overlands instead."

"No argument there. Most Overlanders aren't strong enough to survive the mental adjustments necessary to comprehend the beasts, races, and magic in Aetheaon. I'll always be indebted to you for saving my life," Lehrling said softly. "You didn't have to risk your life for me. You could've continued onward. I hope to somehow repay you—"

"You owe me nothing except your friendship," Roble said. "You've done far more to aid me in understanding and training. I feel indebted to you."

Lehrling laughed. "I'm afraid an old man's training isn't the best repayment. It comes nowhere close."

"It's far better than what I knew. I've had the pleasure of gaining a new friend." Roble smiled and crouched at the side of the fire. "So tell me more about Geowren."

"Why not let a weary ghost rest?"

"So you think he's dead?"

Lehrling's eyes stared blankly for several moments before he acquiesced a nod. "Sadly, I do. Why your interest in knowing more about him? You've only learned about him."

"Like I mentioned, I want to know more about these swamps."

"You wish to explore them?" His voice rose with intrigue.

Roble nodded. "I would."

Lehrling winced as he lowered himself to the ground slowly. He sat near the fire, and warmed his hands. "If it's a guide you seek, you could always ask Odlon."

"He knows these swamps?"

"Yes. Or you could ask his sister," Lehrling said. "She's an herbalist and quite a skilled alchemist. She concocts incredible magical potions, at a hefty price, mind you. Since rarer herbs abound in swamps, she'd probably know her way around better than he. As to whether she'd allow you to accompany her on one of her harvests, only she can answer that. Odlon could relay a message to her for you though."

"I'll ask him the next time I see him."

"You mind if I ask you something?" Lehrling met Roble's gaze.

"Sure."

"Do you really believe it's best we continue searching for Lez'minx's temple? Be honest."

"You can turn back, if you want, Lehrling. You're not required to accompany me," Roble said. "Don't feel obligated—"

Lehrling raised a hand and shook his head. "No, I don't mean it like that. I'd be foolish to depart alone. We're safer traveling together. What I … How comfortable are you about fulfilling the journey to his temple?"

"I'm not *comfortable* about the situation at all. My gut tells me I'm safer and *we're* safer, if I confront him. Besides, he proved he can find us, and in part, he's proven to me he's a powerful being I'm unable to defeat."

"What if he insists you become his loyal subject?"

Roble scratched his bearded chin. "Still sorting through that. I had thought an outright refusal was the best option, but after seeing him wipe out those faeries without physically being in their presence, I have pondered about seeking an alliance with him instead."

"He's not offering an alliance, Roble."

"I know. But would it be a terrible thing if I served him?"

Lehrling's eyes widened. He pulled a pipe and a tobacco pouch from inside his vest. "Surely you jest?"

"Imagine having such power backing you," Roble said.

"Yes, and imagine losing your soul to a … Well, whatever he may be? You don't know his intentions."

"Then I should refuse?"

"Compromise, find an alternative that suits you and him. But if you fully yield yourself to him, he might well possess you and control your mind to do whatever he wishes. You can't sacrifice yourself to a power so dark."

"So he's a dark god?"

"Regardless of *what* he is, he wields dark magics. Why else would he house his temple in the depths of Woodnog Swamps. Have you asked Shawndirea how she likes your suggestion?"

"She's mad enough at me as it is." Roble glanced over his shoulder and watched the sky. He wondered where she had gone and if she was hidden to eavesdrop on their conversation.

Lehrling chuckled softly. "Angry faeries can be full of mischief."

"Or worse," Roble said.

"You're certain she's mad at you?"

"It's obvious she's pissed at me since I put on the rings."

Lehrling nodded. "I didn't want to ask in front of her, but *why'd* you put them on?"

Roble winced and shook his head. "Curiosity, I suppose."

"Did you ... feel any power from them?"

"Nothing really. Only fear and dread after realizing I couldn't take them off."

"Ah, yes, afraid of what Lez'minx might do?"

Roble shook his head and grinned. "No, fearful of what Shawndirea would do because I did not listen to her."

Lehrling grinned. "You see why I chose a bachelor's life, eh?"

Roble laughed. "I once had one."

"Don't get too envious. Do you miss it?"

"No. Although I never sought marriage, I'd never want to be single. My heart aches for Shawndirea whenever she's not near, like now."

"You think she's in trouble?" Lehrling asked.

"No. But she's been gone longer than I expected, which is why I know she's angry," Roble said.

"One thing's in your favor, though." Lehrling puffed his pipe.

"Really? What?"

"Lez'minx prevented Dirk from seeking to dethrone Queen Istrell. Shawndirea must appreciate his help," Lehrling said.

"She's not expressed her feelings concerning that, but it might explain why she wants time alone to sort through her thoughts. For now, Dirk's plans are dashed, but I expect he'll try again."

"Eventually, maybe."

"But even after Istrell learns about what Lez'minx did to protect us, it's doubtful I'll ever find favor with Shawndirea's mother."

"Isn't that true of any mother-in-law though?" Lehrling asked with a sincere stare.

Roble shrugged. "Perhaps. But the fury and contempt Istrell holds toward me ... I doubt such could ever be matched in the Overlands."

Lehrling chuckled. "I agree with you concerning that."

"Istrell challenged me to explore the Black Chasm, remember?"

"I remember."

"Having Istrell as an enemy makes it tempting to serve Lez'minx in some ways."

Lehrling puffed his pipe and cocked a brow. "What's he have to do with her?"

"Someone pulled me out of the Black Chasm before I would've died. Someone powerful enough to open a portal and dragged me through."

"Could've been any wizard or mage," Lehrling said.

"Few people even knew I was there. You were incapacitated at the time, too."

"I'm no wizard."

Roble chuckled. "True! But, you'd have fought me not to enter."

Lehrling nodded. "It wasn't your best decision, especially since your true goal was to impress Queen Istrell, which I'm guessing *didn't* work?"

"Not a bit. This armor kept me alive longer than the rest of the army with me. The others died before my eyes, one by one, along with their mounts."

"The armor has enchantments I've noticed, mostly adapting to whatever climate we're in. I imagine it could protect you from the poisonous air inside the Black Chasm." Lehrling stared at the fire. "Did you have any other enchantments or blessings bestowed on you? Protection spells, perhaps?"

"Only a piece of cloth Shawndirea gave me to breathe through."

"Then that's probably it, more than the armor. Unless Istrell had secretly cast a spell over you."

Roble laughed. "Are you kidding? She sent me there to die, to free Shawndirea from our marriage. Protecting me with magic would be the last thing she'd do."

"True, I suppose," Lehrling said. "The more I learn about Queen Istrell, the more I'm convinced she makes more enemies than allies. But she's unable to sway Shawndirea to find fault in you."

"She has no need to expose fault. I'm doing plenty on my own."

"I've a feeling it'd take far more than wearing magical rings for her to desert you. She loves you too much to allow minor mistakes to sway her heart."

"Minor?" Roble tugged hard at each ring and couldn't budge them. "This is a *major* error."

"I understand how your curiosity got the best of you, but if you suspected Shawndirea would get angry, why'd you put them on?"

Roble displayed a sheepish grin. "Because I thought I could slide them off without her ever knowing."

Lehrling slapped his knee and tried to muffle his sudden laughter. Tears formed at the edges of his eyes.

"It's not funny," Roble said, rising.

"No, it's hilarious."

"In what way?"

"It's Fate's twisted sense of humor. It happens to all of us. We think we can sneak and do something without getting caught, but then irony slips in to ruin the secret."

"Still not funny," Roble said. "Especially not to Shawndirea."

Lehrling wiped away tears. "I imagine not."

"Oh, you don't need to use imagination to see her anger."

"Sorry. She tries to hide it though."

"Around you, yes. For me, it's entirely a different matter," Roble said.

Lehrling stood and walked to his horse. He opened a saddlebag and pulled out some dried jerky and tossed some to Roble. "While we wait for her, we should eat."

Roble caught the strand of jerky, took a bite, and chewed.

"To be honest, Roble, I'd have tried on the rings, too."

"Really?"

"Yes."

"Why?"

Lehrling returned to his place by the fire. "Knowing what your armor's capable of doing, if it were me, I'd have wanted to discover what the rings were capable of doing. Almost any human, dwarf, or elf would've done the same."

"They're windows for Lez'minx to watch us."

Lehrling shrugged. "I believe they do much more than that."

"Like what?"

"We won't know until it's revealed to us, or to you, since you wear them. But they're more than a spyglass."

Shawndirea descended from the sky and hovered near him.

"Well?" Roble asked.

"We're not alone," she replied. "The island's cursed."

CHAPTER 12

"Cursed?" Roble and Lehrling said.

"Why do you think this island's cursed?" Roble asked.

Shawndirea nodded. "Have you not noticed the abnormalities?"

"Other than the island hasn't had rain in years?" Roble said. "The surrounding storms haven't lessened, but strangely don't seem any closer. But after we got drenched and with the creek rising, maybe that's not bad."

"No. It's worse," she said. "If the island *never* gets rain, that's a curse in itself."

"True." No rain explained why all the trees and vegetation were dead. "But for travelers, finding a completely dry place to lodge for the night is no curse."

"It was for whoever lived here," she said. "I've seen their remains and freshly gleaned bones of recent travelers. They died here."

"Couldn't the former occupants have moved and resettled elsewhere?"

"Maybe." She shrugged. "I'd guess they didn't though. As I said earlier, 'we're not alone.'"

Roble stood. Lehrling extended his hand for Roble to help him up. With one swift tug, Roble pulled Lehrling to his feet. "Who else is here?"

"Not a who," she replied. "Some sort of creature lives underground."

Lehrling tapped the burnt tobacco out of his pipe. "What type of creature?"

"A slime creature would be my guess," she said.

Lehrling shook his head. "Not good at all."

Roble frowned and exchanged glances with each of them. "Why's a creature made of slime such a threat?"

Lehrling ran a hand through his beard. "They're almost impossible to destroy."

Roble's eyes widened with surprise. "Why?"

Shawndirea said, "They have no brain or heart. You can't kill them. They're globs of ooze, often composed of strong acid."

"Acid?"

Lehrling nodded. "Yes. Never use a metal weapon you value to slice your way through them. They're so corrosive, your weapon practically melts in seconds. And metal armor won't protect anyone, either. Some are even worse. They attach to you and freeze you to death. If you're lucky to have someone yank you free before it pulls you inside it, you might only lose an appendage."

"You've encountered them before?" Roble asked.

"No. I've heard the tales, and I've seen the results from those who almost died."

Roble frowned. "So you can't kill them? Surely, a membrane of some sort holds the ooze together. Can't you pierce it?"

Lehrling nodded. "But doing so is dangerous. Some slimes divide into smaller halves. Others when split open will gush their acid all over you. If you're lucky, your death is quick."

Roble winced. "Are these slime creatures common in the swamps?"

"No," Shawndirea said. "They don't occur naturally. Usually, they're created by wizards or mages due to their curses."

"If the island is cursed," Roble said, "this devastation is the result of an angry wizard?"

"Probably," she said.

Roble frowned. "For what reason?"

"Reason?" Lehrling chuckled. "Some powerful wizards are pompous. They're provoked by a minor insult and cast curses as stern warnings for others not to trifle with them."

Roble shook his head. "Being friends with a wizard sounds rough."

Lehrling laughed. "Wizards have few friends, which is why they live solitary lives and are shunned by neighboring villages who want no trouble."

"But on this island? This tiny hamlet? What could they have done to prompt such a curse?"

"If it were a trading town for trappers, perhaps the wizard felt mulcted, which is the best possibility," Lehrling replied.

"Or," Shawndirea said. "Someone skinned the wizard's familiar and a vendor bought the hide."

"I hadn't thought of that," Lehrling said. "That'd cause severe anger and immediate vengeance would be sought. A wizard's wrath would be never ending."

"Where did you see this creature?" Roble asked.

"I didn't see it," Shawndirea said. "I saw enough recent evidence on the cellar stairs to indicate its whereabouts."

A worried expression claimed Lehrling's face. "How recent?"

"A few days, maybe a week, based on the coloration of the bloodstains. Not sure what its victim or *victims* might've been."

"Animal bones or human?" Roble asked.

She thought for several moments. "Most likely not an animal."

Roble frowned. "Why do you believe that?"

"An animal's instinctive actions are often smarter than the curiosity of humans, Elves, or other races," she replied. "Curiosity outweighs rational thought."

Roble realized the snide comment was directed at him. He gave a slight grin. "Noted. Which building is it in?"

Shawndirea hovered and pointed. "The one beside the old falling wall."

Roble nodded. "It's not far from us."

"I know."

"Let's check it out," Roble said.

"No," she replied. "Let's *not*."

"We can't leave the island before morning," Roble said. "Doing so would be too treacherous. We wouldn't survive."

"You're right." Shawndirea sighed. "We probably wouldn't."

"We need to know what we're up against."

"*Roble—*"

He drew a dagger and walked toward the building.

"Have you not learned *anything* from your rash decisions?" she asked.

Roble glanced over his shoulder and caught Lehrling's concerned gaze.

Lehrling shook his head. "She's right, Roble. You even admitted such during our conversation earlier."

Roble said, "I don't plan to go to *where* it is."

"So?" Shawndirea said. "For all we know, it could be partway up the stairs, and if it is, you might not outrun it."

"So these slime creatures are fast?"

"Not usually," she replied. "But you'd only find it out afterwards, though."

"True."

Shawndirea nodded. "Good. One thing I sensed about it though."

"What?"

"It knows we're here," she replied.

"How could you know that?" Lehrling asked.

"Its sloshy movements were at the turn of the stairs, and it seemed to hurry upwards. I think it sensed my presence."

Roble looked at the old shack and sighed. "If we can't leave until morning, and you don't want to investigate the stairs, what do you suggest?"

"I could fly over and see," she said.

"Isn't that risky?" Roble asked.

"It cannot fly."

Roble said, "Very well."

She turned and zipped toward the building.

Roble flicked his attention to Lehrling. "How do we defend ourselves against this thing if we can't kill it?"

Lehrling shook his head. "I don't know. But she's right. Confrontation isn't in our best interest."

Roble pulled the end of a large branch from the fire. Flames danced on the branch's tip. "Let's go."

"Shouldn't we wait until she returns?"

"What if she needs our help? We need to be closer to her than not."

Lehrling took a heavy stick from the fire. "I'd rather not follow you, but I like staying behind even less. Seems you're worrying too—"

Shawndirea screamed. A second later, her voice was muffled. Then she was silent.

Roble tore into a sprint.

CHAPTER 13

*R*oble's first fear was Dirk had followed them to the small island. Either he'd taken Shawndirea or one of the Shadowfae archers had shot and killed her. But remembering Dirk's extreme fear, it was highly unlikely her cousin would've returned without a stronger force, which seemed even *less* likely. Lez'minx had certainly left a memorable impression on Dirk.

A colder fear took Roble's breath. Had Lez'minx found them and decided to punish Shawndirea for spell-blocking his vision through the rings?

Silently, he berated himself for allowing her to travel into the swamps with him. She shouldn't suffer for his foolish mistake. His learn-as-you-go attitude was too risky to practice in this realm. His actions not only put his life in danger, but those he loved as well.

This journey to find Lez'minx was one he wished to take alone. But since Lehrling could guide Roble through the swamps, he insisted he come. Lehrling admitted he wasn't an expert guide, and he didn't know where the temple was, provided there was one. But he was familiar with the creatures and races they might encounter.

When Shawndirea discovered they were headed into the swamps, she refused to remain behind. Her magic, she insisted, could aid and protect them. Instead, her magic might've wrought the wrath of a god, a demigod, or a crazed mage or wizard. Until they met Lez'minx face-to-face, they didn't know *what* he was.

"Shawndirea!" Roble shouted. He slowed his sprint to a sudden stop near the shack's opening. He used the flaming torch to light the dried weeds and vines to find her.

Having spent the majority of his lifetime in the Overlands as an entomologist, his keen eyes looked for the tiniest creatures in the most unusual places. This skill allowed him to find rare insects for his collection. In the flickering light, he searched every crack and crevice at the open doorway before he turned his attention to the decayed outer walls.

"Shawndirea!"

Roble's fear-stricken heart caused his chest to ache. He took several deep breaths and exhaled slowly to calm himself. His shouting was foolish. It brought immediate attention to his location, but he didn't care. He'd gladly sacrifice his life to save hers, if necessary.

She didn't reply, and he couldn't find her. He feared the worst and looked for her body in the broken blocks along the wall's edge. His knees weakened, his heart hammered in his chest, and he became lightheaded. He'd never experienced a panic attack, but if he didn't calm himself, he would have one. His vision darkened, his chest tightened, and he was seconds from collapsing. He reached to grab an old post to maintain his balance.

"Lehrling," Roble gasped. "Do you see her?"

Lehrling rushed to Roble and stumbled to stop his thundering footsteps. He used his torch to wash more light in the darkened areas, and sadness filled his voice. "No. You okay, Roble?"

"No."

Both torches illuminated Lehrling's panicked face. His worry to find Shawndirea was evident. Like Roble, he'd sacrifice his life to protect the faery. Having such a devoted friend in a strange realm warmed Roble's heart. More than fate had led Roble and Shawndirea to Bausch's hanging body where Roble took Bausch's armor. The armor was the key that linked them together, and part of the reason they were exploring the swamps.

"She has to be here, somewhere." Roble frantically searched the outside of the building.

Lehrling's hand sternly gripped Roble's forearm. He yanked Roble back. "Watch out!"

At the entrance of the stairwell the sludge-filled beast sloshed forward, making strange gurgling noises as it moved. Without legs, it moved like a giant, sluggish fat snail. It pulled itself forward with the base of its body.

Roble backed away and studied its appearance. He couldn't look away. Part of his fascination came from trying to identify its anatomy to determine *how* it was even alive. After several moments, he located what he assumed was its face. The face was contained *inside* the green creature. It didn't have an actual head or arms or legs. It crawled like a slug but its form wasn't elongated. Instead, it was more like a carpet of moving sludge and sloshed side to side. Somehow, it maintained a partially standing appearance as it carried itself up the stairs.

Roble instinctively stepped alongside Lehrling. "Do you think ... it ate her?"

Lehrling swallowed hard. He opened his mouth but no words ever came.

"Mmm-fff-mmph!"

Lehrling pointed. "There she is!"

Roble turned.

Shawndirea was partially enclosed inside a spider's web between a large rock and a fallen beam of another building. Inches away from the web, a glob of ooze dripped off the rock. The spit's acid components ate holes in the bubbling rock. He didn't want to imagine what the spit could do to human or a faery's flesh. He swallowed hard. Had Shawndirea been struck by its spit, she'd have dissolved without a trace.

Roble rushed to Shawndirea and set his flickering torch on the cobblestone. With his forefinger, he thumped the hairy spider trying to spindle more webbing around her. The spider dislodged from the web and sailed a short distance through the air before landing in a pile of dead ivy. He carefully peeled Shawndirea's fragile wings from the sticky web. He pulled the thicker webbing from her mouth.

"Are you okay?" he asked.

She nodded and wiped away the stickiness around her mouth. She frowned and tried to locate where the spider had landed. He recognized her vindictive expression. He pitied the spider should she locate it.

"Other than the gummy webbing on my face and wings? I'm fine," she said. "But be careful. The slime creature shoots its acid drool much farther than I anticipated. I dodged but didn't see the spider's web."

Roble peeled the web from her delicate wings. After they'd gotten most of it off, he grabbed his torch on the cobblestone. The rock hit by the creature's spit had stopped bubbling and absorbed the acid. However, half the stone was gone.

"Roble!" The panic in Lehrling's voice matched the fear in his eyes. "Let's leave while we can!"

Lehrling took his flaming torch and hurled it at the ooze creature. Almost immediately, the torch was extinguished and absorbed by its gelatin body. The flame caused no obvious damage.

Knowing Lehrling couldn't move as quickly as he, Roble said, "Run!"

Lehrling scrambled and ran.

"There must be a way to destroy it," Roble said.

"All the bones indicate no one else has succeeded in doing so," she said, sliding inside his pocket.

"Yet."

"It's highly unlikely we will."

"Can't you use a spell to rip it apart or something?" Roble asked.

"I've told you before, my dear. My magic's for healing and self-preservation."

"I've never imagined a monstrosity like that," he said.

"Give it time, Roble. Trust me, you'll see far worse in my realm."

While Roble ran behind Lehrling, he used his torch's light to guide their steps without worrying about obstructions along the pathway. Roble glanced over his shoulder to check the ooze creature's pursuit. Best he could tell, it wasn't following them, but since they held the only light source, he couldn't be certain.

"It has a face with a mouth," Roble said. "If it's capable of eating larger prey, I'm fairly certain it doesn't need the mouth to do so."

Shawndirea nodded. "You're right. The acid partially dissolves flesh as its slime encapsulates its victim. Afterwards, the slime consumes everything else."

Roble frowned. "You saw a pile of bones? Why doesn't it dissolve those?"

"It probably sucks out the marrow and discards the rest," she said.

"It had a partially dissolved shield inside it. Several arrows protruded from its ... *skin* ... its outer membrane."

Shawndirea nodded. "Some magic enchantments resist acid."

When they reached the campfire, Lehrling leaned over, placed his hands on his knees, and panted. "Perhaps this island wasn't the best choice for staying through the night."

"We had no better choices," Roble said. "It doesn't look like it's leaving the safety of those stairs, though."

"I wish I took comfort in that." Lehrling stood upright and wiped sweat from his brow with a old piece of cloth. "But none of us know *what* it'll do. There's no guarantee it won't make its way to us during the night or eat our horses while we sleep. Someone needs to stay awake until morning. We could take turns."

"I'll take first watch," Roble said. "It'll give me time to figure out a way we can destroy it."

Lehrling's eyes widened in disbelief. "You can't be serious, Roble."

Shawndirea sighed, crossed her arms, and rolled her eyes. "He is."

Seeing her reaction, Roble chuckled. Indeed, she knew how his mind worked, even though most of the time she rejected his proposals and tried to sway him differently.

Roble smiled. "I am."

"We don't even know how to kill it," Shawndirea said. "Your weapons and my magic can't hurt it. It's best to keep our distance until morning and depart. If we don't attack it, we're more likely to all survive."

"We can't let it live," Roble replied.

"Sure we can," she said with a firm brow.

"But if we don't kill it, it'll continue devouring others who explore this island. I don't want that on my conscious. Do you?"

Shawndirea bit her lower lip and slowly shook her head. Her eyes finally met his. "What do you propose?"

He shrugged. "That's why I need to remain awake, so I can figure out a way to kill it."

CHAPTER 14

$\mathcal{D}$eep in thought, Roble sat on the crude remnants of a carved stone block once used as the base of a support wall. The hexagon stone was smooth across the top. He and Lehrling sat back to back easily. Two wooden, support beams that had been atop the stone had separated, fallen, and stretched across the floor.

Lehrling placed several thick branches on the dying fire. Rising embers floated into the calm, night air. Though the night felt pleasant, the thundering storm raged beyond the island's perimeters. Lightning flashed like flickering nets overhead, but no rain blessed the barren island.

After tossing another branch on the fire, Lehrling gave Roble a sharp glance. "If you plan to keep first watch, continue feeding the fire. Without firelight we're vulnerable."

"I know." Roble sighed.

Lehrling grinned. "You're lost in your thoughts?"

"Most of the time."

"Have any ideas on how we might kill it?"

"A few. Whether or not they'd work, I can't predict."

"We could hope it doesn't leave the stairwell." Lehrling gave hopeful smile. "Rather than gamble our lives by trying to kill it."

Roble said, "We've no guarantee it won't seek us."

Lehrling nodded. "Where's Shawndirea?"

Roble pointed to his pocket. "Asleep and always close to my heart."

"I want to sleep, but I can't with a creature like that nearby."

"Don't trust I'll stay awake?"

"Not so much that. With the fire dying, I was getting cold."

"I'll keep a better watch on it." Roble adjusted on the stone block. He looked at his glove and frowned.

"What?"

"My glove's white."

Lehrling stepped closer. "So it is."

Roble grinned.

Lehrling cocked a brow. "I recognize that look. What are you thinking?"

"I think I know the creature's vulnerability," Roble replied.

"From that? How?"

"There's a reason it never leaves those stairs. I should've made the connection earlier." Roble stood.

Lehrling frowned. "I don't understand."

"Would you get the axe from the saddlebag?"

"Sure. Why?"

Roble grinned. "We're going to make a weapon and destroy it."

"With a stone?" Lehrling asked while glancing over his shoulder.

"A sharp, piercing stone."

"What are you talking about?" Shawndirea stood and stretched in his pocket. She took to flight and hovered above them. Lehrling returned with the axe.

"He says he can make a stone weapon that'll kill the ooze creature." Lehrling wiped sweat from his brow.

"Don't be absurd, Roble," she said. "The best swords, daggers, arrows, and axes have failed to stop it, and you think you can destroy it with this rock?"

"Why not? I assume no one else has tried it," Roble said.

"No one would entertain such a foolish attack," she said in a near whisper. Although her reply was curt, interest beamed in her eyes as she watched what he planned to do.

Roble took the sharp axe and scraped a line across the flat top surface. By his estimation, if he hit the stone hard enough, and luck enabled the strike to properly cut the stone, he hoped a third of it broke free. Then, he could sharpen the stone's edges with the axe blade and make it sharp enough to cut through the flesh of almost any animal or beast.

Roble gave Lehrling an even stare. "Step back and shield your eyes."

"That's the *only* axe we have." Lehrling stepped away. "Axes are for chopping wood, not rock."

Roble grinned, closed his eyes, and swung the axe. The blade struck the stone with a quick singing of the metal as it busted through the stone. He opened his eyes. At least a third of the stone dropped to the ground. Instead of one clean heavy slab, the large section had broken into two near equal portions.

Roble shook his head and grimaced.

"Something wrong?" Lehrling asked.

"I hoped for one slab, but this will have to do."

"At least the axe is intact."

"There's that." Roble nodded.

Shawndirea hovered lower and inspected the white stone. "How you can make a weapon capable of killing that thing from *this*."

"It might not," Roble replied. "But, I believe it's the best weapon we have."

"Why?"

"I'll explain later, if it works."

"And if it doesn't?"

He shrugged. "Then it won't matter."

"Roble," she said, "we don't need to pursue or attack it. The only reason we need to engage it is if *it* attacks us."

"True, but I know why it won't leave the stairwell," Roble replied.

"Why?" Lehrling asked.

"Because of these stones."

Lehrling and Shawndirea exchanged glances and frowned.

"When I was getting the spider web off your wings, something crossed my mind," Roble said.

"What?" she asked.

"The creature wasn't put on this island to kill the inhabitants. It's in the stairwell to protect something hidden down below."

"What makes you believe that?" she asked.

Roble shrugged. "The more I've thought about it staying in the stairwell, the more I believe that's the reason for the creature. It's guarding something. The only reason the townsfolk died was because they tried to find a way to get around it."

Shawndirea shook her head. "If you don't think it'll leave the stairwell, why kill it?"

"Curiosity. What's so important for someone to use the creature to prevent others from stealing it."

"If what you say is true, leave it be. It's not worth the risk," she said.

"But what if it is?"

"It's not, Roble," Lehrling said. "Don't let greed dictate your actions."

"This has nothing to do with greed," Roble said evenly. "Riches aren't what I seek. My curiosity lures me, but overall, my motive's to prevent this creature from killing future explorers."

Lehrling regarded Roble's words and nodded. "Fair enough."

Shawndirea shook her head. "You need a better weapon. I'm sorry, but this is a fool's weapon."

"If you don't want me to use this, fine. Then remove the spell on these rings. I'll consult Lez'minx directly about the best way to kill it. Who knows? Perhaps *he'll* intervene and kill it for us. I imagine the slime creature is a less challenge than killing three dozen Shadowfae mercenaries."

Her brow narrowed and her jaw tightened. "All this time you keep swearing you won't serve him? Yet, secretly, you crave his power."

"No, I don't," Roble said. "I don't plan to serve him in any capacity."

"You just said—"

"What I said was to get your attention. Stop treating me like a child," Roble said. "Have *some* faith in me. I've knowledge from *my* realm you've never been exposed to. Just like there are things in Aetheaon I don't understand, your world has yet to gain the full understanding of other matters."

"This isn't one of them," she replied.

"I'm willing to bet my life on it."

Shawndirea placed her hands on her hips. Her face contorted through anger, confusion, surprise, sadness, and desperation. "I'd rather you didn't wage such high stakes. Lehrling, speak to him!"

Lehrling chuckled and shook his head. "What makes you think he'll listen to me more than you? He's in *love* with you … I assure you, he and I hold no such pact."

"Reason with him," she huffed.

"I offer my sword to aid you since I already know you'll refuse any advice from either of us," Lehrling said.

"That's *not* reasoning!" Shawndirea glared at Lehrling.

"No, it isn't. But if you want him to remain alive, we'd best do something to help him. Arguing is ludicrous at this point."

She darted in the air and circled around to hover in front of Roble. She met his gaze. "So you're determined to do this?"

"Yes. I strongly believe it will work."

She scrunched her nose. "Fine. What do we need to do?"

Roble said, "I need twine and a sturdy, straight stick."

With a frown, she said, "You plan to spear it?"

"Something like that."

"I'll get some rope from the saddle pack," Lehrling said.

After Lehrling was out of earshot, she said, "Why must you be as stubborn as my mother?"

"No more than you are."

She gasped and placed her right hand over her heart. "You think I'm—"

"Yep. You're every bit as stubborn as she," Roble said. He used the sharp axe blade to shave away the sides of the white stone. Slivers and bits of white powder cascaded onto the worn floor of the old shack.

Instead of spewing angry words, she thought for several long moments. "Perhaps *that's* what drove the wedge deeper between she and I."

"Probably."

"I don't want that to happen between us." She wiped a tear from her cheek.

"It won't," he assured her.

"How can you be sure?"

"Love stands the test of time," he replied. "I'm sure you're aware of that?"

"It's what every female hopes to secure."

Without stopping his work on the axe, he said, "Every man holds the same hope, too. Shawndirea, there'll never be a day when my heart stops loving or yearning for you. I wish you trusted my decisions."

"I've tried to, but then you have moments when your actions are quite foolish. Like the rings—"

"I know. You don't need to keep reminding me. You're a faery, *not* a harpy."

Her eyes narrowed for a moment. She noticed his slight grin and burst into laughter.

After several minutes, Roble set the first broken piece of the stone atop the remainder of the support stone. He had shaped it to a long pointed triangle. About fifteen minutes later, he set the second one beside it, which was almost identical in size and shape.

"What now?" Lehrling handed Roble long strands of twine.

Roble smiled, placed the axe head on the ground, and set his right boot an inch or so above the head. "We're going to need a new axe handle."

Pushing his boot against the axe, he pulled the axe handle toward himself and snapped the handle free.

Lehrling's mouth dropped open. "Why? Why'd you do that?"

"You'll see."

CHAPTER 15

After several minutes of positioning the two sharp-pointed slabs of stone on each side of the axe handle, Roble tied the twine tightly around them and made a double-blade short spear. The blades were sharp enough to pierce through skin or leather, which held a great advantage, but the weight of the weapon was far heavier than he expected. With a short handle and the heavy rock blades, he could only stab and kill the slime beast by getting close to it.

Should he miss, the stone could shatter if it struck a harder surface. The creature's thin skin membrane wasn't impenetrable, because it swallowed its victims by spreading around and incapsulating them. Somehow, the creature did this voluntarily. Even if a sword or axe cut through the membrane, the creature's ooze held fast and the intrusive cut gelled together. Unlike metal, this stone, he hoped, would prevent the opening from resealing. The stone's components should disrupt the creature's chemical composition. The danger came in the gushing acid and ooze spilling out. He needed to be quick to avoid the acid dissolving his flesh.

"What do you need us to do?" Lehrling asked.

"Distract the creature," he replied.

Lehrling's eyes widened. "Wh-what?"

"Why?" Shawndirea asked.

"I need to plunge this stone inside it. Since the axe handle's short, I have to get close without it seeing me. If it notices me, it'll spit acid on me and I'll die. Or worse, I'll wish I *were* dead."

She frowned. "I thought you were going to throw the spear at it."

Roble shrugged slightly. "The blade's too heavy. If I throw it, I won't have any accuracy."

"See?" Shawndirea said. "You don't need to do this."

"With your help, I can destroy it."

"It can spew acid quite a distance," she said.

"Exactly. That's why I need you to distract it."

"What if there are more than one?" she asked.

"I doubt that's the case," Roble said. "With as little prey as it catches, there shouldn't be more than one. Although I know little about them, I suspect the largest would consume smaller ones."

"Roble," Lehrling said, "I can't run fast and I'm not as agile as I once was."

Roble gritted his teeth and strained as he picked up the weapon and carefully propped it on his shoulder. His shoulder sagged beneath the spear's weight, and he questioned whether he should attack the ooze monster or not. He was strong enough to swing the weapon, but was he fast enough? If he missed, he wouldn't get a second attempt.

He pointed at the building where the creature lived. He took a torch from the fire and handed it to Lehrling.

Roble said, "From where we stand, you can't see them, but there are several pillars made of limestone. Use the pillars to hide. If it spits acid at you, step behind a pillar. They'll absorb the acid."

Uncertainty creased Lehrling's brow. "Is that true?"

"Yes. Trust me." Roble nodded. "Shawndirea, don't get too close but allow it to see you."

"I truly hope you know what you're doing," she said softly.

"We'll soon find out." Roble walked away from the campfire and headed toward the building.

Thunder rumbled in the distance. Faint lightning flickered from the surrounding clouds and offered the briefest amount of light to illuminate the building and the pillars.

Roble pointed. "See the pillars?"

"Yes." Lehrling swallowed hard enough to be heard. "Can the creature see me from this point?"

Roble shrugged. "Hard to say. Throw small rocks in its direction or speak loud enough to draw its attention, but not until I get into a better position."

"When should I throw the rocks?"

"I'll make three short whistling sounds," Roble replied.

Lehrling met Roble's gaze. "Three?"

"Yes. You won't mistake them. I won't mimic a bird."

Lehrling nodded and turned to head to the pillars. "Good luck, Roble, and Goddesses' speed."

"And to you. Don't make yourself an easy target. Stay close to the pillars."

Shawndirea flittered near Roble. "I wonder if your purpose lately is to make me an early widow."

"Believe me, I've every intention of living a long life."

"You have odd ways of showing it. Since this creature hasn't pursued us, you've no reason to attack it. It's almost like you've declared war."

"It's not a battle, but I'm luring it to attack," Roble said. "But should more innocent people die?"

"We don't know that those who died were innocent. Most likely, they were thieves and murderers trying to enter the cellar."

"All who travel to this island cannot be those of ill repute. We aren't."

Shawndirea beamed a smile. "We're the exceptions."

Faint cloud lightning flickered and cast a strobe light effect over the building for several seconds.

"Damn," Roble said.

"What?"

"There's not enough light to see the creature."

"Well, it's the middle of the night."

"I should've brought a torch."

"Not if you plan to sneak up behind it. A flame will draw its immediate attention," she said. "I assume you wish to lure it in Lehrling's direction?"

"Yes. If it leaves the stairwell, I can stab it from behind."

"I never took you to be a backstabber," she said with humor in her voice.

"I'm not fighting another human." Roble sighed, took another step toward the door of the building, and squinted. "I don't see the creature."

"I hope you're right about it not ever venturing away from the cellar," she said.

"Me, too."

"I'll fly closer and see if it's in the stairwell."

"Be careful."

"Always," she replied. "I may need to use magic to get its attention. Once I locate it, I will cast an illumination spell so you can see it."

"Good idea."

Shawndirea took flight. Another brief flicker of lightning revealed the doorway. She entered and after the last bit of lightning vanished, he couldn't see her. Fear crept into his mind, but he shunted it away.

With his recent streak of luck, he half expected to turn and find the ooze beast behind him. He gave a nervous glance over his shoulder, but with limited vision in the darkness, he relied more on trying to hear the creature instead of seeing it. After a few seconds, he was certain the thing was still in or near the stairs.

Shawndirea's body radiated a greenish sheen, and she zipped upwards through the open ceiling of the building. In seconds, she returned to Roble. "It's in the stairwell. I'm not certain how far down the stairs go, but it seems to patrol them. It's on its way up."

"Good. Thanks."

Lightning struck and the top of a tree exploded in the forest on the other side of the swollen creek. Thunder echoed and shook the ground. Roble focused on the fallen wall to the right of the stairwell.

Nervousness creased Shawndirea's brow. "Do you want me to capture its attention so it'll leave the stairs sooner?"

"Wait for my signal first."

"What are you planning to do?"

He pointed. "If I climb to the top of the broken wall near the stairs, I'll have a better vantage point. I won't have to stab it at close range. Once I'm in position, I'll whistle."

She hovered closer and kissed his cheek. "Don't get killed or maimed or—"

Roble sighed. "I don't plan to."

"Few ever *plan* to suffer an agonizing death. Being dissolved by acid is almost equal to burning to death. Perhaps even worse."

"I'd best hurry. I need to scale the wall *before* it reaches the top of the stairs," he said.

"I'll be overhead. When I see it, I'll make certain it keeps its attention on me and not you."

"Just be careful."

Crouched, Roble walked slowly to the edge of the building. Even though the wall had partially fallen, he needed to enter through the old doorway to climb the wall, which meant possibly stepping in front of the creature. While he hoped the ooze monster moved slower than a slug, he had no knowledge of how fast it could carry itself up the stairs.

He hesitated at the entrance, almost fearful to step through. His heartbeat increased, and he was more nervous than he wanted to be. It was good to be cautious, but with all the objections Lehrling and Shawndirea kept giving him, he began to doubt he'd made the right decision.

He readily defended himself against Lehrling's insinuation that Roble wanted the creature dead so he could find hidden wealth below. Roble had not lied. His first motive was to ensure the creature never killed anyone else. And if it was magically created to guard the cellar, something extraordinary must be below this ghost town island. If he killed the creature, he had earned, at the very least, the right to see what the creature had been protecting.

Listening, no sounds of a sluggish, sloshing creature echoed from the stairwell, which was approximately five feet from the doorway. Roble slipped through the door, lowered the stone weapons at his side, and pressed his back partway against the tilted wall.

Shawndirea hovered above Roble. Outlined by a faint, greenish glow, she nodded and motioned for him to climb.

Roble placed one hand inside a gap where two missing planks had once formed part of the wall. He pulled himself upward. He planted one foot into a groove, pushed, and before rising, he gripped the double-tipped spear tightly. The stone head he had carved was almost too heavy for him to heft along with his own weight, especially since he was climbing with only one hand.

He used his feet for leverage, but each time he lifted one foot to climb higher, he lost his balance for several seconds. And during his climb, each passing second was more valuable than the last. His hand, wrist, and biceps ached from the strain of stubbornly holding the spear. But without the spear, he had no need to reach the top of the wall.

Shawndirea appeared beside him and whispered, "Hurry. It's almost to the top of the stairs."

Roble grunted and offered a slight nod. He heaved the spear upward and pressed the handle against the bent section of the wall. The slope allowed him enough surface area to set it down, but the steepness prevented him from totally releasing the handle. With less weight working against him, he raised his right foot and found a place to step higher. Attempting his best balance, he used both hands to grip the spear's handle and slide the weapon into a narrow groove where it wouldn't fall.

Once he secured the weapon, he pulled himself atop the slanted wall and sat. His right arm burned with pain. He massaged his wrist, fore-arm, and his biceps for a few moments. He doubted an hour's worth of rest for his arm was enough recovery for how he planned to attack the creature. He hoped his weakened arm didn't hinder his accuracy. Should he miss, he wasn't going to get another chance.

Shawndirea waved her hands together to the left of the stairwell, close to where the two pillars set with Lehrling somewhere behind one of them. A bright orb of green glowed with enough vigor to brighten the floor and the entrance of the stairwell.

Roble took a sharp breath when the glob of churning acid slopped from the top step onto the old floor. He couldn't tell if it had seen her light or not. He wondered if it sensed his presence. Shaking his tingling hand to ward off its numbness, he whistled, grabbed the spear handle with both hands, and lifted it over his head.

CHAPTER 16

*I*n spite of his aching arm, Roble waited for Shawndirea to lure the ooze creature from the stairwell. He attempted to hide his worry and hoped the darkness prevented Lehrling and Shawndirea from noticing. Although he was certain the weapon would destroy the acid beast, he hated putting their lives in danger by having them distract it. Of course, the best-set plans always appeared better in one's mind than they did in action.

She twirled swiftly in the air and fired a green bolt of energy at the creature. Although her bolt did no harm, it captured the creature's interest. It spat a wad of acid spit at her.

Shawndirea spun, flew upward, and then she descended too close to the creature. Green bolts shot from her hands, but the monster absorbed them. Incredibly it picked up its pace and spat again, narrowly missing her. She dodged but lost her balance and spiraled downward. She caught herself on the rough floor.

A sharp pain stabbed Roble's stomach. He wanted to help her, but even if he ran, he wasn't faster than the creature's ability to cover her with acid.

Tendrils stretched from the acid beast's sides and elongated like an octopus' arms. It reached for her.

Shawndirea lie on the worn floor, shook her head, and tried to gain her composure.

Lehrling growled, stepped into the open, and threw several small stones, which struck the creature with remarkable accuracy. "Are you okay, Shawndirea?"

"I'm fine." Her voice resounded with a tinge of anger.

"Look out!" Lehrling said.

A large wad of spit soared toward her. She rose to her feet and shot into the air. The acid spit splattered in the spot where she had lain.

After she flew into the air, Roble breathed a sigh of relief. He cursed under his breath for having put her into the situation at all.

The ooze monster moved from the stairwell and was almost outside of Roble's range. Holding the spear overhead, he pushed off the wall with his feet and jumped. If he missed and the stone-blade's points shattered, he was dead. Lehrling and Shawndirea could escape with their lives, but he would probably get absorbed by the creature. Dead in an instant.

As Roble descended, Shawndirea screamed. Apparently she had noticed him jump. He stretched his arms outward and extended the weapon as far as he could. The sharp tips of the spear gouged and split through the creature's outer membrane. A gushing pool of acid and goo flooded out from the creature. The heavy stone blades frothed, foamed, and pulled the acid into them.

Roble's momentum set him in motion to land face-first in the acid. His right arm and shoulder burned with pain, but adrenaline surged through him. He tightened his hold on the axe handle enough to vault over the acid pool. He spun in the air and dropped on his back outside the spreading acid pool.

Shawndirea swooped and hovered above him. "Are you okay?"

Pain radiated down his spine and jagged pangs shot through his arms and legs, which riveted a torrent of agony throughout his body. He knees and back throbbed from his impact.

"You did it!" Lehrling shouted.

Roble gave a side-glance at what remained of the creature and grinned.

"I shouldn't have doubted you," Shawndirea said.

"In hindsight, perhaps I should've have listened. It was foolish to put you and Lehrling in danger. You almost were hit by acid."

She smiled. "Almost doesn't count, does it?"

Lehrling's thudding footsteps approached. He placed a hand on Roble's shoulder. "Roble, are you okay?"

Roble groaned and half smiled. "Never better."

Lehrling frowned. "Somehow I don't believe you."

Roble chuckled. "Minus the pain. At least, I missed the pool of acid."

"True." Lehrling offered his hand and pulled Roble to his feet.

"Give me a few minutes," Roble said.

Lehrling nodded. "Sure."

"You never mentioned you were going to jump and stab the slime creature," Shawndirea said with a narrowed brow.

"You were protesting enough as it were," Roble replied. "I can't imagine your reaction had you known—"

Her eyes flashed green, and she pointed a stern finger at him. "You said you'd throw it like a spear, not ram it into the beast."

"Yes." Roble acquiesced a nod. "Originally, that was my plan. But the weight of it wore my arm out by the time I reached the top of the wall."

"Foolish!" Her eyes darkened.

Roble stared at her, somewhat bewildered. Moments earlier, her demeanor had been loving and relieved. Now, she seemed consumed by sudden anger.

"Perhaps," Roble said. "But it worked."

Lehrling nodded. "Give him credit for that. It worked, but how?"

Shawndirea turned her angered gaze from Roble, crossed her arms, and looked at the vanishing acid pool. Her curiosity overcame her anger. She glided above the receding acid. "What magic is this?"

"It's not magic," Roble replied. "It's science."

She met his eyes. "What do you mean?"

Lehrling walked to the edge of the acid. "Yes, please explain."

Roble arched his back, popped his shoulders, and gripped his aching arm. "In short, the creature never left the stairwell because of the stones' composition. They're limestone. Limestone counteracts strong acids by neutralizing and making them ineffective. The creature's outer membrane was probably thick enough to prevent damage whenever it crawled across the stone, but should it suffer a deep enough cut, it'd be vulnerable."

"So you knew the spear would kill it?" she asked.

"I was fairly certain."

She frowned. "But not absolute?"

Before he could reply, the ground shook. A forceful gust of stagnant air rushed up the stairwell and bellowed. Shrieks followed and dark bats flew out of the stairwell and into the night.

"What's that?" Roble steadied himself on the shaking ground.

Lehrling wobbled, and he fought to keep his balance. Roble gripped Lehrling's arm to prevent his fall.

"I'm not certain," Shawndirea said softly. "But since you killed the creature, you must've broken the spell and opened whatever's sealed below."

"Then let's go see what's down there," Roble said.

"That's not advisable," she replied. "You might've unlocked a magical door or a portal and released a creature worse than the acid beast."

"My gut tells me otherwise." He turned and ran toward their campfire.

"What are you doing?" she asked.

"Getting another torch."

CHAPTER 17

*R*oble led the way down the crude stairwell, despite Shawndirea's livid protests. The torch's flames singed and melted thick cobwebs and roasted the plump spiders that constructed them. Using the light as his guide, he avoided the occasional broken steps as they descended.

He offered for Shawndirea to sit on his shoulder or in his pocket but she replied with a sharp intense glare, which meant he should say nothing else to her for a while.

Severe moodiness was a rarity for her, mostly nonexistent since he'd proven he was a man of his word by risking his life to bring her home.

But ever since they entered the swamp, her temperament grew more fiery than she'd ever displayed in the past, even toward her mother, and he found this dilemma strange.

On this journey, she seemed easily riled and tended to lash out. She held less compassion toward him, which was also unlike her. Their relationship had always been respectful, caring, and loving. Was she unknowingly directing her bitterness for Dirk at him? Had Lez'minx somehow cast a spell on her or perhaps one of the dark Fae had done so before it died?

Something troubled her deeply. Although he wanted to discuss her inner turmoil to get to the root of the problem, the timing wasn't appro-priate. Besides, she'd never hold such a conversation openly in Lehrling's presence. Their personal situations were sorted through together in the privacy of their home.

Every time Shawndirea scolded Roble for his impulsive actions without evaluating the risks, Lehrling cringed. Lehrling was docile, for the most part, so his stressed reactions often seemed like he was the one on the receiving end of her tirades. While Roble wanted to smooth things over with Shawndirea, he wasn't about to address her sudden anger because she'd get madder and possibly increase Lehrling's stress.

The farther downstairs they went, the wetter the walls became. Water trickled and dripped down the cold walls. Small puddles gathered between the sunken, rocky stairs. The dank air reeked with the slightly soured aroma of mold and mildew.

The acid beast wasn't a necessary element to protect the depths under the hamlet at all. Who in their right mind would continue downward when nothing but treacherous traps might lie ahead? He chuckled, realizing he *wasn't* in his right mind for allowing his curiosity to persuade his descent.

Shawndirea's wings fluttered softly behind his head. He could picture the scowl on her face during her silent protest down the stairs.

Although Lehrling eagerly agreed to explore the cellar, too, he couldn't hide his nervousness in the torch's glow. Lehrling drew his short sword and Roble slid a dagger into his left hand.

For some reason, Roble was certain no other creatures awaited at in the cellar. The stairs turned back on themselves four times before ending at the opening to a large room. No creatures were visible, and no hungry growls welcomed them.

The burning tip of the stick Roble had taken from the fire offered less and less light, but produced more and more smoke. Soon, only the reddish embers would glow in the dark cellar before total darkness finally enveloped them. He searched the open room and found a stone pot of pitch with two soaking torches. He grabbed one and touched the flame to it. The pitch on the torch roared to light and revealed the contents of the room.

"My word," Lehrling gasped.

Dusty cobwebs covered several crude tables. Piles of rolled scrolls and books were scattered on the tables. A quill with a long black raven feather rested in a ink pot. On one table, a map of Aetheaon was spread out. Heavy glass orbs weighted each corner. A dozen or more unlit candles had melted into their holders years ago.

Shawndirea flew past Roble and used her magic to zap green fire blasts at each candle's stiffened wick. Slowly the room was aglow.

With sudden apprehension, she whispered, "A wizard once lived here."

"Are you sure, faery?" Lehrling asked.

With bewildered eyes, she glanced around the room before she landed on the closest table and ran her hand along the spines of the ancient books. "These are magic volumes, scrolls, and extensive notes. Rare books most likely stolen from another alchemist wizard."

Lehrling eased closer to view the items. His eyes widened.

"What?" Roble asked.

"It can't be," Lehrling replied.

"What?"

Lehrling picked up an unrolled scroll with a dried red wax seal beside the signature.

"The stamp's from a Dragon Skull pendant," Lehrling said in a near whisper. He held up the scroll and studied it.

"That's odd," Roble said."

Lehrling took a sharp breath and stared in disbelief as he looked from the seal to Roble. "It belonged to Geowren."

"How do you know that?" Roble asked.

"His signature is beside the seal." Lehrling pointed. "And that's his dagger on the table. I'd recognize the hilt anywhere. See? His name's engraved on the blade."

Roble picked up the blade and examined it. The dagger was weighted properly, but to Roble's disappointment, this wasn't a throwing knife, but impressive in its own right. The hilt was designed with silver and gold. More than a dozen rubies were inset. This was a prize for anyone who carried it.

"Why would he leave it?" Roble asked.

Lehrling shook his head. "He wouldn't deliberately."

"Perhaps he was trapped here and became a victim of the ooze creature?"

"No," Shawndirea replied. "The creature was probably his."

Roble frowned. "Did he control magic, Lehrling?"

Lehrling flicked his gaze from Roble and stared at her questionably. "Not to my knowledge, no. Why'd you say that, Shawndirea? He was a common knight like myself."

"If this is his writing, there's nothing *common* about him. He was a wizard or at the least, an apprentice of one." She stood atop a drawing of the ooze creature and the details for how to summon it from a certain combination of different ingredients was written beneath it, along with the written incantation.

"If the creature was his, where'd he go?" Roble asked while studying the information of the ooze beast on the aged parchment. "Why did he stay down here?"

Lehrling thumbed through a stack of loose parchments much like the one with the wax seal, only the others were different. "These are entries, like a journal. The other—" He held the signed one closer to a candle's flame to read the words. "This is a letter."

"To whom?" Roble asked.

Lehrling's brow rose. "Queen Taube."

CHAPTER 18

*R*oble looked over Lehrling's shoulder at the parchment. "Queen Taube?"

Lehrling moved the paper closer to the candlelight. "Yes."

"What's it say?" Shawndirea asked.

Lehrling squinted and read the letter aloud:

"My Dearest Queen Taube,

May the blessings of the Three Goddesses be upon you.

I recently discovered King Erik was never killed in the war against the Dredgemen. He was taken prisoner and is possibly still alive. As your, and his, devoted knight, I've taken it upon myself to find where he's imprisoned. Once I've located his exact whereabouts, I shall arrive at Hoffnung's Courts and gather my Dragon Skull brethren together, so we can bring him home safely. And to those who betrayed the throne, justice will find them by my sword. They will pay dearly for these atrocities. Their crimes will not be ignored or forgotten.

Forever in your service,

Geowren

"King Erik lives?" Shawndirea said with a hopeful smile.

"Geowren might be, too." Lehrling wiped a tear from his cheek, his face flushed red, and he was too choked up to speak. Twice, he tried to say something further, but his voice crackled so badly, he shook his head and mouthed, "Sorry."

"Why didn't he ever send this letter?" Roble asked.

Lehrling placed the letter on the rickety table. Taking a deep breath, he braced his hands atop the table, and tried to regain his composure.

"Perhaps his journals give more details," Shawndirea said.

Lehrling's body shook. He reared back his head, laughed, and shook his hands in triumph. "By the Goddesses above! King Erik lives! Greater news could not befall us!"

Ambition overtook him, fresh tears streamed down his round cheeks into his blonde beard, and he thumbed through the parchments. He chuckled and then released a long sigh. "We must find Geowren so we can aid in the return of our King."

"Easy, Lehrling." Roble placed a comforting hand on Lehrling's shoulder. "All in good time."

"Good time?" Lehrling shook his head. His eager smile didn't fade. "We've wondered about King Erik's welfare for so long. Whether he was dead or alive. If dead, where had they buried him? Now, with this news—"

Roble nodded. "It's great news, but *when* did he write the letter?"

Lehrling placed his finger at the bottom of the letter, where Geowren scribbled a date. Lehrling's smile retreated slightly, but the brightness in his eyes didn't lessen. He sighed. "About a year ago."

"That's not too long ago, I suppose," Roble said. "But, we need to find out where Geowren traveled from here. Maybe we can track his steps and find him. It might harder than finding where King Erik is. A person can travel quite a distance in a year's time."

"Yes, you're right." Lehrling took a couple of deep breaths to calm himself. Still, his smile beamed. "I mustn't get too ahead of myself. But Goddesses, what a glorious day! We have you to thank, Roble! Indeed, it's no accident you found and saved me."

"I can't take the credit for *this*," Roble said.

"Your stubbornness to kill the acid beast allowed us to find Geowren's hideout," Lehrling said.

"Don't forget," Shawndirea said. "His stubbornness is what nearly killed us all. If we'd died, all of this remained lost and buried."

Roble ignored her bitter jab. "The best information we can gather is through his journal entries. You said he's not a practitioner of magic?"

"No. He's never worn a blessed trinket or a magical charm, other than his Dragon Skull pendant."

"Then how'd he learn magic?"

From across the room, Shawndirea said, "This might interest you."

Roble turned toward her. She fluttered above an iron box cage. "Is that a torture cage?"

"It could be modified for such," she replied, "but this specific cage was designed to imprison a wizard prisoner and prevent him from using his magic. See the runes welded at the top? I wouldn't fly into this cage. It'd probably drain all my power."

Roble nodded. "So Geowren kept a wizard prisoner? Why?"

"With the right enchantments, Geowren could've transferred a wizard's knowledge and power to use for himself until he developed his own magical strength. It's rare for someone without natural magical abilities to succeed, as one's magic tends to be loyal to its caster. The risks are often greater than any reward."

"Then why risk it?" Roble gripped the iron bars of the cage door.

"To learn spells?" Shawndirea said. "Geowren wrote out a lot of scrolls."

"Why would a wizard offer his spells, even if he was held prisoner?" Roble asked.

"You'd need to ask Geowren. Or the wizard, if the wizard's still alive. Geowren might've tortured the wizard to divulge his secrets."

"Unlikely," Lehrling said. "Geowren never tortured anyone."

"Perhaps not, during the times of peace," Shawndirea said. "But if this particular wizard knew who had taken King Erik prisoner, wouldn't that be enough motive for him to get the information anyway possible?"

"It would for me," Roble said without giving his comment a second thought. He held undying devoted loyalty to Hoffnung, even though he wasn't from this realm.

Holding the cage bars, Roble pictured a trapped, angry wizard set with vindictive urges locked inside the cage. If the wizard freed himself, he'd torment Geowren, and possibly cast severe pestilence on the Dragon Knight. The wizard would've enjoyed every moment Geowren suffered. Looking at the crude tables covered with scrolls, Roble visualized Geowren busily dipping his quill in the ink well and writing various spell methods on the yellow parchments as dictated by his prisoner. He couldn't image the spells being safe for Geowren to use.

An odd crystal ball covered by dust was strangely shaped with an odd color. The ball resembled an eyeball of a large creature. Perhaps it was, knowing Aetheaon's strangeness and some of the most unusual vices he'd witnessed. What parts of his compassion was Roble sacrificing by living in a realm far different than his own. Aetheaon had less governing laws and a kill-or-be-killed mentality in its own right, which was the law for one's survival. Justice here was not the same.

Lehrling nodded. "If the wizard knew where King Erik was? Yes. Any of the Order would go to any length to find the truth, especially if Erik's alive. Our oath is to our King and Queen of Hoffnung. We'd die to defend the throne."

"But how do you capture a wizard?" Roble asked with a slight grin.

"Not easily," she said. "But, it can be done. Generally by surprise or a quick thwack to the back of the head. An unconscious wizard is a powerless one. It's nearly impossible to sneak up behind one, though. One must get past a wizard's circle of protection. Or, drug his wine and wait for the effects to occur."

"Some of Geowren's entries are interesting," Lehrling said.

"Like what?"

"Apparently the wizard controlled the island at one point and was a tyrant. Let me read this:

The townsfolk on this modest island—Polderholm, it is called—were most welcoming, but not their overseer, Mad Vyssisk, a dark wizard. He ordered me taken prisoner when he saw my Dragon Skull pendant. He'd have had my head removed and feasted on my heart and liver had the Three Goddesses not protected me.

At least, I give them the honor and glory, for they allowed me to turn the tables on this crazed wizard, who is not human, but some sort of reptilian. His skin's scaly. His long tail has sharp plated tips that run down his spine. They're weapons in their own right. Confining him without injuring myself was quite the feat.

To my surprise, Vyssisk has been quite insightful in his instruction and taught me magic in ways I've never fathomed. Keeping him alive, for the time being, is in both of our best interests.

However, time's not a luxury in his cellar. Other reptilian soldiers dressed in leather armor, and carrying flimsy shields and iron weapons, have attempted to descend the stairwell but the magical doorway I created has tricked them thus far. I chanced a view of the surface and found that the reptilians had killed all the other humans that once inhabited the Isle of Polderholm. The town's deserted, except for me.

With time fleeting, I gathered poisonous leaves, clumps of peat moss, and several buckets of acrid swamp water. I brought them to the cellar and resealed the magical doorway. After placing these ingredients in a small pit, I cast an incantation from one of Vyssisk's spellbooks, not certain it would even work. It did. Gryme was spawned.

I suppose a little luck came with the magic, as the slime creature could've killed me after maturation. But instead, he—it—has been more loyal than a dog to its master. Instead of using the magic door, which had been slowly draining my own strength, Gryme patrols the stairs. I've developed a fondness for Gryme since he dissolved and ate three thieves who arrived on the island late one evening. They descended the stairs with the intent of robbing and killing me. It was then I learned Gryme could spit acid. Of course, the three thieves were unfortunate to make the same discovery.

Roble rolled his eyes. "Great. I killed his pet."

"You had no knowledge of that." Lehrling chuckled heartily. "None of us did. To it, we were enemies, trespassers."

"When we find Geowren, let's *not* mention that to him," Roble said.

Lehrling cocked a brow. "It'll be our secret."

"How'd he capture Vyssisk?" Shawndirea said.

"He doesn't say. The rest of his written account is brief. This must be the last entry he wrote before he left the island. Gryme remained behind to protect this cellar." Lehrling frowned. "It makes no sense why he'd leave his prized dagger on the table."

"Perhaps he left in a hurry?" Roble asked.

"He must've," Lehrling said. "But if Gryme remained on guard, *what* did Geowren flee from? How'd he escape the island so quickly?"

A blue flash of light brightened the far end of the cellar.

They turned in direction of the light.

"What was that?" Roble slid daggers from the hidden sheaths in his belt.

The light faded.

Roble crept along the edge of the wall. The light shown again.

Lehrling pulled his sword. "Be wary, Roble."

"Yes," Shawndirea said. "Don't forget this is a wizard's lair. Old protection spells might remain. The last thing you want, is to trigger one of them."

"I understand," Roble replied. "But the source of the light is perhaps an answer to a lot of our questions."

CHAPTER 19

*R*oble slipped alongside the wall with his daggers held to his sides. His footsteps fell silent, which would've impressed Crukas, Aetheaon's greatest thief.

The dull, blue light flickered, which revealed something they'd have never noticed had the light not drawn their attention.

The wall he walked along didn't actually meet the other wall. Instead, there was a gap used for a doorway, but the walls' unusual construction was an optical illusion. Looking dead on, the eye projected the two walls meeting, but physically, the corner didn't exist. For all they knew, the wizard or Geowren could've been watching them without their knowledge.

The light shown from the short adjoining narrow hallway, which happened to be a dead end.

Roble eased closer and moved cautiously to the other wall, so he could look into the hidden passageway. A magical blue oval, ever bit Roble's height, shimmered and rippled like a vivid wall of gel-like water. But this wasn't water. It was a magical doorway, a portal. The wave sensations swirling within the oval were almost mesmerizing.

"What's this?" Roble asked.

"A magic portal," Shawndirea said. "It'll teleport you to another place or city."

Lehrling sheathed his sword. He approached the portal with eagerness. "Geowren must've escaped through here."

"Perhaps," she said.

Roble grinned. "Let's see where he went."

"No," Shawndirea said, shaking her head. "Stop allowing your curiosity to get the best of you. It's not safe. We've no idea what's on the other side or where it'll take us."

"But if Geowren took it—" Lehrling said.

"What if he *didn't?*" she said. "What if the wizard somehow got free and took Geowren prisoner? This portal could lead to a hostile city where we'd be taken prisoner or worse, killed."

Roble sighed. He ached to know where the portal led. But rather than enter to satisfy his curiosity, he chose not to argue the matter. Shawndirea was already angry enough from his recent rash decisions. Her anger had somewhat subsided since their discoveries in the cellar intrigued her. To argue about the portal would be several steps backwards.

Roble clasped his hand on Lehrling's shoulder. "She's right, Lehrling. I want to know where this leads as much as you, but what if it's only a one-way passage? Our horses are tethered outside. We can't leave them to starve."

Lehrling ran his hands through his hair and groaned with frustration. "You're right, but we've learned so much. We're much closer to finding King Erik. We shouldn't dismiss the opportunity entirely."

"We're not," Roble said. "But let this information revitalize your hope. Who knows? Lez'minx might be able to answer some of our questions."

"I wouldn't put faith in that," Shawndirea said with a narrowed brow.

"I wouldn't call it faith," Roble said. "Perhaps I can barter."

"With what? He already holds his gifts over your head."

"Everybody wants something," Roble said. "Meanwhile, let's gather some of these papers. There's a woodcutting axe in the corner, which looks better than the one I used for the spear. Geowren's not in any hurry to use these, if he bothers to return at all. Do you see anything useful, Shawndirea?"

She nodded. "Much."

. . .

AFTER SEVERAL HOURS of sorting through the scrolls, books, and bottled potions Geowren had left on the table, Roble and Lehrling gathered armsful of items to store in their saddlebags. Since most were useful in magic, and some were items Shawndirea expressed a need for, they needed to protect them from the heavy rains after leaving Polderholm.

Shawndirea found a cloak flung over a chair. She sensed an enchantment on it, but the true nature of the protective spell she couldn't discern. However, the green plant material meshed together to make the cloak was waxy and waterproof.

They wrapped the paper scrolls and books inside the cloak and tucked them inside Roble's saddlebag. Roble tied the woodcutting axe between his saddle and the bags. Lehrling placed Geowren's dagger into his belt sheath with a sense of pride.

After Roble and Lehrling climbed on their saddles, Roble said, "We didn't get any rest, but it's time we leave."

CHAPTER 20

*A*fter two days of riding the faint remnants of trails covered by shallow water and thickening muck, they never encountered any towns, hamlets, or ruins. They reached one fork along their trail a day earlier. Roble chose the path to the right because his enchanted armor tugged in that direction. Although making his decision based on the impulse was odd, he trusted the sensation. Somehow, he believed their journey would be fulfilled by following the path.

The swampy scenery seldom changed. Roble wondered, at times, if they were lost and traveling in a circle. And if not, they were deep in the Woodnog's Swamps. The only certainty they had was the constant rain, drab fog, and the eerie feeling of something watching from the shadowy trees. Whether those eyes belonged to wild beasts, Shadowfae, or ghosts doomed to wander the swamps, he wasn't certain. They'd gone too far to turn back, and the chance to find a town or seaport was better by traveling east. At least at a port, they could set sail to Hoffnung or Oculoth. He'd rather find an alternative route than to return to Woodnog through the swamps.

Due to the watery paths, no one could detect any fresh hooves or boot prints. Given how the terrain worsened the deeper into the swamps, Roble was not surprised.

Shawndirea's mood switched between being pleasant and in a

moment's notice, she seethed with heated anger. He suspected her rage came because they'd traveled so far into the swamp. He couldn't blame her outbursts because silently, he berated himself for not having turned back days earlier.

The mixed tree canopy of firs and deciduous trees meshed together to form a natural leaking ceiling. Cascading raindrops pelleted the dark, rising waters. Brilliantly colored snakes, unlike any Roble had seen in the Overlands, slithered from the path. Whether venomous or not was undetermined, but he had no intention to investigate.

The howling wind shook the long flowing curtains of wet moss hanging from tree limbs. Another approaching night slowly greeted them.

How much more misery must we endure? Roble thought.

Roble cast a side-glance at Lehrling. His poor companion was drenched. Even with his blanket pulled over his head, Lehrling couldn't escape the rain. Chilled, and perhaps achingly cold, Lehrling's lower lip trembled and occasionally he shook and hugged himself.

They hadn't seen the sun since they entered the swamp and after nightfall, Lehrling would only get dangerously colder.

Due to wearing Bausch's armor, Roble and Shawndirea were unaffected by the weather and seemingly dry. But unless they found a place sheltered from the rain where they could light a fire, Roble feared Lehrling might suffer hypothermia or succumb to pneumonia and die. Surprisingly, Lehrling never complained about the unforgiving climate.

"How are you faring?" Roble shouted over the heavy rain drumming on the broadleaved branches overhead.

"O-o-kay." Lehrling forced a shaky smile. His fatigued eyes pleaded for rest.

"I know you're freezing, Lehrling," Roble said. "I keep hoping to find shelter soon."

"As do I!" Lehrling held the soaked blanket tightly beneath his chin. "You should under … st—stand why folks who enter these swamps seldom return?"

"You couldn't have painted a clearer picture, my friend!"

Lehrling pointed toward a thicker set of trees, a forest that might offer possible shelter. "We go through there!"

Roble steered his horse closer to Lehrling. "Regardless of what's in those trees—dangers or monsters or predators—we're stopping for the night. You must get out of the rain."

"We can't stop," Lehrling said wearily. His eyes grew more tired and his face paled. "Not here. We're easy targets."

"We've ridden constantly for two days and a night in this rain. It's not going to let up," Roble said. "We stop at the first rise of ground where the water isn't pooling. You can't keep riding through this rain."

Anger stirred in Lehrling's eyes. The paleness of his face reddened and spittle flew from his lips. "Damn the rains! I'm not helpless!"

"No one suggested you are." Roble shook his head. "You're one of the strongest men I've been blessed to call my friend. But, we need a fire for warmth, some food, and lots of sleep."

"Good luck lighting a fire in this rain!" Lehrling glared at the forest canopy. "Nothing's dry enough to burn."

"We'll find a way," Roble said. "Perhaps Shawndirea could use her magic—"

"I'm envious of her," he grumbled. "All warm and dry, curled inside your pocket. Must be nice not facing the wrath of the elements."

Roble nodded. He ached to see Lehrling suffer. "We'll find a way to light a fire. We need sleep. Without enough sleep, our minds become delusional. We'll begin seeing things that aren't there."

"Agreed! But tell me, Overlander, do you still desire to explore these wonderful swamplands? Perhaps you could buy a parcel of land to settle?"

Roble grinned and shook his head. "No, thanks. As for further exploration, I've had a change of heart."

"Then you've grown wiser than you appear." Lehrling winked. "Of course, looks can't be trusted in the absence of light."

Roble laughed. *Good. Keep him talking. He jokes, so he's trying to keep his mind off our current situation.*

Lightning flashed and exposed the watery floor beneath the slick, dark trees. Pools of water broke apart and formed meandering streams that flowed around fallen trees, rocks, and wicked shrubs. Another bolt of lightning zagged above the canopy and the shrubs resembled crouched creatures ready to pounce. Heavy thunder rumbled its unforgiving wrath.

As the lightning faded, Roble was certain one shrub was a creature and not a plant. The horses blew air through their nostrils and stamped their front feet, fearful of moving ahead. Roble patted the horse's neck and coaxed the horse forward.

"Easy, Bleys," he said. "What's troubling you?"

Shawndirea stood inside Roble's pocket, stretched, and released a long yawn.

"At least *one* of us got some sleep," Lehrling said with a tinge of bitterness. "You've slumbered in warmth for hours now."

She frowned and glanced at Roble. "Is this true? Have I slept that long?"

"It's been awhile," he replied.

"My apologies," she said.

"None needed," Roble said.

Lehrling grumbled beneath his breath.

Roble grinned at Shawndirea. "You'll keep first watch after we set up camp."

"Here?"

Roble sighed. "No other places have been suitable."

"You call this *suitable*?" she said.

He shrugged. "At least the trees are thicker."

"So we've still not found a town or an abandoned settlement?"

"We'd have stopped if we'd found such a place," Roble said. "But no sign of humans, elves, dwarves, or any other races. No fresh tracks in the mud, either."

Shawndirea sighed. "I know you would've stopped. I find it … odd … that no settlements are here."

More lightning flickered and illuminated the forest. The outline of an old shack became visible, but only for a moment. Under the next flicker of lightning, the shack was gone.

Roble rubbed his tired eyes. "I could've sworn—"

"I saw the old hut, too," Lehrling said. "I swear I did."

"Yes, it was there," Shawndirea whispered.

The remaining dusk-like light was replaced by a deep, thick blackness. Glowing eyes blinked around various fallen trees, crevices, and on low-lying branches. Enchanted was the last word he'd use to describe the forest that snared his mind with horror. In a similar sensation, it nearly equalled entering the Black Chasm.

Wind rustled through the strange trees. The smell of death and decayed leaves wrought an acrid bite when they inhaled.

"I hate to tell you this," Shawndirea said. "But we can't stop in these woods for the night. Not if we expect to live until morning."

"The same thought occurred to me, too, but we're too exhausted to continue," Roble whispered. "Lehrling can't travel any farther or he'll collapse. We're already seeing things that aren't there."

"No," Shawndirea said. "The three of us wouldn't have seen identical delusions. That's not possible."

"Then where's the old shack?"

"It's still there."

Lightning flashed.

She pointed. "See?"

Roble's armor tightened and squeezed around him like the hug of a friend. "We tie the horses and stay in the shack for the night."

"That's not a good idea," she said.

"You have a better one? Because riding throughout the night isn't an option."

Roble tapped his horse's flanks gently and guided it to the shack. He slid from the saddle and tied the horse to a post near the front door. He hurried and helped Lehrling from his saddle before tying his horse beside Bleys.

Roble took bold steps onto the porch. The boards creaked beneath him. No light shone through the cracks around the worn door or the boarded windows. It didn't seem anyone lived inside. Those doubts subsided when he raised his hand to knock and the door opened on its own.

"Welcome, guests," a frail voice said from inside. "Come in and rest yourselves from your travels. I've been waiting for you."

CHAPTER 21

*R*oble hesitated outside the door, contemplating whether to enter or not. None of them had touched the door. He hadn't even knocked. And yet, the door swung open without anyone standing inside the threshold. As best he could tell, nothing *physically* pulled the door open.

"I'm getting delusional, Lehrling," Roble said in a whisper.

"Then you're not alone," he replied.

Several oil lanterns hung on the beams above the porch and flickered to light. Their wicks burned softly, rose to sharp-tipped flames, and cast white beams over them. Two large moths fluttered from the rafters and danced around a lantern. Coiled on the porch supports were a half dozen snakes. They'd walked past without ever noticing them due to the darkness.

Hanging chimes made from the finger bones of humans, elves, or dwarves, rattled in the wind. This macabre decoration made Roble agree with Shawndirea's concern about entering this home. It was not in their best interests. He was ready to turn around, but his armor nudged him closer to the door.

For the first time during his journey into the swamps, chills swept through him, but not from the cold rain or sickness. His curiosity to look inside the old shack equaled his desire to turn and run. Nothing about the verbal greeting seemed threatening, but one could never read intention from a voice or even the possible deception of a gentle smile.

Stunned, Roble glanced at Lehrling. He expected the old man's eyes to widen with fear. Instead, Lehrling continued to shake from the cold. Water dripped off his clothing and puddled around his boots. The soaked blanket around his shoulders slipped from his grip and dropped to the porch with a heavy splat. His longing for warmth crushed any fear he might have had about entering the shack.

Roble realized Lehrling couldn't travel any farther. Not tonight. None of them could. Death awaited them inside this rundown shack, and they'd never survive riding through the swamp another night without sleep. Beyond the porch, at the side of the shack, a shadowy figure with a scythe shifted. Fear jolted him. Perhaps it was sleep deprivation, but he sensed the illusion was no illusion at all. Death's cloaked silhouette was standing in the shadows.

Heat rushed through the open door. After a few more seconds, the light of a fire flickered across the threshold as though a thick curtain had been cast aside to allow the comfort of warmth and light to repel the uneasiness of the cold, empty darkness. Logs in the fireplace crackled. The rich aroma of fresh meaty stew made Roble's mouth water and his stomach growled.

His mind attempted to warn him of how prey becomes blinded to the lures of intelligent predators. However, hunger and exhaustion blocked any attempt of rationality. Even Shawndirea had not whispered a word since the door opened.

"Don't you know an invitation when you hear it?" The woman's crackled. "Either come inside or shut the door. You're letting precious heat out."

"Apologies," Lehrling said, without hesitating further. He stepped through the door and waited for Roble to follow. "May I sit near your fire?"

"Ah, help yourself." She waved her feeble hand in a sweeping gesture. "If you drip water across my floor, clean it up."

Lehrling smiled eagerly and nodded.

The light of the fire only revealed a faint outline of the woman's seated form near the center of the room.

"We will," Roble said.

"You?" She pointed a shaky finger at him. "My magic enchants your armor, but you're *not* the man who requested me to make it."

"No, I'm not." Roble leaned and tried to see the woman's face, which was recessed by the shadows of her hood.

"Why do *you* wear his armor?"

"It's a long story."

She struck a match and lit a candle on the small table beside her rocking chair. As the candle's flame rose, she peeled back her hood. Her white blind eyes peered at him, a ghastly sight, and he feared staring into them for too long might imprison his soul. They were horrifying to look at, and yet, he found it difficult to look away. Her actions indicated—though she was blind—that she could still see. "Well, child, I've all the time in the world. Care to explain why you wear the armor I tailored and enchanted?"

Lehrling sat on the hearth as close to the flames as was possible without singeing his beard and hair. His body shook involuntarily. "You knew Bausch?"

The woman's neck craned slightly. She turned her attention to Lehrling. "Yes, he sought me to tailor this leather armor. I could've blessed it with any enchantment. But, after traveling through the swamp for days, he suffered from a fever. Like you, he was freezing cold, near death, so he begged for armor capable of adapting to the climate."

"Who are you?" Lehrling asked.

"Moorsis." She returned her attention to Roble. "I assume Bausch is dead? Otherwise, he'd still be wearing this?"

"Yes."

Moorsis shook her head slightly and cackled. "I told him to pay homage to Lez'minx for the enchantment on the armor. I suppose he chose not to. As I had told him, magic comes at a price. It's never free. Fool that he was, he didn't believe me. The price he paid was his life."

Lehrling removed his gloves and placed his cold shriveled hands closer to the fire. His skin was almost blue. "He never told me about any of this, about you, or how he had gotten the armor, though I had asked several times."

"And yet," she said, "you're all here?"

"Yes."

Moorsis smiled. "I sense Fae magic in the room. Am I right?"

Shawndirea cleared her throat. "Yes."

A sneer tightened the old woman's wrinkled lips. "Odd you've paired yourself with a human mate. An Overlander one, at that."

Shawndirea's eyes widened and she gave Roble an uncomfortable glance.

Moorsis smiled. "Yes, I see far more than my physical eyes could have ever gifted me with vision."

Roble's stomach growled.

"Young man," Moorsis said. "You need a place to rest. The storms won't pass for weeks. You and your friends help yourself to the pot of stew over the fire. The night will be long."

"What's the cost?" Roble asked.

A wicked smile crooked across her face. "You've a great deal of wisdom at such a young age."

Shawndirea snickered and covered her mouth.

Roble wasn't sure how to take the compliment. It wasn't about wisdom but more about politeness and how he was raised. One should never assume hospitality. Accepting some offers—like the rings he now wore—indebted a person. Since he'd already made that mistake, he didn't want to oblige himself further to anyone else. "I don't know about young, but—"

"The stew's free. Fill your bellies. You have a safe place to stay the night. Also, no charge. The debt you owe isn't to me. Since Bausch never paid homage for his armor, the duty falls to you. I'm sure you're aware. Otherwise, you'd not have journeyed this deep into these swamps." She cackled. "You wear Lez'minx's rings. Ah. He's made certain you'd seek him out."

Roble grabbed a crude wooden bowl. He dipped the ladle and filled the bowl with stew. He handed the bowl to Lehrling, who nodded his eager appreciation. Then Roble filled another bowl for Shawndirea and he to share.

Roble said, "Foolishly, I placed them on my fingers, and now, I can't take them off."

Moorsis howled with laughter. "Often, subtle things snare the inno-cent. But, no matter, you'd have needed to pay homage for the armor."

"I never requested the armor or the enchantment you bestowed on it, either," Roble said. "So—"

"Doesn't matter," she replied. "You wear it. You might not have known the enchantment was there when you decided to wear it, but you soon discovered its unique attributes. Correct? Afterwards, you continued wearing it, so you accepted the armor as your own."

Roble sighed. "True."

"Therefore, you must pay homage for its blessing."

Roble cupped the bowl in his hands and sipped the rich broth. "What's the price exactly? Does accepting the rings and the armor obligate me to be his servant?"

She leaned back in the rocking chair. Her brow narrowed. "That's between you and Lez'minx. I only fashioned the armor. Such is my skill. The armor isn't Lez'minx's, but the enchantment is. He blessed it in favor of the one who wears it."

"So if I discard the armor, I'm free from the obligation?"

Moorsis shook his head. "No, not now. You've worn it far too long. You've imprinted yourself to it, and it's molded to you. In its own way, the armor understands you. It must, in order to constantly maintain your comfort no matter the climate. Do you understand this?"

"Yes," Roble said. "Its impulses led us to your home. But I thought it was leading us to Lez'minx's temple."

She smiled. "You're only a day or more's journey from your destina-tion. Getting there is easy enough, but leaving … that's yet to be deter-mined. But the spell the faery used to tarnish the rings has angered Lez'minx. Remove the spell before you depart in the morning, or your meeting with Lez'minx won't end well."

"He's no right to invade our privacy," Shawndirea said.

"He has every right," Moorsis replied. "Since the rings remain his and his magic's on them, he can view their surroundings to know their where-abouts, so he can retrieve them whenever he chooses. They don't belong to your husband. The bearer has granted Lez'minx access to every conver-sation and every action during the time Roble slipped them on his fingers."

A look of horror and contempt washed across Shawndirea's face. "What? How dare Lez'minx invade our privacy with his magic!"

Moorsis stiffened in her chair at the venom in Shawndirea's voice.

Fury set in Shawndirea's eyes. "Regardless of Roble wearing these rings, Lez'minx has forever violated my trust. Nothing he ever says could lessen my disdain toward him."

"Careful, faery," Moorsis said softly. "Be careful of the insults you lash at him."

"Why?" she asked. "How do you perceive his pretentiousness? Or are you merely an envious pawn mesmerized by his power?"

The elderly woman took a sharp breath. Anger stirred in her strange, white eyes. Her bony hands clenched the arms of her rocker tightly and her mouth narrowed.

Lehrling sat stunned. He lowered his empty bowl on his lap. His eyes flicked from Shawndirea to Moorsis before finally glancing at Roble.

Silence filled the room. A greenish tint encircled Shawndirea and Roble realized she was moments from casting a harsh spell of her own. He'd witnessed her full fury a few times. The outcomes had been devastating. But he understood her anger and it was his fault. Had he not worn the rings, he wouldn't have given Lez'minx direct access to view and listen to their conversations. Of course, Roble would never have considered such a breach of trust.

His grandfather had been a trapper in the Overlands. Because of that, Roble always viewed snares in the physical sense. From this point onward, he needed to factor in unseen things, such as magic, ghosts, and deities.

He stared uneasily at Shawndirea. Moorsis had not moved. He doubted she'd taken a breath. Was she mortified by Shawndirea's confrontation or was her silence buying her time? He suddenly became more uncomfortable. Did Moorsis have direct communication with Lez'minx and was awaiting his directives?

Before Moorsis answered or reacted, Shawndirea said, "Is he a god, as he so dearly wishes us to believe?"

"Silence!" Moorsis bolted forward and pushed herself to her feet. She staggered to gain her balance. Spittle frothed at the sides of her mouth. It was difficult to tell if lunacy had taken hold of her or if Lez'minx possessed her. Her tone was no longer that of a generous elderly woman.

Anger flared in Shawndirea's eyes. Green orbs of energy encircled her hands. Her eyes narrowed and she readied herself to hurl the magical bolts at Moorsis. "Don't try to silence *me*! I've bitten my tongue throughout this entire journey, but learning Lez'minx has spied on us for the past several weeks has enraged me like nothing before. Now, answer me! Is he a god?"

"Don't threaten me!" Moorsis tilted her head back and raised her hands above her head.

"You're an enchanter," Shawndirea said. "I'm not. I was born with my magic. You were not. You're nothing more than a vessel Lez'minx tinkers with. My magic's far more powerful than yours, a hundred times greater, so unless you're ready to experience it firsthand and become a bag of powered bones, return to your chair and answer me."

Roble took several steps backwards, unaware he'd even moved. He'd never seen Shawndirea enraged to this degree. She never boasted her power or threatened to kill someone with her magic. The idea shocked him. She always insisted her magic was to heal. Was she bluffing? Her narrowed eyes and furrowed brow indicated she wasn't making an idle threat.

He understood her anger and the betrayal of Lez'minx visually spying and eavesdropping. He suffered the same emotions, the same anger. His mind backtracked the things he might've freely said about Lez'minx before discovering Lez'minx was listening to everything they said.

He and Shawndirea had discussed their future, been intimate frequently, and during the entire time, Lez'minx was an unseen presence in their company.

Moorsis reached inside her robe and formed a fist. She was holding something tightly.

"Sit!" Shawndirea said.

Perplexed, Moorsis plopped in her rocker. Her mouth hung open but she offered no words. With an old piece of cloth, she wiped spittle from the sides of her mouth. Her complexion paled and she appeared ill. In short, she looked defeated. With a weak voice, she said, "You're right. I was foolish to challenge an Unseelie."

"I'm not Unseelie," Shawndirea seethed.

"Have you deceived yourself, faery? You're every bit Unseelie. The darkness surrounds your rage and you're married to an Overlander human. That makes you Unseelie."

Shawndirea lighted on the floor. She looked at the flickering green orbs of energy glowing on her hands. When she realized the degree of her anger and the power surging through her, the orbs shrank and vanished. She gathered her composure, looked at Roble and Moorsis, and said, "Lez'minx is *not* a god, and I can tell you why."

CHAPTER 22

*R*oble watched Shawndirea with genuine concern. She appeared confused minutes after he thought she might assault or kill Moorsis. The deeper into the swamps, the more unhinged Shawndirea seemed to become. He wasn't certain how to help her.

"Do you know why he *isn't* a god?" Shawndirea asked.

Moorsis turned in the direction of Shawndirea's voice. "You know not what you speak, faery."

"I should've recognized it much earlier," Shawndirea said. "He's *not* a god, Moorsis. Otherwise, he'd have no need to use the rings to spy on us. He'd know our actions and location without the need of using magic-eye portals through inanimate objects. He's a deceiver who projects magic to heighten the *illusion* of his power. Deep inside, you know this is true."

Moorsis lowered her head. Tears leaked down the sides of her nose.

Shawndirea softened her voice. "You worship him because of your physical blindness. He made a pact with you, didn't he?"

Moorsis sat in silence for several moments before offering a slight nod. Her shoulders slumped.

"In return for your adoration, he gifts divination to you. But he requires you to beguile and proselyte others, deceptively forcing them to venture to Lez'minx's temple to offer their homage."

"Magic's never free," Moorsis mumbled. Her body drew into itself even more, as if she wished to vanish.

"No, it isn't. But the price comes to those who choose to channel and wield it. What you don't tell those who've sought you out is that if ever they change their minds—"

"No, that's not true," Moorsis said with a narrow brow. She leaned back in her chair, formed a bridge with her slender hands, and rested her chin atop them. Sadness filled her voice. "I sternly warned Bausch about the repercussions. I've warned others, too, but with Bausch, I was more particular."

"Why more for him than the others?" Lehrling set his bowl down and stood.

Moorsis leaned forward and lowered her head. Roble couldn't tell if it were from shame or if she was sorting for the proper words. She clasped her hands together, seemingly around an object, which made him even more wary. He slid a hand on the hilt of a throwing knife.

"I never had children of my own and viewed Bausch like a son," Lehrling said, his eyes full of fury. "Tell me why you tried harder to warn him."

Moorsis sighed and tightened her wrinkled, veiny hands around the object. "He held a gentleness no others exhibited. Most who visit me have selfish requests. Bausch had an honesty about him. He helped with things around my cottage while I tailored his armor. Understand, after I finished the armor and gave it to him, I wanted him to have it without paying homage. He had pureness in his soul, and I—I blemished it."

Lehrling wiped tears from his eyes.

Shawndirea cocked her head to the side. "While I believe most of that to be the truth, Moorsis, you're not telling us everything. Reveal it now and redeem a bit of your soul."

"What else?" Lehrling asked.

Moorsis' hands shook. "Lez'minx wanted Bausch in particular because he was a Dragon Skull Knight loyally serving Queen Taube. Lez'minx cast the fever on Bausch and made him so ill that he craved healing and became more desperate to find me. When he arrived, I looked in his soul and saw his pure innocence. Knowing the intent involved, I didn't want to make the armor for him. I wanted to shoo him away, scare him into running, but doing so would've sealed his death. Lez'minx insisted I tailor the armor. I did, but not because he commanded me. I was overcome with compassion for Bausch due to his constant chills. He was hours from death when he found my shack. Much like you tonight, knight."

Roble frowned. "Why was Bausch being a Dragon Skull Knight so important?"

"Lez'minx works through many vessels in Aetheaon."

"Like you," Shawndirea said.

"Yes, faery," Moorsis replied. She tightened her hands in a prayer-like fashion near her heart. *"Like me.* He controls spies in every major city. Some are princes who sought great wealth and power and vie to obtain their father's or mother's throne, even if it's by overthrowing their own flesh and blood. But he wants Dragon Skull Knights subjected to him because he had hoped to eventually find where the great dragons were hidden. That's his true ambition. To control a dragon to do his bidding. Since Dragon Skull Knights are in allegiance with the dragons, he must make at least one subservient to him."

Roble exchanged worried glances with Lehrling.

"So this guise was intended for that purpose?" Lehrling placed his hand on the hilt of his sword. "For Lez'minx to infiltrate our order to take the reins of a dragon?"

"Yes." Moorsis sadly shook her head. "Kill me if you must, knight. I've betrayed your Order and Hoffnung's throne."

Lehrling drew his sword. His eyes narrowed. He sensed something not right, apparently, so Roble slid a dagger from his belt.

"You don't get pardoned so easily," Shawndirea said. "You must atone for your atrocities."

Moorsis unclasped her hands and revealed the pendant she was holding. Thunder rumbled outside. The winds rattled the rafters, and the room grew colder. The candles flickered, but never extinguished themselves. A rush of air expelled from the fireplace. The old woman smiled. "That seems fair. What do you require of me?"

"Some answers."

"Such as?"

Shawndirea glided into the air, closer to Moorsis, and whispered, "Is Lez'minx able to hear and see us right now?"

"Get away from her, Shawndirea!" Roble said.

Moorsis grinned madly and nodded. "He's been here the entire time, my dear."

Shawndirea glanced nervously around the room. "Where? What has he used to watch us?"

The old woman gripped the object she'd been hiding in her hands and revealed the emerald pendant she wore on a silver chain. "Through this."

Roble frowned. "So he's been listening this entire time?"

"Fools!" Moorsis rose with deep laughter and rabid madness. Energy flowed around her and shot from her fingers.

Her face glowed with boldness and her voice was not her own. Roble recognized the voice from when Lez'minx had demanded Roble find his temple and offered the magical rings to him.

The whites of Moorsis' eyes became blacker than ink. "You think you've more power than I? Meet your deaths this night!"

CHAPTER 23

*B*efore the wave of energy rushed from Moorsis' hand, Roble scrambled and rolled on the floor. Shawndirea swooped and landed inside Moorsis' hood. Lehrling flung over the sewing table, drew his short sword, and dropped behind the table. With wide eyes, he peered around the edge.

The room shook fiercely. The walls and roof rattled as though the shack would collapse. The destructive force was not from the storm, and the unleashed power was not hers. Lez'minx worked through her. Roble wasn't sure why he understood this, except Moorsis fought to resist Lez'minx's control.

Her contorted body was outstretched like an X, and she levitated several inches off the floor. The magnitude of Lez'minx's power flowing through her caused the veins in her face to swell. Her blind eyes were now like black saucers that led to an eternal abyss. She groaned and her bones crackled. Gurgling sounds rumbled in her throat. Roble pitied her. He doubted she had any control over what was happening. If her body was strained any further, Roble feared she'd be torn apart.

"Where are you, faery?" the voice boomed deeply from Moorsis' mouth. "Test your magic against mine if you think me less than a god, faery. I'll turn you to dust."

Moorsis jerked and her fingers spread wide. Though she couldn't physically see and because of his control over her, she was unable to voice her pain. Death was better than this unnecessary torture, but he hated to be the one to give her such mercy. He readied his dagger.

"I've given you my protection, Roble, but your faery hinders what you can become. Follow the swamp path northeast of this cottage. In two days, you'll reach my temple. I offer truce and compassion for when you find me. I'll spare Shawndirea, if you vow to—"

Roble rose to his feet and flicked a dagger for Moorsis' heart, but instead, the blade shattered the glowing emerald held by the prongs of her pendant. The blade deflected and missed its true mark. Shards of the emerald ricocheted off the floor, the ceiling, and the walls.

Moorsis wailed, dropped face first to the floor, and clenched the necklace tightly in her fingers. She yanked it from her neck and tossed it across the room. Gasping for air, her blackened eyes gradually returned to their milky white, as Lez'minx's power vanished. Profuse sweat beaded on her face. Involuntary groans came with each labored breath she took.

Shawndirea flew from the woman's hood and rose with green flames covering her hands, ready to end the old woman's life. Roble waved his hand, caught Shawndirea's attention, and shook his head. With the emerald destroyed, her link to Lez'minx was gone. Moorsis looked even older and more feeble than before, devoid of her spirit and soul. She resembled one of the undead. A breathing corpse.

"You ... freed me," Moorsis said weakly. "I bid you ... my thanks."

Even though Roble was ashamed for attempting a deathblow with his dagger, he readied a second one, not fully certain Lez'minx's hold was gone.

"In return for freeing me, ask ... what you will ... but," she said, "you best ask quickly. My body grows weaker. Without his pendant, my life ends soon."

Shawndirea cautiously circled Moorsis so she could see the woman's face. "Is he immortal or not?"

Moorsis' hands pressed against the floor. She looked up, as if she were trying to see Shawndirea through blind eyes. "Honestly, faery, I don't know. For many years, he led me to believe he was a god. The blessings he bestowed convinced me in part. I was thrilled by the abilities he granted me. He had found me after I had crawled into the Kryptos Cemetery. I was dying, perhaps breathing my last, and I wanted to die where my husband rested."

"Did you see him or were you already blind?" Shawndirea asked.

"The disease I suffered, which was the same as my late husband's, had blinded me by the time I reached his grave." She coughed harshly. Her body spasmed. "So no, I never saw him, but he helped me stand after he expelled the disease from my body."

Blood leaked from her mouth. She lowered her head against the floor and took ragged breaths.

"So you don't know if he's a demigod, or merely a mage or wizard who flatters himself unwittingly to think others should bow before him like meager peasants?" Shawndirea asked. "Tell us, please. We've tried to sort this out for weeks now."

"How could I possibly know? I've told you how he entered my life," she said softly. Her breathing rasped. She balled her hands into loose fists. If she lived much longer, it'd be a miracle.

"Has he visited you in person since?" Roble asked.

"No. Not since he gave me the amulet you destroyed."

"That's how he kept communication with you?" Shawndirea asked.

"Yes. As long as I wore it, he promised I'd never die."

Roble approached her, still holding his dagger. "Does he have any weaknesses?"

"I don't know," Moorsis replied softly. "I'm sorry I cannot be of more help."

"It's okay," Roble said.

Shawndirea nodded. "What little you've told us is helpful."

"My biggest regret for accepting Lez'minx's gift is not dying and being buried beside my husband." With those words, she took her last breath.

Roble knelt beside her, checked for a pulse, and shook his head. "She's dead."

Lehrling sheathed his sword. "Now what?"

"We get some sleep," Roble said, slowly standing.

"After all of this? Surely you jest. How can any of us possibly sleep?" Lehrling said.

Roble gave him a quick smile. The color had returned to Lehrling's face. He no longer shook from the cold. The fire and hot stew had aided him, but his tired eyes and fatigue remained evident.

Lehrling returned the smile, shook his head, and placed more dry wood on the fire.

"I'll place a protective barrier around the cottage. I'll keep watch while the two of you sleep," Shawndirea said.

CHAPTER 24

The following morning, Roble awakened and felt more rested than he had in days. Shawndirea sat on his stomach with her knees hugged against her chest. She watched the door, deep in thought.

Closer to the fire, Lehrling snored louder than a muzzled grizzly bear. Roble wondered how he had slept through the raucous. Despite Lehrling's opposition to sleep after the confrontation with Lez'minx and Moorsis' death, he had fallen asleep first.

"What's troubling you?" Roble whispered to Shawndirea.

Shawndirea stiffened at his question. Without turning, she said, "You're awake?"

"Or this is an odd dream."

She turned with a half grin and shook her head. "Nothing since we entered the swamp has been a dream."

"I know," Roble said. "But something's bothering you. You've kept your thoughts bottled up. Do you mind sharing?"

"Later," she said. "There's much to do today."

"I agree, but if these things distract you, we're going to enter unknown territory where distractions can get us killed. So, please?"

Her lips twisted in an usual way, which he found incredibly beautiful. "The things I need to discuss you wouldn't understand. So discussing it with you won't remove my anxiety."

"Doesn't hurt to ask, correct?" Roble grinned.

"Twice I've been accused of being Unseelie," she replied.

"Which you find hurtful?" Roble clasped his hands behind his head.

She nodded. "It's horrifying."

"Why?"

Shawndirea pursed her lips. "It means I've abandoned my family's traditions. I'm no longer fit to abide in my mother's kingdom. I fear what our children will be or what they'll become."

"I don't understand."

"See?" she said. "That's why I need to consult other Fae who can determine if I'm now Unseelie."

"I understand. But what do you mean about our children in the future?"

"They'll be Unseelie, regardless. They won't be pure Fae. They won't be welcome in Elvendale."

"Your mother's—"

Shawndirea shook her head. "This has nothing to do with her. She has no control over this, even if she chose to lovingly accept our children. In a sense I've been exiled, but my mother has never openly suggested or commanded it. There are two courts. The Seelie and Unseelie. The path I've chosen has altered my future greatly."

Roble didn't like their children being considered outcasts by Shawndirea's immediate family. They'd be descendants of Elvendale's monarchy on their mother's side, but they'd hold no future right for the throne. No one likes to be shunned. How would this affect them as they matured?

He sighed. "Because of me, your life's grown worse? Do you regret … *us*?"

"No!" She whispered harshly and shook her head. "I treasure what we have. I love and need you always. Your determination to ensure I returned to Elvendale from the Overlands proved you'd risk everything to protect me. Had your friend captured me … I'd be dead."

"He wasn't my friend."

"That's beside the point. You revealed your heart, your love, and your devotion to me, which is why I want to spend my life with you. However, I better understand my mother's fury over my decisions. It's not only because of you. It's due to the Courts. While the Seelie Court won't tolerate my decision and possibly exile me, the Unseelie Court will embrace and cherish the thought at welcoming me."

"Why would your exile from Elvendale please the Unseelie?"

Shawndirea sighed. "Because I'm royalty and broke my allegiance to the Seelie. It sickens me to know they relish in my mother's misery. The fact Dirk sought their help is all the more reason why I don't want to associate with them. It's a bitter realization."

"You despise the Unseelie?"

"No, I don't despise them," she replied softly. "But I don't want to be identified as one, because I'll never partake in their type of magic."

"If others consider you Unseelie, that doesn't make you evil."

"It's how I'll be judged. For those who've known me since birth in Elvendale, yes. They'll consider me vile. It pains me, but their shunning will always cause me pain. You witnessed my mother's reaction when I chose you and rejected my claim to the throne."

"Yes. Don't remind me. But doing so has become a disadvantage."

"No, never."

Roble looked in her eyes. Her love and devotion for him melted his heart. But he didn't want her to lose her nobility and Elvendale's respect. Those were priceless. "May I ask you something?"

"Sure."

"Since we began our journey to the temple, you've been a lot angrier and more vindictive. Why? Does it have to do with what you've explained?"

"Some of it."

"There's more?"

She nodded. "Things I don't wish to discuss yet."

"What about Dirk?"

Her eyes narrowed and darkened. "What about him?"

"Is he the reason for your bitterness?"

"No more than usual."

"Do you regret Lez'minx didn't kill him?" Roble asked.

"I considered it. I really did."

"I know."

"Really?"

Roble nodded. "The hatred in your eyes as you stared at Dirk was obvious. You struggled with the decision."

"That's why I didn't hastily reply," she said. "Dirk would be dead. No loss there. But I'd be indebted to Lez'minx. There are better ways to deal with Dirk."

"Such as?"

Shawndirea smiled. "My mother."

Roble chuckled and then winced. Istrell's wrath when she learned of Dirk's planned coup made him shudder.

"It's not a laughing matter," she said.

"For Dirk's deserved demise, it will be."

Shawndirea shook her head. "But not for Feather. She'll be tried as a co-conspirator, which means her death, too. Since I love her like a sister, I can't allow that."

"Your mother would execute her?"

"Yes. Poor Feather. She's not violent at all. Naive? Yes. But she's never violent. If she understood Dirk's motive, she'd tell my mother."

"Why doesn't she tell Istrell about Dirk's plan?" Roble asked.

"Feather probably doesn't believe he'll attempt the coup. She tries to see the good in others, even when it doesn't exist. She's a blind, trusting soul to those who are evil and corrupt. She believes they'll eventually change," Shawndirea replied. "If Feather's not protected, Dirk will kill her."

"What can you do?"

"I need to get her out of Elvendale. Since I'm not officially banished, I can find and tell her before it's too late, provided I'm able."

"I'll go with you."

She shook her head. "No, that would cause even more problems. With mother and all."

"I understand." Roble sighed. "After what we saw yesterday, I regret not moving Moorsis to Kryptos Cemetery."

Shawndirea smiled. "That won't be a problem."

"What do you mean?"

"Look for yourself."

Roble glanced to where Moorsis had died the night before. Her body was gone.

"What—"

She sighed. "The life Lez'minx had restored to her was not one of luxury. She was a tortured woman held under Lez'minx's control. There's no way to tell how long he kept her alive to do his bidding."

"Her body vanished?"

Shawndirea shook her head. "No. It crumbled to dust. She must've been over a couple of centuries old. Once his spell over her was broken, her body suffered rapid decomposition. Her dust is in the jar on the table. The hardest part for us, provided you want to bury her remains near his, is finding the cemetery."

"She was a victim all these years?"

"She was."

Roble nodded. "She acted reluctant in obeying Lez'minx during our battle last night, but she was too weak to fight him. I believe what she said about not wanting to make the armor for Bausch."

"Me, too."

Lehrling's snoring resounded with an extremely loud gurgling. He coughed harshly and awakened himself. He blinked, rolled to his side, and coughed up phlegm. After clearing his throat, he smiled at them. "Good morning. We survived the night."

Shawndirea rose from Roble's chest and hovered while Roble eased into a seated position. He rubbed his eyes and pushed himself to his feet.

"We did," Roble said. "Now, let's see if we can survive the day."

CHAPTER 25

*A*fter they ate their fill of the stew bubbling over the fire, Roble extinguished the flames. He wanted to do more, like scrub out the pot for Moorsis, but since she was finally free of Lez'minx's hold and found eternal rest—he hoped—there wasn't a need to tidy the place.

Several flickering candles cast an ominous array of shadows on the walls. Roble grabbed the bottle with Moorsis' ashes off the table and walked to Shawndirea at a bookshelf.

Shawndirea studied the spines of a dozen magic books. She cocked her head to the side and pursed her lips.

"Anything worth taking?" he asked.

She grinned. "All of them."

Roble's brow rose.

Lehrling frowned.

She smiled. "I know we don't have much room, but these books and scrolls are invaluable and rare. There's only a dozen. If they fall into the wrong hands—"

"We could burn the cottage down," Roble said.

"What?" she asked, perplexed. "We'd attract more attention to ourselves."

Roble shrugged. "We won't be here afterwards."

"It's possible the fire might not destroy them. Some spellbooks are protected by the owner's incantations."

"Whichever books you desire the most, I'm sure we can take those," Roble said. "We have room, don't we, Lehrling?"

Lehrling laughed. "Not much, unless you want to discard what little food our packs hold. We packed a lot of books and scrolls at Polderholm. Do you plan to become a wizard, faery?"

She leveled a frown at him. "Not at all. Anyone who practices magic has the potential to learn new spells, rituals, and potions. Sometimes the knowledge we learn from others' magic allows us to enhance and strengthen our own spells. Any information I glean benefits us all."

"Some of these books are for dark magic," Lehrling noted. "Not for those who practice in the light."

"I know," She sighed. "Maybe a spell can get the rings off Roble's fingers. Perhaps I can find a spell to protect us from Lez'minx."

"Moorsis was that good at writing spells?" Lehrling asked.

Shawndirea shook her head. "These aren't her spells, but spells Lez'minx worked through her."

Lehrling pulled a book from the shelf and thumbed through it. "The writing's horrendously jumbled and overwritten in places."

She flicked a quick gaze at him and shook her head. "She was blind. What do you expect? She didn't write these down to read. She wrote them, most likely, as a means to record the actions Lez'minx ordered her to do."

"Hmm." Lehrling tucked the book under his arm. "So, Lez'minx doesn't have any knowledge of these books?"

"That'd be my guess," she replied. "Lez'minx didn't dictate them. She probably wrote them from memory so others found them after she died. He never healed her blindness, so he wouldn't suspect she kept notes of his incantations through her. She was only a vessel he crafted his magic through."

"So maybe there are ways to reverse his spells in some of these texts?" Roble asked.

Shawndirea nodded. "It's possible. She was under his control, and most likely, she recorded what he forced her to do."

Lehrling grabbed two more books. "We'll make them fit in our packs, but if the journey to his temple is only a day or so away, you won't have time to read these."

She grinned. "I read fast."

CHAPTER 26

They stepped onto the creaky porch of the shack, and Roble shut the door behind them. He wondered about the type of tree lumber used for the porch that could withstand the prolonged rainy conditions? Mold and lichens formed odd patterns along the wood-grain. With the constant moisture, these boards were slick and treacherous. Oddly enough, walking on the creaking boards didn't indicate any rot or weakness. They yielded to the weighted stress like a tree bent to an extremely harsh wind. Bending allowed survival.

Much like with humans, he thought. The change in one's mindset when exposed to harsh conditions—especially things he never thought existed—had allowed him to survive after crossing from the Overlands into Aetheaon. Keeping an open mind and willing to decipher new information, enabled him to formulate understanding. Everything one saw on the surface wasn't necessarily factual or true. Often the underlying aspects came from things not visible, like magic.

Few scientists could ever accept the things that weren't provable by straightforward physical methods. What separated Roble from his colleagues was his undying curiosity. His innate ability to question everything, rather than take a blind opposition to things that defied logic, allowed him to adapt and survive.

According to Lehrling and Shawndirea, most Overland humans lost their minds and died soon after crossing a rift. Their minds couldn't accept Aetheaon's reality, a place where nightmares were real. Their minds refused to adjust. Because their minds couldn't cope ... death was the only alternate. A mind without hope caused one's body to wane and die.

Roble thought about Deiko, his colleague who threatened to kill Roble with a gun and steal Shawndirea in the Overlands. Deiko wanted to reveal the discovery of a faery to the scientific world. Now that Deiko knew Fae existed, would he hunt until he found a rift to enter Aetheaon? Could Deiko survive such knowledge or would it be more than his disturbed mind could handle?

"Are you ready?" Lehrling asked.

The question jolted Roble. He hadn't realized how deeply his thoughts had taken him. "Yes. Sorry."

The storms from the day before had subsided. The rain was replaced with a light, hanging mist. The cool breeze brought a stagnant, acrid smell from the gathered pools of swamp water. No longer did Death's threat await them at the side of the shack like the night before.

Crickets and frogs sang a constant melody that, in spite of the creepy swamp, was quite pleasant. If one only had the chorus to go by, no one would fear the hidden dangers within the shadows. But Roble had seen the deceptive, true nature of the swamps.

Fog hovered like a yellowish-white veil, which obscured the surrounding trees, vines, and shrubs even more. It was possible they were being watched, but impossible to detect *what* watched them.

"We aren't alone." Shawndirea glided from the porch and flew to the tied horses.

"I sensed that as well," Roble said.

Lehrling glanced nervously at the fog-shadowed trees and rested his hand on his short sword's hilt.

"How long did we sleep?" Roble asked, untethering his horse.

"A long time," Lehrling said with a refreshed grin. His eyes were brighter than they'd been in days. "It must've been. I've not felt this rested in months."

Roble scanned the trees. "But is it day or night? I can't tell."

Lehrling swung onto his saddle. "From what I've been told, that's always a mystery in these swamps. My guess is it's midmorning. Not quite noon or the humidity would make breathing more difficult."

"One aspect neither of you are taking into consideration is *where* we are," Shawndirea said. "The swamps are becoming darker because we're at the border of Unseelie territory."

"So that's bad?" Roble asked.

"Being as I'm from Elvendale? Yes, it's very bad, especially since I don't have an invitation."

"You need an invitation?" Lehrling asked.

"It's not *required*, but to remain on their good side, it's advisable," she said.

"How do you know when you've crossed into Unseelie territory?" Roble pulled himself atop his saddle.

"Woodnog resides on the last pure territory of the Seelie Courts as one travels south. The elves in Woodnog are of the light and worship the day. Where we are now, at least from what I'm sensing, is the in-between. The tension between light and dark continues. Magic from both sides languishes slightly, but that doesn't mean the magic from either side isn't any less deadly."

"What do you mean?" Roble tapped Bleys' flank, and the horse carried him from the side of the cottage onto the narrow muddy path that cut through the trees. When Roble looked over his shoulder to view the cottage one last time, it had vanished.

"Basically," Shawndirea said. "The enclave is where the two Courts draw the line. A truce, so to speak. It's mutual ground where the leaders from both sides convene for whenever certain trespasses have occurred or to settle skirmishes between the two Courts. This prevents one party from entering the other's territory to seek retribution without fear of assassination."

Roble said, "Isn't that still risky? One ruler could set up the other by sending an assassin instead of meeting."

"Both sides generally send diplomatic envoys and attempt to settle the problem. You'd be surprised how well it actually works most of the time," she said. "The enclave is also a place for recruitment."

Lehrling frowned. "Recruitment?"

Shawndirea nodded. "Yes. The Shadowfae soldiers with Dirk were possibly from an assassin guild in the Unseelie territories we've not yet reached."

"Lez'minx had no trouble killing them," Roble said. "Shouldn't he worry about their deaths?"

"Not necessarily," she replied. "His temple's probably in the dimmer areas of the swamps where neither light nor darkness rule, perhaps a recess within the enclave. He's in the astral realm dividing Order and Chaos so he could draw his magical energy from either side or both, ever how he chooses."

"That doesn't give him the right to kill dark Fae," Lehrling said.

"No, it doesn't," Shawndirea said. "However, the Shadowfae crossed into the Seelie's domain. Lez'minx could justify his actions since they were trespassing. The Unseelie Court could deny all knowledge of the assassins to assume innocence."

"Why would Lez'minx's temple be in this enclave?" Roble asked.

"It's highly doubtful he'd have requested your presence if he lived within the Unseelie territory, as all of us would be killed immediately," she said.

Lehrling scratched his beard. His eyes revealed his curiosity. "What's to say that won't happen in the enclave?"

She grimaced. "Blood must never be shed in the in-between. Otherwise, the consequences usher pestilence on the family of the one who spilled blood. Such a curse is far worse than death because the entire family is permanently exiled from their city and the Court. It should never be taken lightly."

"Has this actually happened?" Lehrling asked.

Shawndirea nodded. "Yes. Once. Trust me, no one in Elvendale would ever wish what transpired on their worst enemy."

"So we're safe *inside* the enclave?" Roble asked.

"So to speak," she said. "But once you leave, regardless of which side you enter, there's always the chance of being attacked by Fae who are capable of traveling through shadow dimensions. Often those killed by them never saw their killers. These Fae travel through shadow doors swifter than an eye blinks. They're masters of stealth and highly skilled assassins. Some are probably watching us right now."

Nervousness returned to Lehrling's eyes, and he searched the trees.

"You said the enclave's where the Unseelie can be recruited?" Roble said.

"Or Seelie. However, if someone has traveled to the enclave, it's most likely to hire Unseelie. While I don't actually know, Dirk hired those Shadowfae to fight under his command."

"Why there?" Lehrling asked.

"Two reasons," she replied. "One, Dirk didn't have to enter Unseelie territory and risk his life. And two, those assembled with Dirk to attack us were arrogant *young* Fae with high hopes of rising in the Courts. They're skilled fighters. Instead of thinking rationally, they're more eager to shed blood with their weapons. Older Fae tend to weigh out the situations instead. When you enter the enclave, you might not see a single potential recruit, but hidden in the veil of shadow might be more than a dozen awaiting the first sign of earning gold for a bounty."

CHAPTER 27

*R*oble wasn't certain if they were following the right path. Without the sun for a guide, and no hint of its glow, determining which direction they traveled was almost impossible. Lehrling's primitive compass wasn't reliable in the swamp, either. After several minutes of discussion, they finally agreed to take the only partially visible path.

The drab, yellow fog clung across the forest and prevented the true vivid colors from being exhibited. Weighted, dripping strands of moss and curled vines bent the trees.

The eeriest aspect of these swamps—other than the strange creatures, poisonous plants, and magical elements—was not knowing where they were or what they might encounter next. Lehrling had mentioned that no maps existed for the Woodnog Swamps, and now he understood why. Something unusual messed with the magnetic compass. No one could discern which direction they were headed. Marking landmarks in a terrain that vastly looked similar at every bend offered no true benefit.

So far, Roble couldn't shake the sensation of being lost inside a swampy maze. It was no wonder why people entered these swamps, only to never leave. The deeper they traveled into the swamp, the more he feared they might end up being amongst the victims as well.

"How the Hell did Bausch find his way through these swamps?"

Roble asked. "For him to travel to Moorsis' shack and return to Woodnog so quickly—"

Lehrling shook his head. "I honestly don't know. He was a better tracker than I."

"You think we'll find our way back?" Roble asked.

"We might not find the place we're searching for."

"That's not comforting." Roble laughed.

Lehrling nodded. "It wasn't intended to be. Don't say I didn't warn you about these swamps."

"If all goes wrong, I only have myself to blame."

As Lehrling and Roble rode slowly along the trail, the animals and insects hushed. Only the soft sound of hooves pressing into the muck broke the silence. Pools of water hid beneath leafy colonies of duckweed. The denseness of the water-covering plants was deceptively dangerous, especially within the shadowed swamp. Some water pools appeared solid while others offered unique places for poisonous creatures to hide.

Shawndirea sat on Roble's saddle pack where Moorsis' books were tucked inside. Without heavy rain, it was unlikely the hard book covers would suffer much damage. In her hands she held a small oval-shaped glass over a book's spines and sat with her eyes closed.

Lehrling glanced at her. "Are you napping?"

Without opening her eyes, a frown creased her brow. "No, I'm *trying* to read."

Lehrling cocked a brow, shook his head, and then shrugged at Roble with a slight grin. "With your eyes *closed*?"

Roble peered over his shoulder and watched her for several moments. "Shouldn't the book be *open* in order to read it? That looks like a magnifying glass to me."

She huffed and opened her eyes. "It's a sacred scryer stone, given to me by the Elven priestess, Daena Bellas. It enables me to scan *through* books and remember relevant information concerning spells and magic without having to read each page."

"Where can I get one of those?" Roble asked. "Talk about a timesaver. Having something like that during my studies would have been priceless."

She rolled her eyes and sighed. "They're rare, for obvious reasons."

"What reasons in particular?" Lehrling asked.

"To limit a wizard's or mage's knowledge. Imagine if someone like Lez'minx had possession of this stone. With the proper teleport spells, he could enter any wizard's private library and obtain all his or her knowledge in a matter of hours. Expanded knowledge of such magnitude would increase his power at an exponential rate. Any wizard would become unmatched and he could kill wizards and mages one by one."

"Knowing we're searching for his temple," Roble said, "*why* would you bring the stone?"

She grinned. "I tuck this into a magical pocket in Shadow whenever I'm not using it. He cannot reach it. No one except me can retrieve it."

"How'd Daena obtain such a stone?" Roble asked.

"She made it."

"I see. Why'd she give it to you?"

"Its abilities tempted her until she no longer trusted herself."

Lehrling took out his pipe and filled it with dried herbs from a pouch. "Shouldn't she have destroyed it?"

"Are you suggesting I can't be trusted?" Shawndirea crossed her arms and gave him a shrewd stare.

"No, not at all. But if it got into the wrong hands, like you mentioned … Destroying it would eliminate that from happening." Lehrling took his pipe and extended it to her. "If you'd be so kind to light this since we don't a fire?"

She waved her hand, brought a green flame to her fingertips, and tossed the small flame atop the pipe. Lehrling quickly puffed the pipe to prime the smoldering herbs before the small flame died. He smiled.

"It's good she has control over the height of the flame. Otherwise, your beard would be gone." Roble chuckled.

Lehrling's eyes widened, and then he grinned. "I trust she's used magic long enough to be accurate. I'll keep better watch on ensuring I don't anger her before asking her to light my pipe."

"Good idea. Another safety reason for *why* I don't smoke," Roble said.

Lehrling laughed softly.

"May I get back to reading?" Shawndirea said.

"Of course," Roble said. "Since we're not certain of our destination, you should have plenty of time. For all I know, we might be riding in circles."

Lehrling laughed. "If that were true, we'd be back at the cottage."

"The cottage vanished," Roble said.

"It did?"

"You didn't notice?"

"I never looked back once we decided which direction to take. Perhaps I should've," Lehrling said. "Such a shame Bausch never told me visiting Moorsis to have the armor tailored. I've no idea how he discovered her abilities. We traveled together all the time."

Roble said, "At some point, the two of you must've separated for several days. There's no way he came this far into the swamps and back in a day or two."

Lehrling puffed his pipe and his eyes went distant in thought for several minutes. "Now that I think about it, we journeyed to Woodnog for a spell. He mentioned something about talking to the smith to have his weapons sharpened and his armor patched. He must've learned about Moorsis from the smith."

"He never mentioned leaving Woodnog?"

"No," Lehrling said softly. "I was … attending to other … more personal matters."

"How long was Bausch gone?"

Lehrling chewed on the pipe stem, shook his head, and grinned. "To tell the truth, my memory escapes me."

"Told you. You're getting old."

"My lapse of memory has *nothing* to do with my age." He gave a side-glance at Shawndirea and whispered, "Woodnog has … places where some of the most beautiful Elven maidens serve the pleasantest wines—strong wines, mind you—and … uh … entertainment, so to speak."

"I see."

"I might be missing a week of my life. At least, my mind draws a blank from when I entered the erm, *tavern* and when Bausch found me. Probably took several days for me to sober up, but he had paid my tab upfront."

"Just because I'm reading," Shawndirea said, "don't think I can't *hear* you or that I'm unaware of these *taverns* you speak of in Woodnog."

Roble chuckled and Lehrling blushed dark red.

"And Roble," Shawndirea said, "if ever Lehrling invites you to one of these *taverns*, politely and hastily decline his offer. Agreed?"

"Noted," Roble said.

"No, do you agree?" she said with an icy tone.

"Of course. Yes."

"Not to offend, faery," Lehrling said, "but Roble has no *need* of such a place."

"Nonetheless," she said before going silent.

Roble glanced at Lehrling who held a sheepish grin. "You still miss Bausch. That much is evident."

"Every single day." Lehrling took a sharp breath and held it. When he finally exhaled, curls of smoke exited his nose.

"At our first meeting, I'm confused as to why you mistook me for Bausch and swore I was his ghost," Roble said.

"It was he I saw," Lehrling said. His misty eyes stared into Roble's. "I swear, even now, it was him and not you. I don't understand why my eyes played such tricks on me. Perhaps it was from the shock of witnessing his death and I was helpless to stop it. Remorse, maybe?"

"Recall what Moorsis told Roble," Shawndirea said. "The armor Roble wears has imprinted with Roble. At the time Roble rescued you from the Vykings, the armor still identified Bausch as its true wearer. And no doubt, Bausch's rage at the Vykings for killing him and his fear they were going to kill you, lingered. His spirit sought immediate revenge. Remember, Roble was not in control of his actions, nor did he respond to my shouts for him to take cover. Bausch somehow controlled Roble through the armor."

Chills ran down Roble's spine. "I vaguely remember my actions, and that disturbs me. I'm good at throwing knives. It was something I started practicing when I was a teenager. But my targets were wooden. In some ways, I'm guessing, the armor sensed my abilities and connected with my skills. Only once in the Overlands had I ever considered throwing a knife at someone. That was because the man pulled a weapon on me and threatened to take Shawndirea. Other than that, I'd have never entertained the thought of using a knife to kill an enemy."

"And yet, you did to save me," Lehrling said.

"In part. Again, my actions weren't entirely my own. I understand, now, they couldn't have been. I didn't know the Vykings were a separate race from ordinary humans, and one of them was a demon."

"Part demon," Lehrling said. "They saw Bausch approaching the campfire. Not you. They, too, swore you were his ghost."

"True. But even though they were what they were, it takes a firm commitment to throw a knife at a living person. Much more to throw with the accuracy to kill without hesitation, which, had I fully had control of my faculties, I'd not have done. I'd have weighed the consequences thoroughly because in my world, what I did was murder, even in self-defense. But I never considered it, and I didn't hesitate."

Shawndirea said, "Bausch's hatred toward them was powerful enough to replace your visage with his, Roble. He wanted them to suffer intense fear before he killed them. Bausch sought vengeance and through you, he achieved it."

"How do you know this?" Roble asked.

"Because I wear a piece of the armor and sense its awareness," she replied. "Something else Roble should try is to retrieve Bausch's sword skills. If you concentrated properly, you could link his knowledge, which would benefit you more in your use of fighting with a sword."

"Part of Bausch lives on," Roble said softly.

Lehrling's expressions showed his discomfort about their talk of Bausch, so he changed the subject. "So faery, have you learned much in your reading?"

She sighed. "Not as much as I had hoped. That tome explained how Lez'minx had extended her life and made her his slave, which she detested from the beginning."

"Really?" Lehrling asked. "I'd think anyone would want a longer life."

"She loved her husband dearly. For months she grieved over her loss. She wrote that if she could undo what had occurred between her and Lez'minx, she'd have chosen death instead. She hated the absence of her husband and her mind never recovered. The longer she lived, the more she resented Lez'minx."

"If that's true," Roble said, "why didn't she rebel against his hold earlier."

"In a way, she was. Writing down these accounts as evidence for others was her greatest rebellion."

"Have you found anything about these rings?" Roble asked.

"Unfortunately, no. I have two more books to read. She was a tailor, not a jeweler, so it's quite possible she didn't enchant the rings. You took the rings from a mage, so he might've enchanted them forLez'minx. We might never know who did."

Ahead on the shadowed path, a worn, bent, wooden sign post stood where the trail forked. One pointed toward Kryptos Cemetery; the other toward Purity Lake.

"Purity Lake?" Roble asked with laughter in his voice. "I can't imagine naming anything *purity* in these putrid swamps. Since we've found where the cemetery is, let's bury Moorsis with her husband."

CHAPTER 28

*R*oble studied his armor while Bleys walked along the pathway to the cemetery. A bit of uneasiness passed through him when he considered the armor might be a living entity. He liked its enchantment to protect him from nature's elements, but its abilities to aid his combat disturbed him.

This meant the armor could influence his thoughts and actions. He wasn't certain how much access to his mind the armor possessed?

The trail to the cemetery altered from the wet swampy muck to black, compacted soil. Gradually, the flora changed from thick clumps of floating sphagnum into a bright green carpet of moss with yellow and blue flowers, which was a welcoming sight.

No puddles of water stood in the lower recesses. The tree groves diminished. Pitcher plants and fern fronds increased. Soon, they found themselves in a place where no trees shadowed the path. But the sun didn't bless them with its presence over this glade, either. The thick, gray clouds remained dismal and dim like an iron veil.

Ivy with flowers larger than a man's hand curled and held fast to the wooden remnants of old cottages and structures forgotten in time.

"This was a town?" Roble asked.

Lehrling nodded. "At one time, I suppose."

"Perhaps this was where Moorsis had lived?"

Lehrling rode ahead of Roble toward a sign covered with ivy. He pulled the vines back and revealed the town's name: Tangled Grove. The name had an X carved through it. A smaller sign was attached beneath it with its new name: Glades of Sorrow.

Shawndirea took her scryer stone, chanted whispered words in another language, and extended her hand forward. Her hand and the stone vanished momentarily, as though she had reached into an invisible pocket. This must've been what she had meant by placing them into Shadow.

Afterwards, she stretched, took to flight, and glided to the sign. She peered across the buildings buried beneath lush green ivy and vines. "Moorsis probably lived here."

Roble sighed and swung off the saddle. "The sign at the fork indicated we were headed to Kryptos Cemetery. There's no mention of either of these town names."

She lighted on the sign. "The cemetery's probably here. The town's been deserted for quite some time. The heavy growth of the plants and the fallen structures indicates no one's tended the area for years."

"So Moorsis could've been under Lez'minx's control for years then?" Lehrling said.

She nodded. "Far longer than this town's been absent of townsfolk."

Roble took his horse's reins to let the horse graze. "Can anyone live in these swamps? The island was barren, and so is this town. Neither place suffered constant rains, so each place could sustain a population. It's odd no one lives here since this town isn't in the swamps."

"I agree," Lehrling said. "I'd have never expected to find townships like this in Woodnog Swamps. From the looks of it, this place once thrived."

"Perhaps," Shawndirea said.

"What happened to the folks who lived here?" Lehrling asked. "Moorsis didn't mention in her journal about what happened?"

Tall bamboo-like poles lined several rows of a former garden. Something furry squealed and scurried through the leafy plants. Birds darted from their hiding places and flitted to other shrubs to hide.

Shawndirea shrugged. "She indicated they were afflicted with a disease."

"No survivors?" Roble asked.

"She never said. The town isn't fortified with walls. They lived modestly off the land. Probably a peaceful settlement."

"If they were affable, this wasn't the safest place to live," Roble said. The opposite border of this town was lined with rows of dark trees. "This glade is surrounded by the swamp."

She nodded. "Perhaps after the disease, they fled?"

"Where would they go?" Lehrling asked.

"Who knows?" Shawndirea said. "Those Lizard-men might have attacked them."

"Why?" Roble asked.

"Slaves? Food?" she said.

"Then where is the cemetery?" Roble asked.

"We can search for it," Shawndirea said. "Or, bury her remains here."

Roble shook his head. "She deserves better. Before Lez'minx found her, she expended her last energy getting to her husband's grave."

"We don't owe her anything," Shawndirea said.

"This isn't about debt. She should rest beside her husband," Roble said.

She smiled but offered no reply.

Lehrling cleared his throat. "Here's evidence the people here most likely were invaded and didn't all die from disease."

"What?" Roble asked.

Lehrling used his boot to brush aside a blanket of ivy and uncovered a dead body. Not human. Dried leathery skin clung to the skeleton, which also had a long curled tail. Loose leather armor clung to its remains. A spear remained grasped in his skeletal hand. "This proves the Lizard-men exist. At the very least, they attempted an open attack."

"We need to find the cemetery and leave," Roble said.

CHAPTER 29

*U*sing their swords, Roble and Lehrling sliced their way through the tall grasses and thick vines. No one had entered this small hamlet for the better part of a year. At least, not from the direction they had come.

The architecture of the cottages wasn't notable. They were all identical. No larger structures towered nearby, so they didn't seem to have had a governing body preside over them.

After fifteen minutes of flying and examining the buildings, Shawndirea returned. "The cemetery's on the other side of those two cottages."

Roble and Lehrling hacked their way between the cottages to find a circular patch of land with crude rocks for gravestones. Chiseled names on the headstones identified the person's grave.

"Did Moorsis mention her husband's name?" Roble asked.

"No," she replied.

"What are ya lookin' for?" The voice came from behind a wall of tall grass. "Haven't the dead suffered enough in life? Be gone, ya grave robbers, or I'll be burying the lot of ya in the ground beside them."

They all turned and searched for the one who'd spoken.

"Go on, now!" The tip of an arrow was visible through the wall of thick grass. Slowly, the tip emerged farther and revealed the small crossbow. "I don't want to kill you, but—"

Roble stepped toward the hidden archer. "We've come to bury someone who should've been buried here long ago."

"Who might that be?" The tiny voice crackled.

"Moorsis," Roble replied.

"Moorsis?" The crossbow lowered slightly. "You—you have her body? That's not possible. She died years ago."

"We have her remains."

"How'd you obtain them?"

"It's a long story, but it's the only reason we've entered this glade," Roble said. "She wanted to be buried beside her husband."

Timidly, the gruff halfling—approximately three feet in height—lowered the crossbow and stepped from the curtain of grasses and vines. His clothes and long green cape were woven from leaves and grass, as was his hat, which camouflaged him within the tall grass. He had no beard, but instead, thick blonde sideburns like muffs on his cheeks. His brown eyes were large for his short stature.

"Come," he said. "I'll show you her husband's grave. My name's Dolan."

They followed the halfling and introduced themselves as he hobbled through the circular graveyard. Unlike the grounds surrounding the abandoned buildings, the plots were tended and neat with flowered wreaths adorning the crude stones.

"Her husband's buried here," Dolan said, pointing.

Roble held the jar containing Moorsis' remains. He didn't know whether to bury the jar or to spread her dust over her husband's grave. Burying the jar kept her beside her husband's corpse and prevented the wind from blowing her dust away.

Dolan stepped closer. With a frown, he said, "How long have you carried those?"

"Since this morning."

"How do you know that's her?"

Shawndirea explained how they had encountered Moorsis and the spell Lez'minx placed on her. Then she asked if Dolan knew where they could find Lez'minx's temple.

Dolan shook his head. "No. I've never heard of him. He found Moorsis dying at her husband's grave?"

Roble nodded. "Yes."

"Hmm. Perhaps he spoke to her through the ethereal and took her without anyone seeing?" Dolan said.

"She said a disease spread through your hamlet," Shawndirea said. "And she contracted it."

Dolan frowned. "That was over fifty years ago, which is why I'm surprised she was still alive. The disease was short-lived. Only a handful of the town died because of it."

"We found a Lizard-man's remains near a sign. Did they kill the others?" Roble asked.

"Oh, you mean the Saurians?" Dolan shook his head. "No. They raided and tried to take the town hostage, but they were met with strong resistance."

Lehrling ran a hand through his beard. "You fought them?"

"Oh, no. Another race arrived and defeated a dozen or more Saurians within an hour."

Lehrling frowned. "What race came to your defense?"

Dolan's brow rose and he shrugged. "They looked like frog people. They were fast, agile, and quite skilled at taking the Saurian's weapons. Then they used the weapons against the Saurians. A human warrior was with them."

"Human?" Lehrling said.

"Yes." Dolan studied Lehrling and Roble for several moments. "What are those pendants fastened to your armor?"

"These are worn by Dragon Skull Knights. Was he wearing one?" Lehrling asked.

"Perhaps. I cannot really say."

"Why not?"

Dolan laughed. "I hadn't been born yet. I learned these legends during my childhood. My elders often mentioned a Dragon Skull Knight."

"Geowren?" Lehrling said in a near whisper.

Dolan scratched his chin. "Yes, I believe that's the name."

"Are you the last of the townsfolk?" Roble asked.

"No. Others were with me earlier. They fled when you began chopping through the tall grass," Dolan said. "They're skittish. Me, I wanted to know who was trespassing."

"Trespassing?" Lehrling said. "No one seems to live here."

"You're right. No one lives here," Dolan said with a wink. "Me and my brothers and sisters tend the graves once a week. We also scout the streets to see if any squatters have attempted to resettle our land. It's the least we can do in memory of those before us."

"Moorsis wasn't a halfling," Shawndirea said.

"No, she wasn't."

Shawndirea said, "Who were the original settlers of the Glades of Sorrow?"

Dolan smiled. "Human mostly. My family was a group of refugees slogging our way through the swamps to the south. We happened on this settlement during its prime, and rather than send us on our way, they invited us to join them."

"Where's the former settlement now?" Roble asked.

"They moved to the east through a narrow swamp at Dagger's Tears."

"Dagger's Tears?" Lehrling glanced at Roble with an odd expression.

"You've heard of it?" Roble asked.

"No," Lehrling replied. "It's such an odd name."

"We named the town after the lake, which is shaped like a long slender, curved dagger. At one time, the lake was a large sharp bend in the major river running through the swamps. Now, it has no current or connection to the river," Dolan said.

"An oxbow lake," Roble said.

Lehrling cocked a brow. "I assume a term from the Overlands?"

"Yes."

Dolan said, "It's a lake. A small one. We built our new town on the inner bank. The main river still flows. Other than a sliver of land between the lake and the river, we're almost an island, which gives us better protection."

Dolan smiled and reached for Moorsis' remains. "If you'll allow me, I'll bury her remains beside her husband. Afterwards, if you'd like, I'll escort you to Dagger's Tears."

Roble gave the bottle to Dolan. Dolan removed a small hand scoop from his belt. He dug a hole deep and wide enough to tuck the jar into the earth. He covered the jar and gently tapped down the soil and smoothed it with his hand, making it almost impossible to notice where the jar was buried.

"Come," Dolan said with a slight grin. "It's been awhile since we've had visitors. It proves to be a most glorious day."

CHAPTER 30

*R*oble and Lehrling retrieved their horses, saddled up, and followed Dolan along a narrow path where the tall grasses and vines were bent and the stems were slightly crushed. This was the path Dolan and his brethren used to travel to and from the Glades of Sorrow.

Although Dolan hobbled, he kept his shoulders squared and his head held with a sense of haughtiness. Dolan possessed high self-confidence and didn't fear confronting people over twice his size, as he had with his crossbow.

"Have the Saurians attacked your village since you moved to Dagger's Tears?" Roble asked.

Dolan shook his head. "No. They fear the deeper water in the river and lake."

"Can't they swim?" Roble said.

"They can, but not too well while wearing armor. Although, lately, a group of them have made their presence known."

"What do you mean?" Lehrling asked.

"Each night, they stand across the small lake. A silent threat. They can't cross the water and perhaps, they're trying to find a way to cross."

"What about those frog-like creatures?" Roble asked. "Do they live in the lake or the river surrounding your village?"

Dolan continued walking without glancing over his shoulder. "I've never seen them. I suppose it's possible, but as I mentioned, they're legends. It's doubtful anyone in Dagger's Tears has seen them since."

"Doesn't mean they're not keeping watch over your town," Roble said.

"Speculation on my part won't help you," Dolan said. "I'll introduce you to folks who might better answer your questions."

"What about the Dragon Skull Knight?" Lehrling asked. "Do you think anyone knows his whereabouts?"

Dolan shrugged. "I honestly don't know."

Lehrling sighed. Disappointment sagged his facial features. His fingers tightened around the reins.

Roble offered Lehrling a comforting smile, but the additional toll from this journey also weighed on Lehrling. Losses were difficult to shake off, especially when a stubborn mind refused to quit analyzing a loved one's absence. Some people grieved themselves to death.

Their conversations with Moorsis had been nothing less than a painful reminder of Bausch's unfortunate fate. Any healing of Lehrling's scars for getting past Bausch's murder had been ripped afresh. Now, Lehrling sought clues for whether Geowren was alive or dead. Roble didn't blame him.

Although Roble didn't know many members of the Dragon Skull Knights, except the recent ones dubbed into the Order by Lady Dawn, he understood what it meant for a member of the Order to end up dead or missing. They were brethren and sisters loyal to King Erik and the dragons of Aetheaon.

If the death of a loved one was known, it was a bit easier dealing with the loss, but when no evidence could be found to drive away the specu-lation of life or death, the mind and heart kept hope alive. Lehrling's sentiments to gather his brethren was great and honorable. Because of Lehrling's convictions, Roble felt obligated to offer his assistance.

Shawndirea returned to Roble's pocket and kept silent. She wasn't brooding over any issues and was fatigued. Since she hadn't stirred, he assumed she was asleep.

Dolan walked ahead of them with his crossbow balanced between his hands. After they left the Glades of Sorrow, Dolan was less apprehensive and said little. At least he was honest in expressing his lack of knowledge concerning their questions, unlike the dwarves. Dwarves spun tales, and if confronted about information they lacked, some lofted fictional tales as possible reasons.

THE GRASSY PATCHES DIMINISHED. Their path returned to the bland mire with thick sedge clumps and foul pools of dark water.

The stagnant air hung thick and the overcast sky seldom showed any sign the clouds moved. The swollen, gray clouds offered no rain, for which Roble was thankful. Yet, the threat remained. According to Shawndirea, the wet season was approaching, so any absence of rain would be short.

A strange cry echoed from the wall of reeds and cattails ahead. Dolan stopped and raised a hand. With the sudden change of flora, Roble expected the river to be close. Dolan whistled in reply.

Three male halflings with spears in hand emerged from their hiding places in the reeds. Two female halflings with their armed bows appeared behind them. Like Dolan, their clothing was tailored from weaved plant material.

"All is well." Dolan raised a hand. "I'm taking them to Lady Versis."

"Why?" a halfling with greenish-brown hair asked. His sideburns and eyes were jet black.

"They have questions, Rufus."

"Questions? Are you certain they mean us no harm?" Rufus asked.

"They're Dragon Skull Knights, like the one who aided us many moons ago," Dolan said.

Rufus' frown faded. "They are?"

Lehrling nodded. "Yes."

Dolan frowned. "Had the lot of ya not fled, ya'd know this."

"Fled?" Another male halfling puffed his cheeks and huffed, obviously feigning anger.

"Yes, Hob, you *fled*," Dolan said. "Scrambled through the weeds like wee frightened kittens, the whole lot of ya."

Shawndirea stood inside Roble's pocket, stretched, and flew upward and lighted on his shoulder.

"Look, Merla," a female halflings said. Her sky blue eyes radiated immediate astonishment. "Tis a faery!"

"Don't believe my eyes, Cora!" Merla beamed a smile. "But it is. Never thought to see a faery here. Oh, except all those *dark* faeries. Those, I don't like. They frighten me."

"Frightening sights, they are!" Cora said, coming closer. "What be your name, faery?"

"Shawndirea."

Cora and Merla smiled.

"Lovely name," Cora said. "As is your beauty."

Shawndirea blushed, in spite of maintaining a guarded appearance.

"Oh, yes," Merla said. "Your wings are more beautiful than any butterfly."

Dolan ignored Cora's and Merla's fascination and quickly made introductions. "Now, if we can continue? I'd like to get our guests to Dagger's Tears before the night settles. I'm surprised you aren't already awaiting my return."

Rufus gave Hob an embarrassed smile and a quick shrug. "We were actually returning to the Glades of Sorrow to make certain you were still alive."

"Really?" Dolan said. "I'd have been long dead or eaten had Roble and Lehrling been Saurians. Not a scrap of me left to take back to Dagger's Tears. What excuse would you have given then?"

"Our apologies," Hob said. "Truly."

"Pfft!" Dolan marched past them. "What we lack in height, we usually make up for in spirit! It's what's allowed our survival after we were exiled from Willow Bend. And look at ya now. No wonder our protests went unheard by Willow Bend's council."

Rufus sighed. "We'll do better next time, Dolan."

"The next time?" Dolan said. "Next time for what? Getting *exiled* from Dagger's Tears?"

"No," Hob said. "The next time we're approached by strangers."

"For me, there might not've been a next time … the way you deserted me." Dolan glanced over his shoulder and waved for Roble and Lehrling to follow. "Come on. Dagger's Tears isn't much farther."

CHAPTER 31

*P*erhaps the distance to Dagger's Tears wasn't a great distance from the Glades of Sorrow, but reaching the settlement wasn't without perilous difficulty. Their cautious maneuvering slowed their progress significantly.

Grasses and slick mosses splotched the exposed path. Rotten planks —used to solidify the pathway had sunken ages ago— created jutting sharp stakes and caused more even problems. The visible ones meant other pointed tips might be covered by mud. The adhesive muck beneath the planks fastened around the horses' hooves like a thick glue. The horses' strained steps made sucking sounds.

The horses backed their ears and their eyes widened. Were they able, they might've reared and bolted. Their evident fear indicated how dangerous the path was. A sharp stake fragment might stab the soft frog of their hooves or the animal could break a leg. Such crippling injuries meant the animal would have to be put down, and Roble didn't want that.

Roble swung off Bleys, and sank in mud up to his calves. He held fast to the reins. Without his added weight, the horse could walk better. After using a broken plank for leverage, he worked his way into shallower mud. Lehrling climbed off his horse carefully and followed suit.

Roble and Lehrling didn't need to encourage the horses to keep moving. The horses understood the mire would suck them down if they stopped. Should that happen, Roble and Lehrling couldn't free them. Absent the extra burden of Roble's and Lehrling's weight, the horses moved somewhat easier. The closer they traveled toward the river, the more solid the ground became.

Dolan and his party of halflings practically glided across the plants and mire without leaving a single footprint. Due to the halflings' light weight, tracking them through the swamps was impossible. It made sense for them to travel from Dagger's Tears to the Glades of Sorrow to tend the graves and inspect their former town. They could do so without a trace. Between their lack of footprints and their camouflaged clothing, the halflings made perfect spies.

With this in mind, Roble wondered whether the halflings' motives were truthful or not. Dolan had asserted several times about them being exiled from Willow Bend. *Why* exactly had they been exiled? Usually, exile was a form of punishment, either for crimes or rumors of possible upheaval.

Roble hoped Dolan was telling the truth for how he and his group had become residents in the Glades of Sorrow. But then, the town's original name had been carved out and replaced with a new name. He didn't want to think the worst of them, but his skeptical mind questioned their possible hidden motives.

Dolan had been devoid in answering any question directly. He often lacked complete knowledge, if not fully evading with his vague responses. Of course, Dolan might not know since he insisted he and his party weren't a part of the township during the time of the referenced events.

A gentle breeze brought with it the stench of the river and dead rotting fish. Roble stood on the high river bank. The wide, swollen, brown river didn't flow swiftly. Occasional wind gusts caused dancing ripples on the surface.

They were approximately twenty yards from the river's edge. Dolan led with Rufus and Hob walking to each side of Roble and Lehrling. The wind ruffled their capes. Cora and Merla closed off the rear. The halflings weren't an aggressive race, but they were protective. They seemed more suited for farming or using their crafting skills but overall, they weren't especially suited for war.

As their group neared the water, the mucky ground was harder. Stacked layers of flat stones provided a stable platform for loading and unloading wares from boats or small rafts.

Roble wondered how they managed to move goods to or from the weathered stone dock. Perhaps this was used before the former town became desolate? Whatever the reason, the horses were relieved to be on firmer ground.

No bridge crossed this massive river. Without sunlight, the river appeared darker. Regardless, the deep river was probably filled with fish and reptiles capable of swallowing a halfling in a moment's notice.

Across the river were large cottages and buildings built on high stilts. Fires burned in braziers at the turns of the stairs and on the upper balconies. Strangely, the flames drew one's eyes to them much like a moth traveled toward a lantern. The dismal swamp held little radiance, so it was natural the fires would be seen from afar. And yet, according to Dolan, the Saurians had never attacked their settlement between the river and the crossbow lake.

Dolan raised his hand and faced Roble and Lehrling.

"How do we cross?" Roble said, "We're not leaving our horses on this side of the river."

"Not at all," Dolan said.

"Then we swim?" Lehrling asked.

Rufus and Hob laughed.

"Only a fool would attempt such a feat," Dolan said.

Insulted by their laughter, Lehrling frowned with a heavy angry gaze. "Then how?"

Dolan placed two fingers to his lips and whistled a shrill cry. Afterwards, he reached into his vest pockets and took out two Elven glowstones. He faced the swollen river and tapped the stones together. A beacon of yellow light shot across the water's surface and struck a curved piece of glass on the other side. The light bent and careened at an odd angle and struck another mirrored glass nearby.

From the tall reeds and cattails, several halflings appeared on the opposite bank. They reached into the water's edge, heaved two heavy ropes, and pulled. Two more halflings stepped between these ropes with huge pieces of meat on the end of thick sticks.

The water swashed and rippled with loud splashes. Slowly the top of a large shell emerged. The giant turtle dug its thick claws into the river bend and stretched its huge head toward the clumps of meat. A hungry groan echoed. The size of the turtle captivated Roble. It could easily eat him or Lehrling. The massive jaws could snap and slice through an arm or leg of a Vyking without any effort. The turtle could do the same to a Saurian as well.

The two halflings held the meat out of the turtle's reach and backed up. The turtle pulled itself farther out of the water. The dozen halflings tugging the ropes wrapped them around a harness attached to the rear of the giant turtle's shell. The tension of the ropes increased as the turtle kept following the meat.

"By the goddesses," Lehrling whispered.

The higher on the bank the turtle walked, the tighter the ropes' tension became. Within several minutes, the ropes rose from the river, and a heavy object broke the surface. Water dripped from the ropes and then a ferry platform appeared at the edge of the bank where Dolan stood with the Elven glow-stones.

Rufus and Hob ran onto the platform, wiped away mud from two metal bars that were flush with the raft's wooden boards, and pushed the bars upright and locked them in place. Once the bars were secured, Rufus took one coiled muddy rope and pulled it through a metal eye at the top of a bar while Hob did the same on the opposite side. They threaded the rope through the steel eye and fastened the attached latches to steel anchors barely visible on the stone dock.

Dolan smiled with great satisfaction. "Almost ready."

Roble frowned in disbelief. He glanced at Lehrling and chuckled. "I'd never have believed it if I hadn't seen it firsthand. Is this the reason Saurians haven't attacked Dagger's Tears?"

Dolan lowered the Elven glow-stones and separated them. Their strong light dimmed and slowly extinguished before he placed them in his pockets. "There are worse things than these monstrous turtles under the river's water."

"Worse?" Lehrling coughed and shook his head.

Rufus nodded. "Yes. That's what protects our river town from potential invaders. Several dozen of these muck turtles lurk in the mud along
this river's bend, but Tinker's the largest and the most loyal."

Tinker?

Perplexed, Lehrling gave Roble a shrewd stare. "What could be
worse?"

"Sometimes," Roble said. "It's not best to know."

"It's better to know what I'm supposed to fear so I'm prepared should
I ever encounter it," Lehrling replied. "Especially, if I happened to fall
into this dingy river."

Roble chuckled softly.

"Hurry," Dolan said. "Get your horses on the platform. Just because
Saurians won't swim across the river doesn't mean they won't ambush
us on this bank."

Lehrling and Roble led their horses onto the raft. The raft was
fastened with large steel eye-rings to a lower set of ropes beneath the
water to prevent the raft from being slowly towed away by the river's
current.

After everyone and the horses were on the raft, Cora approached
Roble. "Where's the faery?"

"Asleep," he said.

"We'd like to talk to her," Merla said with broad smile.

Roble peeked inside his pocket. Shawndirea was curled with her
knees hugged to her chest. She shivered and sweat beaded her pale face.

"Are you okay?" he whispered.

She didn't reply with words. Her desperate, pleading eyes glanced
weakly at him. She shook her head.

CHAPTER 32

Shock coursed through Roble. With Shawndirea wearing the armor, she wasn't shaking from the cold. Something else was affecting her.

Since they were in a swamp with mosquitoes and other insect vectors, had she been bitten and contracted a disease? Due to her size, it seemed unlikely an insect had bitten her. In comparison, a mosquito was enormous and an insect she'd defend herself against.

In Moorsis' cottage, before they lost contact with Lez'minx, the *god* had threatened her life for sabotaging his connection through the rings. Had Lez'minx cursed her? And if so, how could the curse be removed?

Dolan pointed and gave instructions for where each person needed to stand while the raft was pulled across the river.

"With the extra weight of your horses," Dolan said to Roble. "I need you and Lehrling to help."

Roble nodded.

Apparently Merla read the worry in Roble's eyes. "Is all okay?"

"Is there a medic in Dagger's Tears?"

"Yes," Cora said. "Why?"

"Shawndirea has gotten quite ill."

Merla gaped and placed her hands to her cheeks. "I hope it's nothing serious."

Roble held back tears and tried to swallow the lump in his throat. "I hope not, either."

Lehrling stepped around the horses to get next to Roble. "What's wrong?"

Roble shrugged. "I've no idea. She has a fever."

"A fever?" Lehrling asked.

"Perhaps. The quicker we get the raft across the river, the sooner we find out," Roble said.

Lehrling nodded and cracked his knuckles. "I'm not as strong as I used to be, but I'll give it my all."

"That's the most any of us can do," Roble replied. He stood beside Dolan and grabbed the rope. "Don't you ever worry that Saurians might figure out how to find and use your raft?"

"No. It's not possible," Dolan said. "The raft only surfaces when the turtle has pulled the underwater ropes to full tension. Otherwise, the raft's useless."

Roble grabbed the rope and pulled with all his strength. Lehrling pulled the other rope. They strained for several minutes, but the raft never budged.

"That's it!" Dolan said. "Put your backs into it!"

Lehrling dug the heels of his boots against the raft boards and tugged harder. He leaned back until he nearly sat on the raft, and pulled with his bodyweight. "It's ... not ... moving."

Dolan stepped in front of him and pulled the rope. "We have to break it free of the muddy river bank. After that, it won't take as much straining to move it across the river."

Gentle raindrops plinked on the river.

Roble's brow furrowed. His biceps burned. He tugged with such force that his heartbeat thudded in his ears. He reached forward on the rope and yanked. He fell backwards but held steady. Heat reddened his face from his exertion. He held his breath and strained every muscle in his arms, legs, and back. He kept pulling until he neared unconsciousness. Finally, the raft broke free of the mud and floated forward.

He dropped to the raft and expelled all the air in his lungs and gasped heavily for an even deeper breath. Pain equivalent to a million needles being stabbed into every muscle in his arms, back, and legs caused him to hug himself momentarily.

He opened his eyes to near blackness, as the invitation to collapse from fatigue overwhelmed him. Lehrling looked worse for wear. He gulped air and kept his eyes tightly closed.

Roble used the rope to pull himself up. His fingers clung to the rope, and he used it to balance and steady his numb legs. He wanted help Lehrling to his feet, but Roble couldn't balance well enough to offer support. If he didn't collapse on the raft, he feared he might plummet into the dark river water. As weak as he was, he'd never get back on the boat. He disliked the idea of being chum for whatever river monsters waited below.

After a few minutes, he regained partial balance and against his aching muscles' disdain, he pulled the rope again. Rufus, Hob, and Dolan worked together to match the strength of his tow.

After Roble released the rope, the raft moved swifter across the river.

Dolan released the rope, leaned over, and rested his hands on his knees. He gulped air. "Okay, they'll pick up the slack for now."

"Who?" Roble asked.

"On the other side of the river," he said, pointing. "They're pulling the central rope that's attached to the raft's underside. The worst part was breaking the raft free of the mud. That's why no one could possibly steal the raft."

Roble panted and wiped sweat from his brow.

"Go on," Dolan said. "Take a seat and rest. You've earned it."

Normally, Roble would protest such an invitation and prove his strength by toiling with the others, but not today. He sat on the raft and leaned against a metal bar. He opened his pocket and glanced at Shawndirea. Her body trembled.

Carefully, he placed his index finger in beside her. She stood and wrapped her arms around his finger. He lifted her and let her lie in his cupped hand. Her pale face was haunting. When her wings had been shredded, she'd never shown any fear. She'd never been so close to death.

Lehrling moved to a crawling position. "How's she doing?"

"Not good," Roble said, softly.

Merla and Cora seated themselves near Roble. Cora opened a small weaved basket. "We've no medicine or herbs, but we have honey, if she's up to eating some."

Weakly, Shawndirea said, "Please."

Merla tore a piece of bread off a loaf while Cora pulled the dipper from the bottle. A golden yellow strand of honey oozed off the dipper and coated the bread.

"If I may?" Merla extended the bread to Shawndirea.

Shawndirea offered a weak smile and stuck her entire hand into the honey. She closed her eyes and licked the honey off her fingers.

"Portia is our healer," Cora said. "She'll know what to do."

"I hope so," Roble said.

"She will," Merla said.

Cora offered a compassionate smile. "You love her, don't you?"

"She's my wife," he replied.

Cora and Merla exchanged perplexed glances.

"You're married to a faery?" Cora said.

Roble nodded.

"Then she's Unseelie?" Merla asked.

Shawndirea frowned but was too weak to protest.

"No," Roble said. "She's of the Seelie Courts."

"She can't be," Cora said.

"It's true," Roble said.

"Cora means she shouldn't be here."

Concern furrowed Lehrling's brow. "Why not?"

"She's entered the depths of the Unseelie territory," Cora said. "You must return her to the in-between unless she's been granted permission to explore this region."

"That would cause her sickness?" Roble asked.

"It could, especially if she has known enemies in the Unseelie Courts," Merla said.

"Does she?" Cora asked.

Roble shrugged. "I don't know."

"No," Shawndirea said in a faint voice. "But, my mother does."

Cora and Merla exchanged puzzled glances before turning their attention to Roble.

"Who's her mother?" Merla asked.

"Queen Istrell."

Merla and Cora scooted away from Roble.

"You know her?" Roble asked.

"We know *of* her." Cora swallowed hard.

Roble grinned. "I'm not fond of her myself."

Merla took a deep breath but her expressions reflected no recognition of any humor in his statement. With a firm gaze, she said, "It's best you *not* mention her mother's name again. Not while you're in the Unseelie territory. Unless you find comfort in immediate death."

"Her reputation is *that* bad?"

Cora's brow narrowed. Anger tainted her soft voice. "I've never been one to agree that all humans are fools, but as lightheartedly as you're acting, you're warming me up to the notion. You've no idea the hatred this faery's mother has stirred within this region."

"Believe me, yes, I do. I wasn't trying to belittle the danger. Istre—"

Cora pointed a stern finger. "*Don't* breathe her name."

"Sorry. She tried to kill me, so I know the levels she'd go to cause disruptions. Her cousin isn't much better."

"Her cousin?" Merla asked.

"Dirk."

Merla and Cora took sharp breaths.

"We know of him, too," Cora said. "He's part of the reason we were exiled from Willow Bend."

"Steady yourselves!" Dolan grabbed the rope firmly. "We're about to hit bank!"

CHAPTER 33

*R*oble braced against the metal pole seconds before the front of the raft struck the river bank. The collision wasn't as bad as he expected.

A dozen halflings descended down the side of the embankment, grabbed the ropes that secured the raft, and pulled it against the bank to prevent it from rocking while the horses were led off.

Dolan was met by others and before he could speak, he was greeted by numerous questions about why he'd brought humans across the river. He profusely explained his reasons.

Cora and Merla helped Roble stand.

"Come with us," Merla said. "We'll take you to Portia. She can formulate a proper treatment for Shawndirea. At best, maybe all you'll need to do is get her to the in-between where her symptoms will subside. At worst, someone has cursed her."

"Merla!" Cora frowned and shook her head.

"Well, it's possible," Merla said in a hushed tone.

Cora said, "Concentrating on the negative doesn't help anyone. Focus on bettering the situation. Maybe we've some herbal teas or tonic—"

"Not to be impolite," Roble said, "but could we skip the unknown prognosis and see what Portia *might* know?"

Cora nodded. "Sorry."

Roble stepped off the raft with Shawndirea cupped in his hand. She looked at him with distant eyes. He didn't know if she could even see him.

"I'll get our horses," Lehrling said. "I'll catch up to you soon."

"Thanks." Roble lifted Shawndirea close to his face. "Don't leave me. Let's hope Portia is able to heal you."

Roble's boots sank in the mud. He struggled to reposition his feet without falling. Once he reached the top of the bank, the path became more solid.

CHAPTER 34

The world surrounding Shawndirea crashed around her like a black sea sucking her into an abyss. Though the cold dark waves didn't actually exist, her hampered breathing was equivalent to inhaling viscous liquid.

Roble's voice echoed through the depths that spanned through continuous caverns of darkness. Light fled from her vision. The inky gray gel enclosed around her and turned to blackness where neither sound nor vision prevailed.

She was helpless, lost, and fleeting from the Realm of Aetheaon and the man she loved. In desperation, she attempted to thwart the sinking sensation pulling her further away, but she found nothing capable of slowing her descent. Her strength fleeted and nausea turned her stomach.

She accompanied Roble into the swamps because she wanted to protect him, but now she was the one who needed rescued. But where she was, he doubted he'd ever find her. Irony was cruel and unforgiving.

The deeper into the Woodnog Swamps they traveled, the harsher she suffered. Unrecognized forces slowly sapped and drained her magic. Now, her life's energy was fading.

Strange as it was, she couldn't pinpoint the source. Her first reaction to these attacks had resorted in her lashing anger. Unfortunately, Roble suffered from her building fury.

She hadn't been bewitched. She never felt the power of a spell cast on her. She should've detected the exact moment when they left the in-between and entered Unseelie territory. Nothing warned her. Not the slightest tinge or even a tingle pricked her mind.

After she'd denounced her right to the throne of Elvendale, the Unseelie should have welcomed her with open arms since as she inadvertently recanted her place in the Seelie Court. A choice she never considered when rejecting her mother's request to take the throne.

For one court to gain royalty members from the opposing court was rare and would be considered a victory.

Could Dirk have somehow gained favor in Siofra's—the Unseelie Queen—eyes. If he had, as he was quite deceptively persuasive at times, the Queen might've sent the assassins with Dirk to kill Shawndirea's mother. After Lez'minx's intervention, when he had killed the faery assassins in one sweeping instant, Siofra might believe Shawndirea had direct ties with this supposed god.

While Dirk possessed unique charms, she doubted Siofra would be beguiled by him. But if by chance she believed Dirk, Shawndirea wasn't welcomed in either court.

Solitary Fae existed, but few ever chose that path. Alliances were necessary to survive against others that wielded magic. Enemies abounded on both sides of the in-between. Collecting bounties on rebellious faeries held rewards prized greater than monetary value. Some assassins enjoyed the thrill of the hunt and the challenge involved, especially when the prey held the magical ability to fight back. Then the challenge was determined by whose magic was stronger. If Shawndirea chose to become solitary, she'd become a target from both sides, as would Roble.

Her advantage of being solitary was being able to draw magic from either court, which didn't necessarily mean she'd become more power-ful. The benefits, though, weren't worth the risk of being hunted. Solitary faeries never lived in peace, except in the neutral in-between, but that was a narrow terrain. She'd be better off to return to the Overlands with Roble.

Those in Elvendale might continue to protect her rather than pursue. She was highly favored above her mother, and she understood why. Queen Istrell ruled harshly. Her bitter attitude soured her most loyal into near revolts at times. The Fae in Elvendale were more disappointed in Shawndirea's denouncement than was her mother. She imagined Elvendale's celebration had Shawndirea accepted the crown.

Shawndirea's greatest enemies were some of her direct family, particularly Dirk. Although he wanted the throne for his own selfish purposes, she understood he'd never be the direct heir. He couldn't survive the trials necessary to assume the throne. Only female Fae survived the series of trials with the exception of one: Oberon.

Oberon was the revered Emperor of the Fae across multiple shadow realms. At least, Istrell held her allegiance to Oberon and insisted Shawndirea do so as well. Shawndirea didn't know if Oberon had ever graced Aetheaon. But surely, he'd been the one to preside over the trials her mother endured to be crowned Elvendale's Queen a century earlier.

If he had issued the trials, none ever spoke of his visit. She suspected Oberon had never announced his presence. He might've chosen a different form altogether. What better way to discover the darker secrets others held in confidence or to learn the names of those who slandered your name?

To her knowledge, no Kings ever presided over the Fae in Aetheaon. That wasn't to say all realms conformed to this ideology. The rulers of Fae in Aetheaon were strictly matriarchs, and probably always would be.

She suddenly realized why Dirk had chosen Feather to be his queen. She could withstand the requirements necessary to survive the trials, and with her as the new Queen, he was betrothed to become the residing King. He could indirectly rule the throne through her. As subservient as she was, she'd never deny whatever he requested with the exception of not killing Istrell. Dirk could devise no scheme worthy of convincing Feather to kill Elvendale's Queen since Feather viewed Istrell as a motherly figure.

Of course, as King, Dirk could mandate edicts and pressure others to comply by insisting *the Queen orders so*. While Dirk could be cunningly persuasive, he was unable to hide the violent repercussions he'd inflict should someone ever stand against him. Few would ever dare question his demands, and those who did would serve as examples for others in the future.

Without Feather or another female to wed Dirk, he remained a strong prince in the Seelie Courts. He could preside over his own kingdom should he choose, but a prince was the highest level of hierarchy Dirk could ever possess absent his marriage to a Queen.

"Why have you forsaken your own?" a male voice within this blackened void asked. His soft voice carried authority and cascaded like riveting thunder quaking through this abyssal pool.

She saw nothing. Blackness and cold blanketed her.

"I haven't," she replied.

"But you have. Marrying a human altered your path for greatness."

"I've no desire … for greatness. I'm content being the Butterfly Queen."

"That's a *minor* title."

"Nothing's minor when I use my blessing to restore the longevity of nature's most beautiful and yet, fragile creatures."

"Don't be a fool, child. The Seelie has great need for you, your wisdom, and your undying compassion. Don't tarnish your calling. You can't balance between both sides. Death's coming for you, even as you hear my words. You've been forewarned. Your future's not with the human. Accept your fate to rule and abandon the silliness of your selfish desires."

"Who are you?" Shawndirea asked.

No reply came. Just emptiness, coldness, and the sensation of plummeting deeper into this bottomless, dimensional pool. She could no longer hear Roble's voice. No blessing of light gave her vision.

Darkness. Constant, thick darkness.

Drifting, falling, light as a feather carried by the softest child's breath.

She felt like she was at the veil dividing deep sleep and eternal rest. If she failed to find her way back soon, she was certain Death's icy, boney fingers reached for her. Death wanted to call her away from her life, and claim her soul and spirit … Forever.

CHAPTER 35

*R*oble followed Merla and Cora up a long wooden ramp to the top floor of the central building. The crudely constructed buildings stood atop tall stilts for the wetter season when the area flooded. Such buildings withstood heavier rains and flooding. The thatched roofs were made from dried sedges, mud, and thick moss.

Shawndirea's breathing remained shallow. Her radiance had faded and her complexion had grayed. She'd not opened her eyes since she lost consciousness.

His focus on her blinded him to his surroundings. He stood outside Portia's door without realizing he'd made the climb. From several stories above the ground, he had a perfect view of the dagger-shaped oxbow lake. All around the lake, fishermen stood on the docks and watched bobbers float on the dingy water. Other fishermen worked feverishly on small flatboats. They brought up their traps in the light of large glowing lanterns.

Merla knocked on Portia's door. A light breeze rattled the wind chimes made from long, hollow bamboo stalks.

"Enter," a soft voice said from the other side of the door.

Merla eased the door open. Light flickered beyond the threshold. "I hope this isn't a bad time?"

"Is there ever a proper time for interruptions?" Portia asked in a light, amused tone.

Merla smiled. "I suppose not."

"What do you need?"

"Dolan met a party in the Glades of Sorrow—"

"Enemies?"

"No." Cora stepped through the doorway. "Allies."

"Allies? You came to this conclusion in so little time? Why bring them into the only safety we have in the swamp?"

"Not without reason," Merla said.

"What reason is there?" Portia asked.

"Roble has a faerie who's deathly ill." She hesitated for a moment. "Not a dark faery."

"I see. Why does he possess a faery to begin with?"

Roble frowned. "I don't possess her."

Cora said, "He doesn't own her. They're married."

"Married?" Portia said. "To one another?"

Portia appeared at the door. With a stern gaze, she met his eyes and searched them. Her eyes disturbed him. They were oddly shaped, with such a bizarre sheen, he forced himself not to look away. He couldn't afford for his actions to be considered rude. She was the host, a healer, and he desperately needed her help.

The halflings had insisted the inhabitants from the Glades of Sorrows were human, but it was obvious she was *not*. Her eyes were similar to those of a fish. The sheen was a second eyelid to further protect them from injury, or perhaps, he reasoned, to allow her to survive outside of water.

After several moments of peering into his eyes, her rigid attitude lessened and she relaxed. She smiled and looked at Shawndirea in his hands.

"Please," Portia said. "Bring her inside. Cora, set a kettle over the fire. Merla, light some dried jasmine and sage. Smudge the rooms. We can't allow any negativity to enter my home."

"Yes, Portia."

Roble followed Portia to a table at the center of the room. Her long brown hair flowed down her back.

She grabbed a thick pillow of moss and set it on the table. "Lie her here."

Roble gently set Shawndirea on the soft moss. Except for the slightest rise and fall of her chest, he'd have thought her dead.

"How long has she been like this?" Portia asked.

"A few hours."

"Good you got her here."

"Do you know how to help her?" Roble asked.

With a worried expression, Portia shook her head. "No. There are things I could try. With your permission, of course."

Roble hesitated.

She rested her webbed hands on the table. He half expected her arms to be covered with scales. But her skin was covered with a thin layer of dark green moss. As best he could tell, this was her hair and not moss adhered to her flesh.

Portia smiled. "To ease your worry, I'm a healer who prides herself in protecting and healing those who enter my home with whatever ails them. For a faery, I'd go even further to ensure her a longer life. I'd never do anything to harm her."

Roble sighed. "I appreciate that."

"Her wings are magnificent," she said. "I've never seen such a beautiful faery in these parts. From her beauty, she must be from the Seelie Courts?"

"Yes." Roble nodded. "She's the Butterfly Queen."

"This is Shawndirea?"

Roble nodded. "You know her?"

Portia laughed softly. "All Fae know of her. Her beauty far surpasses the description told in tales. She's far from the safety of her kingdom. How'd you convince her to marry you?"

"I didn't. She found and chose me."

Her narrow lips formed a sly grin. "I see. Has she shown any other symptoms?"

"None to my knowledge. She's been fatigued. We've had a stressful journey."

"Destination?" she asked in a stately tone.

"We aren't certain."

"Hmm. Rambling aimlessly through a horrid series of swamps and marshes that spares few. Hardly a task for a human and a faery. Only fools wander into this region of Aetheaon. Certainly you have a reason."

"We're looking for a temple," Roble said.

Her eyes flicked to his with uneasiness. "A temple? To which god or goddess?"

"Lez'minx."

She pursed her lips and her odd eyelids blinked. "I know of no such god. We know of many gods, but none by that name. Why do you seek him?"

"It's a long story."

Portia nodded. "In Shawndirea's condition, she's not going anywhere soon. We've got time."

CHAPTER 36

*L*ehrling led the horses to drink at the edge of the oxbow lake. The calm, muddy water reeked of decaying fish, which made him gag.

Along the lake's docks, children carried small baskets filled with dark crayfish and red fish on their heads. Two men tied a small flatboat to a dock post. One remained on the boat deck and passed heavy traps to the other, one at a time.

None of these workers were halflings. All were human.

Geowren, how long since you were here? Are you still alive?

These questions pained him. Perhaps he was becoming too senti-mental as he aged. He longed for the days of his youth when adven-turing didn't take a horrible toll on his mind and body. He wished he could turn back time, not for himself, but far enough to somehow rescue and prevent Bausch's death.

Lehrling had never recovered from the loss. He doubted he ever would. Roble's friendship helped ease the pain, but it wasn't the same. He and Roble were more equals, and Lehrling viewed Bausch like a son.

He wiped hot tears from his eyes with the back of his hand. Receiving word that Geowren had visited the Glades of Sorrow, his hope rekindled that he might discover the Dragon Skull Knight's whereabouts.

After Taniesse and her sisters reemerged, he expected Geowren to return and help reclaim Hoffnung from Waxxon. When he didn't, Lehrling assumed Geowren was dead.

Geowren was loyal to a fault when it came to his duties in the Order. He remained stubborn in his mission to find King Erik alive.

Seated with Lehrling at the Bent Oak Tavern in Woodcrest, before he disappeared, Geowren often said, "I feel it in my bones. He's alive."

"As much as I want to believe," Lehrling said, "there's no evidence."

Geowren wiped beer foam from his black beard. His coal-dark eyes peered into Lehrling's but not in anger. Geowren's eyes beamed with eternal hope. "He lives, Lehrling, as surely as you and I."

"No one's sought ransom."

"This has nothing to do with gold."

"Then what?"

"Power. Revenge."

"By whom?"

Geowren stood and placed several gold coins on the table. "That's what I aim to figure out."

"Hoffnung's crown has no enemies."

"*Any* kingdom has enemies," Geowren said. "The worst enemies are those who never reveal their open hatred for you. So will you travel with me?"

"Where are you headed?"

"To the Woodnog Swamps."

"There? Why? King Erik vanished far north of Hoffnung at the opposite end of the continent."

Geowren grinned. "I know. That's why the swamps would be the last place someone would search."

"That makes no sense."

"It makes perfect sense."

"Then explain it to me."

Geowren sighed. "Ride with me and I will."

"Not without Bausch."

"Where's he?"

Lehrling took a gulp of mead and set the tankard on the table. "Pigsty Tavern. He fancies a barmaid there. I've told him he's wasting his time, but—"

"Let him have his fun." Geowren chuckled. "He's too old for you to be hover over him like a protective father. Don't spoil his fun. Remember how it was during our youth? Nah, we never wanted chaperones. Ride south with me."

Lehrling hesitated and thought about the perils of being a young man infatuated with a beautiful maiden. Hell, being an adult fearful of courting a lady held perils of its own and why he never settled down. "If you can wait—"

"Waiting puts us farther away from finding him."

"What reasoning can you offer that we're not wasting our time?"

"The Black Chasm. The City of Mortel. That's *two* reasons. If you need a third? Tyrann."

"Tyrann? You think he's responsible? He's never ventured outside the chasm. It's his stronghold."

"He plays an integral part in King Erik's abduction."

"How would that benefit Tyrann?"

"I travel to discover the reasons. The Black Chasm neighbors the swamps. Barrier Pass prevents the chasm from expanding east, but if ever the Fae and Elven magic fails along that barrier, the Black Chasm will consume Woodnog. If Woodnog falls, Tyrann's power increases to a level I don't want to imagine."

"You can't enter the Black Chasm," Lehrling said. "None have survived."

"You're not listening, friend. I've no intention of going into the chasm." He placed his hand on Lehrling's shoulder and squeezed. "You stick around for Bausch, if that's your decision. Eventually, you'll let him mature into his manhood. Maybe. Once I find the evidence I expect to uncover, I'll send word to Queen Taube. She'll gather the Order together. King Erik isn't dead. It's more than a gut feeling. Ever since he knighted me, I've felt a bond to him and the great dragons."

"No one's seen a dragon in ages," Lehrling said.

Geowren's black eyes narrowed. "Maybe not, but they're not dead, either."

"Then where are they?"

Geowren shrugged. "I've no idea. Perhaps, they're trying to locate Erik. Their bond's with him, and we're bonded to Erik through our Order and the rituals we swore to partake. Can you not feel King Erik's spirit?"

Lehrling swallowed hard. He wanted to believe Erik was alive. All of Aetheaon wanted to believe, but Lehrling didn't feel the *bond* Geowren talked about. "I wish I did."

"Find a place of solitude, fast, and meditate," Geowren said. "Then you'll feel the bond. Visions will come to you more clearly than I stand before you. King Erik lives but he's hidden and hidden well."

"If you could wait until morning—"

"No time. Do as I say. Fast and meditate. Seek the truth."

"But—"

Geowren chuckled and ran a hand through his black beard. "Bausch is a man, Lehrling. Send word by raven where we're heading. He'll find us. Let him practice his tracking skills."

Lehrling sighed.

Geowren's boots thudded across the dusty hardwood floor, he opened the door, and gave Lehrling a hearty laugh before closing the door behind him.

That was the last time he saw Geowren.

Lehrling watched several lads toting baskets of fish from another dock.

"I should've gone with you, Geowren," Lehrling whispered. Tears heated his eyes.

In retrospect, had he gone with Geowren, Bausch might still be alive. Bausch might've been successful in romancing Sarey. So many things *could've* been different. Lehrling would know Geowren's whereabouts and whatever evidence Geowren had discovered. But, in doing so, he'd altered so many other predestined events that were necessary. Had Bausch remained behind, Roble and Shawndirea would've died in the harsh cold without the protection of Bausch's enchanted armor.

Of course, Lehrling might've died for traveling into the swamps with Geowren.

Lehrling berated himself. He was where he was supposed to be with Roble and Shawndirea. He hated that Bausch was dead and gone, but for whatever reasons the Three Goddesses held, it had been meant to be. Roble and Shawndirea could have emerged anywhere, but they exited at the right place and time that benefited them and Lehrling. He continued to openly express these thoughts to Roble, perhaps to reaffirm for his own benefit instead of Roble's; and yet, Lehrling ignored the obvious. He'd ignored the truth.

No more.

He could no longer live in the past. Mentally, he needed to push forward and never look back.

A smile spread across his face. He glanced at the muddy surface of the lake and for several moments, the image of Bausch's face material-ized as he remembered his apprentice.

"Son," Lehrling said, choking back tears. "I must release my hurt. Your spirit and my fond memories shall linger with me until my death. One day, though I cannot guarantee, I hope we meet again in another realm or on a different plane to reminisce. Until then, my destiny awaits."

CHAPTER 37

*T*wo boys carrying heavy baskets of mussels stopped to admire the two horses at the lake's edge. Their curious eyes indicated they had rarely seen a horse and the boys were a bit fearful.

Lehrling smiled. "Where can I stable these two horses?"

Sheepishly, the boys looked away, turned, and picked up their pace without answering. With the heavy baskets, the boys' steps turned into a slow run.

Lehrling cocked his head to the side and ran his hand through his beard. Perhaps they'd heard him talking to himself and thought he was deranged? He chuckled. Sometimes he questioned it himself.

"Tether them anywhere." A woman at a table on the dock offered a gentle smile. A long string of gutted fish stretched across a table. "Or let them roam. They're surrounded by water, so they can't wander off. No one will bother them. Folks in Dagger's Tears are afraid of horses."

Lehrling regarded her with a kind smile.

The woman was in her late thirties, but her rugged appearance made her appear older. She was dressed in modest clothes with a thick leather apron tied around her waist. Fish scales and blood stains coated the apron. Her hair had loosely fallen from its bun and dry fish scales clung to strands of her hair. A few scales were stuck to her soiled face. After meeting his gaze, she tried to wipe them away. She tucked her skinning knife behind the apron string, left the dock, and headed to him at the water's edge.

Her dimpled cheeks deepened with her smile. He marveled at her sapphire blue eyes. Captivated by their beauty, he held his silence too long.

"Is … is everything okay?" She cupped her hands together while cautiously approaching him. "You … seem out of sorts. Were you *talking* to yourself?"

Lehrling blushed and nodded. "I'm fine. Just sorting through things."

"Out loud?"

"Yes."

"You are?" She leaned forward in keen interest.

He frowned with confusion.

"Your name?" she said. "What's your name?"

"Forgive me for my rudeness. My apologies, dear lady." His face beamed redder. He bowed slightly and extended his hand. "Sir Lehrling of Hoffnung. A Dragon Skull Knight. What's your name, if I may ask?"

She extended her calloused hand, even though it was grimy with blood stains and fish scales. He ignored her chipped stained nails, the fishy mess, and gently kissed the back of her dirty hand.

She was taken by surprise with his kiss. "Collette."

"A lovely name. A pleasure to make your acquaintance."

Blushing, she shook her head. "You're too kind. You and your friend are already the gossip of our hamlet."

"We've only just arrived."

She shrugged. "No matter. Word travels fast. We seldom get visitors but worry often of invasions. Even if we possessed fighting weapons, our numbers aren't enough to defend against any invasion. It's good to have kind knights arrive. It's been a while. A bit over twelve full moons, I'd say."

"Another knight like us visited here?" Lehrling asked.

"Not for some time. Do you know him?"

"He's a dear friend of mine. Well, *if* it was actually him. Can you describe him?"

Collette walked to the edge of the lake, squatted and dipped her hands in the water, and scrubbed them together. After she finished, she stood and wiped hands on the underside of her apron. "His hair and beard were blacker than the night. At first, the mystery surrounding him frightened us. His smile indicated he knew more than what he'd ever reveal. His laughter was delightful, if not sometimes haunting. But, like you, his demeanor was polite. Is that the man you knew?"

Lehrling nodded. His heart raced with excitement. "That's Geowren."

She smiled. "Yes, that's the name he gave."

"How long did he stay?"

"Three days, if memory serves me."

"Did he say to where he was traveling?"

"Southeast to Spellhaven," Collette replied.

"Spellhaven?" Lehrling rubbed his bearded chin. His mind searched. Thinking aloud, he whispered, "Morgana's Cove is a port near there. What would he be seeking there?"

Puzzled, she said, "He never said."

"Sorry." Lehrling waved his hands and shook his head. "Just thinking out loud again."

She frowned. "You talk to yourself a *lot*."

"I'm afraid so." He tried to suppress his embarrassed smile. "Are you sure the horses will be okay out in the open near the lake?"

Collette nodded. "Yes. No one will bother them."

"Because those turtles near the ferry—"

"Oh, they're too heavy to leave the water."

"Good to know." Lehrling grinned. "I'm certain they had their eyes on these horses. I heard their stomachs rumble."

Her brief burst of laughter was soothing to his ears.

"You said the folks here are afraid of these horses? Why?" Lehrling asked.

"They're such magnificent beasts," she replied, "but so large and terrifying at the same time."

"Are you afraid of them?"

"Yes, actually."

"Here." Lehrling gently took her hand and walked her to his horse. He placed her hand to the side of his horse's neck. With his hand over hers, he glided her hand to rub the horse's coat. "See? He won't hurt you."

"Not with you beside me."

Lehrling laughed. "This ol' horse has never hurt anyone."

"What's his name?"

"Patch, because of the large white spot on his flank." Lehrling ran her hand up the horse's neck and then to the side of its nose.

"He's beautiful."

"He likes you." Lehrling slowly pulled his hand from hers. She looked in his eyes with a flattered smile. Even with her rugged appearance, her radiant inner beauty enthralled him, which overshadowed any amount of grime. Her widened smile indicated he'd stared into her eyes for too long. His face reddened and for once during the entire journey he was glad the heavily overcast sky was getting darker, so she couldn't see his heated face.

"Well, thanks to you," she said, "I'm less frightened. I'd have never stepped closer without your invitation."

Collette turned to Patch, rubbed its nose, and sweet-talked the horse.

"I'm surprised you don't have horses here," he said.

Amusement flowed softly in her voice. "We're river folk. We live off the river and this lake now. Ever since those reptilian beasts invaded the Glades of Sorrows, we've lived here. We're limited to the amount of land we can use. So we've no need for horses and don't have enough suitable land for them to graze."

Lehrling nodded. "That's true."

Without looking away from the horse, she said, "What brought you to Dagger's Tears?"

"My friend was told that Portia is a healer."

"Yes" Collette said. "Is your friend ill?"

"No, but his wife is."

"His wife?" she asked with a frown. "I only saw the two of you."

"She's a faery."

Collette pondered for several moments. "A faery?"

He nodded.

"How's that possible? I mean ... well—"

"Marriage between races and species isn't unknown," Lehrling said.

"I know *that*," she replied. "I meant ... consummation."

"Oh!" Lehrling's face blushed even hotter. "Ah, well, due to her magical abilities, she can become the size of a human."

Collette smiled and lowered her gaze. "So can she stay that height?"

Lehrling shrugged. "I suppose she *could*, but you'd have to ask her. Provided she recovers."

"Have hope. Portia's been a blessing to us." She lowered her voice and looked around, making certain others weren't listening. "She's not like us."

Lehrling frowned. "What do you mean?"

"She's different. She looks human but she's not."

"What *is* she?"

"We don't rightly know. Once we were forced from our former village, we found her gathering herbs, mosses, and other items she needed for her incantations."

"She already lived on this island?"

"No, but she helped establish our new settlement. She has great magical abilities."

"In what way?"

Collette smiled. Her eyes brightened as she remembered details. "She somehow dammed the river for us to build the raft bridge. It taxed her a great deal. She held the wall of water for two days, which gave our men enough time to construct the anchored posts on both sides."

Lehrling shook his head in disbelief. "I'm surprised the men didn't sink to their waists in thick mud."

"The riverbed was bone dry."

"Amazing," Lehrling said.

Collette nodded. "She's sworn to protect us in return for food and a place to live." Collette ran her hand down Patch's neck to his back, and then she looked at the saddlebag. One of the scrolls taken from Polderholm stuck out. She stared at it with keen curiosity. "What's this?"

"Something we came across at an island."

She yanked it from the bag. "May I?"

She didn't wait for a reply and unrolled the thick parchment. Her eyes studied the writing but displayed her confusion. "This is a spell scroll. Are you a sorcerer?"

He chuckled. "No. Far from it."

"And yet, you carry this?"

"It was something we discovered."

Collette frowned. "If you can't use magic, why keep it?"

"It might come of use later."

"Can you read it? I don't recognize the language."

"Nor do I. But there are translators."

"Fool's folly," she said.

"There's a tavern by that name," Lehrling said with a grin. "I've visited it several times."

She didn't smile. Instead, she waved the scroll in the air and repeated the words.

Confused by her reaction, he opened his mouth to speak but a sudden disruption captured his attention.

From the docks around the oxbow lake, bells clanged in rapid succession.

"What's that?"

"Time for us to leave the lake for the night. Hurry!"

CHAPTER 38

Although Collette insisted the horses were safe in the open, the cacophonous rattling, alarm bells caused Lehrling to instinctively grab the horses' halters and lead them away from the lake. Before he turned, a dark cloud spread across the gray horizon, much different than the already overcast sky.

This cloud was alive. It moved and approached at a rapid rate. Sharp shrills pierced the air. A stranger sound carried on the wind. The flapping increased its rhythm the closer the moving cloud came.

Three children, carrying baskets of fish, crayfish, and mussels, dropped their baskets and rushed to reach the buildings towering atop stilts. They sought shelter as if their lives depended on it.

"What's going on?" Lehrling hurried to catch Collette with the horses following close behind him.

"Nightfall comes," she said. "And with it, the creatures of the night."

"Why the alarm bells?"

"Bats," she replied without looking over her shoulder. "Hurry."

"They're a danger?"

"On occasion."

"You said the horses would be okay left to themselves?"

"Yes." She nodded. "They'll be fine."

"Then why's everyone fleeing because of the bats? Do these bats attack people and feast on blood?"

"No. They only eat insects."

"So why's everyone running?"

Collette paused and faced him. She offered a patient smile while she explained. "In their feeding frenzies to capture insects, the swooping bats have accidentally hit folks in the head or caused near fatal injuries. The last one injured was a young boy fishing on the dock. The bat struck his back and knocked him in the lake. He almost drown. The bats are quite large and while they don't pose a significant threat, we can't risk such accidents."

"I understand."

"Since most of the insects favor the water, the bats readily feed there," Collette said. "They're earlier than normal this evening. But bats aren't our enemies. They're more beneficial to us by eating thousands of mosquitoes every night."

Lehrling kept his head lowered, as the bats circled from the water and groomed the air along the banks of the lake. The bats' fierce, red eyes glowed like embers. With them came the smell of brimstone, which made him wonder where these bats hid during the day. He'd never seen a bat as large as these. Their graceful acrobatic dives and circles were neat to watch, but with their size and immense numbers, getting caught in the swarm could be deadly.

"Should we pick up the baskets of fish?" he asked. "No need leaving them here to rot."

Two men from the docks stooped, grabbed the baskets, and ran to the line of stilted houses and buildings.

The chirps and fluttering wings increased in a maddening whirl of action. The sky darkened with the blanket of bats, and an odd odor filled the air.

Lehrling sighed. "I can't get used to this constant dusk."

She frowned. "Is there any other?"

"Surely you've seen the sun?"

"No, I never have. Though I've heard travelers talk about it."

Lehrling gaped and his eyes widened. "You've never seen sunlight?"

"One day, I hope to venture outside these swamps and witness it for myself."

"Perhaps you will." He pointed at the scroll held tightly in her hand. "May I?'

"Sorry. I didn't realize I was still holding it. Here."

He smiled and took the scroll. "Would you mind showing me which building Portia's in? I should check on Roble and Shawndirea."

Collette pointed to the large center building. It also set on the highest stilts with a balcony overlooking the rest of the area. "She's in that one."

Lehrling studied the building and the surrounding terrain. Only buildings towered above the soggy, marshy ground. No large trees or thin saplings graced the hamlet.

The folks hurried through the stilts and rushed up the various ramps to the buildings' balconies. Lehrling didn't want to get lost in a wave of people he didn't know. Even though he'd only met Collette, he felt safer being in her company and uncertain how others might regard him.

"I'd be honored if you'd accompany me," Lehrling said.

She forced a smile. "I'd love to, Lehrling, but I'm not presentable to be in Portia's presence. It'd be disrespectful to enter her home as I am."

His heart sank slightly. He enjoyed talking to her and feared if she got out of his sight, he might never see her again. "Ah, yes. If I were covered in all of that, I'd want cleaned up, too."

Collette pointed to a longer building with heavy smoke coming from its chimney. "Attend your business with your friends. In an hour, meet me at the lodge. Everyone will be there. Cooks will prepare our supper from what we've caught in the lake."

The wind carried a delicious aroma. His mouth watered.

"They're already cooking," she said. "I'd best hurry. Don't arrive late. The best fish are served first, as they cannot be dried or preserved with salt."

"I'll look for you there." He smiled and led the horses to Portia's home.

Collette smiled and turned away. She walked swiftly along the worn timber planks to lessen her chances of sinking in the mire. Though he hardly knew her, her absence made him ache. He wanted to talk more and invite her to travel with him, Roble, and Shawndirea—once Shawndirea recovered from whatever ailed her. Nothing would please him more than to see the look on her face when she witnessed a sunrise or sunset for the first time. His heart quickened as he imagined her stunned smile.

What a drab life to be enclosed in a place where the sun never graced the sky. He wondered how he could best offer her the invitation to travel with him?

"You're an old fool," he whispered. "She'd take no interest in traveling with a man twice her age. Especially one who keeps talking to himself."

Lehrling rolled his eyes and slapped his palm against his forehead. He glanced in the direction Collette had taken, fearful she'd seen him holding conversation with himself. But she was lost in a small crowd of children and folks hurrying to get inside.

You must stop talking to yourself.

He laughed at himself and led the horses to Portia's home.

After leaving the horses at the stilts supporting the building, Lehrling was met by Merla and Cora as they descended the long wooden ramp.

"How is she?" Lehrling asked.

"No better," Cora said.

Lehrling winced. "What's wrong with her?"

Merla shrugged and offered a hopeful smile. "Portia's studying the circumstances, best she can. But if anyone can discover the faery's illness, it's Portia."

Lehrling glanced up the ramp. "Could I check in on them?"

Cora smiled. "Sure. We'll walk you up."

"I appreciate that."

CHAPTER 39

When Lehrling entered Portia's home, a heavy wall of smoky incenses greeted him. His eyes burned and he coughed.

Candles flickered from various shelves and tables around the room. A large candle burned on the center table. Roble leaned and rested on his elbows on the tabletop. He stared at Shawndirea's near lifeless form on a soft pillow.

Roble's fingers intertwined like he was in prayer, but he wasn't praying. His attention was attuned on her. He didn't notice Lehrling's approach. Worry furrowed Roble's brow. His eyes were plagued with despair.

Lehrling placed a hand on Roble's shoulder and squeezed, jarring Roble from his near trancelike state. "Any word?"

The lost expression in Roble's eyes didn't have reason for a reply. He shook his head.

Lehrling patted Roble's back and stood in silence beside him. Shawndirea repositioned herself slightly on the pillow but her eyes remained closed.

Her sudden movement brightened Roble's eyes with hope. But after several more seconds, his hope drained. She remained still. Apparently this was the first time she'd moved, at least in Lehrling's presence.

Rather than commenting or luring Roble into conversation, Lehrling remained silent and offered his support by taking a stool beside him. Only if Roble chose to talk would Lehrling speak, which was something Lehrling had learned during his years of growing wisdom. Sometimes silence was more comforting than words.

Roble's worry weighed heavily. It was obvious Roble thought of nothing else than Shawndirea's recovery. Lehrling wondered why Shawndirea's health suddenly plummeted before arriving at Dagger's Tears.

She'd never left Roble's pocket during the ride from the Glades of Sorrows to Dagger's Tears. She shouldn't have been exposed to anything capable of causing such an ailment. *Why* would her health deteriorate at such a rapid speed? Lez'minx had threatened Shawndirea at Moorsis' cottage. Had he followed through?

With Shawndirea in such a condition, near death it seemed, Roble was in no frame of mind to confront Lez'minx in the *supposed* god's temple. Roble's resolve was shattered. He worried more about her life than his or anything else. Seeing the pain of losing a wife made Lehrling question pursuing a relationship with Collette. The current thought was premature at best, but the pain cutting to Roble's core was an ache Lehrling didn't need, not after having lost so much already.

Shawndirea groaned, rolled to her side, and yet her eyes didn't open.

"She seems to be getting better." Portia walked gracefully to the table. She seemed to glide more than walk.

Lehrling was taken back by her odd eyes. He tried his best not to show it. Collette had been right. Portia wasn't like them. She wasn't human—not that it mattered—but he wondered what race she was. Her unusual features weren't familiar to him.

"What's wrong with her?" Roble asked.

Portia shrugged. "I've yet to solve the mystery. Perhaps she's fatigued from journeying into the Unseelie territory? I detect no identifiable sickness. My advice is for you and your comrade join the others at the lodge and eat a hearty meal."

Roble frowned. "No, I can't leave her."

"You do her or yourself no favors by staying. You're tired, wearied from your travels, and without food and sustenance, your health will diminish, too. I'm certain she wouldn't approve of such behavior?"

Roble sighed. "No, she wouldn't, but the last time I left her, she was taken."

"She's safe here," Portia said. "I guarantee. Her ailment isn't getting worse."

"Why would entering the Unseelie territory cause her to get sick?" Lehrling asked.

"Typically, it shouldn't. But, there might be an added strain by crossing the in-between," Portia said. "Perhaps, magics from both Courts fight to possess her."

"That could happen?" Roble asked.

"Rarely," Portia replied. "But it's not impossible within the Fae population. They attribute allegiance to one court, refute both courts, but for one to hold allegiance to both? I've never known any who have taken that path."

"She upholds *only* the Seelie Court," Roble said. "She abhors the Unseelie Court, especially when anyone assumes she's Unseelie."

"Odd."

"What's odd?" Lehrling asked.

"That others sense her Unseelie ties instead of her Seelie tie."

"It's obvious to assume she's Unseelie since she married me," Roble said. "The Seelie reject her since I'm not Fae."

Portia smiled. "Based on their principles, that might be true, but others sense she taps her magic from the Unseelie. However, I sensed automatically her Seelie magic. You'd be surprised that those who verbally reject the opposite court are often secretly drawn to it."

"It all confuses me," Lehrling said.

"For most humans, that's typical. But if she's tapping magic from both Courts, no one knows what the side effects are. Since she's passed through the in-between, or the Fae's Common Ground, she might be overwhelmed by its saturation."

"So what's she suffering right isn't a curse or disease?" Roble asked.

Portia shook her head. "Her body's adjusting to magic unfamiliar to her."

"We should go eat, Roble. I'm famished. You must be, too," Lehrling said. "From the aroma outside, this'll be the best meal we've had in weeks."

Roble flicked his gaze from Shawndirea to Portia.

"She'll be fine," Portia said. "In fact, when you return, she might be awake and hungry as well."

Shawndirea curled into a fetal position. She didn't seem to suffer any pain. She appeared to be sleeping peacefully. Color had returned to her face and her breathing was more pronounced.

Roble glanced at Lehrling. "What do you think?"

Lehrling's stomach growled loudly. He rubbed his stomach and grinned. "That speaks volumes, don't you think?"

"Never let your stomach lead your mind," Roble said.

"I'm not. But I agree with Portia. You'll renew your strength after eating, and your outlook will be clearer as well."

Roble sighed.

"If her condition worsens," Portia said, "and I don't believe it will, I'll send for you immediately."

Roble studied Portia for several seconds and nodded.

Portia offered a warm smile. "I understand your worries. You don't know me well enough to set aside your distrust. But my reputation rests high with the kind folks of Dagger's Tears. My life's dedicated to healing. I'd sacrifice my life to protect those who live here. I'd do so for the two of you, if it were required. So, please, go enjoy a hearty cooked meal, meet the wonderful folks who call this place home. When you return, you'll be more energetic."

"Come." Lehrling patted Roble's shoulder.

"Merla, Cora," Portia said. "Escort our new friends to the lodge so they can eat."

The two halflings offered slight bows and motioned Lehrling and Roble to the doorway.

At the threshold, Lehrling paused. Roble turned one last time to look at Shawndirea.

"She'll be fine, Dragon Skull Knight," Portia said. "Why do Overlanders worry and stress more intently than those in our realm."

CHAPTER 40

*R*oble followed Lehrling and Merla down the crude stairs. The evening breeze lofted the delicious aroma and spiked the intense hunger Roble had ignored. Despite his ravenous appetite, his heart and mind focused on Shawndirea. It was difficult, and somewhat selfish, to leave her while he ate. He doubted he could *enjoy* the food.

He didn't know Portia well enough to suspend his distrust. She didn't seem to pose any threat. But after nearly losing her several times, his genuine worry wasn't necessarily an abnormal reaction.

Lez'minx had directly threatened her, which is why he suspected Lez'minx was the reason Shawndirea was deathly ill. If so, her illness was his fault.

The drifting smell of food caused him to salivate. In a matter of minutes, they were halfway to the lodge with the two large chimneys.

"Smells great, huh?" Lehrling asked.

Roble nodded. "It does."

"You never answered my earlier question," Lehrling said.

Question?

Apparently, Lehrling had talked ever since they left Portia's home. Roble was so deep in thought, he'd never heard anything Lehrling said.

"I'm sorry," Roble said. "What'd you ask?"

"Did Portia have any information about Lez'minx?"

"No. She isn't familiar with his name."

Lehrling frowned. "Nothing?"

"That's what she said," Roble said.

"If that's what she said," Merla said evenly, "she means it."

"I wasn't being disrespectful," Roble said.

Merla shrugged. "No one's more honest and forthright than her. She's a healer and the last of her tribe. It's impossible for her to cast any negative spell, to lie, or to cause anyone harm."

"Impossible?" Lehrling cocked a brow.

"Yes. Whatever she does is returned tenfold to her," Cora said. "She's over two centuries old. She's lived that long because she heals others. To commit evil, even in the slightest, is an automatic death. Due to her age, should she ever succumb to *wishing* evil on another, she'd probably die before she uttered the first word of an incantation. Shawndirea's far safer with Portia than anyone else."

"What could she do, should someone try to abduct Shawndirea?" Roble asked. "If she can't inflict harm—"

"That's not what I said," Cora replied. "She can't cast evil spells to harm others. Protection spells are completely different. It's not evil to defend your life or the lives of others whenever threatened."

Merla interrupted. "So, you needn't to worry about Portia harming Shawndirea nor would she allow any harm to come to her."

Feeling a bit more relieved, Roble nodded. He doubted he'd ever fully stop worrying about Shawndirea until after Lez'minx was dealt with. Lez'minx wasn't one to throw out a threat, so Roble need to take precaution at all times concerning him. His threat on Shawndirea's life still hung and burned Roble's ears. He glanced at the lake. "Where'd everyone go?"

Lehrling explained about the giant swarm of bats. "These were the largest fanged beasts with wings I've ever seen."

"This isn't like the time you *almost* caught a dragonkin larger than a pony?" Roble asked with a wink and sly grin. "Even Boldair doesn't tell tales that tall."

Lehrling's brow rose in question before he laughed. "Oh, no, *that* was fictional and why I exaggerated it because Boldair *was* present. He'd have done no less."

"I have agree with you on that," Roble replied.

"But I'm not exaggerating about the bats, Roble. I swear they—"

Lehrling and Roble ducked at the same time, narrowly missing a trio of huge bats. The *swoosh* of their wings rang in their ears.

"*Now* do you believe me!" Lehrling pointed at the trio spiraling through the air.

"Absolutely," Roble replied. "Impossible to deny."

"Those bats are pests at times," Cora said. "But more beneficial than aggravating."

Merla laughed with a high-pitched, gleeful sound. "Some fish are larger than us. If the townsfolk become desperate, they'd use us for bait."

Roble almost laughed aloud but chose to keep the conversation more informative and serious. "What'd you mean about Portia being the last of her kind?"

"Again, *not* what I said. She's the *last* of her *tribe*."

"What race is she?" Lehrling asked.

"I'm not sure," Merla replied. "All I know is her tribe was south on the river near where the river splits near Spellhaven."

"They're dead?" Roble asked.

Cora shrugged. "It's possible. She doesn't rightly know. A great flood washed away her swamp village when she was a child. She never found other survivors and somehow survived on her own for many years in the hidden depths of the swamps."

"By herself?" Lehrling frowned with curiosity.

"She's never said, but eventually she moved upriver. We first encountered her when we were forced to leave the Glades of Sorrow," Merla said.

"Interesting," Roble said softly.

Cora stopped at the stairs of the longest stilted building. "This is our lodge. The dinner bell hasn't rang yet. But since the bats arrived earlier than expected tonight, I'd say it's okay for us to enter and find ourselves a seat."

Roble nodded his gracious thanks, and he extended his hand. "After the two of you."

"You're our guests," Cora said. "It's only fitting the two of you proceed ahead of us."

Lehrling offered a broad grin. "As knights and gentlemen, we can't impose rudeness by walking ahead of two young ladies. Besides, you know the seating arrangements and can direct us where to sit. I'd certainly hate to find myself in a magistrate's chair."

"As would I," Roble said.

"You've no need to worry," Merla said. "We're all commoners who share the labors equally. No one presides over us. Whatever situations arise are generally handled during a large group meeting where we discuss and decide what's the best for everyone."

"That actually works?" Roble asked.

"You seem surprised," Cora said with a curious frown. "Why?"

Roble chuckled. "Because in my world, problems seldom are settled so easily. It usually turns hostile."

"It works perfectly fine for us," she replied.

"Then you live in quite a pleasant place," Roble said.

"We've no council like the larger towns or cities. No ruler, which is something we prefer. Why should one or a *few* select individuals make all the major decisions for the entire hamlet?" Cora asked. "Such power often turns into greed, giving the overseers the opportunity to make laws more beneficial to themselves by ignoring those who have greater needs."

"It's a far from perfect system," Roble said. "But that's also the problem with vast amounts of diversity and needs. It's almost impossible to achieve equality. Where I lived, total chaos often exploded because everyone's views are more important than the next person's. Common courtesies are rare. Folks don't discuss their needs and goals. They try to scream over those they disagree with. I wish your system could work in my land. I'd have had a more difficult time leaving it behind."

"You're more than welcome to stay with us," Cora said.

Roble shook his head. "While I appreciate the offer, I must decline. I've too many obligations elsewhere."

"As do I," Lehrling said.

Cora opened the door. Merla stepped across the threshold, peered around the room, and then motioned Roble and Lehrling to enter. Within a few seconds of walking inside, Dolan marched to Cora and

Merla with a stern frown. The fierce anger in his eyes almost magnified his stature, and if properly measured, Dolan would've been a giant.

"Where have you two been?" he demanded. "You've been holding me up."

Merla met his glare with one of her own. "Portia requested we aid her a bit *longer*. If you've a problem with that, take it up with her."

The frown disappeared from Dolan's face, and he paled slightly. "Places, please."

Cora said, "As soon as we show them where the plates and utensils are, and where they're welcome to sit, we'll join you."

"You best hope your instruments are tuned," Dolan whispered. "We've not had time to rehearse, and I'm certain you remember our embarrassment the last time *that* happened."

"It'll be fine," Merla said.

Dolan huffed and walked away.

"Come," Cora said. She led them to the line where they could get wooden plates, bowls, and utensils.

"It seems rude for us to be served first," Roble said.

"Nonsense," Merla said. "You're our guests and our guests are always served first. Now, if you'll excuse us, we need to get on stage before Dolan's head explodes."

She and Cora hurried off.

Roble exchanged curious glances with Lehrling. "Stage?"

Lehrling shrugged. "Let them do what they need. I'm too famished not to help myself, rude or not."

"The smell's inviting enough." Roble followed Lehrling to the line where clay plates of hot food simmered.

The door where they'd entered opened and the townsfolk bustled inside.

Lehrling took portions of cooked fish, mussels, and a huge bowl of soup. Roble followed and took the same.

"Let's eat," Roble said, walking to a table.

CHAPTER 41

*A*fter they took their seats, Roble noticed Lehrling kept his attention on the door more than anything else. Roble had nearly devoured all the fish and mussels on his plate while Lehrling hadn't touched his.

"I thought you were *famished*," Roble said. "After eating jerky and dried fruit for days, I'd think you'd welcome freshly cooked food. This is the best I've eaten in weeks, but you've not taken a bite. You act like you're waiting for someone."

Lehrling blushed. "I suppose I am."

"Really? Who?"

Lehrling's face reddened even more. He took his fork and poked at the food. He took a bite. "You're right. The food's wonderful."

"You scoundrel!" Roble said with a broad grin. He playfully thrust an elbow into Lehrling's side. "I should keep a chaperone with you at all times, eh?"

"No-o-o." Lehrling frowned and shook his head. "That's not necessary. It's not like that. I met a woman at the docks while the horses drank. She informed me about the bats before they descended like a mad storm."

"She must be something special for you to watch the door so intently," Roble said.

He shrugged. "I enjoyed the few minutes we talked. She was someone I'd love to talk with a lot longer. A *lifetime* longer."

Roble chuckled. "That's serious insight for a woman you've just met."

"Don't mock me." Lehrling took a bite of fish. He chewed and gulped down the food. "This is the best fish I've eaten in years. Even better than palace chefs cook."

"I wasn't mocking you," Roble said, softly.

Lehrling took another bite, closed his eyes, and savored it. "Food's almost magical."

"I agree. It's the most flavorful meal I've had since entering Aetheaon."

Lehrling said, "Roble, have you ever met someone and during the first few minutes of talking, you feel an immediate connection to the person? I know she's a stranger, but I feel like we've met in—" He paused and chuckled. "In a different life. Sounds preposterous."

Roble shook his head. "No, it's not preposterous. It's a deep connection. Long before I met Shawndirea and left the Overlands, I've experienced the feeling. It's infatuation, which makes the two of you want to spend more time together."

"Kind of like you and Shawndirea?"

"Not at first," Roble replied. "She was infuriated with me because I destroyed her wings."

Lehrling nodded. "Ah, yes. She had every right to be furious."

"Of course. But maybe this woman—"

"Collette." Lehrling wiped his mouth with a cloth napkin. "Her name's Collette."

Roble tried to hide his sly grin. He didn't want Lehrling more flustered, so he averted the temptation to tease his friend any further. "Maybe Collette's the one for you?"

"Oh, no, she's too young for me." Flustered, he shook his head fiercely.

"What's age have to do with it? As far as that goes, what does race have to do with love?" Roble asked. "Until I met Shawndirea, never in a million years would I have ever thought a human could marry a faery, because height differences are a factor. Yet, due to her magical abilities, she's able to become the height of a human if she performs the proper ritual. So, age, my friend, is the least of the obstacles."

"I know I've overthought that issue. But still, she intrigues me. She told me she's never seen the sun during her lifetime. Can you imagine that?"

Roble frowned and thought of such a possibility. "Actually, no. However, these past few days I've wondered if *we'll* ever see the sun again. That's something I've always taken for granted, I suppose."

"Exactly! You see, I'm the same way. And if she were the one for me … I'd love to see her eyes the first moment the sun shines on her face."

Roble smiled when he regarded Lehrling's beaming smile. "That'd be a wonderful moment."

Several instruments strummed from the small stage across the room. Dolan sat on a stool with a dulcimer set across his lap. Cora balanced a bass that was much taller than Roble expected a halfling capable to hold. Merla held a lute. After playing several chords to check their tuning for adequate harmony, Dolan nodded and they strummed a soft melody.

The tables around Roble and Lehrling's were filled with the townsfolk. Bustling and the soft conversation slowly drowned out the music. Roble tried not to feel uncomfortable, but all eyes were on him and Lehrling. Curious questions were whispered amongst the patrons. They were intrigued by their visitors.

A young lady in her late teens approached with a tall pitcher. She set two clay flasks on the table.

She offered a slight smile. "Bitter beer?"

"Please." Lehrling returned the smile. "Thank you."

Roble nodded and slid the flask for her to pour the beer easier. "Thanks."

Lehrling took a swig and his face creased like a prune. "Ghastly."

"Bitter?" Roble said, laughing.

He cleared his throat. "Horse piss would be kinder."

"Where's your lady friend?" Roble asked. "Did she indicate when she'd meet you?"

Lehrling shrugged. "All she said was she'd meet me here. She told me the best fish was served first. She was right about that."

"She didn't warn you about the beer?"

Lehrling rubbed his throat. "Nope. Guess the potential romance is gone now."

Roble chuckled. "That bad?"

"You try it."

"Think I'll pass."

"Quite wise for an Overlander," Lehrling said with a wink. He gasped and his eyes widened slightly.

"What?"

Lehrling lowered his head and looked at his plate. "That's Collette. She just arrived."

CHAPTER 42

*R*oble studied Collette when she stepped through the lodge door and looked around. She seemed excited and a little nervous as her eyes searched the tables. She wore a plain gown and worn boots. Her brown hair was combed neatly and hung around her shoulders. In comparison to the other women in the room, Collette had invested time to make herself more presentable.

"That's her?" Roble asked, nodding at the door.

Lehrling's eyes widened. He quickly looked down. He whispered, "Yes. What should I do?"

"Greet her with a smile," Roble said. "Don't act like a child. You're a man. Be bold and brave. No sense being nervous. Your introductions have already been made. Ignoring her entrance will make her think you aren't interested in her."

"It's not that."

"Then what?"

"She's more stunning than I ever imagined." Lehrling braved casting a glance. He smiled in her direction. She nodded modestly and smiled. He waved and his grin widened.

Roble said, "She's beautiful. Are you saying you didn't notice before?"

"You'd have had to have seen her before. She was covered with fish guts and scales and blood, but even then, her beauty shone through."

"Don't worry about the age difference then," Roble said.

"Why's that?"

"If she went to the trouble of cleaning up in such a little amount of time, she's interested in you."

"I could only hope."

"Don't sell yourself short. I tease you about your age from time to time, but you've still got *some* life in you."

Lehrling rolled his eyes. "Would she really try to impress me like that?"

"If you like a woman, wouldn't you make yourself more presentable before you met her again?"

"Don't I look presentable enough?" He plucked bits of food from his beard and combed his hair with his fingers.

"You look fine," Roble said. "I gave that as a comparison. You'd want to look your best, right?"

"Yes." He looked around to see where Collette was. "Are you sure I look okay?"

"As presentable as any traveling knight's expected to be."

Lehrling raised his right arm slightly and sniffed his underarm. "Gad! The bitter beer tastes better than I smell."

"Calm down."

Lehrling sighed. "I'll try. I don't understand why she'd go to the extra trouble to make herself more attractive when I was *already* attracted to her in the first place."

"You told her?"

"Well, no, not in *direct* words." Lehrling chewed his lower lip. "I hinted. I'm certain I blushed several full sunsets of red while talking to her. Generally, that'd be the biggest hint. Right?"

Roble nodded. "Being as she's never *seen* the sun—"

Lehrling frowned. "I'm being serious."

"Forgive me," Roble said. "Blushing's a definite sign for some. But be yourself. Nothing more than how you acted when you first spoke to her. Don't act cocky, unless you want her running the other direction."

Lehrling shook his head and chuckled. "I can't believe *I'm* your elder and you're giving me advice about women. That's not a bad thing. Obviously, I misread Sarey's interest in Bausch and ruined his opportunity, so I should take advice rather than give it."

"Keep your composure and compliment her. Here she comes."

Collette approached from the opposite side of the table and smiled at Lehrling. "Would you mind if I sit across from you?"

Lehrling quickly stood. "Not at all."

Roble stood as well.

Due to how the tables were arranged, Lehrling couldn't make his way around to help seat her. He motioned his hand instead. "Please."

With a slight blush, she sat. "Thanks."

"Collette," Lehrling said, still standing. "I'd like you to meet my fellow knight and my closest friend and ally, Roble. Roble, this is Collette."

"A pleasure," Roble said with a slight bow.

"Likewise," she said.

After they seated themselves, Roble picked at his food and tried not to start the conversation for Lehrling. Lehrling was obviously nervous. Too nervous for words, so Roble gently tapped Lehrling's foot with his boot.

Lehrling cleared his throat. "You look … lovely this evening."

"Thanks." Collette blushed.

"You were right," he said.

"About what?"

"How great the food is."

"Visitors often find it delightful, but for us, who eat this every day, it gets tiresome."

"I imagine so," Roble said.

Collette turned her attention to him. "May I ask? How is your … the faery recuperating?"

Roble said, "She's not fully recovered. Portia believes Shawndirea had gotten past the worst."

"Good news then?" Collette asked.

"In a manner of speaking," Roble replied.

"Portia knows what she's talking about. She's very knowledgeable."

"That's my understanding," Roble said.

"None have ever said a bad word about her," Collette said.

"Some seem to fear her."

"Reverence isn't fear," Collette said.

Reverence? Roble frowned. "According to the halflings, no one rules over Dagger's Tears. Is that true?"

"Yes."

"Portia seems to hold control over everyone," Roble said. "What you call reverence ... well, let me say ... comes across as fear in the eyes of those who question her authority."

Collette's eyes shifted nervously from Roble's and then to Lehrling's. "She holds no authority. She's equal to the rest of us."

"I was trying to understand her position," Roble said. "So forgive me if I asked more than I should."

She ignored Roble's statement and kept her gaze on Lehrling. "When do you plan to leave Dagger's Tears?"

Lehrling thought for a moment and glanced toward Roble. "After Portia says Shawndirea's well enough to travel?"

Roble nodded. "Yes, once she's safe to travel, we'll move on."

"Where will you go?" With disappointment, she looked intently into Lehrling's eyes.

"We don't know exactly," Lehrling replied.

"Why wander away from Dagger's Tear's safety when you don't know your destination?"

Lehrling opened his mouth to reply, but hesitated and glanced at Roble.

"Actually," Roble said, "we hoped Portia might've known the where-abouts of a temple we seek."

"She doesn't?"

Roble shook his head. "No."

"If she doesn't know," Collette said, "it's highly doubtful I could help you."

Roble smiled. "So far, no one has any information to direct us."

Lehrling said, "Yes, we've traveled deeper into the swamps without any clue of where we're going."

"Dagger's Tears and the Glades of Sorrow are the only places I know." Her eyes beamed sudden hope and her voice became cheerier. "Like I expressed earlier, I hope to travel outside these swamps one day. I'd love to see the things you've seen."

"Dear lady," Lehrling said, "I'd be honored to be the man to show you those places."

Roble's brow rose at the quickness of Lehrling's offer. While he wasn't totally surprised by Lehrling eagerness to fulfill one of Collette's dreams, he didn't want Collette to get her hopes up too soon. Their journey was to find Lez'minx and for Roble to break his ties to the god or demigod or whatever he might be. The trip ahead proved to become even more dangerous.

"Really?" she asked.

Lehrling's eyes were lost in hers. His infatuation had the best of him. Nothing Roble said at this moment could sway his friend from his promise to Collette. Roble had seen the look on other people's faces. When that lost look of being smitten appeared on one's face, he or she never accepted logical advice, even by those with the best intentions. Whether friends, family, or counselors, such advice fell on deaf ears. Often, only one thing became enough to drive logic into the heart and mind of a love-sick fool.

"Over my dead body!" A rugged voice bellowed several tables away from Roble and Lehrling.

Immediately, Roble and Lehrling looked in the direction of the man's voice. Seated at the table was an older man, perhaps ten years Lehrling's senior, but his voice thundered in spite of his small stature. The man wore a thick patch over his left eye. A deep scar traveled from his upper lip, across his missing eye, and gullied a nasty trail across the man's bald head. The anger in his gaze and the tightness of his jaw was evidence of a fury Roble had never seen in another man.

"Father!" Collette said.

The man adjusted in his chair and leaned forward, which took a great deal of his energy, as his left leg was missing from the knee down. He propped upon the stub of his left arm and firmly pointed his right index finger at Lehrling. "You dare enter Dagger's Tears and attempt to fill my daughter's mind with your lofty tales, and try to take her from us? She belongs here, with her family, and not wandering through the godforsaken swamps—"

Collette stood with tears in her eyes. Her face reddened. "I've no hope here, father! None. There's no life in this world of shadows, constant rain, and sheer misery. I always reek of fish! This place is nothing but a prison for me."

"Silence, Collette!" he said. "You've no need for a suitor outside of Dagger's Tears when several hardy men have already asked for your hand in marriage."

"None I'd have myself to be with!" She promptly crossed her arms.

Two of the younger filthy fishermen looked hurt and disappointed by her statement and lowered their gazes.

Dolan, Merla, and Cora stopped playing their instruments and exchanged stunned glances.

Lehrling turned his chair around, smiled graciously, and said, "Sir, I meant no offense to you or your family. I find your beautiful daughter to be one of the finest ladies I've ever had the pleasure of meeting."

"In the matter of a half hour you've come to such a conclusion?" he snarled.

"The brevity seems hasty," Lehrling said. "But how can one *not* see that? She's indeed a—"

In a gravelly tone, he said, "Knight, hold your tongue. You're not amongst friends at the moment."

Roble's hand instinctively slid over one of his hidden daggers. He turned in his seat.

Lehrling noticed Roble's fingers tense and recognized the intense glare in Roble's eyes. He shook his head. "No, Roble."

"I can't accept that as less than a threat," Roble replied in a near whisper.

"I'd have you two knights depart in the morning, *without* my daughter."

"*Father*—" Collette whispered. She wiped tears from her eyes and glanced at the lady seated beside her father. "Mother?"

Her mother glanced at Collette's father with a bit of fright and stammered, "You're being unfair, Jaux."

Jaux leveled a quick frown at her and shook his head. She turned and looked down, suddenly silent. Jaux returned his hardened gaze at Lehrling. "Knight, I'm sure you tell that to all the young lasses from town to town as you and your brotherly knights travel, seeking the fairest maidens to add notches to your belts."

"That's the furtherest thing from the truth, sir." Lehrling's voice shook with anger. "I've no notches on my belt, nor do I ever seek such shallowness in relations. The Dragon Skull Order holds a prestigious reputation with all the cities, towns, and hamlets throughout Aetheaon. As a Dragon Skull Knight, I've devoted myself to Hoffnung, my King and Queen, having denied myself of many things, one of which is marrying and having a home."

"Bit old for that now, don't you think?" Jaux said.

Lehrling fought to suppress his anger. He gave Roble a side-glance. "It's true I'm not as spry as I once was, but—"

"But *nothing*! I'll not have you ride into our hamlet, filling my daughter's head with delusional dreams that lead to her premature death." Spittle flew from his crooked, near-toothless, mouth. He paused to wipe his lips with the back of his hand. "Her home's *here*. Not with you and *not* elsewhere."

Collette fumed as her fading fear of her father suddenly turned to anger. "He's not filled my mind with delusions. Every day I stare at the river and wonder what's to the north and what's to the south of our hamlet. Curiosity causes my stomach to ache. I want more than this life. Forgive me for dreaming about more than *this*. If I choose to leave Dagger's Tears, that's my decision to make, father. Not yours."

"Mind your tongue," Jaux said. "We can't afford the loss of our people migrating to lands unknown. You see my physical condition daily. I'm like this because I helped establish Dagger's Tears."

Lehrling stood. "I've not so much as even *hinted* at marriage. I've not offered a proposal. I said I'd be honored to show her the places she desires to see. That much's true. Why does that draw outrageous hostility from you?"

"You're luring her away from us," Jaux said.

"Preposterous!" Lehrling said. His face reddened.

"Father, he's not offered any proposal, nor have I sought one," Collette said. "But I want to see what's outside these swamps. I'm tired of the meager living and toiling away from morning to dusk with no pleasure in sight."

"What do you expect to find outside the swamps? That you can shake trees and gold coins will rain to the ground?"

"No." Fiercer anger burned in her eyes. "My desire's not for mone-tary treasure. I hope to bless my senses with the rarer beauties my eyes and ears have never beheld."

"Our lives are dangerous enough living *inside* our hamlet," Jaux said. "Far worse lies outside Dagger's Tears, and on the fringes of our borders unnatural creatures constantly seek to destroy us. Why else do you think we fled from the Glades of Sorrow? You're no different than the rest of our community. You're not a knight or warrior capable of defending yourself. You've no magical wards to keep you safe. You're a commoner, as we all are."

Roble stood. His hands rested on his belt.

Lehrling reached a frantic hand to grab Roble's forearm, but Roble stepped outside his reach.

Roble's eyes searched the faces of those seated at their tables. Finally, he rested his gaze on Jaux. "If I may, I'd like to address the room."

Although tired and weary, the other townsfolk lowered their forks and nodded, giving him permission to speak.

CHAPTER 43

"I'll make this brief," Roble said.

"You'd do us all a favor by doing so," Jaux said. His one eye narrowed and his mouth twisted with his angered disgust.

Roble's jaw tightened. He glared at Jaux. "If you're one for bluntness and insults, I can offer that, too. But be forewarned, if your threats escalate, you'd best be ready to back your hostile words with a blade."

Jaux's face softened slightly, but more in response to the angered stares the others displayed toward him. Several men shook their heads at Jaux.

Roble wondered how little the others favored Jaux. His soured demeanor had probably rubbed the majority of the hamlet's attitude toward the crippled man raw years earlier.

Roble took the moment to make his point and sway the townsfolk's support. "To my understanding, no one in Dagger's Tears presides over everyone else. Is that a fact? Or, Jaux, due to your physical condition, you somehow believe your word is law over the others? Do you govern these people?"

Jaux paled and swallowed hard. He adjusted in his seat slightly.

"He does *not!*" a grimy man seated at a table behind Jaux exclaimed. His fury brought spittle to the sides of his mouth, and he appeared ready to bolt at Jaux.

LEONARD D. HILLEY II

Others grumbled in agreement.

Jaux tried to make himself smaller in response to the tension building around him. He sighed. His pale face and jaw grew slack.

"Lehrling and I are Dragon Skull Knights. We never prey on those we visit and we pay for any goods and services we need. We don't submit ourselves to charity, nor have we ransacked any villages. The oath we've sworn demands we uphold our behavior above all others or we're held accountable before our Queen and the Order. Lehrling's a man of honor. He respects everyone he meets. He'd give his own life to defend the crown or any of his friends. Even those he's just met. His heart's far larger and worth far more than all the treasure hidden inside a dragons' lairs.

That being said, I share the same attributes, with one exception. I never take threats directed toward me or any of our knights lightly. I react to defend those within the Order with swift judgment. Often with a blade if the threat's physical. Understand, we're passing through. We greatly appreciate your hospitality. But as for Jaux dismissing our arrival and demanding we leave in the morning, does he have the right to make such a decision?"

Almost all of the older men and women shook their heads.

"Because," Roble said, "my wife's ill. She's with Portia. I refuse to leave Dagger's Tears until she's able to travel. If any oppose our stay, voice your opposition now."

A man with greasy hair and a matted beard sat upright. "Jaux hasn't the authority to dismiss you and Sir Lehrling. We're a community where each person has a say. I vote you stay until your wife's recovered."

"As do I," another said.

"Me, too," an elderly man stated. And the sentiment echoed throughout the room.

The women in the room nodded their agreement.

"We appreciate this," Roble said. "Now, what's your statute concerning a resident wanting to leave your hamlet?"

"None ever have left," another man said.

"Ever?" Roble couldn't hide his surprise. "None of you have ever been outside the swamps?"

He shook his head. "Of course, *some* have. None of our original settlement have ever left to explore what lies beyond the swamps. Over the years, we've gained new residents who got lost in the swamps and sought shelter with us. Since they feared leaving, we offered them refuge. But no one born in our settlement has left. We know the dangers of venturing out on our own and how foolish it'd be to leave our haven."

"Do you oppose Collette's decision to leave?" Roble asked.

Their gazes returned to Jaux. Roble couldn't recall ever seeing a more sour expression on a man's face. The bitterness contained within Collette's father came from a deep place. Roble didn't believe the man was intentionally hostile, but a great deal of his vileness stemmed from his injuries. Jaux didn't seem to have any prosthetics to aid him and apparently suffered each passing day without the ability to leave his chair.

"Folks of Dagger's Tears." An elderly man seated several chairs away from Jaux stood. "How many favor allowing Collette to journey with these two knights? Give a show of hands."

Only three refused to raise their hands. Jaux and two younger men. Roble assumed the two must've been Collete's hopeful suitors in spite of her open rejections.

Jaux slowly gazed around the room at those with their hands raised. He was disheartened, and then suddenly dismayed when he noticed his wife's hand was raised along with all the others. He grumbled in silence and shook his head.

Tears glistened in Collette's eyes. She wiped them away and smiled. "Thanks be to all of you."

"Well, what now?" Jaux asked.

Collette ignored his question and directed her attention to the townsfolk. "Please, back to eating. Blessings to you."

Lehrling faced her.

She smiled. "I need to get some food before it's gone."

After she walked away, Lehrling and Roble sat down. Lehrling shook his head and sighed. "That was … interesting. You've a way with a crowd."

Roble chuckled. "Thanks."

"Of course, the threat of using weapons to those who opposed was quite the majestic touch."

Roble whispered, "Jaux doesn't have many friends in his hamlet, which isn't surprising, given his radiant charm."

Lehrling coughed to cover his laughter.

"I've the feeling that any weapons drawn in Dagger's Tears tonight would've been aimed at him and not us," Roble said.

"A victory, all the same," Lehrling said.

"Is it?"

Lehrling frowned. "What do you mean?"

"We can't take Collette with us."

"Beg pardon?"

"She's not safe with us once we find Lez'minx's temple and confront him."

"We can't leave her here after all of this," Lehrling said. "Imagine her heartbreak and humiliation. Look at her now."

Roble watched her filling her plate in the cook's line. Her face glowed with renewed vigor.

"You dash her dreams now," Lehrling said, softly. "You extinguish her light forever."

"Be honest, Lehrling. Can we possibly protect her against Lez'minx?"

Lehrling took a bite of his food and thought while chewing slowly. His eyes went distant for several long moments. He swallowed. "At the success we've had in finding his temple thus far, Roble, it's highly likely we're *not* going to find him."

"No? What if he finds us?"

Lehrling took a sharp breath and held it, while considering the possibility.

Roble nodded. "He's found us once, and given that Shawndirea's health faded soon afterwards, who knows if her spell overshadowing these rings has vanished? Besides, he vowed to harm Shawndirea because she's important to me. That's what villains do. They attack your loved ones to make you bend to their will or to punish you. Lez'minx would attack her to weaken you. Is that what you want for Collette?"

Lehrling sighed and wiped his mouth. Sweat beaded his brow. "No, it's not."

"Neither do I."

"So you think he caused Shawndirea's sickness?"

"Portia seems to believe it's not, but I can't shake the possibility that he's the one responsible." Roble took a whiff of the bitter beer and pushed away the tankard.

"My suspicions match yours," Lehrling said. He leaned closer to Roble and lowered his voice. "Collette's coming. Can we not mention leaving her here until tomorrow? I'll try to find a way to break the news to her softly. But tonight, I can't bear seeing her—"

Roble nodded and stood. "No need to upset her. Look, I'm going to leave you two alone so you can talk in private. I need to see if Shawndirea's any better."

Collette beamed a smile at Roble.

"Collette," Roble said. "It's been a pleasure meeting you. I need to excuse myself."

Her eyes glistened. "I hope all's well for your faery."

"She's my wife, not a possession."

"Yes. My apologies," she said, nodding. "Thank you for addressing everyone in my defense."

He glanced at Lehrling. "You know where to find me."

Lehrling nodded. "May the Three Goddesses bless Shawndirea and may good news await you."

CHAPTER 44

*A*s Roble made his way to Portia's home, he found his horse and Lehrling's grazing at sprigs of swamp grass under a neighboring stilted building. Bleys raised his head and nuzzled his nose against Roble's hands.

"How are you faring?" Roble asked the horse.

Bleys snorted.

Roble unfastened his bag from the rear of the saddle, slung it over his shoulder, and then he took Lehrling's saddlebag before he continued to Portia's home.

Night insects voiced a harsh chorus from the tall grasses, sedges, the river bank and the few thorny shrubs scattered between the houses. When he reached her home, he ascended the stairs. He paused at the top balcony, leaned on the railing, and studied the area.

The night became more ominous without the slightest hint of the glow of a moon's light. The mystery of the ever thick clouds and fog disturbed him, and nothing from the science he learned in the Overlands explained this phenomenon. It seemed the swamps were indeed cursed to remain in shadow.

The heavy fluttering wings passing overhead indicated the swarming bats were clearing the air of what insects they could find. Unlike most people, he found bats intriguing and held no fear of them, regardless of their size or numbers.

Blazing torches at each corner of every building offered a slight outline of the village. Along the river's edge several watchmen patrolled. Their lanterns bobbed side to side as they followed the shoreline. Several men stood in the glow of a large fire near the ferry where he, Lehrling, and Shawndirea had crossed earlier.

These folks were fishermen and lived off the land. From his observation, they were peaceful, modest people. What weapons did they have to defend themselves from invaders? They had left the Glades of Sorrow without much resistance. Their buildings and homes in the glades were still habitable, only covered with an overgrowth of foliage.

Roble wondered if the giant turtles in the deep muddy river were enough to prevent the lizard-men from crossing and attacking. After seeing the massive turtle that carried the ferry across the water and being told the river was filled with these abnormal giants, Roble would never swim in the river. Even though turtles were slow on land, in the water, they were swifter and could rip a man in half with their powerful jaws.

The small land area between the oxbow lake and the river was outlined by the line of the fiery braziers. If one could view them from the sky, this outline resembled a large, flaming eye. But even these fires were unable to burn through the heavy overcast skies.

The echoes of the patrols alerting one another caught his attention. After their cries, the men at the large fire continued their conversations, but they were too far for Roble to understand them.

Beyond the curve of the oxbow lake, a trail of flickering fire serpentined in an odd fashion until it formed a curved line along the outer edge of the lake. Roble stood. After a minute of observation, he realized these torches were moving toward the other side of the oxbow. None of the guards noticed. Perhaps at ground level they were unable to see the advancing torches. Were these Lizard-men approaching or a different band of possible enemies?

One torch intensified above all the others. It wasn't fiery orange. It shimmered an icy blue encircled by an outer purplish glow. This fiery orb of fire wasn't normal fire. This light was magical; possibly from a sorcerer or something far worse. This arrival probably wasn't from Lez'minx's beckoning, but Roble couldn't be certain.

Roble glanced at his rings in the faint flickering of a glowing lantern on Portia's balcony. The rings' stones remained tarnished like burnt lightbulbs. Despite her sickness, Shawndirea's spell never faded, so Lez'minx was unable to currently track them. This didn't mean the supposed god hadn't discovered their location in Dagger's Tears.

Regardless, the torchbearers were potential enemies. Since the only one capable of using magic inside Dagger's Tears was Portia, she needed to be alerted about the group waiting on the other side of the oxbow lake.

Roble hurried to Portia's door. He raised his hand to rap on the door and hesitated. Various worries and dreads about Shawndirea's welfare shot through his mind. And as he usually did, he imagined the worst of all possibilities. How could he not?

His worst fear was Shawndirea had died. A lump swelled in his throat. *Not* entering seemed a better option than discovering the truth. Once he stepped inside, he'd know one way or the other. Was he ready to accept and cope with the possible loss?

A lesser fear was Portia had taken Shawndirea and fled, as some races considered Fae blood a priceless ingredient in their rituals and spells. Given the obstacles to flee Dagger's Tears, this was far unlikely.

"Come inside," Portia said in an annoyed tone. "Your delay isn't necessary."

Her statement caught Roble off guard. He pushed open the door. Incense greeted him. Candles and lanterns brightened the room. His gaze immediately sought the table where he had left Shawndirea. To his surprise, she was sitting and drinking from a tiny cup.

His face brightened, and he rushed to her. He sighed heavily. "Ah, thank goodness, you're alive!"

A curious smile spread across her face. "Of course, I'm alive. I was in a deep sleep. You thought I was dying?"

Roble frowned. "I wasn't certain what was happening, especially since Lez'minx threatened your life. I feared he might've placed a curse on you."

She took another sip from the cup. "No, he did no such thing. Yet, at least."

"Have you experienced this type of deep sleep before?"

She shook her head. "No, but I was in a safe place."

"Any idea why this happened?"

"Portia and I have been discussing this," Shawndirea replied.

Roble flicked his gaze to Portia. "How long has she been awake?"

"Soon after you left to eat," Portia replied.

"Sorry I didn't stay," Roble said.

"Quite all right. You mustn't grow weaker worrying about me."

"So what caused you to enter this sleep?"

"Portia and I believe it's because I passed through the in-between and I'm near the heart of Unseelie territory. My body, mind, and spirit might've needed time to adjust. Of course, there's also the possibility some within the Unseelie cast resistance spells against me, hoping I'd leave."

"They'd seek to harm you?"

She shrugged. "Their goal might only be to discourage me from going further into their magical flux. But something else might be responsible."

"Like what?" Roble asked.

"Those spellbooks we kept. The ones I read at such a rapid pace."

"How would that affect you?"

"Devouring too many darker spells at a quick rate? I can't be certain, but I grew weaker not long after I tethered them to my memory."

"I'd think that would *increase* your strength," he said.

"It could, depending on the magical ties. Since a lot of those spells are contrary to the magic I wield, it's possible I suffered an internal struggle as my mind attempted to balance the knowledge."

"Tell him what you learned from entering the dream realm," Portia said.

Roble stared at Shawndirea with genuine curiosity.

"I'm still sorting through all of the meaning," Shawndirea said. "I'm can't properly discern everything yet. But it seems the Seelie awaits my return. I was told to not cast aside my ties to the Seelie for the Unseelie."

"By whom?" Roble asked.

Shawndirea's brow furrowed. She pursed her lips. "That's the mystery. He, or she, never revealed a name. Although, I asked."

"More information might come in her future dreams," Portia said.

"Maybe," Shawndirea replied.

Roble leaned his face lower. She stood, rubbed his bearded cheek, and gently kissed him.

He said, "I feared losing you."

"You've not, yet, love," she said softly.

"I've learned to expect the unexpected."

Shawndirea smiled. "Anyone should, regardless of what realm they live in."

Roble glanced at Portia. "Thanks for watching over her."

"Any time. May I ask how you enjoyed your meal?" Portia asked him.

"It was amazing. Far better than I've enjoyed in quite some time."

"And the hospitality?"

Roble chuckled. "I'm sure you'll learn more of that tomorrow."

"Oh? Something I should concern myself with?"

"You behaved yourself, didn't you?" Shawndirea asked with a sly smile.

"As best I could, given the circumstances. But a larger concern awaits beyond the oxbow lake."

Portia's brow rose. "Like what?"

Roble described the line of torches and what he assumed it meant.

Portia smiled. "Oh ... They come every evening and stand throughout the night. They've done this for several months."

"You don't view them as a threat?"

"They're a potential threat, but they can't get past my magical barrier. They've tried and haven't succeeded."

He told of the odd light from an orb.

Portia stiffened and concern overshadowed her face. "That's new. Come, show me."

CHAPTER 45

*R*oble and Portia stepped out onto the balcony with Portia. Shawndirea sat on Roble's left shoulder. A harsh sticky breeze hinted of coming rain. The humidity magnified the acrid odor of the surrounding stagnant pools. The odor didn't bother Portia, but he gagged. How anyone adjusted to the stench was beyond him.

Roble pointed at the line of flickering torches. Near the center was the icy blue glow. "There."

Portia placed her hands on the railing and studied the orb. Her eyes widened slightly with fear. Once she regained her composure, her eyes narrowed as she intently studied the line. "The one holding the orb has not been here before."

"How do you know?" he asked.

"I'd have sensed it."

"But you didn't sense their arrival before I told you," Roble said.

"They arrive nightly and I sensed something different. I assumed it was Shawndirea's magic after she awakened."

"I sensed the sorcery, too," Shawndirea said. "One thing I can tell you about the sorcerer though."

"What's that?" Roble asked.

"It's not Lez'minx."

"That's good, I suppose."

"In a way," Shawndirea said. "But we still don't know who we're about to face."

"How can you be certain it's *not* him?" Roble asked.

"Lez'minx's magic is much darker."

"Will your magical barrier hold?" Roble asked Portia.

Portia clicked her tongue and exhaled what sounded like a slight hiss. "We can hope. Like Shawndirea said, 'we don't know who we're about to face.' Regardless, whomever stands across the oxbow understands Dagger's Tears' greatest weakness."

"What's that?" Roble asked.

"The oxbow doesn't have massive turtles to defend that front. Should the torchbearers break through the magical barrier, they can swim across the lake unharmed. We have no added defense."

"What weapons do you have to defend yourself?"

She spoke solemnly without glancing at him. "We have a few archers, but no trained swordsmen. And my magic, of course. Nothing else, as Dagger's Tears is filled with docile people."

"What about your people?" Roble asked softly. "Merla said you're the last of your tribe."

Portia took a sudden deep breath. After several moments, she nodded. "Yes, I am."

"I didn't mean to dredge up bad memories."

"Decades of time have eased the pain but not the loss."

"Are you're the last of your people?" Roble asked.

"I don't know. But, since I never plan to travel outside of Dagger's Tears, I might as well be."

"What race was your people?"

Portia smiled slightly. "We are half-breeds, the offspring of forest sprites and dryads. Because our characteristics are far different than our parents, we occupied the less miserable marshlands north of here, closer to Woodnog. Our land flourished and we beheld the sunshine, unlike the rest of the swamps."

"What happened?" Shawndirea asked.

Portia shrugged. Tears formed in her eyes. "I choose not to dwell on it. Otherwise, my bitterness would turn into malice and destroy me."

"I understood a massive flood—"

Portia nodded and politely held up her hand to silence him. "Yes, but that flood was unlike anything to ever occur in these swamps. Nothing like it has ever happened again."

A hot blast of lightning zigzagged over the river and ripped a narrow trench through the muddy bank. Thunder shook the sky and the ground. The patrols near the river's edge sprinted for cover beneath the closest building. The torchbearers across the lake didn't waver. They held fast.

Shawndirea stood on Roble's shoulder and walked down his arm until she reached the railing. "You believe someone used magic to cause the flood, don't you?"

"I do."

"Why?" Roble asked.

"The Shadowfae are darker than most understand. They're the worst of the Unseelie, full of spite and viler than an angered demon."

"Why did they directly target your village?" Roble asked.

"Because we're healers. We heal, regardless of race, and we also heal the land. The radiance of our land was reversing the swamps' darkness. The sunlight blessed our efforts, and the more sunlight that shone through the veiled sky, the faster the land healed. They had warned us, but our elders refused to yield to the Shadowfae's demands."

Lightning flickered from cloud to cloud. Drizzling rain spilled steadily. Roble hoped the rain doused the torches and sent the potential enemies away. They held their places, not even shifting their weight. Strangely, the rain didn't dim their torches.

The bluish orb glowed harsher. Roble, Portia, and Shawndirea shielded their eyes and braced themselves. After the intense light faded, the troops stood beneath a protective, magical dome, which prevented the rain from extinguishing their torches.

"Are those Saurians?" Roble asked.

"That'd be my guess," Portia replied. "But at this distance, it's uncertain. They could be Shadowfae."

"If I were stronger," Shawndirea said, "I'd fly over and examine them."

Roble shook his head. "No. Don't even consider it. Especially not in this weather."

Shawndirea offered a tired smile. "I barely have the energy to *flutter*, so don't worry about me trying to determine who they are. But I'd like to know who's taunting Dagger's Tears."

"Me, too," Portia said.

"Why aren't the warning bells ringing?" Roble asked.

"If these invaders get past the barrier, the alarms will sound. Trust me, our watchmen know they're there. Watching in silence allows us a better opportunity to study their intentions, which so far has only been to intimidate us."

The blue orb flashed. A blue fiery streak shot toward the oxbow lake. When the flame struck the invisible magical barrier, the light turned green for a second and quickly faded.

"Your barrier seems strong enough," Roble said.

"They're checking for vulnerabilities."

"If the watchmen are studying them, can't they determine if these are Saurians?"

"They stand exactly far enough away to prevent the human eye from clearly seeing them. The thin layer of mist and fog also obscures one's vision once the temperature drops."

Another bolt of blue fire hurled at the magical barrier. The fiery clash rumbled like thunder, but the fire was absorbed and faded.

"That's a bit stronger," Portia said.

"What's their motivation?" Roble asked. "If they've done this for months without success, to cross the oxbow and barrier, why do they return night after night?"

"Intimidation."

"I understand, but what do they gain should they succeed?"

"If they're Saurians, they hope to ransack the town and take our youth for slaves. The elders they'll eat. If they're Shadowfae, they know I'm here and want me because of *who* I am," Portia said softly. "Let's return indoors."

CHAPTER 46

"Why do the Shadowfae want you?" Roble asked, closing the door behind them.

Portia crossed the room and stood near a trio of tall burning candles. "Because they were unsuccessful in killing off our entire population."

"I thought you were the last—" Roble said.

"To my knowledge, I am," she replied.

"You'd think they'd do that?" Shawndirea asked. "Even if a dozen of you survived the flood, you've been separated. You power is weaker. Why would they pursue you? From what you've said, the Shadowfae are Unseelie. They generally welcome anyone with only a drop of Fae blood into their courts."

Portia shrugged. "My kind are Unseelie but our magic stems from a deeper well, so to speak."

Roble frowned. "What does that mean?"

"Your wife could explain it more in-depth. Essentially, our power's greater than the Shadowfae. But they use vile tactics to magnify their magic. Had they come to our encampment and directly challenge us with their magic, rather than using nature to produce a rampaging flood in the dead of night, we could've destroyed them." Portia's jaw tightened and she turned away. "I'm sorry, but I can't discuss this further."

Sensing Portia's growing hostility, Roble remembered what Merla had told him. Portia's longevity lasted because she never unleashed her magic with wrathful rage. Her reflection on the loss of her people rubbed a raw wound. Any further discussion might rip the scar wide open. He knew how he'd be, if he were in her situation. His wrath would know no end.

Portia noticed the saddlebags Roble had brought inside her home. "What's in those bags? Something magical?"

"Spell books and magic scrolls," Shawndirea said.

"From where?"

"A lot of these we found in Polderholm," Roble replied. "The others came from Moorsis' cottage."

"Moorsis?" Portia's eyes widened. She gently untethered one saddlebag and flipped the flap over. "I've heard of her."

"A swamp witch," Roble said.

"Yes. Her husband's buried in the Glades of Sorrow. But no one knew of her body's whereabouts."

Roble explained how Lez'minx resurrected her to do his bidding. They'd brought her remains to the Glades of Sorrow to be buried with her husband.

"This is the same Lez'minx whose temple you seek?"

Roble nodded.

"Why do you seek him?"

"To be released from these rings." Roble held up his hands. "He cast a spell on them and I can't take them off."

"I see." Portia's brow furrowed as she silently evaluated the situation. "He kept Moorsis his prisoner for all those years? Making her do evil things by enslaving those who sought magical enchantments?"

Shawndirea smiled. "That's putting it politely."

"I don't know him, but now, my interest is piqued," Portia said. "Let me meditate about the situation. If you don't mind, could I read these magical scrolls and books?"

Roble glanced at Shawndirea. She nodded.

Portia sighed. "I need solitude, but I have an extra empty bedroom on the other side of my home. You're welcome to sleep there, through the night. You both look extremely tired. I'll do my best to find the whereabouts of his temple by the time morning comes."

CHAPTER 47

*A*fter Lehrling and Collette finished eating, they left the bustling lodge where the others continued eating and carrying on conversations. He stood near the balcony beside her under the glow of an oil lantern. Several moths circled the flame.

They stood in silence for a couple of minutes. Leaning on the rail, he made several side-glances at her, but she never turned to meet his gaze. Even without the light of the burning wick, Lehrling believed the glowing excitement on Collette's face would've allowed him to see her features in the pitch darkness. Her broad grin tugged the deep dimples in her cheeks. She seemed a whole new person than when he met her at the lake.

Nervous, and uncertain how to start a fresh conversation, he said, "You were right about the meal. I've eaten at royal banquets and the food here is more savory and delightful than anywhere I've been. I ate far more than my fair share."

Immediately, he regretted those words while patting his swollen stomach. He feared she'd think him a glutton. But his words didn't seem to register with her. They drew less attention than a whistling wind through densely leafed tree branches. She seemed in her own little realm, and perhaps her mind visited such a place. Her intense gaze was like a child playing a new game with enriched delight dancing inside her.

Her smile radiated and her voice became giddy. "I'm glad you enjoyed the meal. Oh, I *must* thank Roble for standing up to my father and coming to my defense like he did. I—I'm so excited. I don't know what to do next."

Lehrling smiled, but silently he berated himself for not being the one to have challenged her father. Roble proved his backbone again, but Lehrling seldom displayed an authoritative tone. He wasn't a coward but he hated public confrontations. His voice stammered whenever his anger escalated. But the more Lehrling thought about the situation, the more he liked that he *hadn't* been harsh to her father, in spite of her father's bullying attitude and lashing anger.

Roble might be viewed as a hero for abruptly scolding the old man in front of the hamlet, but Lehrling—had he actually confronted her father —might have later been viewed in a much lesser light, especially if things between he and Collette soured. She might blame him for whatever tragedies they might suffer.

"What should I pack? What should I leave behind?" Collette asked more to herself than to Lehrling. Her voice was softer, almost childlike, and suddenly he viewed their age difference as much broader than before. She'd been isolated for so long that perhaps her mind never fully matured toward independence. Though excited, she didn't understand what it meant to leave her family and Dagger's Tears behind.

He was slightly amused by her happiness and wanted to join her celebration, but the sudden idea of leaving the hamlet caused her to regress. She sounded like a child and not the solemn lady he first met.

She paused and grew silent for several moments. Her brow furrowed and she wrung her hands together.

"What's wrong?"

"How will I journey with you?" Collette asked. "You only have two horses. You've no extra room for me or *my* belongings. Of course I don't possess much. I live modestly, as it is. All of us do. I have a few work pants and tunics that won't take up much room. I suppose I could walk—"

"No lady can walk through these swamps. It's far too dangerous," Lehrling said. "I'd not hear of it."

"Certainly there's no room on your horse for the two of us," she said.

"I'm not *that* big," Lehrling protested with a forced smile, while trying not to show his actual offense. He was fifty pounds lighter than a year earlier and quite proud he'd not gained it back.

"Of course not!" She smiled. "But the mire and quicksand and the streams you need to cross. The more weight your beast bears, the less stability it'd have. Or am I wrong?"

"While that's true, Collette, he's a young, strong stallion and capable of bearing our weight, but—"

"See?" She sighed, rested her elbows on the balcony railing, and clasped her hands together.

Lehrling stared at her side profile. Her sad eyes looked across the darkened hamlet. He wanted to pull her into his arms and comfort her, tell her they'd find a way, but that gave her false hope and wasn't fair. Besides, he didn't know her well enough to be so bold or how she'd respond since she kept herself at a safe distance from him, which was suitably fine. If she fawned over him and constantly fluttered her eyelids when she looked at him, he'd think less of her.

She was a lady. Everything about her indicated such. She didn't display mixed signals, but he stood on the bridge between the hope of being more than friends with her, or her viewing him as an old doting fool. Perhaps, she thought more of him as an uncle or a replacement father.

This raging emotional conflict inside his mind wasn't the only thing he needed to deal with. He'd promised Roble to inform Collette they couldn't take her with them until *after* the situation with Lez'minx was resolved. Seeing her near broken spirit, how much worse would she become when he told her.

"I'll have to walk," she said with a firm nod. The excitement and boldness renewed in her eyes. She stood upright and took a deep breath before facing him. She smiled broadly and placed her hand on his forearm. "It's settled. I'll walk alongside you."

"No, Collette, you *can't* walk. That'd be too foolish to attempt. The dangers are too great. Snakes, poisonous plants—"

"I deal with those things every day, Lehrling. I've snatched poisonous snakes from fishnets and out of the water and cut their heads off with my skinning knife. I can identify a lot of the poisonous plants, as some grow within our hamlet. I'm more than capable of taking care of myself. If anything worse encounters us, you and Roble can protect me, right?" she asked. "After all, you're both knights."

Lehrling sighed and patted her hand.

"Oh, don't you dare tell me I can't leave with you after Roble's remarkable display! Almost everyone voted in favor of me leaving. Do you realize how embarrassed I'd be, having to stay behind?"

"Yes, I understand. Collette—"

She jerked her hand away.

Lehrling stepped closer and in a pleading tone, he said, "I've not said anything either way yet, now have I?"

"Your actions speak loud enough. You said you'd be honored to show me the things my heart desires."

"You've no idea how overjoyed I'd be to witness you beholding the beauty of new lands and seeing the sun for the first time." Lehrling offered a caring smile. "Collette, please calm down. Your emotions are running every which way."

She clenched her hands around the material of her dress and took a deep breath and slowly exhaled. "I'm sorry. You're right. There's just so many ideas rushing through my head right now." She laughed. "I must sound like a brainless fool to you."

"No-o-o—"

"You need to understand though, if you don't mind my prattling."

"I love listening to you."

"From the time I rise in the morning until late in the evening, all I've ever known is cleaning and gutting fish, hanging them on lines to dry, and helping other women wash garments in that nasty, dingy lake. It's constant toil. *Nothing* exciting. Nothing tomorrow will be different. Not *here*. My life's dismal."

Lehrling nodded but offered no words. He wouldn't want to live under those conditions.

"For years, I've dreamed and imagined what's outside our community, but feared I'd never know. Thanks to Roble and you, I'll finally know. I struggle with my fears of seeing it snatched away. It's not real until Dagger's Tears is behind me, a memory. Should something prevent me from going with you while it's within my grasp, I'd become totally devastated. I never act like this. I honestly don't."

"I understand."

"No, you don't. I don't understand my behavior. I've so many pent up emotions and thoughts bursting through my mind that, I'm having a difficult time reeling them in. Thank you, and I need to thank Roble, too, because what you've done and are doing has made me happier than I ever imagined I could become. If that changes, and I'm denied this, I'd rather die." Collette wiped fresh tears from her eyes. "I can't survive the pain of such a broken heart."

Lehrling was a loss for words. He couldn't tell her or deny her the opportunity to leave with them. Roble could protest, and he would, but since Roble had a sturdier spine than Lehrling did, Roble would need to break the sorrowful news to Collette. Lehrling couldn't. He couldn't break anyone's heart like that.

A bright blue fire danced across the sky. Lehrling suddenly noticed the line of torchbearers on the other side of the lake. The blue fiery orb exploded and vanished before it reached the bank of the lake.

"What was that?" Lehrling asked.

Collette looked where the blue fire extinguished and shook her head. "I don't know."

"Who are the torchbearers?"

"We don't know, but they come to the lake border every night."

"For what purpose?"

"We don't know."

A second blue bolt sped through the air, struck an invisible barrier, and vanished on impact.

"But *those* blasts aren't something we've seen before," Collette said.

Lehrling grabbed her hand and squeezed slightly. "Well, that kills the thought of us walking along the lake's edge, huh?"

Curiosity creased her brow. She smiled and looked in his eyes. After studying him, she lowered her gaze and blushed. "I suppose so."

A blast of harsh blue light exploded against the magical barrier and shook the ground. The impact shushed all the insects and night birds.

Cries of alarm echoed from the night watchmen. The alarm bell clattered with extreme urgency.

"Let's find Roble," Lehrling said. "He's at Portia's home, but I'm not sure which direction to go."

"Follow me."

CHAPTER 48

*B*efore Roble carried Shawndirea to the other side of Portia's home, the building's foundation shook. Seconds later, the alarm bell near the oxbow docks clattered with urgency. In spite of his fatigue, he stopped and turned.

Roble glanced at Portia with curiosity. "That was a pretty severe attack."

Portia balanced against the table to prevent falling. "Indeed. If they've not broken through the magical barrier, it won't take much more before they do."

Roble gently placed Shawndirea on the table. "I'll be right back."

"You're *not* leaving me here!" Shawndirea frowned.

"You're too weak to—"

She fumed. "That's for me to decide."

Roble opened his mouth, but she pointed a firm finger and narrowed her eyes even more.

"No," she said, "I need to see what's occurred. Even from a distance, I can advise. Trust me, I won't fly into battle, if that's what you're thinking. I'm not foolish. But Portia needs my help."

"She's right," Portia said. "At this point, I need any magical knowledge available since we don't know the sorcerer we're dealing with.

Besides, we can't waste valuable time arguing. We need to know if they've broken through the barrier."

Shawndirea stepped back and attempted a short sprint into flight, but her weakened wings couldn't lift her off the table. Roble caught her on the palm of his hand. Rather than saying anything, he placed her on his shoulder and walked to the door.

Inside, her stubbornness made him grin. They were the perfect match, though she'd protest, based on his assessment.

They stood at the corner on the balcony. The yellow line of torches flickered across the water. These soldiers had not moved. They held their ground. The light of the blue orb intensified again.

"The barrier somehow withstood their last attack," Portia said. "But it won't last much longer."

"Can you reinforce it?" Shawndirea asked.

Portia stood in silence. Her eyes analyzed what Roble's could not. At least from his perspective, she could actually see the magical barrier that secured the oxbow lake's outer edge. Since her magic constructed the wall, she could see it. "I could try, for what little it'll probably do."

"Why's that?" Roble asked.

"It took days of meditation to properly align the barrier and connect it to the terrain."

Shawndirea lowered onto the balcony rail.

The watchmen of Dagger's Tears rushed with torches to the inside bank of the oxbow. If the barrier fell, the enemy needed to swim across the narrow lake, which benefited the inhabitants should the enemy pursue an attack. Swimming made the enemy more vulnerable than being on foot.

Townsfolk spilled from the lodge and stood along the balconies in the glowing torchlights. Their frightened voices chattered with such intensity that what they questioned and said to one another was a cacophony impossible to interpret.

The sorcerer's orb glowed like a small blue sun. The light was too intense to view directly. The sorcerer held fast, not hurling the bolt, but this could be a distraction to allow his comrades an attempt to find a different way around the barrier.

"What's he doing?" Roble whispered.

Shawndirea's nervous eyes peered into his. "He's funneling more magic. Brace yourself. The next bolt he releases will be the worst yet."

"The barrier's not going to hold?"

Shawndirea shook her head. "I doubt any of the buildings will remain standing after this explosive attack. The buildings could splinter into millions of pieces and kill everyone. This sorcerer has a goal to be as destructive as necessary. Total annihilation might not be enough to satisfy him."

"Silence, please," Portia whispered.

Portia arched her back and raised her hands toward the sky. Her eyes rolled back. The light from all the nearby lanterns dimmed as she pulled their energy to her. The wooden planks of the balcony buckled and creaked.

Roble stepped back and stared in awe. Thick roots formed around her feet and curled up her legs, across the balcony planks, and spindled downward to the wet ground. The mossy hair on her arms stretched into tendrils of ivy and weaved across the balcony rail and down the thick corner posts that supported the building.

Shawndirea drew her magic from the earth and its flora, but he'd never witnessed anything as incredible as what Portia was doing. She was physically becoming one with nature. It was bizarre watching her face and skin harden like thick tree bark. Was she still able to communicate with them?

"Roble!" Lehrling shouted from below.

Roble peered over the balcony and placed his finger to his lips.

Lehrling nodded, shuffled his steps, and then almost fell backwards. Coiled at his feet were ivy vines and roots that connected Portia to the earth. They rustled and writhed like large snakes ready to strike as the ground quaked from the sorcerer's attack on the magical barrier.

The intense, shimmering blue orb hummed with powerful vibration. The hairs on Roble's neck stiffened and his skin tingled. They were standing in an electrical field of magic. With as little time to prepare as Portia had, could she ward off the next powerful strike?

The collision of her magic against the sorcerer's would, no doubt, cause an explosion that might kill them all. He took Shawndirea in his hands and held her close to his chest. She pressed her cheek against him. Her bewildered eyes were drawn toward what happened next.

The warm, humid air strangely cooled like the moment before heavy black clouds released their pent up rain, only this wasn't a natural storm. The power building on the other side of the lake was far worse. So much that the drizzling rain ceased. Fog crept from the river and slowly veiled the river banks like tethering giant ghosts.

A dozen or more yellow streaks of lightning zipped across the sky. All the lightning strands connected and descended in a fierce, single blast and struck the ground near the oxbow's edge. The rumbling thunder quaked and shook the ground with enough force that the orb lost some of its intensity.

Had the sorcerer missed? Viewing the intense, fiery light, Roble expected the abrupt impact to send shock waves hurtling in their direction.

Between the curved tip of the oxbow and the river, a net of energy zipped across the wet ground like a glowing spider's web or a fisherman's flung net. The radiating sparks crackled and zigzagged to the line of torchbearers. The chain lightning was a frightening display of power and scorched everything in its path.

One by one the torches snuffed, followed by the hideous, terrorized screams of something not human, and the silence of death came quickly. Across the oxbow, only the sorcerer remained standing. The glowing orb of power atop his staff dimmed and blackened.

The strange electrical waves of jagged energy crept across the dead bodies and encircled the sorcerer. The chain lightning slowly wrapped his legs and encased him inside a blue fiery cocoon. The sorcerer emitted a harsh rasping sound, and he struggled to get outside of the electrical-fiery web. He reared his head and raised his magical staff. Shouting in his strange language, he sought to either break free or summon his source of magic to return to the orb. But whatever netted around him doused his magic, robbed him of whatever strength he possessed, and after a few minutes of helpless struggling, he dropped facedown in the mud. His long serpent-like tail rose and stiffened for a moment, and as the last of his life faded, his reptilian tail grew limp and dropped to his side.

"You did it!" Roble said. "They're dead, even the sorcerer."

Portia opened her bewildered eyes. Stiff as a tree, she stared across Dagger's Tears at the fading chain lightning on the other side of the lake. Unable to move, she said, "What? I didn't cast a spell yet."

Perplexed, Shawndirea said, "That wasn't you?"

"No. I'm still drawing magic from the earth, but little's available." She blinked slowly. "What happened? What did you see?"

Roble told her about the energy wave that resembled a net of lightning and how it killed all the torchbearers.

"You didn't cast the waves of chain lightning?" Shawndirea asked.

"No." Portia exhaled and closed her eyes. Her roots and tendrils slowly regressed.

"Then who did?" Roble asked.

Portia didn't speak for several minutes. Her appendages continued recoiling and reshaping. When she returned to her normal appearance, she staggered and fell against the balcony rail, too weak to hold herself up.

Roble rushed to side and looped his arm beneath hers to keep her steady and make certain she didn't plummet headfirst over the railing. "Let's get you inside."

Portia panted. Sweat meandered from her dampened hair, down her face, and she braced against him. "Thank you."

Before Roble walked her to the door, Shawndirea climbed on his shoulder. Lehrling and Collette ascended the wooden ramp and stood on the balcony. Lehrling opened the door for them.

"What happened out there?" Lehrling asked.

"We're trying to figure that out," Roble replied. He led Portia to a cushioned chair, and she plopped down. "They were Saurians, but they're all dead."

"Saurians? How could you tell from that distance?" Collette asked.

Portia's head lulled to the side. Only the slits of her eyes revealed she was partially awake. Her transformation had drained her and was taking its toll. She grew weaker by the second.

Roble offered Portia a wineskin. She accepted it with a weak hand.

"When the sorcerer died, his tail stiffened, so I assume they were Saurians," Roble said.

Portia nodded. "Yes. I've no doubts, either. Nothing else in these swamps would've attempted such a challenge."

"Not even the Shadowfae?" Roble asked.

"Most Shadowfae have no need to attack from that direction. Some could fly across the river."

Collette squatted beside Portia's chair. "It sapped your energy to kill them?"

"I didn't kill them," she replied.

Shawndirea sat on the edge of the table near Portia. Like Portia, she remained extremely weak.

Collette shook her head. "They weren't killed by their own race or their own magic."

"I agree," Portia said. She gulped down the contents of the wineskin.

"I had nothing to do with it," Shawndirea said. "I don't have enough energy to fly."

The door to Portia's home flung open and harshly struck the wall. An outlined shadow of someone stood outside the door, but not enough light revealed who or what the visitor was.

"It was I. I killed them all."

CHAPTER 49

*R*oble turned to the doorway with his fingers grasping the hilts of his concealed throwing knives.

"Who are you?" Roble asked.

"Why should I reveal it to *you*?" the female replied. "You're not the host, nor are you her servant. You're a stranger. *I'm* not."

"I'm sorry. I don't recognize your voice." Portia leaned her head against the back of her chair with her eyes barely opened. "Who are you?"

The woman, dressed in leather armor, stepped across the threshold. Her hands clasped around a long staff with a shimmering emerald orb flickering at the top. Her eyes were like Portia's, only a darker green. Her long braided hair was mossy green and hung down her back like curled ivy. Her smile revealed her pointed teeth. "You don't recognize your own sister?"

Portia studied the woman's face. Her eyes widened with sudden recognition. She gasped. "Daphne?"

"Yes."

Tears, thick like beads of oil, etched meandering paths down Portia's cheeks. "I thought I was the only one who survived the flood."

Daphne's face almost glowed. She rushed and embraced Portia. "Quite a few of us survived, sister. We scattered to different areas of the swamp after the flood. It took me years to find other survivors. I suspect the more I hunt, the more of us I'll find. We're not easy to kill, but our magic's weaker when we're apart from one another. That's why I'm regathering our tribe."

"Where are the others you've found?" Portia asked with concern and great interest.

Daphne's uneasy gaze passed from each of those in the room. She hesitated her answer.

"It's okay. They can be trusted," Portia said.

Her eyes remained uncertain, untrusting. "Perhaps. But I won't risk it. I'll reveal that with you in private."

"I understand, sister, but I'm too weak to be alone. Did you travel here with a party?"

"Aqese and Ki'wese are examining the dead Saurians and await my return. They expect you to return with me."

Portia frowned. "I'm in no condition to travel. They're welcome to come inside."

Daphne smiled. "I'll inform them."

"The attackers are Saurians?" Roble asked.

"Yes." She studied Roble's eyes for a long while. Her eyes narrowed when she gazed at his rings. She scoffed.

"How'd you find me?" Portia asked.

"I sensed your aura as we were heading upriver. You seemed troubled, stressed. After seeing the invaders, I understand why. What placed you in such a weakened state?"

"I attempted to summon a petrification spell to bind them to the earth and have the mire suck them under," Portia replied.

Daphne pursed her lips and cocked a brow. "*That* depleted your energy?"

Portia nodded. "Yes."

"My dear sister, have you been out of practice for so long that such a simple spell depletes you?"

"I had no time to prep beforehand."

"Still—"

"I know," Portia said with a tired smile.

"Journey with us and rebuild your strength," Daphne said.

"To where?"

"Linden-hold."

"The flood destroyed it ages ago," Portia said.

"It's our home. If enough of us return, we can heal the scarred land and return it to the prominence we knew, where we thrived. But should the Shadowfae attack again, we'll be prepared."

"Dagger's Tears needs me."

Daphne shook her head. Her eyes narrowed. "They use you."

"That's not true," Collette said. Lehrling placed a gentle hand on her shoulder.

"Isn't it?" Daphne eyed Collette harshly. "What does Portia contribute to your hamlet other than her magic? Bit by bit her strength has been taken because of your greed."

"Don't blame them," Portia said. "This was my choice. I was tired of living alone. I want to heal the afflicted, regardless of what it costs me. It comforts me."

"The cost's more than you should suffer. What have they given in return?"

"A home. Protection."

"*You* protect *them*," Daphne said.

"In a sense, yes. But, sister, they've welcomed me as a part of their extended family. They supply my food and gather whatever herbs and ingredients I request for magic."

"*We* are your family. Our kind. Never forget that."

Portia sighed. "Until now, I thought *I* was the last of our tribe. I'd given up on anyone else surviving."

"You should've been able to locate us, like I located you."

"I tried."

"Recently?"

Portia looked away. "No. Many years ago. I've accepted this as my home."

Daphne waved her hands in the air and spiraled. "Home? *This?*"

Shawndirea crossed her arms. "For two sisters who've not seen one another for decades, this isn't the most friendly reunion."

Daphne frowned. Her eyes shimmered like silvery dew in harsh sunlight.

"Why scold her?" Shawndirea said. "You could restore her strength with your magic."

"Well, faery, she'd not be in this weakened state had she not chosen to live where others continuously sap her power." She faced Portia. "Do you not understand why you're so weak?"

Portia shook her head. "I've not given it much thought. I've never experienced this level of feebleness until today. I've always kept my strength, even to heal others, and even when I healed this faery."

Shawndirea and Roble looked at her with sudden curiosity.

"You healed me?" Shawndirea asked.

"Of course." Portia shrugged. "Somewhat, anyway. Enough to awaken you. Perhaps rejuvenation would be a better term. You were a bit askew."

Roble frowned. "Why didn't you tell me you could awaken her?"

Portia ignored his question and returned her attention to Daphne. "I've done as I know to do, sister. To heal those who come to me and never harbor wrath against those who've done us wrong. Had I sought vengeance, my life would've already ended."

"*This* place isn't your home," Daphne said. "In fact, this town's the reason you nearly died tonight. By trying to perform a simple spell. Your magic's not what it should be. You've not regenerated your aura. Your mantle's razor thin. Do you know why?"

"I'm sure you'll tell her," Shawndirea said.

Daphne's jaw tightened. "Sister, as half-dryad, we draw our greatest strength from the forests, from the *trees*. Dagger's Tears is barren and stagnant. Your hut's surrounded by water, *not* trees. Not the magical life source *we* need and desire in order to maintain our strength. Sunlight's also essential, but not seen in the depths of these cursed swamps.

"The spell you attempted earlier would've killed you had we not intervened. Your tendrils reached deep into the stagnant mire to search for kindred trees, but the nearest tree is far beyond your grasp. Instead of drawing magic from nature, nature sapped you. Your death would've ended the magical barrier and opened the way for the Saurians to cross easily."

Portia took a deep breath, closed her tired eyes, and shook her head.

"Another reason you're weakened was because the Saurian sorcerer was drawing his power from your magical barrier. It's quite possible his next launched bolt would've ripped the barrier in half and allowed their invasion to be success."

Shawndirea's anger lessened and she uncrossed her arms. "That's a valid interpretation."

Daphne gave Shawndirea a shrewd side-glance, rolled her eyes, and shook her head. "Without trees, you've not been able to renew your magic, Portia. Each time you've healed others, your energy lessens."

"So if you and her magic are drawn from the fertile life of trees," Roble said, "why couldn't she draw from the land here? The soil in most swamps is composed of layers of dead matter and sphagnum mosses, which is the best quality to enrich trees and plants outside the swamp."

"Even you, Overlander, should know that you can't draw life from the dead. Since these swamps are cursed, the dead matter was stealing her magic and life without her realizing it. The land's cursed. The only reason we survived in Linden-hold was because our combined energy birthed new life into the earth. Our magic slowly dissipated the curse, which caused the Shadowfae to despise us even more."

Portia nodded. "How do we know Linden-hold still exists? Could we find it?"

"We've mapped most of the southern Woodnog Swamp region. Linden-hold remains to the north, based on my memory of familiar landmarks. However, decades have passed. Some places no longer exist. As to our former settlement? Most likely, it's in ruins. However, with the bond of our regathered tribe members, we can rebuild it. Once we've reestablished it, sunlight will bless our tribe again."

Collette gave Lehrling a bright hopeful smile.

"You've mapped the region south of here?" Roble asked.

"Yes."

"I'd love to study those maps, if you don't mind."

Daphne gave him a curious stare. "Daring enough to venture deeper into places where even holy deities never tread?"

"Actually," Portia said, "he and his party are looking for a temple."

"A temple?" Daphne asked with curiosity furrowing her brow.

Roble nodded.

"Whose temple?"

Portia adjusted in her seat. Her tired eyes glanced at her sister. "The name's unfamiliar, but he's insisted Roble finds him. His name's Lez'minx."

"Lez'minx?" Daphne's eyes widened.

"You know him?" Portia asked.

"You know him, too," she replied.

Portia shook her head. "I do not."

"Ah, but you do, sister. Only by a *different* name. He's one of us."

"What's his true name?"

"Runefel," Daphne replied.

"Our brother?"

"The same." She glanced at Roble. "I noticed your rings. Has he bewitched you with them?"

"For a time. I can't get them off," Roble replied.

Daphne chewed her lower lip and shook her head. "Humans are so gullible."

A slight grin stretched on Portia's lips.

Shawndirea giggled.

Roble frowned.

"What'd you hope to gain by wearing these rings?" Daphne asked.

"I wanted to see what they did."

"He never told you?"

"No."

"Why be such a fool?" She didn't await an answer. "What'd you learn about the rings?"

Roble cleared his throat. "He used them to spy on us."

"Our brother." Daphne sighed and looked at Portia with a sly grin. "Still up to his old tricks."

"Indeed," Portia said.

"You remember what he did to us the final time we saw him before the flood?"

Portia nodded. "I shall never forget. I swore he'd regret that, but after the flood, my hope of repaying his ill deed was washed away."

Daphne glanced at the rings again. "We should keep our voices lowered, lest he hear us."

"Shawndirea cast a spell to prevent him from using the stones as looking glasses," Roble said.

A wild grin spread on Daphne's face. Her pointy, sharp teeth made her smile more sinister. "Good. He'll be caught off guard when we confront him."

Lehrling's brow rose. "You'll help us?"

"Oh, what we have in mind has nothing to do with the solution to your problem. Roble's far more indebted to Lez'minx than what he's yet revealed." She came closer and slid her hand along his leather chest piece. "His magic flows through your armor, too, does it not?"

Roble nodded.

"Instead of diving an inch, you dove fathoms."

"Can you remove these rings?" Roble held his hands out.

Daphne shook her head. "No. Only he can. The true question should be, 'Will he?'"

"You don't think he will?" Roble asked.

Daphne shrugged. "It depends on the value of what he wishes to con from you."

Lehrling sighed with relief when he looked at Roble. "At least we know we're not confronting a god or a demigod."

Daphne chuckled. "A god or demigod would have more mercy than Lez'minx. He's incapable of such. What's he demanding in return for these … gifts? Let me guess. Devoted loyalty? Reverence?"

"He's never told me, but he threatened Shawndirea's life. For that, I plan to find him," Roble said sternly. "Once I find his temple, he won't enjoy our encounter."

Daphne was humored by his statement. "He doesn't have a temple. He lives in a cave beneath a massive swamp oak, much like a worm burrows in filthy, slimy mud to hide."

"He killed several dozen Shadowfae mercenaries," Shawndirea said.

Daphne's face withered. She sighed. "He's an expert in making enemies. This time he might've gone too far."

Portia nodded. "I agree. Since our brother's a common enemy to Roble and his party, it's time we take action and join his cause, sister."

"My dear Portia, you're right. It's long overdue."

CHAPTER 50

*T*he following morning Roble awoke in Portia's spare room with renewed energy. With his senses heightened, he was more alert than he'd been during their entire journey through the Woodnog swamps.

Shawndirea's face glowed with radiance while she slept. He gently nudged her, since she'd been so drained the past several days.

Her eyelids fluttered open, and she smiled at him.

"How do you feel this morning?" he asked.

She stretched her arms and yawned. Her brightened eyes searched the room. "Oddly, I feel energized."

"Me, too."

"I feel *spritely*." She smiled, moved her wings, and hovered above the pillow. She zipped across the room and back. "I've regained my strength, but I'm bursting with liveliness I haven't possessed for days. It's almost … magical. Wait—"

"What?"

She placed her index finger to her lips and motioned to the door. Her odd frown heightened his curiosity.

Roble walked to the door as she flew along beside him. Before he reached the door handle, a humming sensation filled the air. The hairs on his neck rose and his skin tingled beneath the armor. The humming sound was similar to fluorescent lights in the Overlands, but the prickling along his skin indicated something more hung in the air.

He grabbed the door handle and turned.

"Careful," Shawndirea whispered and fluttered upward.

Roble nodded and slowly pulled the door inward. The humming increased and the pulses radiated a pleasurable warmth. A giddy feeling passed through him.

Standing at the table where Shawndirea had undergone her deep sleep were Portia and Daphne. In the center of the table, a large luminous, yellow Elfstone pulsed a steady glow of light.

Portia beamed. She showed no signs of weakness from the night before. Her face held more color than when Roble first brought Shawndirea to her. Portia's features had altered from the appearance of a drought-sickened plant to a regenerated one after a healthy summer rain. Hope renewed in the brightness of her eyes.

The newness and revived glow in Portia's features reinforced Daphne's explanation of how the swampland was draining Portia's aura. Roble never noticed how drained Portia was at their first meeting, but now, after her vigor had returned, she had come close to death.

"Good morning." Portia said to Roble and Shawndirea.

"It's a far better morning," Shawndirea replied.

Daphne smiled. She rolled out a large parchment on the table and Portia placed heavy objects at the map's corners. "While you slept, I sketched a map of the swamp territory to the north where Linden-hold once thrived. Of course, this is from my memories before the massive flood, so some landmarks might not remain."

Roble stepped to the table and studied the map. "Where do you expect Lez'minx to be?"

Daphne placed a finger to the northeast of Dagger's Tears in what looked to be a thick wooded area. "Here."

"The Ruins of Saggy-nook?"

She nodded.

"What's there, besides the ruins?" Roble studied her crude map.

Portia smiled. "As children, before we were shunned and set off to establish Linden-hold, we spent a vast amount of time playing in the old ruins, over a century and a half ago. The ruins were once occupied by Orcs, and a few artifacts we found support that theory."

"Orcs?" Roble asked.

She and Daphne nodded.

Daphne said, "Some artifacts indicated humans were there as well. One was enslaved to the other, as neither race would co-exist peacefully. We believe the Orcs were the ones in power, though it can't be proven."

"What caused the town's demise?" Roble asked.

"Not a town. Saggy-nook, the name we called it as children, was an incredible city at one time. Its real name we never knew since we couldn't read the language carved into the grand entrance ways. Most of the city sank beneath the swamp's mire over time."

Shawndirea frowned. "Why would Lez'minx reside there?"

Daphne shrugged. "The massive swamp oak was near the center of the city and beneath its giant roots are catacombs where we loved to hide and explore. Even as children, we sensed its well of unending magical power and fed off its source to increase our own. Even if the lower regions of the city have sunken, the oak's far too massive to ever be engulfed."

"Wouldn't the overly saturated ground rot the roots?" Roble asked.

Daphne smiled, almost mockingly. "For a normal tree, Overlander, yes. But magic protects the tree."

"Then," Shawndirea said, "Lez'minx wields the tree's magic for his own benefit?"

Portia glanced at Daphne with grave concern.

Daphne nodded. "Yes, he must."

"Then we've a greater problem than we thought." A worried expression claimed Shawndirea's features.

Lehrling frowned. "What?"

"Daphne and Portia draw their magic from the trees." Shawndirea clicked her tongue against the roof of her mouth, and then she crossed her arms. Her eyes revealed the depth of her thoughts, which were overshadowed with equal concern as the two sisters. "Such a tree, already empowered by powerful magic, could wreak total devastation against other cities if someone properly siphoned the magic for his or her own use. If that's Lez'minx's magical source, he'd be worse to confront than a demigod or demon."

Lehrling's brow rose. He swallowed hard. "W-w-worse?"

Shawndirea said, "He killed nearly two dozen Shadowfae assassins in an instant. I imagine he could do far worse." She looked at Daphne. "Did you know he was capable of murder?"

Daphne took a sharp breath and after a few moments of thought, she shook her head. "No. He's always been prone to his mischievous pranks. He never physically harmed anyone. But, understand, neither Portia nor myself have seen him since the flood. I wasn't certain he was still alive."

Portia nodded. "He's hidden himself well."

"Why haven't either of you sought to return to Saggy-nook?" Shawndirea asked.

"It was a fondness of our youth," Daphne said, "but not a place to set up residence."

"Why not?" Roble asked.

"Ghosts," Portia said. "Strange magic-feeding creatures are attracted to the magical tree and ventured in, which is dangerous for anyone who wields magic."

"Why?" Roble asked.

"They drain their magic from anything. Whenever they capture someone or something with magical abilities, they feast until the life source of the individual shrivels," Daphne said.

Lehrling frowned. "Why attack others for magic, when they could feast on the tree's source of magic?"

Daphne said, "Being near the tree is overwhelming and cause the feeders' minds to grow into a frenzy. They're intoxicated by the flow. They often turn on one another, crazed by the sudden flux, and some of the fights turn bloody. Those who feed directly on the tree never live long. The rush of power causes them to explode like old wineskins filled with new wine."

"This influx never affected you?" Shawndirea asked.

Portia folded and rested her hands against her stomach. "We were new to our abilities, so our spells and desires were basic. We had no reason to gorge on the excessive magic wells. We never understood the driven need of these creatures and wizards. Hidden behind the soft, winged leaves, we watched from the boughs. We questioned and we learned through observation. However, the longer we watched, the less we viewed the tree as a sanctuary. We witnessed more death than advantages and often battles ensued for control of the tree. Peace never resided there.

"As children, these bloody battles between overzealous feeders, mages, and wizards frightened us. After we got caught between two dueling wizards, we vowed to never return. As an adult, I realize the dangers of returning since I better understand magic. Our arrival might merely be taken as a challenge to any others tapping into the tree's source."

"So, if Lez'minx lives with access to this wealth of magic, why's he interested in me?" Roble asked. "I'm hardly someone—"

"It's not *you* he's interested in," Portia said. "It's his ability to work *through* you to lessen the toll on himself."

"How?" Roble frowned.

Shawndirea smiled. "Magic, my dear, always comes at a price. How many times must I say this?"

"She's right," Daphne said. "Some wizards and mages imprison and sacrifice slaves in order to use the darkest sorceries while lessening the cost for themselves."

Lehrling's brow rose. "Are you serious?"

"Quite."

"I never fathomed such a thought."

"Others are far worse," Portia said. "Have you considered what Tyrann does to maintain the darkness shrouding the City of Mortel?"

Lehrling shuddered but didn't reply.

"Roble," Portia said. "This is why Moorsis did whatever Lez'minx demanded of her. Probably why he enticed you with the burden of the rings."

"He's never asked me to do anything except to find him," Roble replied.

"Therein lies the danger," Daphne said.

"Why?" Roble asked.

Shawndirea's brow narrowed. "Yes, why?"

"If he's at the tree, he could be luring you so he can sacrifice you and the faery. With the proper blood sacrifice, he can funnel greater quantities of the tree's magic without suffering direct repercussions."

"Dear Goddesses!" Lehrling gasped. "Roble, we mustn't go."

"Oh, but we must," Daphne said.

"Are you mad?" Lehrling said, angrily.

"No, but to save our brother from himself, we've no better opportunity to confront him," Daphne replied.

"You're mad," Lehrling said. "It's his territory and his power outweighs yours, Portia's, and Shawndirea's combined! We won't survive this."

"The only ones capable of reasoning with him are his kin," Daphne said.

Portia nodded. "Most likely, he thinks us dead, too. If so, it better explains why he's so angry and seeks to inflict massive pain on others without fearing repercussions. He's like a spoiled child enacting his retaliation for the massive flood that destroyed Linden-hold and his family."

"You can't justify his actions," Roble said.

"Perhaps not in your world," Daphne said.

"No. In any world, nothing grants one the obsessive need to become an executioner."

Daphne eyed him fiercely. "I'm certain your faery explained how things work in our realm? Has she not?"

"She has but—"

"No. You don't understand what it's like in a world where magic reigns supreme. You haven't a clue," Daphne said. "Your actions prove it. You appreciate magic, as long as it benefits *you*, but for whatever reason, you won't accept its full understanding. When one is wronged by magic, or loved ones are killed by it, or as in our case, an entire village is destroyed because of the wielder, those capable of using magic have every right to retaliate."

Roble's eyes narrowed. "Doesn't that make the one seeking vengeance the same as the one he casts against?"

Daphne stared at him in silence for half a minute, never flinching or looking away. "No. It's justice. There's no equal ground when it comes to casting magic. It's always more about how to outmaneuver the other to gain the upper hand, to take advantage of an enemy's vulnerability."

"Shouldn't magic be respected?" Roble asked. "Shouldn't it be used to benefit and not harm others?"

"Of course," she replied. "But like men who carry swords or any weapon, shouldn't those only be used to protect the weak?"

"Yes."

"And yet, kings and queens send troops to invade other cities or small townships whenever the mood strikes them. They ransack and take whatever wealth the weaker hold. Whom does *that* benefit?"

"No one," Roble replied. "Magic should be viewed sacredly and respected. Its essence requires tribute in order to properly wield it, but that's too often ignored, with little thought to the possible repercussions."

Portia scoffed. "An Overlander dares to lecture *us* about magic?"

"I'm not lecturing you." Roble shook his head and then met Daphne's gaze. "Were you ever an apprentice?"

Daphne's jaw tightened. Her strange eyes almost glowed. "We're half dryad and are *attuned* to magic. We've no need to be apprentices."

Roble shook his head in disbelief. "Anyone capable of tapping into the magical resources should be properly trained. Without guidance, magic will be misused. Not everyone's pure in mind and spirit. Very few ever are. If one can't control his or her emotions, the havoc caused by unleashing uncontrolled spells is immeasurable. Were the Shadowfae faeries Lez'minx killed directly responsible of the flood you accuse them to have caused? "

"How dare you!" she spat. "You come from a world where magic faded long ago and you want to tell *us* how to behave?"

"Faded?" Roble glanced at Shawndirea with confusion. "Meaning magic was once a force in the Overlands?"

Shawndirea nodded.

"Yes, you fool. Those still capable of using magic have hidden themselves or wisely found breaches in the veil and passed through to our realm or other realms where magic flourishes."

"You ever consider magic's less accessible in my realm because of the abusive practices sorcerers conducted centuries ago?" Roble asked. "Who's to say such won't eventually occur here?"

Daphne's anger lessened. She broke eye contact, sighed, and reflected on his words. She nodded. "That's a possibility, Overlander."

Shawndirea said, "We're all on the same side. We've no reason to hash out such a bitter debate about formalities. Although, at another time, it might be critical for each of us to reflect on magic's true usage in our lives. Roble and I need to find Lez'minx for our purpose, and apparently, that's your desire as well."

"You're correct, faery," Daphne said softly. "Though it pains my pride to admit it, your husband's chastisement isn't without merit. I, along with so many others, have taken the use of magic for granted. But, I must add, we can't confront our brother without using magic to defend ourselves. I'm guessing you're not opposed to that?"

Roble held his hands out, palm-side up. "All I want is to be released from his rings and any commitment he desires from me. I'm not going to witness his death. Nor do I wish him harmed. I want freed from his bonds. Whatever you find necessary when you find him, I'll leave that at your discretion."

Daphne smiled. "Fair enough."

CHAPTER 51

*R*oble stood at the table and traced his finger along the river on the map of the swamp. "Why are there so many ruins in the swamps?"

Daphne said, "Kingdoms, over time, fall. Terrains change. Fertile, prosperous places alter over time. Climate changes. Rains cease in some regions while increasing in others. The wind's direction modifies. These elements are often beyond our control. The living either adapt, move on, or perish. Magic doesn't dispel nature's intentions. However, a lot of the ruins in Woodnog's swamps came *after* the raging flood."

"If you'll forgive me for being blunt," Roble said.

Daphne, Portia, and Shawndirea glanced intently at him.

"I mean no ill-will or criticism. It's merely my curiosity—"

Daphne's eyes narrowed. "A cat holds less curiosity than an Overlander."

Portia chuckled. "Please, sister, let him speak. As with anything, receiving answers for his questions is how he will learn."

Daphne sighed. "Very well. Go ahead."

Roble took several seconds to carefully reflect on his words before speaking. He didn't want any further resentment from Daphne. Her bitter taste toward Overlanders was obvious. "Based on your earlier statement, why do you believe the Shadowfae are responsible for the destruction of your village? What proof do you have?"

No anger surfaced on Daphne's features. "What occurred ... as is forever etched in my mind and has scarred my heart... the flood came like a sudden tidal wave. It wasn't the product of continuous, excessive rains. On that particular night, a heavy, dark force drifted with the wind. Evil saturated the night breeze. Portia, Runefel, and myself were standing outside on a balcony watching the first moon rise when the eerie breeze cut through the trees. The flood wasn't nature's doing."

Portia nodded. Sorrow claimed her eyes and voice. "I remember. We attempted to form a shield of protection around ourselves, but we didn't have enough time to prepare. We clung to one another as the large wave of water crashed around our village. I stood between Daphne and Runefel. We desperately clutched to one another. The immense pressure of the water's volume drove us deep underwater before the current yanked us apart. The dark water prevented me from seeing where they'd been taken. My world went black."

"As did mine." Daphne wiped tears from her eyes.

"I'm sorry," Roble said with genuine regret. "I understand your anger. My anger would be as furiously heated as yours. But, how do you know the Shadowfae were behind it? Could it not have been a dark mage or wizard? Or from another?"

"Time's wasting." Daphne rolled up the map. "It's best we head upriver while the day's early."

Portia looked at Collette. "You need to stay in Dagger's Tears."

Collette's eyes moistened with tears. A hurt expression overtook her facial expressions. She shook her head. "No. Lehrling promised to take me with them."

"It's not safe for any of us," Daphne said. "It'll be difficult enough for Portia and I to protect our party as it is. But Lehrling and Roble have faced battle. They're trained for combat. You put all of us at risk."

"Roble?" Collette glanced at him with desperate eyes.

"I agree with them," Roble said. "I told Lehrling the same thing while we were eating."

Hurt overshadowed her. She turned to Lehrling. "Why'd you let me believe I could leave with you? Why didn't you tell me?"

"Collette," Lehrling said, softly. "I didn't know how to tell you. Honestly, I didn't. I hoped to discuss it further with Roble—"

"You must take me with you," Collette said. "I can't stay behind. Not when you promised I could go."

"Hastily." Roble gave Lehrling a slightly hardened stare. "We can return for you after this has been taken care of."

"No!" Collette wiped away tears. "That won't do. I must go."

"Roble," Lehrling said, sheepishly. "Is there not a way we can take her?"

"We only have two horses," Roble said.

"She can ride with me," Lehrling insisted. "Or I can walk alongside her."

Daphne frowned. "You walking only *impedes* our journey. For us to be successful, Lez'minx ... Runefel must be taken by surprise. Any advanced notice of our arrival and we're all dead."

"*Please,*" Collette said.

"I'll stay behind," Lehrling said sternly. "Travel on without me."

Shawndirea gasped. "*Lehrling!*"

Roble's eyes narrowed. "You'd forsake helping a friend who saved your life on more than one occasion?"

"I'm no match for him. I can't fight magic."

Roble's tone became sour and bitter. "I might not have been directly knighted by King Erik, but Lady Dawn knighted me. I'm part of the Order. If this be your decision, so be it."

"You've given me little choice," Lehrling replied.

"Love can be so blind," Roble whispered.

"Coming from a man who risked his entire life and the world he knew to bring a faery into a realm to where he's a stranger?"

"Careful," Shawndirea said. Her eyes darkened.

Daphne cleared her throat. "Before this escalates into swords being drawn—"

"That'd never happen," Roble said. "I'd never attack a friend. No matter how much I disagree with his ideology or his extreme lack of common sense. Besides, he'd be no match for me and he knows it."

Lehrling lowered his gaze. Regret made Roble's heart ache for the sting of his insult.

Daphne sighed. "I have a proposal."

Lehrling and Collette turned their attention to her. "What?"

Daphne looked at Portia. "I may regret this."

Portia shrugged and laughed softly.

Daphne rolled her eyes. "*Love* is why dryads never seek communion with humans. It's maddening. We have room on our rafts for Collette. But once we reach Saggy-nook, our protection ceases until our affairs with Runefel are settled. Do you understand?"

"Yes," Collette said. "Bless you."

"Save the blessings for yourself," Daphne said. "You'll need them. As for you, Lehrling, since you've allowed passion to sway reason, she's your responsibility once we confront Runefel. She'll have you to thank or curse for whatever happens to her. None of us are to blame. Can you live with that?"

Lehrling swallowed hard and remained silent for several moments. His eyes searched the floor, and he didn't glance at Collette or Roble for support in making his decision. Finally, he nodded. "I will."

Collette rushed to Lehrling, wrapped her arms around his neck, and squeezed tightly.

"Then, let's prepare to depart," Daphne said. "Within the shadows, our enemies await."

CHAPTER 52

*R*oble stood beside Daphne at the river's bank. The rest of her party paddled their rafts to the bank, so everyone could step aboard. Collette and Lehrling stood a fair distance away. Collette embraced her friends and her mother and held what few possessions she wished to take with her.

Shawndirea and Portia conversed, but outside Roble's range of hearing.

Aqese and Ki'wese helped Collette onto a raft. Roble admired the architecture of the rafts, which were shaped like large, flattened canoes but the stems were coiled tendrils that resembled thick ivy vines. For all he knew, the stem necks were constructed from vines. Near the center of the gunwales were small masts with narrow sails that shimmered like meshed spider webs. The olive-colored wood camouflaged with the water and the rafts were hardly noticeable, especially from a distance. He imagined in the areas where the trees further darkened the water, the rafts were invisible.

Both of Daphne's companions wore hooded cloaks, almost the exact color of the rafts' wood. Their faces were grained like polished lumber, which he found incredibly odd. Their complexions benefited them by allowing them to blend into the trees. A few times they glanced and glared at him for rudely staring at their features too long. He meant no disrespect. He loved the diversity and unusualness of the various races in Aetheaon. His intrigue was more than his curious mind could handle.

Daphne's skin radiated as she overlooked the river. A cool breeze flowed past them. The mossy tendrils on her arms rose and swayed like minuscule blades of grass.

"You never answered my question earlier," Roble said. "So I must assume you've no actual proof the Shadowfae were responsible for the flood."

"Assumptions can get you killed," Daphne whispered without the slightest glance in his direction. Her tone indicated she was tired of his repeated questions.

"Is that a threat?"

"Not so much a threat than it's advice. Advice that might aid your survival this time tomorrow."

Tomorrow? That soon?

He attempted to quash his rising apprehension. After all this miserable time sloshing through swamplands, he'd finally confront Lez'minx, but what did he gain by doing so? Worse, he feared what he might *lose*.

As much as he admired Portia and Daphne's abilities, their ambitions for confronting their brother were far different than his own, especially Daphne's. She wasn't as effective at hiding her inner anger and rage as Portia. Most of the time, she didn't try. Her meeting with Lez'minx or Runefel—his *real* name—wasn't going to be affable in any way.

Runefel had somehow soured her affection toward him. Her need for vengeance outweighed any former cordial familial ties. Daphne wasn't like Portia. Daphne seemed capable of inflicting pain and suffering on those who crossed her without a second thought or any remorse. Portia didn't seem to possess the ability to do the same.

Daphne's strange eyes stared across the river. Her gaze indicated she was brooding and perhaps planning what she'd do after they found her brother. Although he'd rather not meet Runefel, he had no other choice if he wanted freed from the rings' bondage. However, he feared Daphne might actually kill Runefel, and if so, Roble's opportunity to be released from the rings might never come.

What happened to bound magic once its wielder died? He hoped death ended the magical ties the sorcerer had cast. That seemed the most reasonable, but nothing in Aetheaon was *ever* reasonable. It was a tossup. While he wanted the rings pried off his fingers, he didn't want to lose his armor's unique abilities to acclimate to the surrounding climates to comfort him.

The standing silence between he and Daphne was almost stagnant. She refused to acknowledge his presence even with a slight glance and kept her gaze straightaway.

Roble knew it was best to keep his silence. He needed to choose his words carefully. His uneasiness about Daphne's potential motives prevented him from doing so.

"You don't have any proof the Shadowfae caused the flood, do you?" Roble asked.

Daphne turned her head slightly and her eyes darkened as she regarded him. From his periphery he witnessed the blue sparks crackling on her fingertips but he kept his eyes locked with hers, which easily could be considered a challenge. A sheen glazed her eyes like a thin layer of blue frost. A chill jolted him. He fought hard not to look away from her frozen pools of misery. Her captivating gaze was luring. Once he understood she was trying to lull him into some form of hypnosis, he broke eye contact.

She laughed softly like whispering hummingbird wings, which echoed inside his mind; laughter meant only for him to hear. His jaw tightened. He sensed her arrogant triumph and the dominance of her power over him. He'd never been exposed to that type of drawing power, but he understood that she could, in the matter of minutes, force his mind into submission. Her capabilities were far more dangerous than he and the others had credited her. She was the complete opposite of her sister. He doubted Portia recognized the drastic change in her sister's aura since they had been apart from one another for years. Portia's weakened mind lowered her perceptiveness.

After the soft ringing laughter in his head faded, Daphne glanced at him and smiled.

"I sense the dark power behind what caused that flood," Daphne said. "It's why I journey through the swamps the way I do. I must rejoin our kindred and restore Linden-hold to its original power."

"From my understanding of the Shadowfae, their numbers are broad and differ in many ways. Most aren't evil, at least no more evil than some Seelie, but they are considered outsiders, shunned by the Seelie, as they're not *pure* Fae," Roble said. "Does this coincide with the truth?"

Daphne nodded. "Yes."

"Aren't you and your sister of the Unseelie Courts?" Roble asked.

"To some degree, yes."

"Some? Wouldn't it be either or?"

"Must we squabble over semantics?"

Roble shrugged. "Call it what you will. All I want is to understand why your near hatred stems toward an entire group of Fae, rather than narrowing your bloodlust to the rightful party that's guilty of—"

"Careful, Overlander," she hissed. Her eyes displayed a darkened pool that resembled swirling ink. "Don't meddle in the affairs that don't concern you. You've seen what happens to my enemies, or is your memory too short?"

"I'm not your enemy."

"Not yet," Daphne replied. "You seem determined to become one."

"No. I'm not against you. I only wish to understand your intentions before I defend your cause with my life and the lives of those dearest to me. You admit that you and Portia are Unseelie. Why then would the Shadowfae, who are Unseelie want to cause you great harm?"

"Because we favored bringing light into these shadowed swamps," Daphne replied. "Our understanding and use of magic is far stronger than theirs."

"Why did they oppose your actions? They don't have to journey into your town."

Daphne shrugged. "Their hideous features makes them seek the shadows. They may have viewed us as a threat; not fully understanding our intentions. At no time had we ever sought to bless the entire swampy regions into fertile workable lands. That would only invite humans to further corrupt and distort what we worked so hard to achieve. We only wanted *our* town that way."

"Did you ever express that to them?" Roble asked.

She leveled a frown at him. "They never offered us such a chance."

"So, in return, you've no intention to seek a peaceful negotiation?"

Daphne sighed angrily. "Why do you continue to prod and poke questions at the tender place in my heart and mind? At the moment, I've set my attention on traveling to protect you and your party. Must you evoke my hospitality? Would you rather have my wrath instead?"

"No, of course not," Roble replied. "But why not set your anger toward the few Unseelie who are responsible instead of initiating a war with the entire Unseelie Court?"

Daphne's jaw tightened. Rather than replying, she stepped on the raft and kept her attention turned away from him to end their conversation. They couldn't reach mutual ground, but he wasn't angry and hoped she didn't insinuate he was.

He had, however, provoked her to nearly attacking him. The lightning sparks flickering on her fingers had been a warning, but somehow she kept herself in check. It hardly served her purpose to kill a Dragon Skull Knight in the presence of a peaceful hamlet and in view of her sister.

Why had Portia convinced herself and the townsfolk that she could never turn her wrath against another soul without shortening her life. Daphne's approach and outlook was the opposite. She held no reservations about starting a war against the entire Unseelie Court. The proof of her power was evident when she destroyed the Saurians and their mage.

He wanted to examine the site where she'd electrocuted the creatures, but they lacked the time. Within a half hour, the rafts would be ready, and he'd only worsen his stance with Daphne if he took the time to investigate. Yet, he wanted to see the actual damage of her power as well as examine the anatomy of the Saurians.

When Portia altered her appearance by drawing the earth's magic, she exhausted herself. Had she possessed more power, what was she capable of? Would she have increased the magical barrier, or would she have done as Daphne and killed them all? Could she have even done so?

After his conversation with Daphne, did she now perceive him as an enemy because they didn't see eye-to-eye? Of course, he didn't have any basis for his counterarguments, as he'd only recently learned about their courts.

Portia seemed genuine in her view of her responsibility. Acting on her inner rage and wrath reaped severe repercussions. Perhaps someone else had taught her this? Had Daphne deceived Portia such during their youth to bolster her own power and lessen Portia's?

Roble glanced at Portia, who continued her enlightened conversation with Shawndirea. Both held partial smiles. Shawndirea met his gaze and her smile broadened. A warmth filled him with comfort and joy.

Fate's direction for individuals was often unpredictable. Shawndirea had been destined to find him. They were meant to be together. But, Fate could be cruel as well and snatch precious blessings from those who had received them. He hoped the confrontation with Lez'minx didn't cost them far more than Roble's acceptance of the rings. By the end of the next day, they'd all know, either way. His gut twisted from worry.

CHAPTER 53

$\mathcal{L}$ ehrling watched Collette hug and kiss her mother, several elderly women, and other friends and family members. Her captivating smile brightened the otherwise gray, damp misery that clung to Dagger's Tears. She seemed the only light to shine during the overcast morning.

Her father had been carried onto the lodge balcony where he sat on a broken barstool. He wore a scowl and hatred heated his eyes. His disdain wasn't particularly aimed at any of them, and seemed his general disposition. If Collette noticed him, her acknowledgement didn't reflect in her eyes. Lehrling almost wanted to pity her father for his physical disfigurements but more for his embittered outlook at the world.

He had an incredible daughter and a good wife, from what little Lehrling knew of both, and yet, the bitterness snared him with blindness to what blessings remained in his life.

While Lehrling was happy knowing Collette would leave the dismal hamlet, he worried that her haste might cost her or someone else in their party a premature death.

He glanced from Collette to Roble. Roble stood on the river's bank talking to Daphne.

Regret crawled through Lehrling's chest and seeped into his mind for standing against Roble's sound advice about leaving Collette in

Dagger's Tears until after their confrontation with Lez'minx was finished.

Roble's advice had been in Collette's best interests, but Lehrling ached to see the hurt and brokenness in her eyes when she was told to remain behind. The hot tears streaming down her face were more than Lehrling could handle. If he hadn't stood up for her against Roble, he might never see Collette again, even if he returned to Dagger's Tears later.

She loathed Dagger's Tears and her inability to venture outside its borders. As broken as she had been, he feared she might harm herself if left behind. Or, when Lehrling finally returned, she'd have nothing to do with him, perhaps feeling scorned by him. Either way, he'd lose her.

While Lehrling couldn't predict he'd eventually marry her, his heart ached with the hope that he might. Despite their age difference, he didn't believe he'd ever meet another woman with Collette's warm generosity and kindness. He shook his head and scolded himself. "You're an old fool."

But hope was what kept anyone alive, even in the most depressing situations, and Lehrling had survived several bouts against death. He considered retiring his sword and investing his final years on a small farmstead, gardening and raising sheep. Riding was hard on his aging bones. Besides, the younger knights were more effective in defending the crown.

He released a tired sigh and watched Collette give her final good-byes. Some brought her small gifts for her journey, and while they continued talking, he couldn't get past spouting his stubborn words at Roble.

Lehrling wondered what damage he might've caused their friendship by challenging Roble. Even though he didn't know Roble all that well, he couldn't stand the thought of driving a wedge between them. Roble was a strong-minded man determined to defend those who could not. He would serve Hoffnung's crown quite well. Since Roble was much younger than Lehrling, Lehrling didn't know what type of grudges Roble might harbor whenever he felt slighted. Roble was quick to use weapons without a second thought whenever he felt threatened.

Roble didn't perceive Lehrling as the slightest threat. He outright downplayed Lehrling as no challenge should they take up arms against one another. While Lehrling could've argued that in sword-to-sword combat he'd have been the victor, Roble possessed the greatest advantage with the use of his throwing knives. Even the best swordsman was no match against Roble's precision.

Lehrling needed to right his wrong with Roble, since he'd opposed Roble in the presence of others, instead of discreetly. Two knights should never argue in public, as it weakened the Order's unity. Lehrling planned to thoroughly apologize in private once the opportunity came. Until then, he prayed to the Three Goddesses that Roble might forgive him.

Lehrling watched the others ready the rafts and the conversing sounds around him faded. His focus turned toward Geowren and what had become of his fellow Dragon Skull Knight. His former best friend and mentor had stood on this bank not too long ago. Although Lehrling would never tell anyone he could almost feel the presence of his dear comrade, that was exactly what he felt inside his soul.

Was Geowren still alive? If so, Lehrling needed Geowren's assistance now more than ever. From his own calculations, they needed all the help they could get to confront Lez'minx. He wasn't quite sure why Geowren had chosen the direction in which he was traveling. Perhaps Geowren had given misinformation to mislead those pursuing him? That was possible. A lie sometimes benefited one through harrowed situations. If Geowren was on the run because his life was in danger, a lie was justifiable.

Collette took his calloused hand in hers and jarred him from his thoughts.

"Are you ready, my love?" She beamed at him.

He returned an uncertain smile but didn't oppose holding her hand. His eyes studied hers momentarily, but he couldn't determine if her words were meant to appease the onlookers or if she looked at him with the same hope he did for finding his life mate. She didn't hesitate in grabbing his hand. No quiver or distaste resounded in her voice, and he couldn't find any deceit in her eyes. A strange sensation rushed to his heart and his stomach twisted with slight excitement, which was a feeling he'd not had since his youth.

Her fingers intertwined with his, and she smiled at him while they walked. Two young lads carried her belongings behind them.

Her smile soothed Lehrling, and her grip on his hand didn't lessen. He read her actions as genuine and not for display to suit herself and those around them.

The last thing he wanted was for Collette to become collateral damage, due to his selfishness and shortsightedness to satisfy her desires in leaving Dagger's Tears. He hoped he could keep her protected.

CHAPTER 54

From the corner of her eye, Shawndirea watched Roble talk to Daphne while she conversed with Portia. Even from the distance between her and Roble, Shawndirea discerned the anger and hostility rising inside Daphne.

Shawndirea shook her head. How'd Roble always find ways to chaff others into anger? While it never seemed intentional, he did it more often than not. He pried for information to gain understanding for others' actions. But in Aetheaon, actions didn't directly correlate with reasoning. He delved for knowledge because he was cursed with his duties as a *scientist*—as he called his bizarre obsession in the Overlands —but in her realm, this wasn't how to find resolutions for problems.

In spite of his inquisitiveness, she never wanted to quash his want for discovery.

Portia continued talking about Daphne and how she had never expected to ever see her sister again. And now, they were preparing to find their brother.

Shawndirea graciously smiled and nodded, but added little to the conversation. Portia deliberately spoke rapidly to prevent Shawndirea from adding any input. Portia also gushed about the revived hope of reestablishing Linden-hold without considering how her absence would cost the folks of Dagger's Tears.

While Portia talked, Shawndirea reflected on the dark pool to where she'd been taken during her deep sleep and the voice that told her to accept who she truly was. This hadn't been a dream or nightmare or delusion. She'd been taken to have her attention focused in a new direction—a direction she'd have never thought of otherwise, due to the current distractions in her life.

Although she didn't know, nor could she discern whom had spoken to her, the voice radiated a familiarity she couldn't explain. For some reason, she sensed she knew the being pointing her toward the proper path. She only wished he'd have revealed his name or said something to jar her memories enough to dislodge it.

Secrets. Why must secrets be kept?

Portia droned on.

Shawndirea thought more about her deep sleep and what she'd discovered after awakening. Something else had been revealed to her. It was an issue she couldn't yet tell Roble, although she needed to. But Roble didn't need another distraction.

Distractions set forth unforeseen dangers, but he needed to know. She wanted to tell him, but based on prior confrontations Roble had experienced, she forbade herself from letting him know. She ached to keep any secret from him, but withholding this one hurt her most of all.

Merla and Cora joined Portia and Shawndirea. Tears welled in the two halflings' eyes.

Portia stopped speaking when she glanced at them. "My dears … what's wrong?"

Shawndirea cocked a brow. *Has she no clue?* Was Portia so self-absorbed she couldn't see how attached those in Dagger's Tears were to her?

"We need you here," Merla said.

"No." Portia shook her head. "I've happily served my purpose in Dagger's Tears."

"You can't leave us," Cora said. "You mustn't."

"I've taught you which herbs to use for healing potions and the proper way to make poultices with blessed mud, herbs, and oils. You can readily take my place," Portia said with a smile.

"No," Merla said. "Your presence offers us much more than your healing abilities. You're the light within this drab hamlet. Without you, our hope perishes."

"That's—"

Dolan stormed to them and stopped. He huffed and his eyes narrowed with anger at Portia. "What's this I hear that you're *leaving* Dagger's Tears?"

Portia quickly explained her reasons for why she must leave.

"Unacceptable!" he said. His chest rose and his hands formed tight little fists. "If ever a place has needed you, it's us. Not off on some delusional trip, hoping to find a lost city that probably no longer exists. Believe me, after our exile, we traveled looking for a place of unity and hope. A place we could call home. At first we thought it was the Glades of Sorrow, but our town was attacked and decimated. We packed up and settled Dagger's Tears. You joined us. We received you as family. One of our own. Last night we suffered an attack again."

"You wish to leave us?" Cora wiped away tears. "Who's going to stop them when they return again and you're gone?"

For a moment, Portia was a loss for words. Her eyes viewed them with pity. "I—I don't—"

"Bah!" Dolan frowned and waved her off. "You're no different than those we placed our trust in years ago."

"Believe me," Portia said, "I'm not leaving to cause you harm or to leave you vulnerable."

"Yet, you are!" Dolan spat.

"What if I return for you—"

"What if?" Dolan said. "What *if?* We-e-l-l, what if *I* were the height of a human? Huh? What if I could walk on water or fly like a bat? None of these aren't possible, nor will they ever be. What if's are generally spoken about things that won't happen, so if that's your promise, I won't bank on it. We won't ever see you again."

"Dolan," Cora said, shaking her head. "Don't be rude."

"Perhaps we should gather sugar-coated mushrooms and make a delightful loaf, eh?" Dolan said. "I'm tired of others letting us down and leaving us to fend for ourselves."

Portia's eyes widened. "I never realized the degree of your bitterness, Dolan. I'm quite surprised."

Merla frowned at Portia. "You *never* noticed?"

"I tended to ignore his childish outbursts," Portia replied.

Dolan sighed and looked at Cora and then to Merla. "This leaves only one thing for us to do."

"What's that?" Cora asked.

"We travel with them," Dolan replied.

"You can't—" Portia said.

Dolan pointed a stern finger at her. "We can and we will."

"You don't realize the dangers," Portia said.

"We saw real dangers last night. Had it not been for your sister frying those lizard fiends like fritters, we'd all be dead," Dolan said.

"I tried," Portia said.

"Save it!" Dolan held his palm toward her. "You need our protection as much as we need yours."

"There's not enough room," Portia said.

Dolan laughed heartily. "Not enough room? For four halflings? We fit into the tiniest of places. No one will notice."

"Shawndirea," Portia said, "please explain to them?"

Shawndirea shook her head. "We've no time. Roble's motioning that it's time for us to get aboard."

CHAPTER 55

*R*oble handed the last crate of supplies to a hooded dryad while carefully watching where he placed his feet in the mud. He didn't want to slip and lose a leg to a massive turtle beneath the muddy water.

Even though the turtles weren't visible, air bubbles popped on the water's surface. He'd been around enough lakes and ponds to know these bubbles came from turtles exhaling.

Roble stepped back and his foot slipped on the slick mud. He'd have fallen into the soggy earth but someone caught him from behind. Strong hands positioned themselves, held him upright, and prevented Roble from getting stuck in the muck.

"Thought you could use a hand," Lehrling said, embracing Roble. "Or a *couple* of hands."

Roble halfway laughed, nodded, and then slapped a firm hand on Lehrling's shoulder. "Thanks."

Roble walked to the top of the bank without hardly a glance at Lehrling but laughed with a tinge of embarrassment.

"Roble," Daphne said in a firm even voice. "You and Lehrling load your horses onto the second raft."

"We can ride," Roble said.

Daphne shook her head. "No. You'll never keep up with us."

"There's a path alongside the river." Roble pointed.

"An uneven path and often that pathway leads *away* from the river due to tributaries and fallen trees. If your real interest is in removing those rings, you need to ride *with* us. Otherwise, you'll arrive several days after we have. I won't wait for you."

Roble sighed. "Can your raft support two large horses?"

"They support far more weight than most small ships. We dryads know our strengths and limitations when it comes to woodworking," she replied.

Shawndirea frowned. "I never thought dryads could harm a tree."

Daphne leveled an even stare in response. "We didn't. The lumber for these two rafts came from a human logging yard as they rampaged through an Elven forest. The spirits of the trees were gone, but we wept and blessed each board while constructing these rafts. These vessels, though small, are far sturdier than any ship in Hoffnung's navy."

Shawndirea wiped a tear from her eye. "I'm sorry. That must've been devastating."

"No less than you weaving a cloak from butterfly wings," Daphne replied.

Fresh tears welled in Shawndirea's eyes.

Daphne returned her stoic attention to Roble. "Yes, the raft can safely carry your horses."

Roble looked at Lehrling. They shrugged and retrieved their horses.

Dolan, Cora, and Merla hurried their stubby legs to the river's edge. Portia walked briskly behind them. She scolded them under her breath.

"What seems to be the problem?" Daphne asked.

"These three wish to travel with us," Portia replied.

"Nonsense," Daphne said.

"Try and stop us!" Dolan leapt on the second raft where Roble and Lehrling led their horses.

Cora and Merla didn't hesitate to follow him.

"Do you understand how ludicrous your actions are?" Daphne asked.

"What I understand is that we're going," Dolan said.

"As am I," Rufus said from behind Dolan.

"Suit yourself." Daphne glanced at an agitated Aqese. "If we need to lighten the load, toss them overboard first. Use them as bait if necessary."

Aqese nodded and grinned at Dolan.

"Bait?" Dolan's face creased with anger.

Rufus' face tightened and his eyes grew fierce. He started around Dolan, but Dolan shook his head and placed a gentle hand on Rufus' shoulder.

"It be as it is anywhere we travel," Dolan said. "Because of our size, other races think us inefficient."

"Isn't right," Rufus said in a harsh whisper.

"No, it's not. But it means we must work harder to prove our worth."

AFTER TRAVELING eight agonizing hours on the muddy river that occasionally narrowed into a wide shallow creek without a consistent current, Roble couldn't believe he was physically and mentally exhausted. The best part of the journey had been the lack of rain, but without sunlight, the drab depressive aura remained, and had drained the heightened renewal of energy the glowing Elfstone had given them.

In the shallowest sections of the river, everyone—including Daphne and Portia—had to get off the rafts and pull until they reached deeper water. Pulling the raft carrying the horses was the hardest part, but they couldn't risk a horse breaking a leg on the rocky bottom of the river.

These shallow areas darkened with thicker trees, hanging vines, and unusual curious reptiles. Strange ferns and orchids flourished on small islands of dirt and in the cracks of large trees and rocks. Had this been a place in the Overlands, Roble would've viewed this as an unexplored paradise. But Aetheaon wasn't a place of serenity, especially not in the darker places that housed creatures and magic wielders. Neither welcomed intruders into their abode.

Lehrling and Collette smacked biting flies and mosquitoes as the bloodthirsty insects landed on their faces and any exposed flesh. Shawndirea spent most of her time zapping these nuisance insects with tiny blasts of heated light.

Large butterflies with metallic-colored wings drifted past on the slight breeze while other smaller butterflies puddled on the soggy river bank. Occasionally, a worn, weary butterfly drifted to Shawndirea to be blessed and have its tattered wings restored.

Due to the darkness caused by the thick canopy and the constant overcast skies, fireflies lit up the forest, which might've been more beautiful and relaxing if not for the occasional, glowing eyes of beings at different levels amongst the trees.

In spite of the humid, hot air, a chill shot down Roble's back. They were being followed. By what, he wasn't certain, as he'd never gotten a full glimpse of any of them. Their luminous eyes increased the farther upriver the rafts drifted. These beasts coveted the shadows but didn't seem worried about letting Roble and his party know of their presence. Whatever they were, they were getting bolder.

Shawndirea sat on his shoulder and occasionally whispered her concerns about the eyes watching them. She expressed that members of the Shadowfae were following them.

Daphne seemed to have sensed these unwelcome stalkers as well, but she remained quiet. Her companions, Aqese and Kilwese, each controlled a rudder of the two flat rafts. The small sails caught the slight breeze and drifted near a sandy wide shoreline. Jutting up from the sand were ancient broken pillars.

Daphne motioned toward the sandbar. "We stay the night here."

"In these ruins?" Lehrling asked. "Out in the open?"

She flicked her narrowed gaze at him. "Yes."

"Where are we?" Roble asked.

"The Ruins of Evendusk," she replied. "At least, that's my guess. I don't recall any other ruins."

"Who lived here?" Lehrling asked.

"Dark Elves." She stood in silence for several long moments, while studying the writing on the cracked and broken pillars rising from the sand. "They lived here several centuries ago. From what historians have written, the city had been a prosperous one."

"What caused its demise?" Lehrling asked.

Daphne shrugged. "Your guess is as good as mine. The historians could never define the actual reason the city fell into ruins."

"You know we're being followed, correct?" Roble asked.

"Yes. I'm aware. They seem more curious about who we are," Daphne replied. "Had they wanted to attack, they'd have already done so. But be prepared, in any case. Don't let down your guard."

Dolan slowly turned his head. His fearful eyes searched the shadowy trees on the opposite bank. Cora and Merla held small bows with tiny arrows that would most likely infuriate whatever they shot rather than kill it. They were too nervous to step off the raft. He took a deep breath and tried to muster his courage.

Rufus stood upright, crossed his arms in an attempt to look bold, but his eyes displayed his nervousness. He glanced with uncertainty at Dolan.

"This ... this doesn't look like a safe place to spend the night," Dolan said.

"Either we set up camp here," Daphne said, "or we drag these rafts into the next deep section of the river. Then who knows how much farther upriver we travel before we reach another suitable place to camp. Night falls soon. Do you want to drift on the river during the darkest hours of night?"

"Not particularly," he replied.

"You were warned to stay behind," Portia said. "It was your own stubborn decision to travel with us."

Partially angered by the reminder, Dolan leapt from the raft onto the pebbled sandbar. A snarl formed on his lips and he huffed. He eyed the opposite shore lined with thick trees and snaky coiled, leafy vines. Ferns and dense brush filled the area between the tree trunks. He stood with his boots partway sunken in the sand and gripped his bow firmly.

Aqese and Kilwese pulled the rafts onto the small pebbled beach and then helped Lehrling and Roble unload the horses. Afterwards, they slung their quivers over their shoulders and readied their bows, standing near the rafts. They watched the opposite river bank.

Lehrling walked his horse toward a fallen pillar. He pointed at the dark shadowed recess against a hillside above the sandbar. "There's an opening above us."

Bones and skulls littered the sandbar beneath the opening.

Roble flicked his gaze to Daphne. "We're not alone. Someone still lives in the tunnel."

"Or some *thing*," she replied softly.

"That doesn't concern you?"

"It does, but whatever lives inside will prevent what's following us from crossing the river." Daphne studied the dark opening. "Send the halflings in to investigate."

"Hey!" Dolan snarled.

"I jest, Dolan," Daphne said in a bland monotone without any humor. "Let's gather driftwood and build a large fire. We split the night-watch into three short shifts with two individuals. Come morning, we load up and sail to our destination, which by my estimation is four to five hours more, unless we hit more shallow points."

"That requires *surviving* the night," Dolan said.

"Quite an accurate evaluation, halfling," Daphne said. "All the more reason to remain vigilant. Which shift do you intend to keep watch?"

"I doubt I'll sleep a wink," he replied.

"All the better!" Portia said, smiling.

Roble shook his head. "Lehrling, come with me. Let's go see what's in the opening."

"Are you mad?" Lehrling asked with a raised brow.

"No. But we need to know if it's a creature or if by chance there are goblins or Ratkin living there. If it's only creatures like wolves or a bear, we've a stronger possibility of not being attacked. If it's goblins or Ratkin ... we'll be mobbed during the night."

Lehrling swallowed hard. "Or as soon as we look into the opening. Perhaps we'd be safer waiting for *it* to emerge?"

Roble frowned. "Come on. We're knights for God's sake."

"Goddesses' sake," Lehrling corrected.

Roble shrugged. He walked along the worn, sandy path that ascended at a forty-five degree angle and led to the opening that over-looked the sandbar and the river. With the sprigs of grass and mossy mounds, he couldn't discern the recent unidentifiable footsteps.

"Look, um, Roble," Lehrling said softly, while following behind. "I've been meaning to apologize for my behavior back in Dagger's Tears. You know, for opposing your opinion—"

"No need. I'm past it." Roble kept his attention on the opening and didn't glance at Lehrling.

"Are you sure? Because if you're leading me up here to prove a point about my bravery—"

"What's to prove? You're a Dragon Skull Knight, chosen by King Erik. He'd have not chosen you if you weren't worthy."

"Don't mock me, Roble."

Roble turned at the top of the path and headed to the opening. "I'm not mocking you. What makes you think that?"

"This. Leading me up here with you in front of our party, in front of Collette."

"You've nothing to prove. You've already won Collette's heart. She's hardly stopped holding your hand during the journey and her eyes peer into yours with pure affection."

"Roble!" Lehrling said in a harsh whisper. "While I'm much older and more experienced than you, I still regard you as a better warrior. I'm actually learning *more* from you than you are from me."

"Better?" Roble laughed. "Why? *I'm* the fool who refused to listen to Shawndirea about these rings and got us into this mess to begin with."

"I'm not so certain I wouldn't have done the same as you," Lehrling said. "With the armor you have and the blessing Moorsis gave under Lez'minx's power, I'd have wondered what benefits the rings offered, too. Any knight from any kingdom wouldn't have hesitated to test the rings' powers."

"Is that so?"

Lehrling nodded. "Yes. When you fight magical mages and wizards, swords and axes are of little value. Why do you think the dwarves engrave runes into their weapons? Some tattoo runic symbols on their faces, hands, and bodies. Dwarves can't wield magic, but they can readily defend themselves against it. So, if this is a public test, leading me here—"

"Lehrling, I'd never deliberately place you in harm's way, and I'd certainly never embarrass you in front of Collette."

"What are you doing, Roble?" Shawndirea asked, flying behind him.

"*He* wants to find out what's in the opening," Lehrling said.

Roble said, "I want to know what we're dealing with. I don't intend to provoke it."

"Is that so?" Shawndirea asked.

"Yes."

"If it's Ratkin or goblins, do you think it wise for the *two* of you to face them? Either could rip you to shreds before you properly defended yourselves. Most likely, it's not goblins though."

"No?" Roble asked.

Shawndirea shook her head. "No. Goblins prefer the mountains, not swamps. According to Dwarven tales, the goblins were eradicated completely."

"She's right, Roble," Lehrling said. "I've heard many a bard's tale about the final confrontation between the dwarves and goblins. Many noble dwarves died that day, but the slaughter of the goblins has remained the tales of legend ever since."

"Did you ever consider whatever straggling goblins that happened to survive might have retreated into the swamps?" Roble asked.

"Swamps are not their habitat," Shawndirea replied.

"No? Hey, people change and adjust. I did," Roble said with a slight grin tugging the sides of his mouth.

Lehrling grinned. "That's true."

"Humans adapt to most anything," Shawndirea said sharply. "But other races do not. You could never move a city of elves into the heart of the desert; just like you could never enslave the Saurians and successfully move them from the swamps. Goblins would never settle in these ruins."

"One less hostile creature to worry about then," Roble said.

Shawndirea sighed. "I wonder if your curiosity isn't anything other than a death wish."

"It's not," Roble said. "I assure you I want to live a long life."

"You've an odd way of expressing that," she replied.

Roble's brow tightened as he processed her words. He nodded. "Perhaps. But I'd rather be the one surprising potential enemies than getting surprised by them."

"Either way doesn't allow longevity," she said.

"Running only gets you shot in the back," Roble said. "That much I've learned while being in your realm."

A roaring rhythm echoed from inside the opening.

"What's that?" Lehrling asked.

"It's not an animal," Shawndirea said softly.

"Then let's see," Roble said.

Before either Shawndirea or Lehrling could offer protest, Roble stepped into the dark opening. They followed.

CHAPTER 56

*R*oble stepped into the shadowed recess of the hillside. "We need some light. Lehrling, do you see anything we could light for a torch?"

"Do bones burn?" Lehrling pointed. "There are a lot of large bones on the ground."

"I suppose if they're dry enough," he replied.

"Light draws too much attention," Shawndirea said.

"I can't see in total darkness," Roble said. "A torch—"

She sighed. "I meant *firelight.*"

Shawndirea focused on her hands momentarily. Soft greenish light encircled her hands, which offered enough light for them to see the crude pathway.

"This path isn't what an advanced city would've used for an entranceway."

"It wasn't," Shawndirea replied.

"How do you know?"

"From what I can tell, this crude path was bored through the outer wall *after* the city's prosperity ended."

Water splashed heavily against rocks farther ahead.

"A waterfall?" Roble placed his hand against a tarnished marble pillar that held the compacted soil and rock into place.

"Sounds like it," she replied.

Lehrling followed behind them. "I smell smoke."

"As do I," Roble said. "It's faint but carries on the sour air."

Revealed by the greenish glow on Shawndirea's hands were more bones, a few reptilian shriveled hides, but no obvious discarded weapons of the victims.

Roble knelt and studied the long intact skeletal remains that were almost as long as he was tall. The long jawbone held numerous teeth. "This appears to be a skeleton of a crocodile-like animal."

Lehrling leaned down. "What's that exactly?"

Roble gave a quick explanation.

"Never heard of such a thing. They must be a tasty creature, as there seems to be a lot of their remains," he replied.

"Apparently so, but these creatures didn't crawl into the crevice," Roble said.

"Something brought them up from the river?" Lehrling asked.

"No. If these were in the river, we'd have seen them."

"Then how'd they get here?"

"I don't know," Roble said. "But believe me, these are aggressive hunters in my world. They rest on the shorelines and when they're in the water, you'll occasionally see their eyes crest above the water. Nothing like that was in the river."

"Be careful where you step," Shawndirea said in a near whisper.

"Why? What's wrong?" Lehrling asked.

She said, "Roble's right. These bones aren't from creatures here."

"You're confusing me," Lehrling said. "And I don't like that."

"There's a rift in the realm barrier nearby," she said.

"Do you believe that's why Evendusk fell?" Roble asked.

In the greenish glow of her hands, her eyes peered into his. "Not through this rift. It's not large enough for an army to pass through."

"It's more recent than when Evendusk fell, too," Daphne said, standing behind Lehrling.

Lehrling clutched his chest and let out a brief shout. "Heavens, priestess! Announce yourself instead of sneaking up behind us!"

"Sorry," she said, "but Portia and I felt the magical tug of the rift. I thought it best for us to venture inside and warn you. Luckily, Shawndirea senses these things as well."

"Does the rift lead back to my world?" Roble asked.

"It's difficult to know without crossing through," Shawndirea said.

"I advise against it," Daphne said. "It's far too risky, as the rift could close."

"Close?" Lehrling's hand tightened on his sword's hilt.

"It's true," Shawndirea said.

"Apparently Evendusk lies on a realm barrier, which means different rifts might've occurred over time," Portia said. "The realm wall might be too thin in this area."

"Something resides in these ruins," Roble said. "Otherwise, there wouldn't be so many skeletal remains along this pathway."

"Maybe," Daphne said. "Or maybe *not*. It could be that once a creature passes through one rift, something else enters through a different rift and feasts on it."

"A double rift?" Shawndirea asked.

"That, or the two are superimposed," she replied.

"That's even more dangerous," Shawndirea said.

In the greenish glow of Shawndirea's light, Portia's eyes widened. "Shh! We're not alone."

Lehrling slid his blade from its sheath. Roble pulled two daggers from his belt. Lehrling looked at Roble. "Did you hear something?"

"All I hear is splashing water," Roble replied. "Do you hear anything other than that, Shawndirea?"

She placed her index finger to her lips and nodded. She flitted to his shoulder and whispered, "What we hear isn't a physical sound, but rather an attempt to enter our minds, to locate and determine who and what we are."

"Roble," Lehrling said, "we should retreat to the river bank. *Now*."

"I'm afraid it's much too late for that," Daphne said. "They know we're here. Anything less than an immediate confrontation is death."

CHAPTER 57

*R*oble glanced at Daphne, uncertain of what he should do. In the pale green orb of light that encircled Shawndirea, Daphne's face appeared grim, her eyes piercing, and she stiffened, almost like petrified wood.

"Protect your minds," she whispered inside Roble's mind.

Her lips never moved and her words weren't audible. She spoke telepathically to him. Had she done the same with the rest of their party since she had said, '*minds*'?

He gave a side-glance to Shawndirea, and she placed a gentle hand to his cheek. "We're dealing with psionic beings."

Daphne glanced at Shawndirea harshly.

Silence! Daphne's voice rang inside Roble's head. Lehrling shook his head and placed his hands over his ears. The voice boomed and echoed. A ringing sensation throbbed in Roble's ears as though Daphne had shrilled the word at her highest octave.

Roble focused his thoughts on Daphne, but he didn't know if she could detect his words like he'd heard hers. "*What should we do?*"

"*Don't retreat,*" she replied. "*Move toward the waterfall.*"

He feared following her command would prove suicidal. Fleeing, as Lehrling had insisted, seemed the best option, given the present circumstances.

Lehrling looked in Roble's eyes. His brow furrowed. He whispered, "How am I hearing you inside my head?"

Portia grabbed Lehrling's arm tightly and turned him toward her. She flung her thoughts into his mind, *"Think your thoughts. We can hear you. Speaking aloud allows them to locate us faster."*

Lehrling frowned but obeyed. *"How's this possible?"*

"A spell hangs over this narrow passageway," Daphne said, *"which allows intelligent beings to converse or read the thoughts of others. A delicate but rare type of spell, but quite beneficial whenever a group of thieves or invaders enter a city and wish to refrain from physically voicing their conversations. However, in our case, using this form of telepathy is the deadlier, sharper side of a two-edged sword."*

"Why?" Roble and Lehrling asked at the same time.

"The more we speak, the faster they pinpoint our location. So move onward. Try to not phrase thoughts in your minds."

"That's impossible," Lehrling said.

"Yes, it's a horrible flaw for humans," Daphne said. *"But try."*

Roble held his throwing knives at his sides. Not thinking or questioning things inside his mind or anyone's, for that matter, *was* impossible. Human minds were constantly driven to think, even when one didn't want to. The brain's activity sought and craved understanding, even during sleep, which was why dreams crept in and why nightmares often held partial truth and caused fear to awaken the dreamer. But nothing could shake them out of this living nightmare.

Bright light shone at the end of the path where they stood and revealed they had less than twenty yards to walk. The wash of light under normal circumstances would've been received as inviting, but Roble believed they had somehow triggered the sudden light by getting too close to where the inhabitants dwelled.

Lehrling took a sharp breath and held it. Although none of them stepped forward, the subtle sounds of their breathing and slight adjusting movements of their hands to their weapons were amplified. The longer they stood on the path, the more Roble felt exposed. It reminded him of a nightmare he'd had during his childhood. One where he had been seen by an unknown entity and wanted to run, but his body became paralyzed by fear. He couldn't will himself to swiftly escape and dropped to the ground, trying to crawl away.

"*Go!*" Daphne said.

Roble started to step forward but his leg had grown heavy. Fear seized him. His eyes studied the edges of the carved tunnel in the glow of the light shining in. He couldn't see any enemies, but he *felt* their presence. The sensation flooding through him didn't come from one being, but from many.

In the same manner he expressed his thoughts to the others in his party, he felt others—strangers—feeling outward for him. The best he could describe it was how bats used echolocation to hone in on insects to pinpoint accurate strikes to capture their prey.

"*Move!*" Daphne said.

Roble took a cumbersome step forward and slapped his hand against the earthen wall to steady himself. Pebbles and dirt spilled to the ground.

"You okay?" Shawndirea asked.

Roble nodded and attempted to take another step.

The most worrisome part of moving forward was not knowing what type of creatures they were about to encounter. He'd seen plenty of unusual species since his arrival in Aetheaon. Confronting his first monster in Devils Den should have been enough of a deterrent to convince him to stay in the Overlands. Adaptation for survival was not in his favor by staying with Shawndirea, but his love for her and his distaste for the Overlands persuaded him to abandon his previous life. Going back home to reside permanently was not an option.

His next step forward was easier, and he continued stealthily walking through the narrow tunnel. If he accidentally stepped into a rift, he feared where he might end up. *Which was more dangerous?* he wondered. *Stepping through a rift or facing the creature or creatures with the ability to read their minds?*

"*The rift's more dangerous,*" Daphne said.

Roble's face heated, realizing that anything he thought could be read by the others in his group. No secrets hung between them if revealed by their minds.

He listened with his mind, and attempted to read the thoughts of the others. He could only hear Lehrling's fearful thoughts and his deep concern that they were heading to their demise. Portia, Daphne, and Shawndirea were absent of thought or perhaps, as Daphne had insisted, they successfully shielded their thoughts. Of course, they could use magic, which allowed them better protection. Since they weren't human, perhaps they had better control over their thoughts.

As the rushing splashes of the waterfall became louder, the light brightened even more at the end of the tunnel. The air moistened with a richness of earth and minerals.

Roble stopped at the end of the carved-out tunnel, which overlooked a stone-tiled floor about eight feet below where they stood. At least that was his estimate of the drop in the brightness of the large Elven glowstones placed into the pillars around the water pool. Not an impossible descent, but one that required a bit of careful footwork, so as to not plummet headfirst onto the floor below.

Roble counted eight pillars surrounding the water pool. The Elven glowstones cast a yellowish-white hue like pleasant, bright sunlight washing over the massive room. The underground waterfall spilled from the rocks above but the pool capturing the cascading water didn't overflow.

Four carved, marble statues of robed figures with swords and shields stood at equal distances and encircled the pillars. The hoods prevented him from determining what race had once lived in this city. The architecture was phenomenal and displayed the majestic nature of the civilization now absent from Evendusk. Everything was buried, not only in ruins, but in mystery.

While he wasn't sure, the quarters before him seemed to be former gardens. Thick leafy vines coiled around the pillars and partway up the statues. The offered lighting blessed plant growth and several of the vines had large, colorful flowers blooming. Others held heavy seedpods.

With the lighting and the access to fresh water, the place was habitable, and yet, it had been abandoned more than a century earlier. That is, except for whatever killed and feasted on any stragglers bold enough —or foolish enough—to enter the ruins. Curious treasure-hunters were probably some who met their demise.

No large carnivorous creatures moved about. At least none were visible from Roble's vantage point. The only activity was tiny moths flitting from flower to flower and fireflies flicking their lights on and off.

Daphne moved to Roble's right. She stood and gazed on the lit area below.

Roble gave her a side-glance. "What now?"

Confusion furrowed her brow. Her eyes hunted the pillars and statues below. After several minutes of silence, she finally said, "I'm not certain."

Lehrling lowered his sword and shook his head. "These gardens were spectacular and are peaceful."

Daphne nodded. "That's the deceit. Be alert. We're being watched."

CHAPTER 58

*R*oble would've agreed with Lehrling about the peaceful solace these gardens offered, if not for the piles of white bones lining the walls. It was impossible to lower one's guard knowing violent deaths had occurred within these ruins, especially when the unseen enemies could be anywhere.

Telepathic tendrils reached for his mind. These silent, mind-searching probes softly brushing the edge of his thoughts weren't Portia's, Daphne's, or Shawndirea's, as he recognized their non-spoken thoughts when they entered his mind. The mind-reachers in these ruins probed, blindly, it seemed. Even though he couldn't see these dwellers, there was no denying they were here, somewhere.

Lehrling gripped and squeezed Roble's shoulder harshly. He turned Roble and pointed at the corner of the compacted dirt ceiling beyond the waterfall. Fearful, gasps escaped Lehrling's open mouth. If Lehrling wanted to speak or scream, his terror prevented him from doing so.

Narrow, silvery eyes reflected in the glow of the Elven stones. Two overly large, insect-like creatures clung to the ceiling. Their bodies were flat like beetles but their mandibles were fierce, long, and sharper than a sword. On the inside of the mandibles were several dagger-pointed edges. Given the beetles' immense size, they possessed enough strength to pierce through the strongest armors. Neither his sharpest dagger nor

303

Lehrling's short sword could penetrate the exoskeleton of these insect horrors.

An unrecognizable voice crept inside Roble's mind. "Caution or your fate will be like those who entered before you."

"Anyone else hearing this?" Roble asked in his thoughts.

"Yes," Shawndirea, Daphne, and Portia replied.

"We don't take threats lightly," Roble thought.

"It's not I who threatens you," the voice replied.

"Who are you?" Daphne asked.

"First, tell me, how many are in your group?"

Roble studied the areas around the pillars and the waterfall, but he didn't see anyone. "Why should I give you that information? It'd only give you an advantage."

"Don't be a fool," the voice replied. "I wish to aid your escape. Nothing more and nothing less."

"Like those who were killed before us?" Roble asked.

"Like you," the voice said, "they chose to argue *instead* of listening."

"The beetles on the ceiling ... Are they yours or is it one of them that speaks?"

"I've no part of them. They're what killed the other parties that entered our gardens. Unless you heed my warnings, they'll feast on your bodies as well."

"Your gardens?" Shawndirea asked. "You're a resident of Evendusk?"

"Yes."

Shawndirea exchanged glances with Daphne.

Daphne shook her head. "Impossible."

"It's true. I'm the last voice of my people," he replied.

"Then reveal yourself to us," Roble said.

"I can't. The moment I become visible, we all die. Now, yield to me your trust."

Roble shook his head. "That's difficult, since I can't find you and don't know with whom I'm dealing."

"Fool," the voice said with immediate distaste. "You, I take, are the foolish warrior standing on the ledge, slightly ahead of the others."

"I'm a knight, but hardly a fool," Roble replied in thought.

Shawndirea snickered in his ear and his face heated. He thought of the rings on his fingers and winced.

"Sorry." She kissed his cheek.

The voice continued, "Warriors use brute force far more often than commonsense. That's why so many have died where you stand. Warriors have deaf ears and ignore the soundest advice."

"If the beetles left behind the piles of bones, commonsense doesn't come into play. No insect is capable of negotiation," Roble said. "Seems a foolish thought to entertain. Extermination is the best solution."

"With your metal weapons?" the voice said.

"Yes."

The hidden speaker roared with echoing laughter.

Roble winced.

"Your ignorance reigns above your rationality."

"How?" Roble asked.

"Their exoskeletons are harder than any armor the best smith can fashion. Your weapons won't penetrate their shells. No warrior has yet found any physical weakness or vulnerability. Hundreds have tried and failed."

"There's always an exception," Roble replied.

"Every warrior's ghost before you thought the same."

"Roble," Lehrling whispered. "We should retreat."

Laughter echoed in their heads from the unseen one. "In seconds, beetles will fill the tunnel and you'll be surrounded because you've chosen to waste your time arguing with me."

"So, you set us up?" Roble asked.

"Not at all. I asked a simple question and you refused to answer. Yet, you continue to squabble. The blame falls on you. I could've helped you. Instead, you debate. Still think you're *not* a foolish warrior?"

Roble took a sharp breath. Anger overshadowed him. He glanced over his shoulder into the darkened tunnel. Clicking sounds from the beetles' leg sheaths rubbing together echoed in the darkness.

"You can't rely upon metal weapons," the voice said. "In case you didn't notice, there aren't any swords or metal armor on the floor. Time's a fleeting commodity. The only metal here is whatever metal you've brought inside. There's a reason for that."

"What is that?" Roble asked.

"The beetles spit acid that melts metal. Are you ready to tell me how many are in your group, or do you wish to be reduced to piles of bone?"

"What difference does it make now?" Roble asked.

"See? No rationality. Your stubbornness will be your death."

"There are five of us," Shawndirea said aloud.

Roble felt the heat of her angered glare directed at him.

"Finally, a voice of reasoning." His voice held a tone of relief and a slight sigh.

"I happen to agree with Roble in giving away too much information. Why's our number important?" Daphne asked.

"I could only read the minds of two men. The foolish one and the cowardice one beside him. I sensed others capable of blocking my mental probing, so I assume some of you use magic?"

"Yes."

"How many?"

"Three," Shawndirea replied.

"Three? Good. Perhaps it's enough."

"Enough for what?" Roble asked.

"Get off the ledge, if you hope to live," the voice said.

"Who are you?" Roble asked.

"Is my name important at the moment?"

"You said you'd—"

"*Still* you argue. Sephar'ris is my name. Let's hope you've not wasted so much time as my name be the last spoken one you hear."

CHAPTER 59

*R*oble stepped off the edge of the bored tunnel and dropped onto a narrow rock jutting from the wall. Shawndirea flew from his shoulder and hovered above him.

The rock where Roble stood was supported by the top of a broken pillar that once met the ceiling as a buttress. He offered his hand to Lehrling. Lehrling stooped and clasped it.

From the tunnel came the high-pitched hungry shrills of massive hurtling insects. Their hard exoskeletons clattered against one another as they fought and scurried to reach their prey ahead of each other.

"Jump!" Roble shouted, still clutching Lehrling's hand. Lehrling closed his fearful eyes, mouthed a prayer, and took what Roble could only define as an actual leap of faith.

Lehrling landed on the narrow top of the rock beside Roble, but his footing wasn't sound. He teetered to the right, his boots slipped, and his weight yanked Roble with him. Somehow, Lehrling completely missed the broken edge of the pillar, which would've given him adequate footing to correct his balance.

Roble's free hand desperately slid along the edge of the cracked wall, until he frantically gripped a thick root. He held fast and struggled not to lessen the grip of either hand, but holding Lehrling's dead weight strained Roble's right arm and shoulder. Lehrling flailed his free arm and blindly grabbed for any solid object to steady himself, but nothing was within his reach.

"Use the pillar for support," Roble groaned.

Lehrling stiffened his legs and placed his feet against the pillar, but the slick wet moss prevented him from steadying himself.

Roble looked at the tunnel opening and hoped Portia or Daphne noticed his peril and could offer some assistance. Instead, Daphne grabbed Portia's hand and turned her sister to face the giant, scuttling beetles rushing toward them. The sisters raised their hands and chanted in a strange language. A flickering fiery wall roared into a hellish gate of heat across the tunnel.

Several beetles squealed, their armored legs clattered like slamming steel shields, and their fire-engulfed bodies barreled past Daphne and Portia and plummeted out the opening and crashed on the marble-tiled floor below. The heat of their blazing bodies nearly scorched the side of Roble's face. Shawndirea thrust an icy bolt of air to lessen the fire's effect on his head since he lacked a protective helm. His armor absorbed the majority of the flaming heat from the neck down and yet, he continued struggling to hold Lehrling's hand.

The dying beetles hit the floor and flipped onto their backs. Their burning legs and antennae curled and flailed, slowly growing tighter and crisper until death claimed them. Regardless of how tough their exoskeletons were, fire was their greatest weakness. Their insides were roasted by the intense heat.

Roble pulled the root harder, trying to maintain what little footing he had, but the strain of Lehrling attempting to find footing against the pillar was overbearing. He was thankful Lehrling wore thick leather and not heavy plate or steel. Otherwise, Roble could never have held Lehrling for as long as he had.

"Hold on, Lehrling," Roble groaned.

Roble pressed his chin to his chest and focused his strength in holding the root for leverage. He held fast until he thought his shoulder would dislocate itself, but he never surrendered to the agonizing pain. Although the fall wasn't far enough to *kill* Lehrling, Lehrling had sustained severe injuries from falling in the past and he couldn't risk Lehrling becoming immobilized in the middle of the swamp. Getting Lehrling to safety outside the ruins would prove too difficult.

Lehrling grunted and after several weak attempts, he placed his hand into a narrow crevice. He gripped the rough rocks tightly, which helped stabilize him and lessened the strain on Roble's arms and shoulders.

Roble struggled to hold Lehrling's hand and keep him from plummeting to the marble floor.

Lehrling pulled himself partially upright and rested his feet against a large crack in the pillar. After Lehrling secured better balance, Lehrling dove forward and landed on his stomach. He clung to the rock with his free hand.

Roble released the root and Lehrling's hand. He turned, pressed his back against the rock wall, and panted. While trying to regain his composure, Roble scanned the ceiling near the waterfall where the other large beetles clung. They were gone. Had the fire frightened them? Perhaps. Or perhaps, the painful cries of the burning beetles had signaled the others into hiding.

No longer using telepathy, Sephar'ris said, "Well done. You killed at least three of them."

"Show yourself," Roble said in between panting.

"I can't. Not yet."

"Why not?"

Sephar'ris didn't reply.

The fire wall Daphne and Portia created filled the inside of the tunnel. The outside air pressure funneled the flames all the way to the entrance side.

"If any beetles were inside the tunnel, the fire has destroyed them. We have a safe passage out," Daphne said. "As for you, Sephar'ris, reveal yourself, if you wish any further aid from us."

"I tell you the truth. I can't. For if I do, all of you die with me."

Short of breath, Roble said, "The other beetles have retreated, for now. I doubt they'll return to attack for a while."

"Although daunting, the beetles aren't what I fear the most," Sephar'ris said.

"What causes your greater fear?" Daphne asked.

"The rifts," he replied.

"We sensed a rift," Shawndirea said. "Perhaps more than one."

"Yes, there are at *least* three," he said. "Perhaps more."

"Why do the overlapping rifts trouble you?"

"You don't understand."

"Then explain it?" Roble said, angrily pushing himself to his feet.

"Warrior—"

"Knight," Roble seethed.

"Knight, I can *not* speak logically with you."

"Why not?"

"Because warr—*knights* often aren't led by logic."

"I'd be happy to debate that," Roble said with a harsh stare.

"I'm certain you would!" Sephar'ris. "Again, proving my point."

Even though Sephar'ris spoke aloud, the high ceiling caused his voice to echo, which made it impossible to distinguish the vicinity from where he spoke.

Sephar'ris sighed. "Rather, they tend to use brute strength and aggression to get what they want. Like now, your anger indicates—"

"My anger, as you put it," Roble said, "stems from the fact that we almost lost our lives. I've little patience to put up with your charade—"

"Charade?" Sephar'ris said in an abrupt tone. "I assure you this is no charade."

"Then—"

"Look, don't make demands of me," Sephar'ris replied. "Or else, I'll cease talking and leave you to your demise. You've yet to witness the real danger in this place. Without my further assistance, you'll trigger what guards these portals and you'll die."

Roble crossed his arms and tried to suppress his anger. "My apologies. Please shed more light on this."

Sephar'ris kept silent for the better part of a minute. "The reason no one before you survived is because a bullheaded warrior led them to their deaths. Every … single … time. Warriors think brute strength can defeat everything before them. None ever killed any of these beetles. Perhaps you, warrior, will let that seep into your thickened skull. You didn't kill the dead beetles on the floor. The mages, or whatever they are, used magic to destroy them. Not you or your weapons."

"Yes," Roble said. "No need to hammer the point. But I'm not as thick-skulled as you'd think. Skip the prattling and get to the point."

"*Roble!*" Shawndirea hissed in a firm whisper.

Silence hung between them for several minutes, until Roble exchanged glances with Lehrling and then Shawndirea. Both shrugged.

"Enough of this." Roble grabbed the large root and prepared to climb to the opening where Portia and Daphne stood. "Let's leave this place."

"Wait," Sephar'ris said in a softer tone. "Perhaps my judgments have been too hasty, based on all those who blatantly ignored my warnings in the past. I plead to those who wield magic. Please offer your power to release me."

"What must we do?" Daphne asked.

Shawndirea flew to the broken pillar where Roble and Lehrling stood.

"Repair the rifts."

Shawndirea frowned. "Repair them?"

"Yes."

Shawndirea glanced at Daphne. The two exchanged puzzled expressions.

"Where are they?" Daphne asked.

"They overlap above the water pool," Sephar'ris replied. "And are hidden inside the waterfall."

"How many?"

"Two I'm certain of, but on occasion, a third rift emerges between them."

"I doubt our combined power is strong enough to seal these rifts. Not since they're so close together," Daphne replied.

"You must try," he replied in a weak voice mixed with sorrow. "It's the only way I can be freed."

"What do you know about the rifts?" Portia asked.

"If they remain unsealed, chaos will emerge in full force. Nothing will prevent worser things from entering our realm. Hope will be dashed forever."

"How do you know this?" Roble asked.

"Because I'm the last of those who lived here long ago."

CHAPTER 60

"The last?" Roble offered his hand to help Daphne step off the ledge onto the top of the broken pillar.

Lehrling had climbed down the thick ivy vines that encircled the pillar. He waited to help Daphne and Portia to the floor.

"Yes," Sephar'ris replied.

"How long have these rifts existed in Evendusk?" Daphne turned in the direction of the water pool.

"The formation of the rifts were Evendusk's downfall," he said solemnly.

"Several rifts materializing so close together couldn't have occurred naturally," Daphne said. "I've never encountered such a combination of rifts before. I've heard of a double rift only once. These inside the waterfall didn't occur on their own, did they?"

"No. She'zist and her coven performed rituals at an altar where the water pool now sets. They bent edges of different realm barriers until they weakened and formed narrow rift slits. These allowed us to pass through to other realms and others from those realms could come to us." Sephar'ris' voice broke with sadness. "Their hope was to increase our strength and power by forming alliances with civilizations in other realms, but that didn't happen. Instead, we suffered several invasions, which cost the lives of thousands in our city."

"What happened?" Lehrling asked.

"None of the realms She'zist connected to held peaceful races. All were hostile. They entered at such a rapid pace that we had no time to defend ourselves."

Shawndirea flew closer to the waterfall, studied it for several moments, and then darted back to Roble. "She didn't intentionally open more than one rift at a time, did she?"

"I don't believe she ever intended for more than one to be opened at the same time. She thought she could open and close them at will. But while she discovered they were easy to open," Sephar'ris said. "They couldn't be closed quickly."

Roble frowned. "Why didn't she seal them?"

"She tried. But she failed. Forming and opening the rifts was too easy, which all of us had thought to be suspicious. Closing them became an *impossible* task."

"Why?" Roble asked.

"Because she and her coven stood at the rift column when the first invasions came, they were the first to die. Even if they could've cast a protective spell, they didn't have time. They weren't prepared. The monsters came through first, killed the witches, and then retreated through the rifts. Their soldiers came next to kill our remaining population."

"How'd you survive?" Lehrling asked.

Sephar'ris ignored the question. "Those of us who held magical abilities were summoned to close the rifts. We failed, too. After three different races plundered us, the rift portals became heavily guarded. Those beetles you encountered are the current guardians. Perhaps the last."

"Why are they the last?" Roble asked.

"What's left for them to take?" Sephar'ris asked. "They've destroyed everything we held sacred. What valuable gems and precious metals we possessed were taken through the rifts. All that's left of our city are ruins. Hulls of shops, houses, lodges, and the palace are in shambles. The beetles guard the rifts to prevent anyone from invading their realms."

"What races passed through into Evendusk?" Daphne asked.

"Goblins were one. The others ... I've never seen before."

"Goblins?" Lehrling said in surprise. "Did they return through the rifts?"

"No. They resided here for a short time. Then they left our city and dispersed into Aetheaon."

"Other than the beetles, what opposition do we face once we try to seal the rifts?" Daphne asked.

"No one knows," Sephar'ris replied. "Other monsters could lie in wait should anyone tamper with the rifts."

"And you want *us* to seal the rifts?" Roble asked.

"Not *you*, obviously, since you can't wield magic."

"I'm aware," Roble said angrily. "But if Evendusk's witch coven was unable to seal the rifts, what makes you believe *three* attuned to magic can be successful?"

"Four," Sephar'ris said. "I'll assist with my magic."

"So four?" Roble said. "Against whatever might flood through those portals? That's too great a risk for us."

"Not as risky as it might've been a few days ago," he said.

"Why's that?"

"A stranger came to this forsaken garden, apparently drawn by the power of the rifts. He was a dark wizard, a sorcerer unlike any I've ever seen. His power astounded me." Sephar'ris's voice quaked. "Before he arrived, I wasn't the only voice protecting others from the portals. Three of my brethren were hidden with me. This man, or *demon*, I should say, sucked their spirits into himself. Their essence, though pure, he took and tarnished by adjoining them to his soul."

"That's possible?" Roble whispered.

Shawndirea nodded.

"Why'd he spare you?" Roble asked.

"A question I've mulled for days now," Sephar'ris said softly. "Perhaps he left me as a witness? To alert others? I don't know."

Daphne frowned and walked closer to the water pool. "Do you know this wizard's name? Was it Tyrann?"

"No," he replied. "Tyrann I'd have recognized, as I crossed paths with him long before the formation of the Black Chasm. This darker wizard is more vile and has greater evil than Tyrann. Tyrann never leaves the City of Mortel."

Daphne nodded. "Any idea who this was?"

"Mors … that's what his minions called him. He arrived in a black carriage with a horse from the abyss."

Roble and Lehrling exchanged troubled glances.

"You know him?" Sephar'ris asked.

Roble nodded. "Yes. He's the Plague-bringer. He destroyed most of Glacier Ridge. He has raised armies of undead and even a dead dragon. He's a necromancer."

"I realize his power. He's still adding numbers to his army. When he left Evendusk, he called to life more than a thousand of our dead to serve him. Those we had revered in life are now fallen as his undead."

"A thousand?" Roble shook his head. "If that many followed him, they'd have left an obvious path. No such evidence disturbs the tunnel we entered or the garden grounds."

"Indeed not," Sephar'ris said. "With his immense power, he formed a portal from the rifts and ushered them through."

"Did he leave with them?" Daphne asked.

"No. Not through the rift portal. He closed it soon after they departed, after killing the guardians that opposed his meddling with the rifts. That's why I think we can finally seal these. Unless new guardians have replaced them."

"He sent the army through?" Roble said. "To where?"

"I've no idea. After they went through, he got on the black carriage and a magical whirlwind carried him away."

Roble looked at Daphne. "Where do you think he sent them?"

"The possibilities are endless, Roble. Perhaps he suspended some-where to release at another time."

"He can do that?" Lehrling asked.

"Yes. As a necromancer that has Death following him, he can suspend resurrections at will. Frightening to comprehend." Daphne wrung her hands with worry. "If one could predict his first major attack, we'd be able to attempt a counterattack against him. As it is, he's accumulating an army that no one will be able to count."

"Can you seal these portals?" Roble asked.

"Let me consult with my sister and Shawndirea."

CHAPTER 61

*R*oble scanned the tarnished architecture of Evendusk's garden pillars and pools. He wished he could've seen the city's former glory. He could almost picture the interactions of those who had passed through these prosperous gardens.

After much deliberation with Portia and Shawndirea, Daphne finally said, "We might be able to bend the rifts into one roughly combined corner. Doing so prevents any of these rifts from being used. But more importantly, no further invasions from other planes will attack through these portals. Yet, we have a problem."

"What?" Roble said.

Daphne swallowed hard. "We need a sacrifice. One pure in heart, mind, and soul. Performing such a sacrifice requires dark sorcery that none of us are willing to do."

"There are no other options?" Roble asked. "We can't allow these rifts to remain open. Mors has the ability to manipulate them for his purposes."

"I agree." Lehrling stepped closer. "There has to be another way."

Shawndirea looked in Roble's eyes. "We know of no other way to seal these planar rifts. Should we only close one, it'll trigger immediate responses from the other two. All three must be sealed at once. Otherwise, the invading guardians will kill us all."

"I volunteer," Sephar'ris said softly.

Roble and the others frowned and looked in the direction of Sephar'ris' voice. For the first time, his voice didn't echo. He was closer to them than they expected.

"What?" Roble placed his hands on the hilts of his throwing knives.

"Sacrifice me," Sephar'ris replied. "It's the only solution to satisfy what's necessary to seal the openings."

Lehrling appeared puzzled. "You're willing to do this with such little thought?"

"For as long as I care to remember, I've offered warning after warning to those who've adventured here. Yet, no one heeded my warnings. Hundreds of treasure-seekers lost their lives."

"You're not responsible for their willingness to sabotage their own fates," Shawndirea said.

"Perhaps not, but the weight and toll of it all is more than I wish to bear. Sealing these rifts prevents future deaths from the foreign guardians."

Lehrling's brow furrowed. "But you're Evendusk's last survivor. You hold the truth and the legends of your city. You should be the city's historian orator so visitors know what occurred here."

"That's not entirely true," Sephar'ris said.

"What isn't?" Roble asked.

"Me being the last survivor."

"You're not?" Lehrling asked. "You said Mors took your other comrades."

"That occurred," Sephar'ris said. "But my explanation wasn't clear."

Daphne's eyes narrowed. "What do you mean?"

Sephar'ris slowly materialized in front of them. They gasped. "I didn't survive."

"You're a ghost?" Roble asked.

"Yes. An apparition," Sephar'ris replied. "I'm not the last survivor, per se. I'm the last living *voice*. My essence is of a purity you'll never find in the living. I remained, along with my brethren, in the hopes to warn the living of the dangers in our gardens."

Roble glanced at Daphne. "Would his proposal even work with him being in spirit form?"

Before Daphne offered a reply, Sephar'ris said, "I'm a part of Even-dusk, and as such, it's vital you use *my* essence to thread these rifts shut. Nothing else will achieve such a feat."

Roble stared in near disbelief at Sephar'ris. The pale figure of the man hovered several inches off the tarnished tile floor. If Sephar'ris' image reflected his living form, he must've died fairly young—in his mid-twenties or early thirties. He wore a cowl that didn't cover his bearded chin and the sleeves of his robe concealed his hands. In his near transparent form, his face looked almost human, but his eyes indicated he wasn't.

The hem of his robe hid his feet. The silvery pendant hanging on the chain around his neck flickered silver in the lighting, which gave his eyes an odd glow.

Daphne sighed. "He's right, Roble. If he offered himself as the sacrifice, and since he's in spirit form, we could bind those three rifts into one corner and block the passage from either side. He'd become the tethered anchor and seal them shut forever. No blood would be shed, so it wouldn't be dark sorcery, either."

Roble said, "Is that how you'd want to spend eternity, Sephar'ris?"

Everyone gave Roble an odd glance.

"Have you become a priest, warrior?" Sephar'ris asked with a slight smile.

"No," Roble replied. "Not at all."

Sephar'ris offered a brief moment of laughter. "It's not suitable for those who've killed as warriors. No redemption."

"I seek none. Connecting the three rifts with your essence won't be a short-termed imprisonment."

"My sacrifice won't be imprisonment at all," he replied. "It'd be my honor to seal these rifts to preserve what's left of Evendusk. As such, it means I'll forever become a part of the city. Tying the rifts together by the threads of my essence grants me guardianship over the ruins. I'll protect others who venture here."

"Your bold sacrifice impresses me," Roble said. "I'm curious, though, what more could be done to ensure we lessen Mors' power before his final confrontation."

"What confrontation?" Sephar'ris asked.

"For what he's been doing throughout Aetheaon, he's preparing for a major assault on the kingdoms. Eventually, he's going to be met by armies ready for war. Not everyone will lie down. A majority will fight."

"Maybe. But each soldier that dies fighting his undead will reemerge as one of his soldiers," Sephar'ris said. "His armies continue to increase as his enemies diminish."

"I know. That's why we should try to thwart his ability to summon those he sent through the rift."

"What are you thinking?" Daphne asked with a curious stare.

"If you're able to seal these rifts," Roble replied, "perhaps it suspends Mors' armies indefinitely? Perhaps it'll block his control over them?"

"It'd prevent his access from those armies, but only through these rifts," Daphne said. "He might pull them through a different portal."

"Does he have such power?" Roble asked.

"I don't know," Daphne replied.

"No, he doesn't," Sephar'ris said.

"How do you know this?" Portia asked.

"He has the power to raise the dead," Sephar'ris replied. "But the only reason he could use the rifts was because they were already open. He manipulated the guardians into attacking one another, and while they did, he used his demon minions to destroy those guardians. But he can't form portals at will. Roble may be right, and I pray he is. Shut the portals and prevent Evendusk's former residents from becoming Mors' pawns in battle."

Shawndirea glanced at Portia and then to Daphne. "Are we in agreement to use our magic to shut these rifts?"

Portia and Daphne nodded.

"A final word of warning." Sephar'ris looked at Roble. "Once their incantation begins, the guardians will attack."

"You said Mors had destroyed them," Lehrling said.

"He destroyed those guarding the rifts when he was here," Sephar'ris replied. "However, new ones might've replaced them. Or some of Mors' minions might await inside the rift portals. Take caution."

Roble nodded.

Sephar'ris said, "May the gods and goddesses protect you. The two of you must keep the three sorceresses safe. The odds for your success is limited, but fight you must."

CHAPTER 62

*R*oble pulled two sharpened daggers from the sheaths on the back of his belt. The blades' silvery edges gleamed in the bright glow of the Elfstones. On the opposite side of the water pool Lehrling had drawn his short sword. Sephar'ris' image hovered outside the waterfall.

Roble turned his attention to the splashing waterfall that vanished into the pool as the hidden rift captured the water. He remembered stepping through the rift inside Devils Den when he first entered Aetheaon. The rift had been hidden in the deep cavern, and he wondered for a several moments if, on the other side of *this* rift, someone stepped through a waterfall, would they pass into the Evendusk?

Daphne took a pouch of reddish brown grains from the inside of her robe. She walked a circle around the water pool while pouring the red grains to form a circle with Shawndirea and Portia on the inside with her. After she completed the circle, she stood equal distances from Shawndirea and Portia. They all faced the water pool.

Sephar'ris turned toward Roble and slowly glanced at each of the others. "Though there's no time to discuss where you venture after Evendusk, may the richest blessings be bestowed upon each of you. I can never offer enough gratitude for what you've done for me today."

"We've not succeeded," Daphne said.

"Even your offer at risking your own lives—"

"We understand," she replied.

Sephar'ris offered a gracious bow. "My thanks to all of you."

Daphne, Portia, and Shawndirea raised their hands above their heads and began chanting with their eyes closed. Seconds later, a cool air rushed through the city tunnels. The temperature plummeted.

Roble's hands tightened on the hilts of his daggers. He wasn't certain what to expect, and the fear in Lehrling's eyes indicated his friend didn't, either. Roble wished their fighting party was larger than it was. He didn't like the possibility of a single guardian emerging from a portal, but with how his luck normally played out, dozens of guardians would swarm them.

His gaze flicked briefly to Shawndirea. Her eyes were closed. She was encapsulated by the growing circle of protection and focused on drawing her magic from the earth. Not certain of what might happen during the next few minutes, he wished he'd consulted with her in private to lessen his apprehension and to express his love for her in case the incantation ended catastrophically.

Unseen waves of energy flowed. The hairs on the back of his neck stiffened. A tingling sensation ran down his spine and chill bumps radiated across his arms. The energy force increased more and more. Roble readied the daggers and attempted to take a step forward but the magic lining the protective circle pushed him backwards. The air thickened and any movements he made were as sluggish as trying to run through chest-deep water.

The circle of reddish brown grains Daphne had made slowly levitated and swirled and formed a wall around them.

Roble trembled with fear.

The rising wall enclosed around Shawndirea and the dryad sisters. They were inside *with* the portals. Anything coming out of the portals would attack them directly. He and Lehrling couldn't intervene, as they'd been instructed.

Roble struggled to move but his legs were heavy like steel anchors. He screamed to warn Shawndirea but his words were silenced. No sound came from his mouth, though he tried multiple times to shout.

Overcome by concern and possible betrayal, he glanced at Lehrling. Lehrling stood petrified, as he watched the floating reddish-brown grains disperse tiny green sprouts that rapidly extended leaves and weaved together like a magical curtain of vines. The vines serpentined, knitting and meshing together, and bit by bit, his view of Shawndirea was being blocked.

How could he and Lehrling protect them when Daphne had prevented them from entering the circle? She never forewarned about building a barrier to keep he and Lehrling out.

Movement from behind Lehrling captured Roble's attention. He shouted, "Run!"

Lehrling didn't hear Roble's desperate cry, nor did the word echo in Roble's ear.

Roble turned toward Lehrling and pushed against the invisible force that fought to hold him in place. He didn't know if the resistance was from the circle's magic or an unseen entity lurking in the shadowy ruins. Had Sephar'ris been wrong in claiming he was Evendusk's last voice or had he deceived them?

Roble didn't have time to ponder and even less time to react.

Roble leaned forward, lowered his head, and pushed his weight against the viscous air. Every muscle ached for the short distance he managed to move.

Lehrling looked from the circular ivy wall and gazed directly into Roble's eyes. He must have read Roble's panic. Lehrling turned as a giant beetle dropped from the ceiling. The cumbersome insect was not immune from the thick atmosphere shrouding the garden ruins. It dropped in slow motion, almost hovering as its legs thrashed and kicked.

Lehrling pushed off his left foot, apparently trying to dive to the side, but instead of a rapid fall to the ground, he hung in the air, momentarily cradled, while steadily descending in the same manner a fallen leaf drifts softly to the forest floor.

A viscous gel suspended them and hampered their movements. The helpless beetle maneuvered from its attempted attack but now it was confused by the sudden alteration of the terrain. Time was somehow lapsing, but he and Lehrling didn't have any real advantage. The slowing of time or whatever was responsible prolonged any attempted defense. He wished the lapse occurred with the beetles and whatever else might emerge from the portals. That'd give them the upper hand.

Lehrling slowly drifted to the ground, and Roble continued pushing through the invisible viscous medium. He gained several more steps but the strain sapped his strength. His inability to inhale deeply drained him, too. His vision blurred, darkened, and his heartbeat hammered inside his head. He was seconds from losing consciousness.

Roble's lungs ached and the drowning sensation pressing against his chest caused him to stop fighting his way through the gel-like barrier.

A blinding light gleamed inside the vine-enclosed circle where Shawndirea stood. He was helpless to defend her or himself. Gasping, Roble tried to see but the gardens darkened, in spite of the light. His knees buckled, everything spun in slow motion, and he fell backwards with less speed than a falling feather. He was near blacking out. The frightening sensations shrouding him was similar to the atmosphere in the Black Chasm, except this air wasn't toxic. It was too thick to breathe.

Roble's movements were like suspended animation. Everything outside the protective circle moved painstakingly slow, and was enough to challenge the most tenacious monk's inner patience.

Was Daphne to blame for the pausing of time, or should he be trying to locate the one responsible?

By the time Roble sat on the floor, Lehrling was lying on his side and his eyes stared lazily at Roble. No pain reflected in his eyes, but the heaviness of his eyelids meant he was fighting sleep or possibly death, if he couldn't breathe, either.

The maddening bright light inside the tall cylindrical vine wall flashed with tiny rays escaping through the narrow slits in the foliage. Roble attempted to analyze what was occurring inside the circle, but the harsh light prevented it.

The large beetle finally rested on the floor. Its hard carapace scraped across the rock as it landed on its back, lifeless, and its legs curled in death.

Roble tried to push himself to his feet to check on Lehrling, but the surrounding, invisible force prevented him from rising. With the exception of the dead beetle, no other insects or attackers had revealed themselves … yet. Since everything moved in slow motion, it was difficult to determine. Observers cloaked with invisibility could be nearby, so possible dangers still existed.

Roble wondered if the magical circle prevented guardians from emerging from the rifts and attacking. Their combined power was strong enough to incapacitate him and Lehrling. Hopefully, the rifts had melded sufficiently to prevent further attacks.

Still gripping his daggers tightly, he slowly raised his hands in a defensive manner. That's when his heart nearly froze. The gems in his rings suddenly flickered and brightened. Shawndirea's spell no longer clouded them. Since she'd focused her mind and magic to aid Daphne and Portia, Shawndirea's spell on the rings must have weakened and allowed Lez'minx to use the rings once again.

The gemstones glowed brighter and sent a tingling sensation through Roble's fingers and up his forearms. The thickness of the air around him melted, and he could move freely. He took several deep breaths and pushed himself to his feet.

Lehrling's heavy eyes closed. Roble took a cautious step toward his friend. He half expected the viscous wall to hamper his movements, but the barrier was gone. He hurried and helped Lehrling sit up.

Lehrling panted, frowned, and rubbed his forehead.

"What happened?" Lehrling asked.

Roble shrugged, while trying to analyze his surroundings.

For the first time since the magical ivy cylinder had enveloped Shawndirea, Portia, and Daphne, Roble could hear. Their voices chanted in a language with a soothing melody. The blinding light inside the protective circle hummed steadily but with a slight undertone. The sound of the waterfall was no longer audible.

"You okay?" Roble offered his hand to help Lehrling stand.

Lehrling nodded. "I couldn't breathe."

Roble pulled Lehrling to his feet. "Me, either. It had me worried for several minutes."

Lehrling's eyes widened. "Your rings."

Roble nodded. "I know."

"Are there no guardians?"

"We've no way to know," Roble replied. "Daphne hedged us outside their circle. If anything emerges, we've no way to intervene."

"The beetle—"

Roble shook his head. "No. It was here before they began the incantation."

"No." Lehrling pointed. "It's moving."

CHAPTER 63

$\mathcal{T}$he beetle lying on its back rocked back and forth and attempted to right itself. Its legs twitched. Roble rushed to it with one dagger raised above his head.

The blade couldn't penetrate the beetle's thick chitin exoskeleton, but with it on its back, it exposed its most vulnerable spot. Between its head and the thorax were soft connective muscles not covered by chitin, which allowed the insect's flexibility.

Roble brought down the blade and plunged it into the tender muscles. The beetle shrieked and its body writhed. Its armored legs thrashed. Due to its enormous size, the dagger didn't sever the head from its body. He yanked the blade free and stabbed repeatedly, until only a narrow strip of muscle attached the head to the thorax.

Liquid oozed from the wound and dripped into a growing pool on the floor. Although the beetle wasn't completely dead, it was dying and even if it flipped over, its mandibles were useless.

"Do you see any other beetles?" Roble said.

He and Lehrling scanned the ceilings and the shadowed edges of the walls.

Lehrling shook his head. "Best I can tell, no more are above us."

Roble studied the glowing gems set in his rings. "What do I do about these?"

"How'd they reactivate?" Lehrling stepped closer.

"I'm not certain," Roble replied. "But, once the stones started glowing, the choking air thinned, which allowed us to become mobile and breathe again."

"You think Lez'minx is protecting you?" Lehrling frowned but his voice trembled.

"Seems so."

"I shouldn't," a voice said.

Lehrling and Roble stared at the dying beetle where the voice had emitted. They exchanged troubled glances.

The beetle's lobbing head craned. Its giant, obsidian eyes shimmered while examining them. For a moment, their reflections were visible in the compound eyes' sheen like a mirror. The illusion soon faded. The glassy dark eyes glowed and ignited like flickering fire. The voice continued, "I should've watched you breathe your last breaths and die."

"Then why didn't you?" Roble pulled his knives.

"I've need of you."

"Lez'minx?" Roble said.

Lehrling gasped and gripped the hilt of his sword without hesitation.

"Aye, it's me, though not in the most prominent of vessels," he replied. "It suffices for now."

"Free me from your binding rings," Roble said firmly.

"For what reason?"

"I'll be enslaved to no one."

"Enslaved? That's how you view the rings? That they've *enslaved* you to me?"

"Haven't they? I see no alternative."

The beetle exhaled a strange shuttering sound that could be nothing more than a sigh. "What harm have I caused you? When have I ever hurt you? I've rescued you twice though."

"True. But when we last spoke, you threatened to kill Shawndirea, my wife," Roble said, unable to calm the anger in his voice.

"Mere words during moments of haste," Lez'minx replied. "I've no intention of harming either of you. Let's skirt past such remarks."

"Such words aren't easily forgotten. I won't dismiss them from my memory, ever."

"Overlanders savor grudges," Lez'minx said. "My apologies. I've every intention for you and her to prosper."

"For a price," Roble said.

"And what price is that?" Lez'minx asked.

"Servitude."

"You've mistaken my intent. I can offer you anything you desire. There's no limits to the power and wealth you could have."

"By serving you? No. I'm not interested."

"I've only asked you to meet me at my temple and hear my proposal."

"Your temple?" Roble laughed.

"That amuses you? Why?"

"Because I know your true real identity. You're *not* a god or a demigod. You don't *have* a temple. A shrine you've built to yourself, perhaps, but it's not a temple. You don't have devoted worshippers."

"Humor me, Roble. How'd you find this ... *incorrect* information?"

Lehrling opened his mouth to speak, but Roble shook his head and motioned for Lehrling to remain silent. He glared into the beetle's eyes.

"I have secrets," Roble said, "just like you have secrets."

"You're in the Ruins of Evendusk, so you are seeking my temple. You're less than a day's journey in reaching me," Lez'minx said. "I'm impressed."

"Don't expect my adoration once we find you," Roble said. "That's not my objective."

"Do you not fear what I'm capable of doing?"

"Why should I fear what you might do anyway?" Roble asked. "You use guile and threats to have others obey your demands. Just to enlighten you, people who do that aren't worshippers. They're victims, fearful of your bullying demeanor."

"Do recall. I killed a few dozen Shadowfae in the blink of an flickering wisp."

"Yes. I witnessed the unnecessary slaughter. You've created a vast number of enemies within the Shadowfae because you murdered those mercenaries. Those enemies are coming to find you."

"You're taking their side, Overlander?"

"No. But since your rings are bound to me, they assume I'm under your hold, which makes me their enemy as well. I'm not vested in your underhanded affairs. I've no part in your agendas."

Lez'minx hissed. "Understand something. Not only did I protect you, I protected Shawndirea when Dirk was set to imprison her."

"That somehow grants you my loyalty?"

"Shouldn't it?"

Roble said, "Your conceit for how the realm should behold you holds far more vanity than a god would ever display."

"You're right," Lez'minx said. "Most gods wouldn't tolerate your belligerent, defiant attitude. Perhaps I should kill you here?"

Shrills echoed from inside the protective circle where Shawndirea, Portia, and Daphne continued their chant.

"What was that?" Lez'minx asked. "I sense a great magical binding force. What's happening around you?"

"Nothing that concerns you." Roble pressed the rings' gemstones against his dark armor.

"What's Shawndirea doing?" Lez'minx asked. "Seems she's channeling a powerful spell."

"You're making assumptions, which means you're *not* omniscient. Kind of kills your boast of being a god, doesn't it?"

"Whatever she's doing weakened her spell to cloud your rings. For something to require that much attention, she must be participating in a ritual—"

Roble frowned. "It doesn't concern you."

"You *might* need my assistance," Lez'minx said in a near desperate tone.

"I'll take my chances." Roble looked at Lehrling. "Use your sword to severe the beetle's head from its body."

Lehrling nodded and drew his short sword. He brought the sword over his head, and decapitated the beetle. The ricochet clashed like two heavy swords striking one another. Lehrling winced from the jarring pain. "Will that stop him from talking?"

Roble shrugged. "Perhaps for now. I need to cover these rings with thick mud or clay until Shawndirea can recast the spell."

Lehrling scraped the tip of his sword along a crevice between a slab of marble and the claylike substance of the wall. He rubbed a thick glob over each stone in Roble's rings.

The pure white light inside the ivy cylinder ignited upward like a thick laser beam. Lehrling and Roble shielded their eyes. Several seconds passed before the light slowly dimmed and they could glance at the circle.

Dried, crumbled leaves on the brittle ivy vines dropped to the floor. The crisp vines bent under their own weight and dissolved into cascading red dust.

Shawndirea's wings drooped. She sat on her knees and leaned forward while balancing with her hands. Sweat streaked her face. She panted and kept her eyes closed, trying to regain her composure.

Roble rushed to her. "Are you okay?"

She offered a slight nod. "Give me a few minutes."

"Sure."

Afraid to touch or move her until she was stronger, he looked at where the waterfall had been. Instead of a waterfall, a column of white crystal rose from the water pool to the ceiling. The crystal shimmered like wet ice. No water dripped down the sides. Sephar'ris' image was visible about midway up the crystal.

Portia stretched prostrate on the floor. Shallow breaths escaped her narrow mouth. Daphne lie outstretched beside her. Neither attempted to rise. Soft groans rumbled in their throats.

"Not to alarm anyone," Roble said, "but Shawndirea's spell to block Lez'minx's view through the rings has been broken."

Daphne's and Portia's eyes flicked open. They gazed in his direction but were too tired to raise their heads.

"You're certain of this?" Daphne asked.

"He spoke to Lehrling and I just moments before your incantation ended."

Shawndirea gasped and looked at his rings.

"Then he knows we're with you?" Portia asked.

"He questioned what was happening, but he couldn't see you because of the thick ivy," Roble replied.

Daphne sighed and pushed herself into a seated position. "We've not much time. I hope we've not lost the element of surprise. As long as he doesn't know Portia and I are with you, we maintain the advantage."

CHAPTER 64

*R*oble waited fifteen minutes before Shawndirea gained enough strength to step on his hand. She placed her fingers to her temples and winced.

The white crystal column containing Sephar'ris' frozen image, pulsed. A beam of energy flowed outward, much like Daphne's healing stones she used the day after defeating the Saurians.

"Are you okay?" Roble asked.

Shawndirea nodded. "I'm fine. Drained is all."

Daphne stepped closer to Roble and examined his rings. She offered a weak smile. "Good. You did the right thing by coating these rings with clay. Perhaps in a few hours, Shawndirea will gain enough strength to cast a new spell over them."

Shawndirea nodded. "It shouldn't take that long. My strength's returning faster than I expected."

Daphne smiled and nodded. "That's due to Sephar'ris' blessing, spilling out from his essence in the light."

"His sacrifice was a worthy one," Roble said.

Daphne nodded. "Indeed."

Shawndirea straightened and arched her back. Her wings no longer drooped and the color returned to her face. "I'll cast a new spell over the rings in a few minutes. Does Lez'minx know what we were doing?"

"No. He asked," Roble said. "I refused to tell him. But, he knows we're in Evendusk."

"He said that?" Portia asked.

Roble and Lehrling nodded.

Portia glanced nervously at Daphne. "Does he know we're here, too?"

Roble said, "He didn't mention either of you. He fished for information, but I didn't give him any. Instead, I mentioned that since he didn't know, he couldn't be a god."

"I'm sure that went over well," Daphne said with a shrewd grin.

Roble shrugged. "He threatened my life."

"Our brother mustn't know we're with you," Daphne said. "Otherwise, he'll be prepared, and he might kill us all."

Roble frowned. "You're his siblings. He despises you that much?"

Portia cleared her throat. "No. But he'll be fearful of what we might do."

"Shawndirea," Daphne said. "Allow Portia and I to assist you with the incantation. Rather than block him, we should track his whereabouts. We need to find him before he finds us."

"You plan to kill him?" Lehrling asked.

"That's probably what he'd expect us to do," Daphne said.

"Is that your intention?" Roble asked.

Daphne wiped sweat from her brow and forced a smile. "Let us worry about the confrontation and how to negotiate with him to free you of those rings beforehand. For the moment, the rest of our party should join us where they'll be safer."

Shawndirea gazed at Sephar'ris. Brightness set in his frozen eyes and a content smile widened on his face. "He looks at peace."

"He chose to serve this purpose," Daphne replied. "He's forever a part of Evendusk. He's a true guardian and binds the three rifts together."

Worry furrowed Lehrling's brow. "I'll get Collette and the others. They're not safe outside since Lez'minx knows we're here."

"Go fetch them," Daphne said.

Lehrling eyed the crude broken pillar that led to the exit tunnel. "I can't possibly scale the wall. Not by myself. Is there another entrance?"

Roble followed the rough stone street from the crystal pillar to the far wall. Large rocks had fallen and blocked the street long ago, which was why a new tunnel was burrowed to get to the ruins. "The main passageway collapsed years ago."

"I'll go inform them," Shawndirea said.

Roble glanced at Daphne. "Are all the beetles in the tunnel dead?"

"It's doubtful any *thing* survived the fire," she replied.

CHAPTER 65

Shawndirea glided through the smoke-filled tunnel and passed over several charred beetle carapaces. The lingering, acrid aroma of the burnt insects left a choking, nauseating smell. She covered her nose as she flew. Any moss or mushrooms that had clung to the rocks were shriveled into black, crispy plant matter. The slightest vibrations of her delicate wings caused these plant remnants to dissolve into darkened ash and fall to the tunnel floor.

The degree of heat from Daphne and Portia's fire was beyond her comprehension. She had seen dryads' power in the past. Dryads drew their magical energy from the forests. The crude carved tunnel didn't host trees and hadn't been invaded by thick roots, either. Dryads tended to use their power to protect their tree homes but seldom did they possess enough strength to thwart a group deforesting an area. Many perished after the trees they were linked to died.

The spell for the wall of fire had been instant without any prior preparation by Daphne or Portia. Their fire hadn't been a single wall to seal one end. The roaring fire blasted through the entire tunnel, singeing and killing anything in its path. She had never met a dryad with the ability to cast fire spells, which was concerning. Fire could consume forests, so it was an unwelcomed element by general consensus for dryads to use.

She wondered about Lez'minx and why Daphne and Portia despised him enough to kill him. What had he done to scorn them? Although Daphne kept denying her murderous intent with mere words, her eyes betrayed her. Her facial expressions revealed her lies.

Shawndirea was fairly confident Roble had noticed, too, which was why he kept pressing Daphne for further information. Yet, Daphne avoided giving a direct answer. What did they intend to do to Lez'minx and why?

She doubted she'd get these answers until *after* Lez'minx was killed, provided that was Daphne's true intent. His premature death left her and Roble with the dilemma of the binding magical rings. While she believed Lez'minx's spell ended with his death, Daphne had sown enough doubt that his magic might outlive him. If so, they couldn't leave it to chance.

Somehow, Roble needed to persuade Lez'minx to release him from the rings *before* Daphne and Portia confronted their brother and performed whatever hostilities they plotted. Thus, their need for secrecy and their hope Lez'minx didn't learn his sisters were traveling with Roble and Shawndirea. They needed the element of surprise, which hinted he might be stronger than they.

Faint light appeared about ten yards from the tunnel's mouth overlooking the river's edge. She increased her speed until she noticed the outline of a body lying on the floor. She dipped slightly and hovered in place while examining the scorched body. No corpse had been on the floor when they entered. Only the bones of previous victims had been on the path.

After a minute or so, Shawndirea assumed the corpse was one of Daphne's party paddled the raft. He had fallen victim to her fiery spell and died. But a closer look and she realized the bones were of a little person and not one of the dryads. His death wasn't intentional, as Daphne probably had no idea he had entered into the tunnel.

Uneasiness tensed her stomach. Tears crested in her eyes. Because of the severity of the burns, she couldn't determine which halfling had died.

"You must claim your rite and accept the power of who you truly are," a voice whispered inside her mind.

Shawndirea stiffened for a moment and then flitted toward the tunnel entrance.

"Don't flee," he said. "Power and authority await you."

She recognized the male voice from her deep sleep. More disturbing, she remembered this sovereign voice when she was a child.

Chills shot through her.

"Have you not discovered how your magic has changed since you crossed the in-between?"

"I've gone mad." Shawndirea placed her hands to her temple.

"Not mad. *Enlightened*. A grand difference."

"Until you reveal to me who you are, you're only a figment of my troubled mind," she replied.

"Your place isn't with the human—"

"Roble's my husband. Nothing changes that. I chose him and he has chosen me."

"He's in danger for as long as he stays with you."

"I can protect him," she said.

"Can you?"

"Yes. I'm confident I can. He trusts me."

"Trusts you?" A slight chuckle rumbled inside her mind. "And yet, you've not told him everything about you, have you?"

Shawndirea took a sharp breath and bit her tongue. How'd this phantom voice know her secrets?

"I know all about you," he said.

"Who are you?"

A gentle rumble of laughter rang in her ears and slowly faded.

She peered down the dark tunnel. Roble and the rest of their group slowly approached in the shadows. She tried to push the thoughts from her mind and regain her composure.

Daphne paused where Shawndirea hovered. In the darkness, Daphne noticed the scorched body beneath the faery's glow. "Who's this?"

Shawndirea fought tears. "I—I'm not certain."

Lehrling carried a flaming torch and stopped where Daphne and Shawndirea were on the tunnel path. His voice choked. "It's one of the halflings."

"Yes," Daphne replied. She sighed.

"Oh, no!" Portia placed a hand over her mouth. "What have we done?"

"We protected ourselves," Daphne replied. "That's what we did. Sometimes, casualties occur."

Portia's eyes narrowed as she glanced at her sister. "To you these halflings are nothing. But for me, they're my friends."

"They were warned," Daphne said with stiff coldness.

"Warned?"

"I told them to remain in Dagger's Tears," Daphne said. "Did I not?"

Portia glared.

"Sister, none of us had any idea a halfling had followed us into the tunnel," Daphne said.

Tears trailed down Portia's face.

"I'm sorry," Daphne said. The coldness faded in her voice and genuine remorse weighed upon her features. "I truly am. I hate that this happened. I do. But understand, its death would've been far worse had one of those giant beetles attacked."

"It?" Portia said. "He or she had a name."

"I phrased my words poorly," Daphne said. "Please forgive me."

Portia knelt beside the smoldering body. The charred, blistered flesh prevented any recognition.

"It's regrettable," Roble said. "But Daphne's right about the pain those beetles would've caused before killing him or her."

Portia gasped, whimpered softly, and walked to the tunnel exit.

"It was unforeseeable." Daphne shook her head. "We barely had time to defend ourselves from the beetles' attack. We didn't have time to think—"

"We know." Shawndirea rose in the air and darted to catch Portia.

ROBLE GLANCED from the dead halfling's body and looked in Daphne's tear-filled eyes. She possessed no hardened exterior, and for the first time, she revealed deep passion he'd not seen in her before. Perhaps she'd suffered so much loss that she shielded herself by portraying a calloused outlook to those around her. Sudden regret crushed her facade. "None of us blame you."

"That's not true," Daphne replied. "Portia will never forgive me."

"You saved our lives," Roble said.

"Indeed," Lehrling said, unable to hide his sadness. "Accidents happen."

Roble nodded. "I'd have never expected any halflings to enter the dark tunnel without us. Dolan is too timid."

"I know," Daphne said. "Yet, I can't relinquish my guilt."

Roble took her hand. "Come on. We need to return to the others."

She accepted his hand and nodded. He had half expected her to pull from his grip. Her cold skin was odd with little bumps and grooves similar to tree bark. Though cold, a flux of energy flowed through her skin and provided a tickling sensation as her power massaged his flesh. The odd sensation was pleasant.

"Perhaps I've misjudged you," Daphne said.

"I have you," Roble replied.

"Is that so?"

He nodded. "Yes."

"You probably saw me for what I wanted you to see, but in truth, my heart isn't petrified," she said.

"I'm beginning to see that." He grinned.

Her lips formed a quick grin, which disappeared in the blink of an eye. "I envy Shawndirea."

"Why?" Roble asked.

"She sacrificed her right to the throne of Elvendale because of how much she loves you. Despite you being a human, she looked deeper. I somewhat see what drew her to you. You're not like the humans in Aetheaon, and certainly not like Overlanders I've encountered before."

"No, he's certainly not," Lehrling said.

Daphne smiled. "I've a feeling there's a reason she sought you in the Overlands. Fate has everything to do with you being in Aetheaon. It's no accident you're here. Perhaps this is why my brother wishes to control you. He must've sensed that when you obtained your armor. When our paths cross his tomorrow, you'll be freed of those rings. He'll release you from all future obligations."

"*What* did he do to make you hate him as thoroughly as you do?" Roble asked.

"That's a story for another day," Daphne replied.

CHAPTER 66

$\mathcal{U}$sing Lehrling's torch to guide him, Roble led the way to the tunnel entrance. Small shadows appeared and stood blocking the opening before they could exit.

"Have you seen Rufus?" Dolan asked. "He said he was going to examine the cave to see if you were all right. But that's been quite some time ago."

Merla nodded. "Yes, we became more concerned after the blazing fire spewed out the tunnel."

"Is a dragon in there?" Cora asked.

Shawndirea regarded them with teary eyes. She looked at Roble.

"No dragon." Daphne's voice cracked when she attempted to say more, so she looked away.

"What happened?" Dolan's face tightened with fear. "Is he okay?"

Lehrling lowered the torch and looked down.

"No. He's ... not," Portia said.

Cora and Merla gasped.

Dolan tried to look around them into the darkness of the tunnel. "He's dead?"

Daphne nodded. "I'm afraid so."

Dolan sniffled. "How'd he die?"

"The fire," Daphne replied.

"No dragon? Then what caused the fiery explosion? We felt the heat near the river bank," Dolan said. "If there isn't a dragon, magic created the fire?"

"Yes," Daphne said with remorse. "My sister and I cast a fire spell."

The three halflings' eyes hollowed in disbelief. Portia wrung her hands together.

Anger narrowed Dolan's gaze and his voice became harsh. "You killed Rufus? Your magic, you said, was *always* used to heal others. And yet, you killed our friend and brother."

Portia closed her eyes. Tears spilled and ran down her cheeks. "The spell was made in haste to protect us."

"It didn't protect *him*," Dolan said through gritted teeth. "Now, did it?"

"In all fairness," Roble said, "they didn't know Rufus was in the tunnel."

Dolan pointed a stern finger. "You keep out of this, Overlander. All was well until you and Lehrling and Daphne came to Dagger's Tears. Portia would never have done such a thing without her sister's assistance."

"None of us knew Rufus had followed," Roble said. "Had the fire not killed him instantly, his death would've been much slower and more painful."

Dolan pulled a dagger. The blade reflected in the torchlight. "I told you to keep out of this!"

"Careful." Roble slid a hand over a throwing knife.

"As I recall," Daphne said. Her remorse faded and anger coated her words. "You were all told to *stay* in Dagger's Tears, were you not?"

Balls of red flames rose on her hands.

Shawndirea shook her head. Her fingertips glowed green. She glared at Daphne. "No! No one else needs to die."

"That depends on Dolan," Daphne said. "Put the blade away."

Dolan watched the flames dance on Daphne's hands. His eyes seemed to entertain that he still wanted to attack.

Cora placed a hand on his cheek. "What's done is done, Dolan. We don't want to lose you, too. Let's ... let's go get Rufus' corpse."

Dolan brushed her hand away and glared at Daphne. His hand tightened on the dagger's hilt as though he might attack. "Magic can't protect you from everything."

"Dolan," Cora whispered. "Don't make us lose you, too."

"Not today, you won't lose me at her hand," Dolan said. "I won't give her the pleasure of killing another of us. Hers is coming. She has no remorse for our loss."

"That … isn't true," Daphne said.

Dolan rammed his dagger into its sheath and pushed his way past Roble and the others.

"Allow me to help," Roble said.

"Do us no favors," Dolan replied.

"Here." Lehrling offered Dolan the torch. "You'll need this. It's mighty dark inside."

Dolan paused and stared into the flame. He shrugged, nodded, and took the torch. "Thanks."

Cora and Merla followed Dolan. They weeped and wailed aloud.

Daphne turned and watched the three halflings walk away. "What happened was not done purposely. I hope you search your hearts and understand I'd never use magic—"

"Be gone," Dolan said. "Let us concern ourselves with the loss of our brother."

Nightfall darkened the dark sandy river bank as Roble and his friends left the entrance. They made their way down the narrow pathway to join the other dryads near the river's edge.

Daphne joined Aqese and Ki'wese at the supplies and the horses. A small fire flickered atop the sand-covered pebbles. Before she said anything, she glanced at the tunnel and shook her head.

"There's nothing I can do to ever make this right," Daphne said. "Is there?"

Portia leaned and hugged her sister.

"What's wrong?" Aqese asked.

Daphne's eyes narrowed. She pulled from Portia's embrace, turned, and faced him. "Why'd you allow a halfling to follow us?"

"We understood they were to watch out for themselves," he replied in an even tone. "You were quite adamant they were on their own."

A wash of various emotions crossed her face. She turned to Roble. "I knew they should've stayed at Dagger's Tears. Now, I've more enemies to contend with."

"Rufus' death isn't your fault," Roble said.

Lehrling nodded. "I agree."

"I appreciate that," she said. "But your opinions won't alter Dolan's hatred toward me."

"Anger's part of the grieving process," Roble said.

"He's more than angry. He'll seek vengeance. I saw it in his eyes. I recognize the look, as it's beamed from my eyes for decades."

Shawndirea landed atop Roble's left shoulder. "Once he's had time to process the situation, he'll settle down and his anger will lessen."

Portia shook her head. "If it were Cora or Merla, that might be true. But Dolan … Dolan's different. He designated himself as their leader after their exile. He feels responsible for them. With Rufus' death, he's not only angry with you, Daphne, he's angry with himself."

"While that may be," she replied, "we don't need any further contention before confronting Lez'minx tomorrow."

"It's best we sort through that elsewhere." Ki'wese pointed at the river. "We can't camp alongside the river. It's too dangerous."

On the other bank, curious eyes glowed within the dark, scrubby brush and the bent leafy trees. As Roble had expected during their journey, they were being watched and followed.

Daphne noticed the eyes and nodded. "Where do you suggest we set up camp?"

Ki'wese said, "The tunnel's the safest place."

A look of horror struck her momentarily; more, it seemed, in having to enter the tunnel where Dolan was than in confronting whatever watched them from the other side of the river.

Roble understood Ki'wese's suggestion was sound. They were safer inside the tunnel than exposed on the riverbank. Besides, Daphne and Portia had cleared and killed everything inside the tunnel, which unfortunately included Rufus.

While Roble didn't fear Dolan, he knew none of them would get a moment of sleep tonight, as Dolan's actions were unpredictable.

CHAPTER 67

Getting the two horses to follow the jutted, narrow pathway to the tunnel entrance wasn't an easy task, but with Aqese and Ki'wese's help, Roble and Lehrling coaxed the horses there. They needn't worry about their horses being stolen or eaten by whatever watched them from the other side of the river.

At Roble's suggestion, they built a fire inside the tunnel's mouth, so they could watch the river. If anything swam or flew across, Roble and the others held a better vantage point.

Roble thought it odd the watchers' eyes glowed in the absence of light. Normally, nocturnal animals' eyes were only seen in the reflection of light and remained otherwise invisible. He kept reminding himself that what was *normal* in Aetheaon was often contrary to what he knew in the Overlands.

Aqese tended the fire while the rest of the group divided and situated themselves with their backs against the wall while facing one another. They took Roble's advice since Dolan had made his threat.

Dolan was unstable after Rufus' death. Sometimes, extreme grief spawned violent vengeance when someone blamed another for a loved one's death. Grief often clouded judgment. Even though Dolan was nowhere in sight, his anger and rage were hotter than the dancing campfire flames.

Daphne focused her attention at the shadowed area where Dolan and the halflings were. She was aware of his anger.

Cora and Merla's sobs echoed midway down the tunnel and were haunting. Strangely, Daphne's half broken expression revealed her troubled soul.

When Roble first encountered Daphne, her stoic aura was frozen and seemingly uncaring, but after learning about the fire killing Rufus, her rigid persona faded. He worried her sudden grief would weaken her confrontation with Lez'minx the following day. The last thing they needed was for her to be distracted.

He never thought her resolve could be shaken. Shaken meant she was somewhat weaker. Was this why Portia told Cora and Merla that she couldn't use magic to inflict harm on innocent bystanders? Was Daphne held to the same restrictions?

Even if it were the case, Daphne never deliberately used her magic to kill Rufus. Rufus' death, although misfortunate, had occurred because his curiosity had led him to the wrong place at a most unfortunate time. She never sought to kill him. She didn't know the halfling was there. From Roble's perspective, she didn't have time to calculate and formulate a spell. She and Portia cast in haste. Despite Roble and Daphne's former odds with one another, he'd defend her should Dolan attempt to harm Daphne.

Portia's brow furrowed and she embraced Daphne. Daphne whispered apologies to Portia.

Collette leaned her head against Lehrling's shoulder. Her eyes were heavy. She was closer to sleep than the rest of them. Lehrling's gaze fixated on the fire. A slight smile curled on his lips as Collette intertwined her fingers with his. Roble recognized the glee of a new love. He thought it a shame that Lehrling and Collette couldn't have a more picturesque setting. Reaching such a place could be weeks away or might never occur, depending on what transpired with Lez'minx.

Cora and Merla stopped their wailful cries. The tunnel grew quiet except for the soft, crackling fire.

"What happened?" Roble whispered to Shawndirea.

"How should I know? Perhaps their grieving's over for now?"

"Or their wall of fire missed one of those beetles?"

She shook her head. "Doubtful. The halflings are coming our direction."

A flickering light glowed farther down the tunnel and intensified as they slowly approached. Cora held the torch and led the way. Dolan held Rufus' burnt body over his shoulder. Merla wiped tears from her eyes.

Dolan stood at the fire and his serious stare passed to each of them and then narrowed at Daphne. His evident anger and his elongated shadow made him appear several feet taller than his actual height.

"Use your fire to turn the remainder of his body to ash." Dolan set Rufus' charred body on the tunnel floor beside the fire. "Might as well complete the process so we can set his ashes adrift on the river tomorrow."

Lehrling regarded the body and winced. Collette gasped and pressed her face against Lehrling's chest. She hid her eyes and covered her nose to escape the smell.

Rufus no longer resembled a halfling.

"Dolan," Daphne said. "His death was not—"

"He's at peace," Dolan said. "Let's leave it at that."

Portia said, "Don't let your anger overshadow the truth of the situation. We barely had time to use the spell we chose to defend ourselves."

"If we all had died," Daphne said, "where would that have left the rest of you?"

"So sacrificing *him* to save yourselves—" Dolan said.

"He *wasn't* a sacrifice." Daphne's eyes narrowed with fiery fury. Her briefly weakened countenance rebounded, and she returned to her normal, nonchalant expression. "We didn't know he was foolish enough to enter the tunnel."

The rigid Daphne had returned. As she rose, Dolan stepped back in fear. Roble slid his fingers over his daggers.

"His death wasn't deliberate," Daphne said. "But, continue your accusations, and I can show you what a *deliberate* death is. Do you wish to challenge me?"

Dolan's lips tightened and his eyes darkened. His hand rested on the hilt of his dagger but his fingers were lax. The uncertainty in his eyes indicated his fear was far greater than his need for revenge.

"Wait!" Roble stood.

"Overlander," Dolan said, "this doesn't concern you!"

"You're right. It doesn't," Roble replied. "But it concerns whether you live or die. Before you allow your emotions to direct you through Death's door, understand that Daphne *didn't* kill Rufus."

Everyone turned to Roble in surprise.

"Don't lie to spare her guilt," Dolan said.

"I'm not lying. I've no reason to spare her the agony of remorse if she had actually killed him."

"She cast the wall of fire spell!" Dolan's face tightened with fury. Spittle sprayed from his lips. "She even admitted it."

"The spell was cast by Daphne *and* Portia," Roble said. "Do you wish to kill Portia, too?"

Dolan shook his head. "The wall of fire spell was Daphne's idea, not Portia's. Portia only yielded her assistance and Daphne funneled Portia's magic. I doubt Portia even knew what spell Daphne planned to use."

"Yes. None of us deny the spell Daphne used, Dolan, but Rufus was already dead before any magic was dispelled," Roble replied.

Daphne looked surprised.

"What makes you think that?" Dolan asked.

Roble walked to Rufus' body and knelt beside it. He pointed at dark grooves that carved deep into both sides of the halfling's abdominal region. "These are the wounds a giant beetle inflicted on him. He was dead before the flames ever filled the tunnel."

Dolan knelt and studied the wounds. He pressed his fingers against the side of the wound and pushed the flap of charred skin aside. Clear ooze and dark blood leaked from the gaping hole. The deep wounds resembled a curved blade of a sharp sword. "You sure?"

Roble nodded. "Even the blistering caused by the fire couldn't hide them. Did you see the hulls of the beetles' shells."

"We saw one," Dolan said.

"They were massive," Cora said, sniffling. "At first, we thought the shell was a chest plate."

"Those beetles are why Daphne and Portia cast the fire spell," Roble said. "There were more inside the ruins, too. Most likely, Rufus was attacked by one that dropped from the ceiling."

Cora and Merla looked to the tunnel's ceiling.

Dolan released the flap of skin to cover Rufus' puncture wound. He glanced at Daphne and offered a slight bow. "My apologies. My judgment was in haste. I'd never have seen those puncture marks if the Overlander hadn't pointed them out."

Daphne weighed his words for a few moments in silence. "Your reaction's understandable, Dolan. My attitude was brash toward you at Dagger's Tears when I insisted you and your party remain behind. Regardless of my words then, I'd have done everything within my power to save Rufus from the beetle had I known he followed us. I hope you recognize this as the truth."

"As would I," Portia said. "And you know this."

Dolan nodded slowly. His eyes teared. "We've lost so many of our kind."

"As have we," Daphne said. "I fully recognize your pain. Portia and I'll do as you request with Rufus' remains. I wish we could've intervened and protected him."

Cora wiped a tear from her cheek. "Thank you."

Aqese and Ki'wese stood and gently lifted Rufus' remains and carried his corpse outside the tunnel entrance.

After they returned, Roble said, "Tomorrow may prove more treacherous than today. Get some sleep. I'll keep first watch."

Daphne smiled. "Your offer's appreciated, but Aqese and Ki'wese will stand guard outside. Portia and I will watch this end. None of the beetles should've survived, but we're better equipped to destroy them than you. You need your rest. You must be sharp-witted when we find Lez'minx. A tired mind's more susceptible to the cunning tricks he'll attempt to confuse you with tomorrow."

CHAPTER 68

$\mathcal{M}$orning came quicker than Roble ever imagined. Ki'wese shook Roble's shoulder until he awakened. Roble eased into a sitting position, blinked and looked around until his eyes focused clearly.

"Sleep doesn't put off the inevitable," Daphne said with a slight smile. "Lez'minx awaits."

Ki'wese turned a large hunk of meat on the spit above the fire. Juices dripped from the caramel-colored meat into the flames. The smell reminded Roble of bacon, and his stomach growled with aroused hunger.

Lehrling sat against the cave wall with a big portion of meat in his hand. He cheeks bulged as he chewed a bite much larger than his mouth could handle. Juice dribbled from the sides of his lips as he smiled.

Roble stared in question. "What are you eating?"

Ki'wese said, "Wild boar. Several were on the riverbank rooting around. Help yourself."

Roble rose to his feet and walked closer. On the other side of Ki'wese's feet was the massive head of the three-eyed boar with black twisted tusks that could shred through the flesh of any animal.

"Where's everyone else?" Roble asked, as only he, Ki'wese and Lehrling remained at the tunnel entrance.

"Daphne, Portia, and Shawndirea are searching for herbs," Ki'wese replied. "The halflings are scattering the ashes of Rufus along the river."

"By themselves?" Roble looked at the river.

"No. Aqese is with them. They're safe, if that's what worries you."

"And Collette?" Roble asked, glancing toward Lehrling.

Lehrling swallowed and cleared his throat. "She wanted to help Shawndirea find herbs, and she hopes to find some fresh fruit."

Ki'wese laughed. "Less chance of that occurring."

Roble grinned, turned to the spit, and peeled off a thick piece of boar meat. As he devoured it, he couldn't avert his attention from the interesting patterns on Ki'wese's skin. From a distance, one might mistake these markings for tattoos but up close, the dark lines were exactly like the tree rings on a stump.

"What troubles you?" Ki'wese asked.

Roble realized he had been staring too long again. "My apologies. I find those patterns on your skin fascinating."

"Why's that?"

Roble shrugged. "The lines ... they remind me of tree rings."

Ki'wese studied Roble for several seconds. His curiosity turned to disgust and then he frowned. "So were you a destroyer of trees, like other humans?"

Roble shook his head. "No. Almost any human in the Overlands has seen woodgrain and a tree stump."

"That's why dryads fled your realm a century or more ago to reside in ours and others. Overlanders are the most destructive beings I've witnessed. They've no regard for the sanctity of forests, rivers, or seas. I'm surprised your kind has survived as long as they have."

"I'm not like them," Roble said.

Ki'wese looked intently into Roble's eyes and gave a solemn nod. "You speak the truth. Shawndirea would never have chosen you for her husband if you were."

Lehrling chuckled.

Ki'wese flicked his gaze to Lehrling. "Something amusing?"

"Their first encounter wasn't as romantic as—"

Roble glared at Lehrling. "Now's not the time."

Lehrling's eyes widened. "You're right. I'm sorry."

"Once you've finished eating." Ki'wese stood. "Put out the fire. I need to find Aqese and prepare the rafts. I hope you've gotten sufficient rest. We must carry the rafts over the shallow pocket in the river. I suggest you eat your fill. We won't have a chance to eat again for quite some time. Let's hope this isn't the last."

Ki'wese left the tunnel and descended the narrow path.

Roble took another bite of ham. While the taste was savory, he didn't want this to be his last meal. Few people ever chose what their last supper would be, so it was pointless to speculate.

CHAPTER 69

Over a half hour passed while they hoisted the rafts over the rocky, shallow section of the river and then reloaded the horses and their supplies. Roble sighed and wiped sweat from his brow.

His fatigued knees trembled. Shawndirea slept on his shoulder. After she, Portia, and Daphne returned with their herb pouches filled with leaves, she said little at all. She was exhausted, but not as weary as she was when she slipped into the coma-like sleep. Was her mental and physical strength enough when they finally confronted Lez'minx? Were any of them strong enough?

Roble would give his life for hers, should the circumstance ever arise, and she'd do the same for him, as she truly loved him. But she could hardly defend herself at the moment, and she didn't have enough energy to protect them. Sealing the rifts with Daphne and Portia had weakened the three of them. The overly thick atmosphere had drained Lehrling and himself, too.

After Rufus died, the halflings were stricken by grief and immense sorrow. Their zeal was gone.

Roble stared at the rings on his fingers and then at the river's bend. In a few hours, their journey to find Lez'minx would be over, provided Daphne was correct in where he was hiding. For Roble, this expedition seemed like he was hunting prey rather than pursuing an affable conversation with an enemy. He intended, one way or the other, to be freed from the rings. He imagined nothing less than a major confrontation. While he held no advantage in the fight, he hoped Daphne and Portia's threat was enough to sway Lez'minx's mind to release Roble.

Exhausted, Lehrling lie down on the raft with his back against a wooden crate. His eyes were closed and Collette was pressed against him, deep in sleep.

Apprehension tightened Roble's stomach. He worried about how the confrontation would end. In so many ways, he regretted bringing Shawndirea and Lehrling with him. Both had insisted he not go alone. Retracing their journey thus far, he'd have never gotten to this point alive without them. He'd have been lost days earlier. He wouldn't have found Moorsis' shack by himself, either.

Yet, the longer Roble pondered about their journey, the more he reasoned that Lez'minx had purposely directed them along a path he'd chosen. None of their encounters had been by chance. After all, Lez'minx had rescued them twice, thus attempting to somehow cement a bond between he and Roble. Lez'minx used the situations to persuade Roble's loyalty.

In some ways, Roble was tempted to accept at least *part* of Lez'minx's terms, if only to save Lehrling, Shawndirea, and the others traveling with him from certain death. But Roble refused to give his loyalty to a proposed *god*.

Being a stranger in Aetheaon, Roble thought the rings could give him advantages over unexpected enemies, which would be beneficial. Deep down, he'd never blindly and submissively offer his allegiance for someone else to control his actions; especially after Daphne and Portia had revealed Lez'minx's mischievous nature. Lez'minx's purpose for luring Roble, Lehrling, and Shawndirea into the depths of the swamps could be to kill them or to manipulate them to become his servants.

Roble didn't know Lez'minx's scheme, but if worse came to worst, he hoped Lehrling's and Shawndirea's life would be spared.

While deep in thought and watching the muddy river, Daphne slipped up alongside him without him noticing.

"Can you see it?" She pointed.

"What?" Roble replied.

"The branches of the Great Tree," she said.

He followed the direction of her finger. Through the dim, woven canopy, long crooked tree branches stretched to reach across the river. Mist and fog rose on the river. Roble took a sharp breath and held it. The faint outline of the Great Tree's rugged, gnarled branches slowly materialized.

The massive branches forked outward and upward like giant arms wide enough for horse carriages to travel like roadways. Some branches disappeared into the heavy overcast sky.

Roble had never seen tree branches as wide and long as these. Yet, the branches were all he could see. The trunk remained far beyond his view. If he guessed the distance, the trunk was at least a mile or more away. The giant tree defied all feasible traits possible for any tree species. The distance these heavy branches stretched from the tree's trunk seemed impossible. None seemed to have rotted or any signs of decay, and yet, nothing supported their weight. It was almost magical ...

Roble shook his head. It *was* magic. Nothing else explained the phenomenon.

Blinks of red, yellow, and emerald lights flashed from the different fireflies drifting through the mist. Frogs bellowed and peeped along the river's marshy edge. The strange bird cries echoed and blended together.

"Spectacular?" Daphne asked.

Roble met her gaze. "Beyond spectacular."

Daphne motioned to Aqese. "Pull the rafts ashore and tie them. We walk the remaining distance to better ensure our brother doesn't see our arrival."

"What about the horses?" Roble asked.

"They stay aboard the rafts. With all the underbrush, they'd be more a hindrance than a help," she replied.

Roble leaned and shook Lehrling's shoulder. Lehrling's eyes opened in surprise. "We're here."

"Saggy-nook?" Lehrling eased up and rubbed his eyes. "So soon?"

"She told us it wasn't much farther," he replied.

Lehrling nodded. "I know. I just hoped to sleep longer."

Collette pulled away from Lehrling, stretched, and yawned. She stared at the closest tree branch in disbelief.

Dolan, Merla, and Cora helped paddle the raft to the riverbank.

"How close does the river flow to the tree's trunk?" Roble asked.

Daphne said, "The river bends well before we see the tree's center or the Ruins of Saggy-nook. From past experiences, if we don't go ashore now, we won't get another chance. The river becomes more rapid and the jagged rocks prevent us from reaching the shore."

Lehrling stood, arched his back, and groaned. He clasped a firm hand on Roble's shoulder and smiled. "These old bones insist this is my last arduous journey, friend."

"Let's hope it's not the last journey for each of us," Daphne said with a firm stare.

Lehrling's smile retreated.

"Is Shawndirea okay?" Daphne peered at the faery.

"She's slept since we left the ruins," Roble replied. "It's not as severe as before."

"Gently wake her," Daphne said. "None of us can afford to be mentally unguarded."

"We need her insight," Portia said. "She might detect what we cannot. She's attuned differently."

Roble nodded.

Aqese looped a long rope around a tree root and tied the raft while Ki'wese did the same on the second raft.

Roble nudged Shawndirea. She opened her eyes, blinked several times, and smiled at him.

"How do you feel?" he asked.

She stood and expanded her wings. "Rested. Why?"

"We're here."

"I figured as much."

"Shh!" Daphne placed her index finger to her lips.

All the sounds of nature grew deadly silent.

"That's impressive," Roble said.

Daphne glared. "They weren't responding to me."

"Then what?" Collette asked.

Daphne glanced at Portia. "Runefel's nearby. Do you sense him?"

Portia nodded. "Yes."

"Shield your mind, sister. The same goes for Shawndirea, Aqese, and Ki'wese. Our brother mustn't know we're here."

"Lez'minx?" Lehrling whispered.

Daphne nodded. "Now, please, keep silent. He mustn't know we're here or it's too late for all of us."

Shawndirea frowned. Her eyes searched through the trees and the canopy. "I sense a powerful force."

"I told you," Daphne said. "Our brother—"

Shawndirea shook her head. "It's not your brother I sense. I recognize *his* power, but this ... this isn't him."

Portia's brow raised in question, as did Daphne's.

"It's probably the tree's magical aura," Daphne said with an even smile. "Portia and I both feel akin to it."

"Yes." The mossy hair on Portia's arms stood slightly and bent with the gentle breeze. "Its power is stimulating."

"No, I feel that, but the stronger sensation isn't the tree, and it's not Lez'minx, either," Shawndirea said.

A troubled expression tightened Portia's brow. "I sense what she speaks of now. Do you, sister?"

"Unfortunately ... yes," she replied.

The halflings looked at the riverbank with apprehension.

Aqese extended his hand to Daphne and helped her onto a massive tree root. She accepted and followed the root to the bank. Once she reached the bank, she looked at Dolan. "You three can remain behind with the horses, if you wish."

Dolan shook his head. "We didn't journey with you to be onlookers. We came to fight with you and in Rufus' honor."

Daphne regarded him with renewed respect.

"Very well, but only if you remain silent and comply with our advice," Daphne replied.

Dolan gave a firm nod.

Roble gripped Aqese's hand and stepped from the raft. Their determined eyes met with mutual coldness, not for one another, but each knowing their mission. While for different reasons, both would soon end. How the finality of the meeting played out held no certainty.

Roble stood on the giant tree root. A surge of energy jolted his feet and moved through his calves. He didn't need to assume the root was connected to the Great Tree. No other plant had ever sent chills through him. This energy radiated with magic. He couldn't explain how he knew this, but in his mind, he understood. He quickly stepped off the root.

Once Roble's feet were steadfast on the bank, Aqese clasped Roble's shoulder and nodded his appreciation with a slight grin. The already dim forest and river grew darker, colder. The slight misting rain stopped, and for several long moments, complete silence enveloped them.

"Be on guard," Shawndirea whispered to Roble. "We're *not* alone."

CHAPTER 70

*R*oble slid two throwing knives from his belt and held the blades, ready to fling them in an instant.

Ki'wese used a machete-like blade to slice a path through the thick dead brush. No evident path lie before them. Unlike the other areas of the swamp, the ground was almost dry, and yet, the sandy soil was undisturbed by any previous footprints. If anyone had walked through this area, it'd been long ago.

Other than the thick, meandering roots of the Great Tree, all the smaller brush and bramble were dead and shriveled to the core. The larger trees seemed healthy but their leaves were a dull greenish-yellow.

Had these plants been alive, Ki'wese wouldn't cut a path through them since he was a dryad. They'd find another way to reach the Great Tree.

"Why's all the scrub brush dead?" Roble whispered.

Shawndirea shrugged. "I don't know."

Daphne whispered into his mind. "The Great Tree is consuming the life of its neighboring plants."

"Why?"

"A possibility for reasons comes to mind," she replied. "One, perhaps the tree's diseased and dying. Thus, she's drawing sustenance to maintain her own life. Or, someone's pooling and siphoning too much of her magic for ill-gotten gain, which could kill her. Either way, she's forced to sap the surrounding plants. My guess is the latter. Runefel has steadily drained her magical well for his own greedy pursuit. Namely, his want to control you, and for the purpose of killing the Shadowfae you encountered days ago. Both require a lot of magic, if no blood sacrifices were done concurrently."

Whispering sounds rasped in the darkened tree branches overhead. Fast-moving creatures zipped from branch to branch in the canopy. Either magic cloaked them or they moved too swiftly for Roble to see. Perhaps both.

The fluttering, delicate wings reminded Roble of a dragonfly fighting to free itself from inside the netting of a butterfly net, but these creatures were not suffering. They were actively following Roble.

Whatever they were, they observed Roble and his party, but the creatures remained reluctant to approach or allow themselves to be seen.

"Should we turn back?" Roble asked in his mind.

"No. That's what they want us to do," Daphne replied. "But they don't seem to be acquainted with Runefel."

"What makes you think that?"

"They'd have already attacked and taken us to him."

"What are they?" Roble asked.

"At this point, it's difficult to know. Being this close to a tree filled with magic, we're liable to come in contact with almost anything," she replied.

"Don't forget," Portia said. "As children, we witnessed a *lot* of carnage in these ruins from those lusting to obtain more magical power or trying to claim the tree for their own."

"Which means," Daphne said, "we might encounter skirmishes or be attacked before we find Runefel."

"I'm aware," Roble said. "What makes you think he was successful claiming the Great Tree's essence?"

"If he killed a couple dozen Shadowfae assassins from halfway across the swamps, he has access to magic that exceeds his knowledge and abilities," Daphne said. "Even I and Portia combining our strengths could not perform such a feat without an enormous magical boost. This tree feeds on its surroundings to maintain its essence, as you called it, but the height of the energy issuing outward stimulates any of us with the ability to cast spells. The closer we get, the more overwhelming this sensation becomes. Should we become giddy and act unusual, you need to know, it's because of this outpouring of magic flowing through us."

"It makes you giddy?" Lehrling asked.

Daphne nodded. "The flux of energy is more than we can handle until we acclimate."

"If that's the case," Roble said, "why do so many try to murder others to obtain—"

"That has to do with the intention of one's heart," Daphne said. "Lust and greed are negative attributes that become magnified the closer one gets to the tree's trunk. But those are prominent inner traits to begin with. Obsession overtakes their reasoning. They don't care who they hurt or kill. Portia and I never seek magic due to lust and greed. As children, we always fed modestly from the tree's magic resources. Runefel, however ..."

"Shh!" Shawndirea placed her index finger to her lips and nodded to the right of the path Ki'wese was hacking.

Ki'wese lowered his blade and everyone grew silent. "What?"

"Listen," Shawndirea whispered.

The thumping rhythm was faint but grew steadier and a bit louder.

"What's that?" Roble asked.

Lehrling's brow rose. His eyes narrowed as he cocked his head to listen. He gasped. "Orc war drums?"

Portia glanced at Daphne with apprehension. "Orcs?"

"I've only heard their war drums once," Lehrling said. "That was half my lifetime ago, during my first sea voyage as a Dragon Skull Knight, shortly after King Erik christened me into the Order. The sound of Orc drums is unmistakable, even after all these years."

"Where'd you encounter Orcs?" Roble asked.

"Cinder Isles at the outskirts of the Ashen Sea."

Portia looked at Lehrling. "Are these Orcs sounding their battlecry?"

Lehrling shrugged. "Battlecry? No. Probably not. The drums might be signaling a warning to others of their arrival. I don't rightly know. I heard the drums as our ship sailed past their isles. From what I know about Orcs, a battlecry is their loud roars before they rush and remove your head with an axe."

Daphne swallowed hard. "It *can't* be Orcs. Not in the middle of Woodnog Swamps."

Shawndirea nodded. "I think it is."

"Why would they be here?" Lehrling asked.

"The ruins, we believe, was once their city," Daphne said. "Though it's merely our speculation based on the carvings."

"How would they get that far from the river?" Roble asked. "The only trail we have is the one Ki'wese is making. No one's taken this direction for many years."

Daphne nodded. "Yes, that's true. Another inlet is farther upriver. I chose to stop here to lessen our chance of being seen, which was the best choice, given the Orcs arrived before us."

"What now?" Ki'wese asked.

Daphne looked at Roble. "What do you wish to do? Turn back and hope for another time to confront Runefel, or do we take our chances and hope for the best?"

"What do you wish to do?" Roble asked.

"Portia and I will continue toward the Great Tree," she said. "Our agenda doesn't change. We can't allow ourselves to be veered off our path. It's time Runefel understands he must answer for his misdeeds."

Lehrling frowned and shook his head. "We're no match in a battle against Orcs. Even a small band of Orcs could destroy us before we attempted any defense."

Dolan considered what Lehrling said and cleared his throat. In spite of his nervous demeanor, Dolan said, "Cora, Merla, and I are going to the tree."

Lehrling glanced at him in surprise.

Roble looked at Ki'wese. "Keep clearing a path. As for Lehrling and Shawndirea, they—"

"I'm going," Shawndirea said.

"As am I," Lehrling rubbed an index finger across his silver Dragon Skull pendant. "At best, if there are Orcs ahead, they're not in large numbers. Most likely a scouting group sent from one of their ships else-where. That doesn't make them any less deadly."

"My guess is they're not here for the magic tree," Roble said.

"No," Daphne said. "Most likely not, which might make them even more dangerous."

"In what sense?" Roble asked.

"If this had once been their land and city, perhaps they wish to reclaim it," she replied. "In which case, anyone they encounter becomes their enemy."

CHAPTER 71

*W*hen the drumbeats became louder and eerily similar to a steady heartbeat, Roble placed a hand on Ki'wese's shoulder and asked him to stop clearing the path. The sharp blade hacking through the dead branches might capture the Orcs' attention. Dead leaves and twigs rattled and crackled, even with the faint whispering of a razor-edged machete slicing through them.

Pushing their way through the thick, dead underbrush was not an easy endeavor, either. Some branches had sharp barbs that clung to their leather armor and cloth robes. Without armor, they could easily sustain deep cuts and possible infection.

The winged creatures in the canopy continued darting out of sight but never lost their interest in following Roble and the others.

Roble pushed aside the last two dead tree branches. They reached a clearing where the soil faded and they stood atop aged, tile stone. Sprigs of dead weeds stood in the cracks and grooves of the tiles.

Several feet to their left, a giant gnarled tree root snaked toward the Great Tree. Ruins of crumbled stone walls lie in jagged piles, where weather, time, and the huge tree roots had carved their way through the former city barriers.

The height of the root stood higher than Roble's six-foot stature. He stared in awe at the towering Great Tree in the distance. *No wonder the soil's bone-dry and the underbrush was dead.* For the tree to sustain itself, it needed a vast amount of nutrients, and it claimed whatever sustenance necessary to survive.

Even though they reached the clearing, the Orcs weren't there. The hollow, deep thudding on the drums had not lessened, and seemed closer, but where exactly the Orcs were positioned remained a mystery.

"Careful," Lehrling said. "They've probably concealed themselves at a higher vantage point."

Roble nodded. He searched the long root as he followed it. The root extended at least forty yards from where they stood and connected to the massive trunk. Its height increased the closer to the tree they came.

"There." Daphne rushed to his side, placed a gentle hand on his shoulder, and pointed. "There! See the crevice in the trunk, near the old door opening of the higher level?"

Seated in a circle, around a small glowing fire that somehow produced no smoke, were six muscled Orcs dressed in dark metal plate sleeveless armor. A seventh Orc stood with a decorative staff raised in his right hand. He wore dark cloth robes and chanted while two Orcs beat a constant rhythm on the drums.

Roble marveled at their massive size. Any of them was three times his width with huge biceps and thick chests, shoulders, and backs. They needed no weapons to tear his limbs from his body. Their blackish-green skin and their dark armor made them nearly invisible against the tree's mossy bark.

Regardless of their size, he imagined they could run swiftly. For several minutes, he contemplated turning back. Had it not been for his damned curiosity, he probably would have. Before he whispered his fear to Daphne, the standing Orc stopped chanting, opened his eyes, and stared in their direction.

Lehrling mumbled curses under his breath, and Roble cursed mentally. The seated Orcs turned and noticed them. Roble and Lehrling stiffened in terror. They couldn't retreat now. To run, they'd become prey. To stand their ground almost ensured quick deaths, but Roble hoped they could end with a peaceful resolve.

The shaman spoke in a language Roble had not heard voiced in

Aetheaon. The six seated Orcs growled as they watched Roble and his party.

Roble held the fierce moment of intense fear unlike anything he'd ever experienced before. The Orcs were much larger than the Vykings. Their thicker muscles made them hulks. A throwing dagger probably wouldn't pierce an Orc's skin.

"Don't run," Daphne said. "Above all else, don't show any fear."

"That's easy for you to say," Roble whispered.

"I'm terrified," she replied.

"You hide it well," Roble said with a slight chuckle.

She gave him an even side-glance. No laughter tugged the edges of her mouth or lessened her glare. She was more serious than any other time they had spoken.

"Of course, you hide your emotions quite well." Roble broke their gaze.

The six Orcs slid their hands on the thick hilts of their double-sided axes and heavy hammers that were on the ground before them. The Orcs rose to their feet more fluidly than Roble could've done. Their metal weapons scraped across the stone floor.

Their strange orange-yellow eyes fixated on Roble and then to Daphne and the others standing behind Roble. Their thick, heavy brows tightened into intense glares. Their expressed rage in their low, rumbling growls could make a lion flinch.

Veins snaked down the Orcs' arms while they held their heavy weapons. Each giant axe and warhammer probably weighed fifteen to twenty pounds. They turned the heavy weapons in their hands like tinker toys.

Roble thought of several odd epitaphs for his gravestone, some of which were humorous, but he never spoke them aloud. It didn't matter if he did. None of the Orcs would bother to chisel one should they kill him.

Daphne spoke aloud in a language he didn't understand, which captured the shaman's attention. His intense facial features weakened. His angered gaze turned to curiosity and sudden interest. The six warriors turned their attention to the shaman and awaited his reply.

"She told them we wish them peace and blessings and our battle is not with them," Portia whispered to Roble.

"You think they're open for peaceful coexistence?" Roble asked.

"Depends," Daphne said.

"On what exactly?"

"How much they hate humans," she replied.

Roble exchanged glances with Lehrling, who appeared more nervous than ever.

The Orc shaman set the end of his staff on the stone floor. He motioned his comrades with his left hand. The six warriors nodded and sheathed their weapons.

"That's a good sign, right?" Lehrling asked.

"It would appear so," Roble said.

"For now," Daphne whispered.

The shaman walked away from the smokeless campfire. With the six menacing warriors behind him, they ambled their way to Daphne. As they came closer, Roble noticed several Orcs had suffered severe injuries. A line of drying blood crusted from a hole in one's left side and down to the upper part of his thigh.

Due to the shape and depth of the wound, the Orc must've been stabbed with a sharp-tipped spear or a pike. A dagger or most short swords probably couldn't have pierced his thick skin. With the amount of dried blood, the puncture wound was deep, but the Orc walked without the slightest hint of pain. Other Orcs had lacerations on their faces, their muscled arms, and exposed chests.

Thick yellow tusks protruded from their mouths. Some tusks were sharp and even the broken ones were frightening to behold.

The shaman voiced his reply in the language Daphne had spoken. After several minutes of bantering, Roble understood what they were saying. The shaman's name was Uksen. Roble marveled that this unusual language made sense. Someone had cast a translation spell to make it possible for them to understand one another. Or, had the Great Tree allowed it?

"We're the last survivors of our fleet," Uksen said. "We were sailing to the Cinder Isles when Vykings attacked us. We lost several ships, and our Chief's son, Borgess, was one of the casualties. Our vessel caught the swell of high waves and strong winds forced us to Aetheaon's shoreline."

"Why'd you come so far inland?" Daphne asked. "Deep into these swamps?"

Uksen took a deep breath and sighed. His weary eyes were troubled. "Our ancestors once ruled these swamps. Where this tree stands was once our greatest city, Nozord. It has long been lost and forgotten in time."

Daphne nodded. "My sister and I have believed this for years. We thought Orcs once ruled this city, but we could never read the language carved into stones."

"Yet, you can speak it?" Roble asked.

Uksen leveled a harsh, imitating stare at Roble. Roble cringed. "She speaks our *modern* language, human. *Not* our ancient one carved into our monuments."

Roble offered a humble nod and eased a few steps back. He hoped slight submissiveness could avoid a heated confrontation. Uksen, like the other Orcs, looked easy to offend, and he doubted any of them were capable of smiling. Their aged wrinkles creased deeper frowns and indicated they growled in anger a lot. He never wanted to be on the receiving end of their wrath.

Strange tattoos were carved into Uksen's face. He had nose, cheek, and chin piercings. His earlobes drooped from the weight of heavy gold rings. The other six Orcs' body art resembled Uksen's. His headdress flowed down his back with large dark feathers. The greenish-black skin of his face made his yellowish-orange eyes gleam brighter.

When he exhaled, the huff through his nose was a rough snort. His large tusks seemed to make breathing more difficult.

"What do you seek?" Daphne asked.

"The staff I carried was destroyed in our battle against the Vykings. Without it, my power is weaker. Legend tells that our greatest shaman ancestor, Thull, is buried in these ruins. I seek his staff. It's an artifact that will enhance my magical abilities. We're in need of healing," Uksen said.

Daphne looked confused. "Thull?"

"Yes," Uksen said in an raspy tone.

Shawndirea stood on Roble's shoulder and cleared her throat. "You'll not find any remnants of Thull in Nozord."

Uksen flicked his gaze at her. "Why not?"

"Mors summoned him from the dead and used him and his power to fight in the Battle of Hoffnung," she replied.

Uksen snorted. His voice lowered to a gravelly growl. "Who's this ... *Mors?*"

"He's a necromancer," Roble said. "Thull ... his skeleton was destroyed during the battle."

Uksen growled and ground his tusks. The other Orcs replied with the same aggression. "Where do we find Mors?"

"He's known as the Plague-bringer. He comes and goes, vanishing in a magical whirlwind," Roble said. "He's building an army to destroy all of Aetheaon's major cities."

"He's your enemy?" Uksen asked.

Roble nodded. "Yes."

Determination set in Uksen's eyes and his thick jaw hardened. "Since he desecrated Thull, he's our enemy, too. Since he's your enemy, we're allies. We'll hunt him. Once he's found, we'll stand by your side in battle. What he's done can never be forgiven. Not in this life or in the lives hereafter."

Roble started to offer his thanks but the most injured Orc toppled forward, clutched the deep wound in his side, and collapsed at Uksen's feet. His comrades formed a circle around him and knelt. Uksen inspected the wound. He looked at Daphne and shook his head. "Without the staff, our hope to heal him and ourselves is gone."

Daphne gave a reassuring smile. "Not necessarily."

CHAPTER 72

$\mathcal{R}$oble left the semi-circle of Orcs and joined Lehrling, Collette, and the halflings while Shawndirea, Portia, and Daphne attuned their magic to aid in healing the injured Orc.

In disbelief he marveled at the Orcs, a mighty and yet frightening race, far more massive than he anticipated and beings more suited for nightmares. Seeing these Orcs firsthand amazed him, even if they purportedly hated humans.

A glowing dome from the combined magic formed over Uksen, the injured Orc, Shawndirea, and the dryad sisters. After several minutes, the injured Orc opened his eyes and sat up with a horrifying grunt of surprise. Uksen smiled, placed a gentle hand on the Orc's shoulder, and offered words of assurance that all was well.

But not all was well.

After the dome vanished, Shawndirea dropped and crumbled to the ground. Roble ran to her lifeless form. With tender care, he eased her onto her back. Her weak eyes opened.

Roble said, "Are you okay?"

She offered a slight nod. "Fatigued. That's all."

He placed his hand beside her, and she crawled on his palm where she collapsed again. She snored softly.

"Why is she so weak?" Roble whispered.

Daphne's eyes expressed her concern. "Being so close to the Great Tree, she shouldn't be. She has no need to draw magic from her abilities when the tree's essence is like an overflowing river."

"We're in your debt," Uksen said. "How can we assist you?"

Daphne looked into Roble's eyes for a moment before she faced Uksen. "We've come to Nozord to find my brother. Our confrontation might prove difficult and dangerous."

Uksen thought for several moments. "We've not encountered anyone. Though we've not been here long."

"He would not be on the outskirts," Daphne said. "But, on the other side, where the pools and old fountains are."

"We could scout the gardens," Uksen said. "Should we find him, we'll restrain him and alert you when he's captured."

"I'm afraid it won't be that easy," Portia said. "His sorcery is strong."

Uksen chuckled and the other Orcs laughed. "That might be, but our trinkets and the weapons I've blessed are resistant to magic whenever an enemy targets us. These items don't resist healing magic, for which we're grateful."

"We are happy to aid you," Daphne said.

Uksen turned his gaze to Roble and then to Lehrling. He frowned. "I recognize your dragon pendants. You're Dragon Skull Knights who serve King Erik of Hoffnung?"

"Queen Taube, now," Lehrling said.

"And Erik? What of him?" Uksen asked.

Lehrling summarized King Erik's disappearance and the possibility of his most likely, unfortunate death.

Uksen's saddened eyes looked at the broken tile floor. He shook his head. "He was always generous in his trades with our isle. We had wondered of his absence for quite some time."

Lehrling's brow rose in surprise. "He ventured to Cinder Isles?"

"Periodically."

"That's odd," Lehrling said.

"Why?" Uksen asked.

"It's odd that he'd venture to your isle without our Order," Lehrling said.

"Can a king not venture to wherever he wishes?"

"Of course. Usually, though, such travels ... it's just odd he'd put himself and our kingdom at risk."

"You perceive us as a threat?" Uksen asked.

"I recall only one voyage where I and other Dragon Skull Knights sailed within sight of Cinder Isles," Lehrling said. "We heard your war drums."

"Was Hoffnung's crest on the sails?"

"Of course."

"Then the sound you heard was most likely a hail of welcome."

"We sailed past," Lehrling said.

"I see. Perhaps the others with you didn't share his unbiased attitude?"

"That may be."

Uksen shrugged. "King Erik never came alone. He was always well guarded, as any king should be. He's the only human king we viewed as non-hostile to our people. He and Hoffnung have never been viewed as an enemy." He offered a smile that appeared shrewd due to his large tusks. "You and I may talk further at another time. For now, let's see if we can find the one you seek. What's his name?"

Daphne said, "Runefel ... But he has deceived Roble and Lehrling into calling him, Lez'minx."

"If he's here," Uksen said, "we'll find him."

CHAPTER 73

A half hour later, Roble sat against the mighty root of the Great Tree with Shawndirea curled on his palm. Like before, she was unresponsive, deep in sleep, and he feared for her life.

Daphne sat beside him. "She's not awakened?"

Roble shook his head. "No. Any idea why this has occurred again?"

Dolan and the other halflings studied the carved markings in the stone wall and the floor without words. The gloom overshadowing them remained evident. Their thoughts had not strayed far from Rufus' death. Collette and Lehrling sat lost in their own conversation nearby.

Everyone was drained from the long journey, especially Lehrling and himself. Roble wondered if the long journey had sapped Shawndirea.

Roble peered up the Great Tree's trunk, unable to get an estimate of how tall the massive tree was. Clouds and a low curtain of fog hampered his vision. Not much had changed in the dismal atmosphere that hung over the swamps.

Portia joined Roble and Daphne. Her interest was also on Shawndirea's well-being.

"When we cast the healing spell together," Daphne said to Portia, "did you sense anything amiss?"

Portia shook her head. "No."

"Neither did I," Daphne sighed. "Her collapse makes no sense."

"I know," Portia said. "Magical essence abounds all around us. She should have the well flowing through her, like we do. The spell shouldn't have drained her. It *couldn't* have."

"Something has," Roble said.

"Someone or something is trying to inhibit her magic. That's obvious. It's almost as though she becomes ill with every spell she casts."

"You've never experienced this before?" Roble asked.

Daphne and Portia shook their heads.

"Here?" Daphne said. "No."

"I should've known it was you! I sensed that familiar, aggravating feeling from years ago, but I thought you died ages ago."

Daphne turned in the direction of Lez'minx's voice. In a harsh tone, she replied, "You should be so fortunate."

Everyone's attention was immediately drawn toward the shout. Roble was stunned to see a strange creature roped and tied and being dragged by two Orcs. He didn't look like Portia or Daphne at all, which puzzled him. Despite his much smaller size, he possessed incredible strength in his ability to resist their tugging.

"Is this the one you seek?" Uksen asked.

Roble, Lehrling, and the halflings stared at Daphne and Portia with obvious confusion as they awaited their answer.

Daphne and Portia rose and nodded. Daphne appeared agitated while an affectionate smile came to Portia's lips.

Roble had expected Lez'minx to look like his sisters, but he was nothing like them. He wasn't a god, but he looked like what most people in the Overlands would assume to be a demon. From the waist down, his muscled legs were covered with thick coarse hair. His cloven feet dug in the ground, adding slight resistance for the Orcs to pull him, in spite of their great strength.

His red hair flowed in neat, twisted strands down to his shoulders. His radiant face could be considered handsome with his neatly trimmed beard and mustache, if one ignored the other aspects. Two goat-like horns protruded and curled backwards on his forehead.

Lez'minx was a satyr.

When Lez'minx's eyes met his sisters', his resistance in following the Orcs lessened. Fear widened his strange eyes. He flicked his gaze rapidly from one person to the next, almost as if he were calculating a quick route of escape.

"I never imagined our reunion would require such *forcefulness*," Lez'minx said. His voice was smoother than warm honey and revealed no bitterness or hostility. "If you wished to talk, you could have asked, without the escort and ropes."

"You'll not escape us so easily this time," Daphne said with sheer coldness. Roble involuntarily shivered.

Uksen walked to Daphne and held a crooked staff and a small harp. "We took these from him."

"You keep the staff," she said.

Uksen studied the staff for a few moments before acquiescing a slight nod.

"That's mine," Lez'minx said in a sweet tone. "It'll do you no good, Greenskin. It's not attuned to you. You've no use for it, so give it back."

Uksen's brow furrowed. He turned and faced Lez'minx. For a moment, he offered the staff before anger narrowed his eyes and he gripped the staff tighter. "Sneaky. Trying to seduce my mind with the gentleness of your words? Do so again and find your head over there."

A grin spread on Lez'minx's face. "Keep the staff, Greenskin, and the longer you hold it, the more you'll be willing to do my bidding. Ask Roble."

Uksen took the staff in both hands and bent it.

"No!" Lez'minx said. "Daphne don't allow him to break it!"

Daphne ignored his protest and cast her glance at Roble. "State your peace. You only have a short time before Portia and I do what must be done."

Lez'minx gaped.

Roble frowned and strode to Lez'minx. When Lez'minx fought against the two ropes tied around his neck and attempted to break free, the two Orcs tightened their hold on the restraints.

"You must free me, Roble," Lez'minx said. He stared in Roble's eyes with the purest sincerity. "I beg you."

"Remove your spell on these rings. I want them off my fingers and to have no further ties to you. I've no idea what your sisters plan to do with you, but before they seek their revenge, break the spell," Roble said. "Free me."

Lez'minx stretched his neck and looked past Roble. "Revenge? So it's true? What do they plan to do?"

"I told you, I don't know. Ask them, not me."

"I've done nothing to them. *Ever.*"

Roble shrugged. "Again, an argument you need to discuss with them."

Lez'minx's eyes shifted nervously, and he noticed Shawndirea in Roble's hand. "Your faery ... she's injured?"

Roble looked at Shawndirea's curled form in his hand. He tried to show anger at Lez'minx, but his voice broke. "I—I don't know what's wrong."

"It wasn't my doing," Lez'minx said. "I swear it. I had no idea you were this close to my home. But I assure you—"

"Just remove the spell on the rings," Roble said.

"Haven't I done more to protect than harm you? I've never caused you any harm." Lez'minx's eyes shimmered and his tone held soft musical rhythm.

"Just—"

"Don't be so hasty to disregard the truth, my dear Roble," Lez'minx said. "I never meant you any ill will. In fact, I saved your lives. That's worth something."

Roble's jaw tightened. As much as he despised Lez'minx for the rings, he found himself feeling pity for Lez'minx and wanting to help him. Surely, it had something to do with Lez'minx being a satyr. "While appreciated, Lez'minx, the fact remains that you deceitfully used your magic to spy on us without our consent. That violates trust on so many levels. You should've told me the price for wearing the rings."

"A price? Yes, everything has a price, or haven't you figured that out yet?" Lez'minx whispered. "If you'd known what benefited me from your wearing the rings, would you have ever worn them?"

"No. I wouldn't wear them at all. But at least I'd have been informed."

"Fair enough. Look, I didn't cause Shawndirea's sickness," Lez'minx said. "You must believe me."

"You threatened her life," Roble said. "That's why I'll always hold some doubt to your denial."

"Yes. I'll remove my enchantment on the rings," Lez'minx said, "if you'll do one thing for me?" Lez'minx's eyes and voice revealed his genuine fear.

"I didn't come to bargain," Roble said.

Lez'minx grinned. "Oh, but you *did*."

"I insist you remove these rings."

"They're going to kill me, aren't they?" Lez'minx asked.

"I don't know their intent as they've not confided in me."

"What *do* you know?"

"Whatever they've planned does not bode well for you," Roble replied.

"Do you know their reasons?"

Roble shook his head. "No."

Lez'minx kept his gaze focused on Daphne and Portia. He was stalling at Roble's simple request.

"What are you waiting for?" Roble asked, frustrated.

"The second I release you from the rings, they're going to kill me."

"If that's their intention, they're going to do it anyway. That much I know. They said for me to confront you first, but even if you don't remove the enchantment, their minds have decided it'll happen anyway."

Lez'minx nodded. "I see. Did they give any hints as to why they wish to kill me?"

"They've never said they're going to *kill* you."

"Well, harm me then? Keep me prisoner for their wanton needs?"

"Your sisters have—"

Lez'minx frowned. His eyes bore into Roble's. He whispered, "They're *not* my sisters."

"That's what they've told us."

"And you believe them?" Lez'minx rolled his eyes. He huffed. "Of course you would, Overlander. You believed I was a god, after all. Gullible."

"They're *not* your sisters?"

"No ... Do I look *anything* like them? That, in itself, should leave nothing to question."

"They're quite insistent, but I questioned the possibility when the Orcs brought you to us and I saw that you're a satyr."

"Yet, you have doubts?"

"Not anymore."

"That's good. Then perhaps now you can better determine what their true intention is. They want me dead," Lez'minx said.

"For what reason?"

"For being jilted?"

"Jilted?"

"Surely, even an Overlander understands the reputation of a satyr? I understand we're legends and lore in your realm."

Roble nodded. "You used your charm on them? Why? They're dryads."

"Half-dryads. It doesn't matter what they are. Their attraction toward me was, well, strange nonetheless, but we developed a different, special type of bond. They had pursued me and not the other way around. I never charmed them, as you put it. Later, I wanted to leave, to move on, but they used their nature spells to prevent me from escaping. That is, until the great flood. During their distraction to stay alive, I managed to escape their tendrils."

"You caused the flood?" Roble asked.

Lez'minx shook his head. "No, but I know who did. And I'll *never* divulge that information, so don't bother asking."

"Why'd you pretend to be a god?"

"Why not?" he replied. He shrugged and a snarl curled on his lips. "Overlanders know no differently. My kind have always been pranksters."

"That's another reason why it's hard to believe anything you tell me."

Lez'minx offered a genuine smile. "I understand. However, I hope you can detect my truthfulness right now, as my life is most likely in jeopardy. You seem a rational person. One capable of discerning the intentions others have."

"If you truly believe that about me, why'd you bother deceiving me about who and what you are?"

"You took Bausch's armor," Lez'minx said. "Another way my magic saved you and Shawndirea's lives. Bausch never paid homage for the armor, and once I discovered what had happened to Bausch, I used the opportunity to beguile you since you're an Overlander. I shouldn't have, but had it worked, I'd have a servant to work through. To your credit, you're far wiser than the majority of Overlanders who've entered our realm. Most don't survive six months."

Roble frowned. "I've no idea what happens after you disenchant the rings, but I'll find out before we leave you with them."

"And if they wish my death?"

Roble shrugged. "They'd need a good reason."

"So you would defend me?"

"I didn't say that. But if they've lying about their relationship with you, I won't allow your death if I can prevent it. I don't know how much I can protect you since I know no magic."

"Very well," Lez'minx said with a huff. "Turn your hands palm-side down so I can see the gemstones in the rings."

Roble placed Shawndirea in the crook of his elbow.

"Any tricks," Daphne said, still from a distance. "And the Orcs will slit your throat, Runefel."

"My name's Lez'minx!" Anger flared his nostrils.

Daphne said, "All the same, you've been warned."

His anger turned to indignation. "Best you remember who has the greater power between us, Daphne."

"That's why Portia came with me."

Portia's brow creased with confusion as she glanced at Daphne in regard to the statement.

Lez'minx took a deep breath and broke his gaze with her. His eyes softened as he looked into Roble's. "No tricks. I swear it. I realize it's too late to gain your trust, but I hope you'll reconsider."

Roble recognized the depth of Lez'minx's hostility toward Daphne, and if the satyr wasn't bound with ropes, he'd probably attack her.

Lez'minx sighed. "Turn your hands."

Lez'minx's throat rasped. He cleared his throat and spat green snot on each ring. "There."

Roble leveled an even stare and his jaw tightened. His hands tightened into fists.

"Easy. It's not an insult. It's the only way to inactivate my binding spells so you can remove the rings," Lez'minx said in a soft whisper. "I know you're skeptical, but think about it. Without my saliva, no other wizard or mage could undo the spell."

Roble looked at the glob of snot on the gemstones. His stomach turned.

"You only have a few minutes to take them off or you'll wear them forever."

Despite the acrid taste at the back of Roble's throat, he did as Lez'minx requested. For all Roble knew, this could be a test or it might be the satyr's twisted sense of humor.

Before Roble twisted the rings, he studied Lez'minx's eyes. A hint of eager laughter brightened the satyr's eyes. If anyone could witness the gleam in a jester's eyes before he unveiled his folly, Lez'minx gaze certainly mirrored it. For a moment, Roble expected Lez'minx to burst into laughter, but he remained in utter silence.

"Go on," Lez'minx said. "What're you waiting for?"

"If this is an underhanded—"

"Where's your trust?"

"In you? I've already established *why* I have none," Roble said.

"Why be like that?"

"With all you've done?"

Lez'minx's eyes narrowed. "In time, you'll understand that, although I schemed, I was never your enemy. But the longer you tarry, the more I believe you don't want to break our bond. It's fine if you don't, as I'll continue to protect you. For small favors, of course."

Roble's jaw tightened. He twisted the left ring and without any resistance the ring turned, and he slipped it off his finger. He did the same with the other one.

"See?" Lez'minx beamed a smile.

Roble stared at the two rings covered in viscous green slime, dropped them on the old tile floor, and crushed them under the heel of his boot.

"Hey!" Lez'minx said. "Do you realize how long it took to craft those?"

Daphne and Portia stepped to each side of Roble. They took the ropes from the two Orcs, nodded their appreciation, and faced Lez'minx.

"Brother, it's been a long time," Daphne said.

Desperation set in Lez'minx's eyes as he looked at Roble.

"What are you going to do with him?" Roble asked.

"Your business with him has ended," Daphne said. "It's best you attend to Shawndirea."

"No, your charade ends now," Roble said. "Privately, if you wish, or I can tell everyone what this is actually all about."

Daphne's eyes glowed fiery red. Her face withered. "Don't threaten me, Overlander. You haven't your faery to protect you. And if you stand in our way, you might lose her, too."

"No," a voice thundered from a large branch of the Great Tree. The sky darkened. "He has us!"

CHAPTER 74

*S*hawndirea drifted, lower and lower, and deeper into the strange black, purplish abyss. She didn't struggle to prevent her fall, as the place didn't frighten her as it had the first time she entered this deep sleep.

Although she held no fear, she was confused. What kept drawing her consciousness out of her body and causing her to delve into this unusual endless place.

"Have you made a decision?" the male voice asked.

"About?"

"Which Court have you chosen?"

"I'm Seelie," she replied. "Nothing's changed that."

"Your actions have changed far more than you realize," he replied. "You can *never* be recognized as pure Seelie any longer. You know the reasons why."

"Then why bother asking?"

"Because I wanted to know if you've thought about the repercussions of your actions."

"I have."

"And?"

"Nothing's changed."

"Nothing?"

"No," she replied. "If sent back in time, I'd do it all the same. No changes. No remorse."

"Then *awaken*! Now!"

CHAPTER 75

*R*oble stood between Lez'minx and Daphne. Their anger and resentment toward one another vanished. Their attention was drawn to the shimmering glints of silvery wings descending from the tree canopy.

With the sudden darkness shrouding the ruins on the outskirts of the Great Tree, seeing the creatures hovering around them was difficult. Roble didn't need to question if the sounds of these winged creatures were the same as the ones following them toward the tree.

Shawndirea opened her eyes and shook her head. She pushed herself to her feet and looked upward.

"What have you done?" Daphne whispered to Roble.

Roble didn't respond to her question. His attention remained on the tree's higher levels, where a bright orb intensified. He had no idea what was occurring, but Shawndirea took to flight and landed on his shoulder. She pressed herself against his cheek.

"I'm glad you're awake," Roble said. "Are you okay?"

"Yes."

"What happened?"

"Now's not the time," she replied. Facing Lehrling and the others, she whispered, "Whatever happens, don't pull any weapons, or you're dead."

Uksen spoke commands in his orcish language. The other Orcs nodded and crossed their hulkish arms to show they held no weapons.

"What are these creatures?" Roble asked, as the bright orb lowered like a falling bubble.

"We're about to find out," Shawndirea replied.

"Oberon," Lez'minx whispered. He crouched behind Roble to hide.

When the orb hovered less than fifteen feet above the floor of the ruins, an assembly of a hundred or more armored faeries formed a large circle with their swords drawn. Another circle of faeries hovered above them with loaded crossbows and long bows.

"Oberon?" Shawndirea's eyes brightened and she gasped. She flitted to the tile and knelt.

Daphne, Portia, and the other dryads knelt, while keeping their gazes fixated on the floor.

King Oberon's feet touched a high knot on a massive tree root. The bubble surrounding him vanished.

Roble stared at Oberon in awe. Several seconds passed before he realized he'd stopped breathing.

"Bow, you fool!" Shawndirea whispered harshly.

Roble dropped to both knees without a second's thought. His eyes met Oberon's. A jolt of electrical energy surged through Roble's body but he couldn't look away.

At Roble's side, Lez'minx had fallen prostrate and sobbed heavily, whispering his confessions to the king.

Horns protruded from the king's head. His regal eyes radiated. His countenance was solemn. Without speaking, he commanded fear, respect, and honor.

Even the Orcs bowed. Lehrling and Collette clung to one another and bowed with apprehension. The halflings cowered, blubbering sobs not quite as loudly as Lez'minx's.

Oberon's great presence was so overpowering that Roble wondered why the king bothered to have an armed entourage. When Orcs offered their submission without resistance, Roble doubted any enemy could draw a weapon to attack.

Roble couldn't explain the mixed emotions rushing through him. The pit of his stomach twisted with excitement. His heart hammered, and he was so overcome by the intense supernatural energy that he became light-headed.

"Court has come to order," a female said from the shadows. A few seconds later, she marched past Roble and his party, stopped at the base of the massive root on which Oberon stood, and she faced the crowd.

"Court?" Daphne whispered.

"Siophra?" Shawndirea said softly.

"You know her?" Roble asked.

"She's the Unseelie Queen."

"Order!" Siophra said through tight teeth. Her opal eyes pierced the gloom and fixated on Lez'minx's sobbing form.

"What atrocities have made it worth summoning me to this realm, Siophra?" Oberon asked in a stern tone.

"Your servant." She pointed at Lez'minx.

"What has he done?"

"He murdered twenty-six Shadowfae renegades!" Her eyes blazed her fury, and she never looked away from Lez'minx.

"What do you say of this, Runefel?" King Oberon asked.

"He goes by Lez'minx now," Daphne said.

Siophra flicked her gaze at Daphne. Venom coated her words. "One word more from you and you'll be petrified kindling."

Daphne pressed her face to the cracked floor tile.

The air turned icy cold. Roble felt it for a moment before his armor acclimated.

Oberon shook his head. "Lez'minx? Why the name change? Still trying to hide?"

"Hide? Yes. But not from you," he replied.

"From whom?" Oberon asked.

"The two dryads, Daphne and Portia."

"I suppose there's no reason to entertain why?" Oberon chuckled.

"No."

"Your brother, Pan, has thought you dead for quite some time," Oberon said. "He believed the massive flood you requested had killed you along with the others. The guilt he carries weighs heavily. He'll be relieved to learn you're still alive."

"I'll happily explain what occurred," Lez'minx said.

"Don't think your actions are forgiven," Oberon said. "Why did you kill the Shadowfae?"

"They were going to kill Roble. They planned to kidnap his fair wife, Shawndirea, so they could overthrow Elvendale's throne."

Oberon glanced at Siophra. "Did you know of this?"

Siophra's hardened gaze became suddenly troubled. She faced Oberon. "This is the first I've heard of this."

"Shawndirea," Oberon said. "Is his statement true?"

Shawndirea stood and nodded. "It's how Lez'minx describes."

"Who was the leader of this rebellion?" Oberon asked.

"That's something I wish to know, too," Siophra said icily.

"My cousin, Dirk," she replied.

"Dirk?" Oberon frowned and stared into the distance.

"He's Seelie," Siophra seethed. "What ... How'd he get Unseelie to follow him?"

"It would seem," Oberon said, looking at Siophra, "you've not keep a tight watch on your infantry."

"I know precisely—" Siophra began.

"Careful," Oberon said, interrupting. "Lest you incriminate yourself further."

"Incriminate myself?" Her brow furrowed.

Oberon shifted his feet. Anger thundered in his voice. "You called them *renegades*, did you not? And if so, why haven't you dealt with them well before now? There's only one reason I can think for why you haven't. You wish to see Queen Istrell's throne taken by the Unseelie."

Siophra's mouth gaped. "That's not true!"

"So you knew nothing about this plot?" Oberon asked.

"Nothing at all." Siophra shook her head. "I swear it."

Oberon studied her intently for several long moments. Siophra met his gaze, knelt to one knee, and quaked.

"What became of Dirk?" Oberon asked.

"He fled," Lez'minx said.

"You let him escape?"

"I offered to kill him for Shawndirea since he threatened to take her, but she declined," Lez'minx said.

"She declined because you offered to do it in return for her allegiance," Roble said.

Shawndirea cast a harsh stare at him.

"Is what the Overlander said, true?" Oberon asked.

Lez'minx shuddered. "Yes. Yes. I offered that."

"I should strike you dead." Oberon drew his sword.

"No, Your Highness, please," Lez'minx said.

"He's not the only guilty one here," Siophra said. "The Overlander killed one Shadowfae, too."

Oberon's jaw tightened. "Did he now?"

"To be fair," Roble said.

"Don't question my fairness," Oberon replied.

"I'm not, but in my defense, the dagger I threw was intended for Dirk. I nicked him, but the dagger went past him and struck one of the Shadowfae. My intention was to kill Dirk."

Oberon smiled. "Interesting. You'd kill Dirk without hesitation?"

"He threatened my wife," Roble replied.

"Shawndirea?"

Roble nodded.

"Your wife!" Siophra spat.

"She is."

Perplexed, Siophra looked at Shawndirea. "How could you betray your mother and the Seelie Court? Don't think I'll usher a welcome to you in my Courts."

"Did I make such a request?" Shawndirea said through gritted teeth. "I'm still Seelie."

"No, you're not!" Siophra's face contorted from bitterness. "And you're not one of us, either! I won't allow it! I'll see you dead first!"

"Careful, Siophra," Oberon said. "You're threatening *my* daughter."

Siophra's hand went over her heart. She gaped and her eyes widened. Her knees buckled.

Confused, Roble glanced at Shawndirea and she was the mirrored, shocked image of Siophra.

Siophra said, "Wait a minute. *She's* your daughter?"

Oberon smiled. "Yes. Istrell and I once considered marriage long ago, when she carried Shawndirea. But since my duties across the realms requires too much time, we decided against marriage."

Shawndirea swallowed hard. Tears formed in her eyes. "I thought I recognized your voice … Wait, you've been talking to me during those deep sleeps I've fallen into. That was you, wasn't it?"

"Yes," Oberon said. "Over the decades, I've spoken to you in your dreams. I've whispered my blessings for you on the moonbeams that graced your room at night. I've visited your mother's palace many times and watched you grow. I brought you many gifts, but you probably don't remember."

Tears spilled down her cheeks. "You … you called yourself Beron?"

"Yes." Oberon's face glowed. "You were always so elegant and grace-ful. I knew you were destined for greatness. So many times I wanted to reveal who I was, but I'd have to explain why I was never around."

"You approve of her marrying an Overlander?" Siophra asked.

"No, I don't," Oberon said.

"I can't do as you requested," Shawndirea said. "I will *not* annul my marriage to Roble."

"I no longer ask that. Not after learning about his strength and integrity. For an Overlander, it's obvious how much he loves you, and he's willing to give his life to protect you at all costs. That's rare in any realm. But why have you kept secrets from him?"

"Secrets?" Roble said, glancing at her.

Oberon said, "Tell him. The time's long overdue."

"Here? Now?" she said. "I think—"

"No," Oberon said. "If it's privacy you think you need, you've had more than adequate amounts of opportunities before. *Now* is the appro-priate time."

Shawndirea sighed. She lifted her hands upward, chanted a beautiful melody, and shifted from her faery form into her human height. She walked to Roble, took his hands in hers, and placed them on her stomach.

"We're going to have our first child." Tears flowed down her cheeks. "A son, I think."

Tears crested in Roble's eyes and spilled. "A son?"

She nodded.

Roble grinned, pulled her tightly into his arms, and embraced her. Lehrling stood nearby wiping his eyes with one hand while his hugged Collette with his other arm.

Siophra faced Oberon. "Has the court session come to a close with this … *good* news?"

"No," Oberon said. "I'm afraid not. I must dispense proper punishments. The Orcs are free to leave to set up camp or sail downriver. Everyone else must stay."

CHAPTER 76

*R*oble held Shawndirea closely while the Orcs walked past. Uksen handed the staff to Lez'minx, but a few seconds later, Siophra took the staff away.

"How long have you known?" Roble asked Shawndirea.

"Before we ventured into Woodnog Swamps," she replied.

"Why didn't you tell me?"

"You'd have protested my traveling with you; worse than you already had."

"Of course I would've. Or I wouldn't have gone."

"Confronting Lez'minx was a necessity," Shawndirea said. "Had we not found him, he would've eventually found us."

Roble stared into her sparkling emerald eyes. "All this journey, I thought you resented me because of the rings and the journey."

"I'm sorry for lashing out at you so much. I think it's because of my pregnancy," she said.

Oberon walked to them. Six faery guards with swords and shields formed a semi-circle behind the King.

Oberon said, "Your pregnancy with a human was also the reason for why you kept falling into deep sleep. But I could converse with you during those times."

"I wish you'd have told me years ago who you really were," Shawndirea said.

"As do I," Oberon said. "But we have lots of time to catch up. I hope to spend time with your child in the near future, too."

"Yes." Shawndirea smiled.

Roble regarded Oberon for several moments. Shawndirea's eyes were the same color as her father's. "Will our baby be okay? You mentioned her have problems because of the baby being half human."

"Your child should be perfectly fine. The toil suffered is Shawndirea's alone. The further along she becomes, the less she'll succumb to those deep sleeps. Now, if you'll excuse me, order needs restored."

Oberon took to flight and returned to his vantage point atop the giant tree root.

"Shawndirea, my dear daughter," Oberon said. "Because of your marriage to Roble and because your children will not be pure Seelie, you can never rule over Elvendale, even if your mother offers you the rite. Siophra has made it clear she won't welcome you to her Courts. Perhaps this is due to your contention with Istrell?"

In shame, Siophra lowered her gaze and nodded.

"Even though Shawndirea's nothing like Istrell?" Oberon asked.

"I perceive Shawndirea's nothing like her mother, but should I invite her into my Courts, the tension between Elvendale and the Unseelie Courts would magnify. If you've a hint of Istrell's stubborn behavior, Oberon, you know I speak the truth."

Oberon laughed. "I remember quite well, and it's another reason I couldn't see the marriage working. No offense, Shawndirea."

"None taken. I can't think of a time when my mother placed others before her. She never has. I've never been free of her bitter contention. If she smiled, her face might shatter," Shawndirea said in a serious tone.

Siophra reared her head and laughed in a high shrill until tears formed in her eyes. After she composed herself, she wiped away tears and looked at Shawndirea. "I'm truly sorry. I shouldn't laugh at your expense."

"No need to apologize," Shawndirea said. "I'm not laughing because I meant what I said."

Siophra released a long sigh. The sudden laughter made her countenance glow. "I'm tempted to invite you into my Courts solely to irritate her."

"No." Oberon shook his head. "There's too much contention between the courts. It's time for a truce to mend the two. I have a solution."

"What?" Siophra said.

"My blood flows in Shawndirea's veins, which makes her royalty. She deserves a throne to rule from," Oberon said.

Shawndirea shook her head. "No. It's not what I want. I'll not have it. I'm content with being the Butterfly Queen."

"As I've told you before, that's nothing more than a title. No throne comes with those duties."

"I understand and I'm content with that."

"No," Oberon said. "I've need of your counseling to bring balance between the Seelie and Unseelie Courts."

Siophra eyed the King shrewdly. "What do you have in mind?"

"Do tell." Shawndirea placed her nervous hand in Roble's.

"You've already renounced your ties to the Seelie throne in Elvendale, and due to possible retaliation from your mother, you can't be accepted into the Unseelie Courts. You're a faery without a home or proper court. The best resolution is for you to rule the In-between with a Court for you to govern."

"Splendid idea!" Siophra clasped her hands together.

"Father, no," Shawndirea said. "This isn't what I want."

"It's not what you want, but it's what you and your children *need*."

"Where would we reside? I've no armies," Shawndirea said.

"All of that will be established."

"Roble and I have matters to attend to."

"Your residence in the In-between won't occur immediately. It takes time to build a castle. Once established, you'll have an army. Your children will be properly trained, educated, and protected. As the queen, you'll oversee the new kingdom and you'll be the mediator between your mother and Queen Siophra."

Shawndirea squeezed Roble's hand.

He looked into her uncertain eyes. He smiled and kissed her forehead, hoping to comfort her.

She smiled back. "This was never part of my plan when I sought to find you."

"I know."

"You're okay with *this*?"

"From what I've witnessed over the past few weeks, and knowing your mother firsthand, your father's right. Someone needs to negotiate between the two courts."

"I don't think I'm the suitable choice," she said.

"Why not?"

"My mother will resent me even more."

"I'll speak with your mother before I leave Aetheaon," Oberon said. "Do you accept?"

Shawndirea nodded.

"Good. Next order is what to do with Lez'minx," Oberon said.

Lez'minx trembled and slowly made his way to stand at the foot of the massive root. He tucked his bearded chin and averted direct eye contact with Oberon.

Oberon frowned and looked at Queen Siophra. "How many Shadowfae did Lez'minx kill?"

"Twenty-five. Roble killed the twenty-sixth," she replied.

Oberon nodded. "What punishment do you wish enacted on Roble?"

Roble's hand tightened around Shawndirea's. He never expected his fate played into the punishments.

"None," Queen Siophra replied. "He didn't intentionally aim to strike the Shadowfae faery. I've no doubt he intended to kill Dirk instead."

"Noted," Oberon said. "And Lez'minx?"

Siophra studied the satyr for over a half minute. "He's your servant. Since he's Pan's brother, I'll accept whatever punishment you deem fitting."

"Very well." Oberon eyed Lez'minx. "Are you ready to accept your fate?"

"Yes, Your Highness," Lez'minx said. He bleated and clamped a hand over his mouth. "Apologies."

"Queen Siophra, Lez'minx becomes your servant for a quarter of a century. One year for every Shadowfae he killed. He must do whatever unpleasant menial duties you request. For the next twenty-five years, his

magic will be stripped from him. Had these Shadowfae not been renegades, the punishment would be harsher."

Queen Siophra nodded her acceptance.

"As for you." King Oberon pointed a stern finger at Daphne. "You
threatened my daughter's life and—"

"I had no idea she was your daughter," Daphne said. "I beg your
forgiveness, and hers."

"Whether she was my daughter or not, isn't what matters. You
deceived the Dragon Skull Knights into believing Lez'minx was your
brother, which is the furtherest from the truth. You planned to use your
magic to harm my servant because you felt spurned." Oberon formed a
white orb on his right palm and blew into it. Icy snowflakes gusted
toward Daphne, and froze her in place. Her appendages hardened and
splintered. The sheer look of terror etched in her face.

Oberon directed his gaze at Portia and the two male dryads. "Let this
be a warning. I'm under the impression she also deceived you with her
true intentions. Is this correct?"

"She tricked me," Portia said. "I wasn't fully aware of her intentions
until several minutes before you appeared. Ki'wese and Aqese? I don't
know about them."

Aqese said, "We sailed the rafts. Nothing more. From our understanding, she wanted to gather those who once lived in Lindenhold
before the flood. We didn't know Daphne, other than by recognition
when she first requested our aid."

Oberon instructed them to take the halflings to the rafts and return
them to Dagger's Tears. They left without hesitation.

"What about us?" Roble asked.

"After a feast, some wine, and a good night's sleep, I'll have you
escorted outside of Woodnog Swamps. Where's your destination?"

"The City of Woodnog," Shawndirea said.

Oberon waved his hand and a large banquet table materialized near
the Great Tree's trunk. "Eat your fill. The table never goes bare, and the
wineskins never empty."

CHAPTER 77

Seated at the campfire, Roble smiled at Zauber. "That's how we returned to Woodnog. It's a shame we didn't met Shawndirea's father *before* going into the swamps."

Shawndirea smiled.

Boldair stoked the campfire with a long stick. "That be a mighty fine, and yet, quite a *long* story, if I have me say. Tell me, Overlander, you have a knack for storytelling. Perhaps, secretly, you be a bard?"

Dwiskter laughed and elbowed Drucis. "An Overlander bard! Can ya imagine?"

Boldair groaned.

Drucis downed his tankard. "I don't know. If he happened to tell tales about his realm, nobody'd believe it, and dat, Boldair, might make *his* tales more sought after than ya own!"

The smile drained from Boldair's face and Dwiskter's laughter faded.

"You 'ave a point." Boldair looked at Lehrling. "Where's dis Collette? She didn't ride up with ya. Parted ways, so soon?"

Lehrling sipped his stout and shook his head. "No. Due to the dangers we might face with the Plague-bringer, I asked King Oberon to send her to Woodnog where she'll hopefully be safer."

"Dat's a good idea," Boldair said. "I'm not certain if we should head into the City of Woodnog early tomorrow or wait another day to recuperate from all this stout. Some of ya will 'ave a horrid headache on the morrow."

"Aye!" Drucis said.

"Tis a shame." Zauber ran his hand through his long beard. "That your father couldn't aid us in this battle, Shawndirea."

"The battle isn't his. That's what he said," she replied.

"While I suppose that's true, we could use all the help we can find," Zauber said. He rested his hand on a stone portal. "This portal appeared a few hours ago. We've been hoping whomever built this would send us aid through it."

"Still no word from other Dragon Skull Knights?" Lehrling asked.

"No ravens. No word," Zauber said with a smile. "But we mustn't allow hope to die."

"Hope never dies." A deep voice said from the dark pathway cutting through the trees. On horseback, he left the woods and rode through the dead portal beside Zauber. "A Dragon Skull Knight never yields, either."

Lehrling stood at the campfire. His eyes widened in surprise. "Geowren?"

"Aye, ol' friend!" He grinned. He dismounted and was fiercely embraced by Lehrling.

"I feared you were dead," Lehrling said. "It's been so long."

"You should've journeyed with me, as I requested."

"Tell us what you learned," Lehrling said.

Geowren combed his thick black beard with his fingers and laughed heartily. "That's a long story, and one that'd require many tankards and half a roasted wild boar to pry the tale from my mouth."

"Then you're in luck!" Boldair said. "We've plenty of both. While I can't speak for the others, I'm keen on hearing new stories."

"Every word," Lehrling said in awe. "Please, tell us what you've discovered."

"Before you begin," Zauber said. "Answer one question for me."

"Certainly," Geowren said.

"Does this long story give us helpful information in finding a way to defeat Mors?"

"Mors?" Geowren frowned. "Who's he?"

"The Plague-bringer."

The old portal suddenly gleamed bright blue. Rippling watery waves sloshed.

"Step back!" Zauber said. "Perhaps our hope is renewed."

An arm reached through the watery portal, and seconds later, out stepped a thin, wiry man dressed in black.

Zauber offered a shrewd frown and soon beamed a smile. "Crukas? What's that you carry?"

Crukas held a lantern. Seconds later, four Ravenfolk and four more Dragon Skull Knights emerged from the rippling portal. A female halfling with a scar above her eye stepped through, too.

Crukas showed the lantern to Zauber. "If we find the proper way to activate this lantern, we have the way to defeat Plague-bringer."

Zauber smiled. "Please join the others around the fire. We'll bring you food and drink. Tell us how you obtained this and how it can defeat Mors."

THE END

ACKNOWLEDGMENTS

I extend my heartfelt appreciation to my beta reader, KC Riley-Gyer, whose keen eyes captured errors I missed and graciously highlighted them for me.

I greatly appreciation the fantastic job KC Riley-Gyer did in updating Aetheaon's maps for better clarity.

This book's exceptional cover design by Ellie Douglas brought this story to life. https://www.authorellie.com/covers

ABOUT THE AUTHOR

Leonard D. Hilley II grew up a quiet, shy kid with an inquisitive mind. Learning to read at an early age, he fell in love with books. He read every book he could get his hands on and stacks of dark comics about ghosts, monsters, and creepy things that stalk the night.

Like a lot of boys, he caught beetles, wooly bears, butterflies, and had an ant farm. When he was ten, his interests in science increased even more after seeing a professor's insect collection. Soon he set out on his quest to build his own collection. He learned to rear butterflies and moths to obtain perfect specimens. He learned botany, gardening, and set his goal to become an entomologist.

At eleven, he watched Star Wars on the big screen. His imagination soared. Soon after, he discovered Roger Zelazny's Chronicles of Amber. Six months later, he had written the first draft of a novel. A novel he later discarded, but the characters stuck with him. Years later, these characters came to life in Shawndirea, which Hilley intended to be a background novella for Devils Den. The characters, however, refused to be ignored and took the opportunity to unveil Aetheaon in their first epic fantasy. Lady Squire soon followed.

Shawndirea was Hilley's farewell to butterfly collecting. Those who have read the novel understand why. He has taken Ray Bradbury's advice to heart: "Follow the characters." He does. He follows, listens, and take notes—often never knowing where they're going to take him, but he's never been disappointed in the results.

Hilley earned a B.S. in Biology and an MFA in Creative Writing to combine his love of science and writing.

Sci-fi Titles: Predators of Darkness: Aftermath, Beyond the Darkness, The Game of Pawns, Death's Valley, The Deimos Virus.

Epic Fantasy: Shawndirea (Aetheaon Chronicles: Book One), Lady Squire (Aetheaon Chronicles: Book Two), Frosthammer (Aetheaon Chronicles: Book Three), Shadowfae (Aetheaon Chronicles: Book Four), and Devils Den.

UF/PR: Succubus: Shadows of the Beast (Nocturnal Trinity Series: Book One), Raven (Nocturnal Trinity Series: Book Two), A Touch of the Familiar.

YA UF/Paranormal: Forrest Wollinsky Vampire Hunter; Forrest Wollinsky: Blood Mists of London; Forrest Wollinsky: Predestined Crossroads.

YA Mystery: Dee's Mystery Solvers

www.ingramcontent.com/pod-product-compliance
Lightning Source LLC
Chambersburg PA
CBHW060220030726
47499CB00004B/1120